What You Wish For

Détra grinned at him. She had never grinned at him before. A stunned Hunter rose to his feet and moved to stand before his lady. The uncertain way she looked at him and around herself corroborated her claimed confusion. He looked into her eyes, eyes oddly bereft of scorn for him. Mayhap the chalice had granted his heart wish, after all. A second chance to begin anew with his lady wife.

He reached for the chalice when she lay a hand on his arm.

"I do not even recall your name," she whispered.

Her touch bored holes through his garment, searing his skin and unleashing his desire. He fought against the urge to pull her flush to his body and kiss her lips in full for the first time. And Lord help him! He wanted her to kiss him back as badly. Wanted it with such force he could almost taste her from where he stood.

With the possibility that she could finally fulfill his heart wish, his desire for her flourished, becoming fiercer.

He cleared his throat before he spoke. "Hunter is my name."

Praise for
A Perfect Love

"A perfect ~~

"Exciting . . . alive."

the Wishing Chalice

Sandra Landry

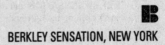

BERKLEY SENSATION, NEW YORK

THE WISHING CHALICE

A Berkley Sensation Book / published by arrangement with the author

PRINTING HISTORY
Berkley Sensation edition / February 2004

ISBN: 0-425-19458-2

BERKLEY SENSATION®
Berkley Sensation Books are published by The Berkley Publishing Group,
a division of Penguin Group (USA) Inc.,
375 Hudson Street, New York, New York 10014.
BERKLEY SENSATION and the "B" design
are trademarks belonging to Penguin Group (USA) Inc.

PRINTED IN THE UNITED STATES OF AMERICA

10 9 8 7 6 5 4 3 2 1

For Elizabeth Laiche
with heartfelt gratitude

Prologue

THE cry of a newborn baby dragged Isabel from a deep sleep. Disoriented, she sat up in bed and pushed a strand of hair away from her face. Heart tumbling, she listened for the sound to repeat. It didn't. After a moment she realized she'd been dreaming. Again. A dream that reoccurred with haunting frequency since that day, a year ago, when she'd lost her baby to a miscarriage.

Isabel fought the longing filling her heart. Not only had she lost her baby but she'd also learned she would never be a mother.

Maybe it was for the best. Her marriage had fallen apart soon after that, and with her lifestyle there was no place in her life for a baby anyway. Of course, her parents would have disagreed with her. They'd had no qualms about dragging Isabel with them all over the world. Not that she resented them for that. Being exposed to different cultures and customs had made her life incredibly rich.

And yet, at times, she had felt quite lonely.

Swinging her legs to the side of the bed, Isabel pushed the old sadness aside. It was dark in the room, and as she reached for the lamp, her hand struck the bedpost. Rubbing her stung fingers, she tried to remember where she was—not an easy feat considering she'd been on the road for the past year.

A citizen of two countries, a resident of many more, Isabel had always lived a nomadic life. When her father died, three years ago, her mother had insisted they move from Europe to her native America, maybe in the hopes of recapturing the joy of life that had died with her husband. But after a year of roaming the country aimlessly, Isabel's mother had also died, leaving her alone at the age of twenty-three.

An ill-advised marriage, a miscarriage, and a divorce later, Isabel had left America behind and returned to Europe. At twenty-five, she was a woman with no ties, no family, and no place to call her own, and she liked it that way. She sold her drawings and paintings at art fairs in various European cities, moving on to a new place once boredom set in, which happened quite often. Thankfully, she was financially solvent and could afford to live as she pleased.

With her eyes finally adjusted to the darkness of the room, Isabel stepped out of bed. Her bare feet touched a soft rug as she fumbled her way to the bedside lamp. The soft light revealed heavy mahogany furniture that spoke of old times, English proper, and well-lived life.

Her late grandmother's English cottage!

A new sense of loss filled Isabel. She hadn't known her grandmother well; in fact, she had visited her only a few times. Yet the thought of her grandmother as a safe harbor, a possible anchor to her rootless life, had been a comfort Isabel hadn't realized how much she'd cherished until it was lost forever. With her grandmother's death, she was now officially alone, the last of her family.

Chasing the sadness away, Isabel sought the antique wardrobe in one corner of the room. From its perfumed drawers she lifted a T-shirt and a pair of panties. She quickly donned them, covering her naked body before she glided over smooth, hard wooden floors to the bedroom door. Stepping into a softly illuminated corridor, she found her way to the staircase and down into the foyer. She halted for a moment, familiarizing herself with her surroundings, since she'd arrived only the day before, then strolled to the back of the house where the kitchen was located. Once there, she flipped on the light switch and crossed the cold stone floors to peek through the window into the small garden on the back of the house.

A new day was dawning amid dark clouds.

On the kitchen counter she found everything she needed to make tea—thanks, no doubt, to her grand-mother's housekeeper, whom, it seemed, Isabel had also inherited along with this cozy cottage. As she waited for the water to boil, memories of her father flooded her mind. He had stubbornly clung to the traditional English way of preparing tea—no microwave-boiled water and, God for-bid, no tea bags for him—even though he'd always been ready to learn and adapt to new customs wherever they lived.

Often Isabel wondered about his reasons. Had he been trying to hang on to his English heritage? Or was it a deeper feeling of home, even if home lived only in his memory and heart?

Would she ever know what home was?

AN HOUR LATER, ISABEL IGNORED THE PROMISE OF RAIN in the heavily clouded day, slung her backpack over her

shoulders, and left her cottage. The weak morning sun
dared occasional peeks from behind gray clouds in a teasing childhood game of peekaboo as Isabel ambled down
the old cobblestone streets.

Even from a distance she could see St. Mary's sand-
stone spire. As she approached it, its graveyard, where her
grandmother was buried, became visible. Stone tombs,
shrouded in mist in the overcast day, spread out like a
barren crop in front of the neo-Gothic church. Cautiously,
Isabel meandered between the ancient and undisturbed
tombs, looking for her grandmother's grave. The stones'
inscriptions of the Herbert family, dating back to the
1800s—her grandmother's being the most recent—came
into sight. These unknown names were all relatives of her
father, Isabel realized. Her relatives.

Maybe her father should've been interred here, she
thought. And yet his wishes had been to be cremated and
to have his ashes spread on the Thames. Likewise, her
mother's ashes now belonged to the Mississippi River.

Where would hers end up?

As she often did, Isabel sought refuge in her art to
chase away the sudden loneliness that beset her. Her pen-
cil busily sketched what would later become a painting.
As she drew St. Mary's graveyard, she already knew the
various nuances of gray she would use to depict the true
feelings of the picture. After she finished she looked at
the drawing and shivered at the desolation and sadness
expressed there, the emptiness of extinguished lives, the
relentless constancy of the passing time. No matter the
subject, drawing had always had a calming effect on Isabel, and yet today it had stirred deep doubts within her.

Restless, she collected her supplies and took to the road
toward Lake Windermere. Walking was another way she
calmed herself down, and she knew this area offered wonderful hiking places. She would try them another day.

This morning she would stick to the lakeshore. Concentrating on the rhythm of her breathing and the beating of her heart, Isabel efficiently closed the world out, until serenity took over.

Losing track of time, she plodded on until her lungs were about to burst with the effort. She slowed her pace, catching her breath as she glanced at her wristwatch, surprised that a whole hour had already passed. Meanwhile, the wind had picked up speed, and the dark clouds that earlier hovered in the distance now approached menacingly.

Maybe she should turn around.

Directly in her pathway stood a hill of mud and debris from the recently dredged-out lake. Isabel veered inland to avoid the mess when she stepped on something hard. Catching her fall, she looked down to find part of the offending projectile protruding from the earth. She unearthed it and scooped the object up. It was a heavy chalice, pewter maybe, certainly old. Isabel took it over to the lake and washed the encrusted mud off, revealing three huge blue stones. Could they be real sapphires? They were of a rough cut and rather dull, not at all like real gems. Probably glass.

Normally, Isabel wouldn't think of keeping it—she had no use for collecting objects in her nomadic life—but her artistic eye appreciated the symmetry of the high-relieved stones and the whole beauty of the chalice.

Chalice in hand, she was ready to turn around when lightning streaked the sky. From the corners of her eyes, she caught sight of the remnants of an old castle on a hill, less than a mile away from where she stood. Its silhouette of round and square towers stood stark against the darkening sky. Under the roaring of distant thunder, Isabel took up the grassy hill toward the castle, mesmerized by it. Surely she had time to explore it before the storm arrived.

A couple of hundred feet away from the castle, Isabel stopped, her breath caught in her throat, a slight tremor running through her body. She'd seen many castles in her life; some so well preserved you could easily imagine the people who'd lived in them, others crumbling ruins that gave little indication of what they truly looked like. But none had captured her interest as this one. There was something about it, like a painting you must stare at for hours before you had your fill of it, before you understood it, before it became part of you.

Lightning streaked the sky again, this time above the castle, framing it in light for a fraction of a second, like the flash of a photographer's camera.

The scene etched deeply in Isabel's mind. She reached for her backpack, for her art supplies, wanting to draw it, paint it, freeze the image in time, but an urge to get closer to it stopped her hand in mid-motion and pushed her feet forward instead. The wind picked up sudden momentum, slapping her short hair over her eyes. Futilely Isabel pushed the bangs away while her free hand firmly held the chalice.

Ignoring a warning not to trespass, she jumped over the steel cable surrounding the property, thankful there was no one in sight. She approached the ruins, taking in the ivy-covered wall and a crumbled tower. Two other square towers and a round one still stood mindless of the disrepair surrounding them. A low wall enclosed part of the side of the castle where a garden must once have grown. She crossed under an archway, which seemed to stand by sheer stubbornness since the walls that held it no longer existed, and walked into a small yard. Before her stood the entrance to what once was a medieval castle.

Isabel entered the castle to the echoing of her own footsteps. For a moment the air inside was deathly still, then a chilling draft swirled around her body and a musty smell of damp stone wafted to her. A sudden batting of wings spooked her and Isabel screamed, almost dropping the chalice from her hands. Letting out a nervous laugh, she realized it was only a bird flying through the hole-gapped roof, leaving behind a wave of dust in the air.

The place sure reeked of an eerie atmosphere, Isabel thought as memories of childhood tales her father used to tell came rushing to her. "There isn't a castle in England," her father used to say, "that doesn't harbor a haunting ghost."

Laughing at the absurd thought, Isabel proceeded through the shadowed room until she reached a steep stone stairway with no handrails. For a moment she hesitated; the stairs didn't look very safe and they led to a second floor swallowed by darkness. She shook her head and moved up anyway. She wasn't a little girl anymore; darkness and ghost stories didn't scare her. Besides, she never walked away from new situations. In fact, she thrived on them. And she wanted to see the upper floor of this castle.

Midway up the steps a whistling hissed in her ears. Isabel refused to be cowed. No haunting ghosts, just the wind caught in the tunneling walls, she told herself, shivering with the dampness of the place. At the top of the landing she stopped and perused her surroundings. A little light infiltrated through the many holes in the roof and walls, illuminating the corridor ahead. To her right, a few steps from where she was, a frameless door marked the entrance to one of the square towers she'd seen from outside.

As if compelled by an invisible force, Isabel ambled to the door, walked through it, and found herself inside the tower. For a brief moment she thought she caught the scent of rosemary in the air. Standing in the middle of the room, Isabel turned around slowly, taking notice of the large arched window on one of the walls and the crumbling remains of a fireplace on the other. Thunder rumbled outside and she looked up to a partially missing roof. A drop of rain fell on her face as lightning flashed across the sky. Moving farther inside, Isabel found herself near the fireplace, somewhat sheltered from the weather outside.

For a moment she watched the brief flashes of light revealing the shadowed room, wondering if she should wait the weather out or just venture back to the cottage. When sudden warmth began creeping up her body, Isabel frowned. She knew the heat couldn't be coming from the dark, cold fireplace behind her. Her gaze strayed to her hand holding the chalice, from where the heat seemed to originate. The chalice's blue stones glowed like embers, emanating a soothing blue light. In disbelief Isabel stared at them. Were they really glowing? When she brought the chalice closer, from deep within a mist began to form, swirling up and around Isabel like tongues of blue opaque smoke. With the plume, the essence of rosemary also rose and the heat spread faster over her body.

The hair on Isabel's arms rose in warning as an image began to emerge from the mist. At first in barely recognizable shapes, then slowly taking form like a holograph projection, it became so real Isabel could swear that if she reached for it she'd be able to touch the people the image revealed.

Instinctively she stepped back, but for some reason she couldn't drop the chalice. The mesmerizing, glowing stones and the blue mist had her transfixed and she was unable to tear her gaze away from the vision. Unwillingly she stared at a beautiful woman in the last stages of pregnancy, dressed in clothes of a bygone era, sitting by a fireplace while a dark, handsome man looked adoringly at her.

Isabel could feel the warmth from the lit fireplace, could see the vibrant color of the woman's auburn hair, could even feel the joy in the woman's heart as if she were the woman herself.

Disturbed, Isabel turned her gaze to the man. His clean, male scent suddenly overpowered the more feminine bouquet of rosemary. A sudden desire to reach for him, to touch his bronzed face, to be the object of his admiration assaulted Isabel. A hint of jealousy rose in her. No man had ever looked at her that way, with such love, such pride.

With her heart constricted to an unbearable pressure, Isabel's hands unconsciously tightened around the chalice. The vision was so real Isabel almost felt part of the ensemble, though she was only an unwitting witness to a picture-perfect family.

Oh, what she wouldn't give to be in that woman's place! To belong, to be part of a family, to carry a child in her womb! The wish sprouted from deep within her heart, uncontrollable, undesirable, irrefutable.

The vision suddenly wavered before Isabel's eyes, like an image reflected in water. The mist swirled faster and faster, enveloping her, its dizzying speed making her head spin.

Images—real and imaginary—fused and separated in a hypnotic pattern. The chalice's blue stones shone brighter as their light escalated from soothing blue to blinding white. Then suddenly the room plunged into total darkness as Isabel, robbed of her last vestiges of consciousness, crumpled to the stone floor.

Chapter 1

Windermere Castle
Cumbria, England, 1315

THE delicate scent of rosemary wafted into Hunter's dreams, awakening him with sweet promises. As he opened his eyes to the shadows of the early morning, lightning flashed through the bed curtains, illuminating his lady wife's sleeping form on the mattress by his side. Her vibrant auburn hair escaped the constriction of a tight braid to fall in fat curls over her fair face.

Thunder roared in the distance as Hunter rolled to his side, bracing himself on one arm to face Détra. The bed frame's interlaced strips of leather complained loudly under his shifting weight, but his wife remained motionless.

A morning chill filled the air, speaking of the need to add new logs to the hearth's dying embers. He shifted, and the coverlet slid off Détra's shoulders, and the temptation of her bared skin, revealed by the disarray of her chemise, spoke of his need for her.

Hunter responded to the latter and reached for Détra.

As he touched her shoulders, her velvety skin seared his fingers and the heat traversed to the lower part of his body in lightning speed. He slid her chemise further down, unveiling the top of her generous breasts, the rosy, tempting nipples. His breath quickened and his eager member jutted forward, rigid and ready.

As always, his body willfully responded with a mind of its own to the sight of Détra's beauty. Heartbeat drumming in his ears, Hunter leaned over and skimmed her shoulder with his lips, her sweet taste flaming his thirst of her, inflating his hope that this morning he could put an end to this miserable waiting.

"Nay, Hunter. Not yet," Détra said, turning away from him.

Disappointment clogged his throat. Since their wedding night, two weeks ago, Détra had denied him his rights. Bothered by her menses on the first few days of their marriage, a terrible aching head keeping her virtually abed for days afterward, she had held him at bay. But then, a week ago, Détra had finally confessed to her late husband's cruel treatment of her. Hunter had tried to reassure her he would never harm her, but Détra had been disconsolate.

It was within his rights to demand her yielding, to force her submission, to make use of her body, but the mere thought of forcing himself on a woman, least of all his lady wife, was immensely distressing to Hunter. The horrible thought that his own mother had undoubtedly been taken against her will and then abandoned to bear his father's bastard alone had instilled in him the desire to never repeat his father's mistake.

And so he had waited, hoping to prove Détra's fears unfounded. But he could wait no longer. If word of his failure to consummate his marriage got out, not only would he be the laughingstock of the whole kingdom, but his control over Windermere Castle would also be in serious jeopardy.

Hunter could afford neither of them.

He gently turned Détra around and took her stiff body into his arms, keeping the chill of the morning away with his body heat. He sought her mouth and kissed her but she kept her lips tightly sealed to his seeking tongue. He lifted from her. "If you but allow me to hold you," he said.

In response she pushed further away from him, as if that were possible, seeing that she already slept on the far edge of the bed.

"I am not William, Détra," Hunter reasoned with mounting frustration. "Surely you must see that. We can no longer be obliging to your fears."

In silence Détra rolled out of the bed and rose, dragging the coverlet with her. The bed curtains fell behind her departing form.

His lady wife's prompt assumption she could turn her back on him and not fulfill her marital duty to him annoyed Hunter anew. Was there more to Détra's reluctance than what she had led him to believe? Had his idealized image of her veiled his mind to the truth of her heart?

But what could that truth be if not what she had told him?

Hunter jerked to his feet to stand naked before her. She held the coverlet tight over the chemise she always wore to bed, covering her body to his gaze. Lightning flashed outside the window and fell in incandescent streaks upon her, but for the first time, her beauty failed to move him. She stood before him like a statue—a beautiful, unattainable, lifeless form of a woman.

Before his lady wife's tearful revelation a week past, Hunter had mourned her detachment toward him but had not understood; then he surmised her manners were in truth an unfortunate outcome of her difficult former marriage. Détra was not a woman to laugh easily, to appreciate a jest or converse naturally. Efficient in the care of the castle and its inhabitants, she had time for naught else but her duties and obligations.

With the exception of her marital duty to him, which she skirted with great mastery.

"We can no longer avoid this matter," Hunter said.

"If you take me against my will, and there is no doubt you can for your strength is greater than mine, then you are no better than William."

Blood rose to his face. "I need not use my strength against a woman, for I have every right to your compliance. You were given to me by king, our marriage blessed by God and made legal by men. You are mine, Lady Détra."

"Neither you, nor the king, not even God have ever considered my wishes at all." There was such bitterness in her voice, such stubbornness in the way she defiantly pointed her chin at him, that Hunter began doubting every word she had ever spoken to him. "What about my choices?" she cried suddenly.

She spoke of choices as if he had been given many in his life. What choice had his heart those many years ago when he first caught sight of her beautiful face? What choice had he in having been born a bastard of unknown sire?

Had he reached higher than he should have when he wedded Détra? Hoped more than he deserved? Wanted more than fate was willing to give him?

And yet, when the opportunity arose, he took it, and, by God, he would offer no apologies for having done so. A woman's lot in life was to be wedded for gain of land, power or protection, and not always to her benefit. And yet, though he had gained land and power through her, he had vowed to protect and care for her. And he intended to do so. He wished to go even further. He wished to offer her his heart, in which she seemed not interested at all.

Refusing to consider the chilling possibility Détra might have given her heart to another, he countered, "You bewail having no choices, and yet it looks to me you have made yours. You have chosen to deny the marital rights that are due to me as your lord and husband—"

"A bastard son of a village witch shall never be my true lord nor husband," she spat.

The slur slapped Hunter with such a force he almost staggered back, his heart slamming against his chest. Finally the truth was revealed, lifting the veil from his eyes. Fool that he had been to think a highborn lady would overlook the circumstances of his birth. Mad that he had been to think Détra could love him.

Wounded pride made Hunter square his shoulders. The old mask of indifference fell over his face like a well-worn glove.

"A bastard I am," he whispered. "And yet, I am also your husband and lord. Keep your heart to yourself, my lady wife, if that is your wish, but your loyalty and obedience I shall have. You would do well to remember that."

If wooing Détra had proved impossible, he would try no more. But by God, she was his wife, and though their marriage had turned out to be naught akin to what he had once envisioned, his wife she would remain.

Rain began falling outside with swift violence. Lightning dazzled the chamber with sparkling streaks of light as thunder reverberated within the stone walls.

A tempest outside to match the tempest in his heart.

He reached to Détra but she evaded his hands, running away from him and tripping over his garment chest. With the lid open—he had forgotten to shut it the night before—and Détra's weight, the trunk toppled over, its contents spilling out.

Hunter lifted Détra from the floor but she fought his hold of her. "Cease your struggles," he demanded. "I will do you no harm."

"Bastard!" she hissed, pounding his chest with her fists.

The slur hurt him anew as ire rose in his heart. He fought against the debilitating emotion, warring against the need to take Détra to bed and consummate his marriage as quickly as possible, knowing that by doing so he would terminate the dream he had cherished for most of his adult life.

Out of the corner of his eye Hunter noticed his chalice lying on the floor amidst his spilled garments. He had always kept the heavy pewter chalice hidden from prying eyes. He pushed Détra away, hoping to reach the chalice before she noticed it, but when he darted a glance back at her, he realized she had already seen it.

Now he would have to find another hiding place for it. Still, Détra could not possibly know of the chalice's significance to him, or its supposed magical powers. Hunter had never spoken of it to her, or anyone else for that matter. The only remaining possession of his mother, and as such invaluable to him, Hunter would share the chalice with no one, least of all Détra.

As Hunter took the chalice in his hands, memories of his mother gifting it to him on his fourteenth birthday, days before she had passed away, flooded him. Her words of that long-ago day echoed in his mind. "This is a gift from the heart," she had said. "Your heart it shall read, and your wishes it shall fulfill."

Heart wishes! Hunter snorted. His mother had believed in the chalice's magic powers, though it had never benefited her, as it had not him, for naught had been given freely to him or by magical powers. He had paid a dear price for all he had accomplished in his life.

Their overlord had taken an interest in him and paid for Hunter's fostering, his horse and knightly accouterments, and to this day, Hunter still owed the man knightly services. Hunter had obtained the golden spurs of knighthood after long years of hard work and enduring endless taunting by the noble young men who believed he had no birthright to be a knight. And his latest largesse in life—Windermere Castle and Détra—was a just reward for Hunter having saved the king's life in battle.

Nay, the chalice had naught to do with any of it.

He lifted his gaze to his lady wife—his heart wish and greatest disappointment—and her cold glare congealed his soul. There was no magic in the entire Christendom, let alone in a small chalice, that could transform his lady wife into the lady of his heart, or convert their arid life together into the vision of hearth and loving family he dreamed of.

Unable to withstand the sight of his wife's antagonistic glare, Hunter turned his gaze to the chalice. Sudden warmth invaded his body and the azure stones of the chalice began to glow like bright stars in the darkest night. Before his unbelieving eyes, a blue mist spiraled from within the chalice's depth, slowly forming an image. Hunter stared, unable to avert his gaze until the vision completed, revealing his heart wish—his lady wife carrying his child in her womb, sitting by the hearth and looking at him with love in a portrait of perfect harmony.

Hunter's breathing deepened, his heartbeat slowed, his heart filled with joy, pride, love, and then disbelief.

What manner of powers did his mother's chalice truly possess? Was it mocking his innermost desire or foretelling his heart wish?

A strong scent of rosemary suddenly engulfed Hunter, as if Détra had just doused herself with the fragrance. "Détra," he whispered, then suddenly remembering where he was and who was there with him, he fought to drag his gaze from the vision and face the cold reality of his lady wife's presence.

Darting a glance over his shoulder, Hunter found Détra standing behind him. Her blanched face could not hide her horror. Was she also seeing the vision? Hunter stared at her as she stared beyond him to the blue mist of his heart wish. Then with a sudden jerk, she pulled his arm, trying to reach the chalice.

Instinctively, Hunter pulled away, but Détra had latched onto his arm and now his hand, the hand that held the chalice.

"Nay," she cried. "I do not accept this."

The vision faltered as they fought for possession of the chalice. The mist swirled around them, enveloping them, possessing them in a dizzying speed. Hunter's head spun as whimsy and reality fused in a surreal moment. The chalice's blue stones flashed a last, blinding light before the bedchamber plunged into utter darkness. Robbed of consciousness Hunter toppled over to the floor, taking Détra with him.

Chapter 2

VISION blurred, senses muddled, Hunter fought for clarity of thought. His head ached with a dull throb; his fingers tingled alongside his body. Lifting heavy arms, he pressed his palms against his temples and closed his eyes, listening to the rain falling outside. Moments later, he opened his eyes again and stared at the ceiling, waiting for the bedchamber to halt its dizzying spin.

He dragged himself to a sitting position on the hard stone floor, struggling to clear his mind. *Deus!* What had happened?

His unfocused gaze found his lady wife's motionless body sprawled on the floor by his side. Hunter scurried to her side. "Détra," he called, but there was no response.

He touched her pallid face, then moved a lock of auburn hair covering her eyes. The small lump on her forehead was surely less worrisome than her clammy skin underneath his fingers. With mounting trepidation Hunter leaned over her chest and listened to her heart. Shaking his head uncomprehendingly, he lifted, unable to accept the absence of a heartbeat.

Dread made his skin crawl. He shook her, at first gently, then a little rougher, hoping for a reaction, any reaction. Naught.

Détra could not be dead!

The mere thought spun Hunter into action. He took her in his arms and settled her in their bed, then rushed to the door and bellowed for help. His outcry resounded like thunder down the stone corridor and into the great hall below.

As he returned to the bed, he caught sight of the chalice lying on the floor not far from where they both fell. As he picked it up, the first memory that assailed him was of the vision the chalice had revealed, the second, Détra's angry rejection of his heart wish.

Could the chalice be responsible for their collapse? The thought perplexed and intrigued him as he set it on the table and returned to Détra's side. His mother had believed in the chalice's magical powers. He had been witness to its manifestation. And yet, according to his mother, the chalice was supposed to fulfill his heart wish and grant him the wife of his dream. How had he ended up holding a lifeless wife in his arms? The vision had revealed them happily together, not eternally separated.

Hunter refused to accept Détra was dead. He would not allow her to die. Even though she loved him not, even though she had flatly rejected him, she was still his wife. She was still his.

He donned his breeches, then returned to her bedside. Moments later, Maude, Détra's maid companion, finally rushed in.

"What happened?" Maude cried.

What could he tell Maude? Surely not that he believed his chalice had caused Détra's demise.

"Détra tripped and hit her head," he said. "She is not breathing. Send for the village's healer, at once." There was no time to waste. Death would not rob him of his dream. He had despaired of conquering Détra's heart, but he had not considered being without her.

As Maude stumbled out of the bedchamber to do his biding, Hunter turned his gaze to his lady wife. He thought he saw a slight tremor, an almost imperceptible twitch of her eyelids. Had he imagined it?

"Détra," he called, approaching the bed. For an infinite moment there was no response, then her body began to shudder. He had not imagined *that*. Détra had indeed moved. She was not dead.

Relief washed over him.

Détra's body jerked, and, opening her eyes, she lurched forward, gasping for breath as if emerging from a pool of water. She half lifted herself from the bed, taking in big gulps of air.

"Easy, easy," he whispered, supporting her back with one arm until her breathing eased and she lifted a confused gaze at him.

"What happened?" she asked, still gasping. "I feel like I have just returned from the dead."

Hunter flinched inwardly at her uncanny remark. And as she seemed not to remember what happened, he used the same excuse he gave Maude. "You fell and hit your head."

"Oh," she whispered, scooting back against the pillows. Her hand immediately went to the bump on her forehead and she winced; then, lifting both of her hands, she halted them in front of her, flexing her fingers.

"They tingle," she whispered, a perplexing expression on her face. She rubbed her eyes, as if to clear her vision.

Remembering the tingling in his own hands when he regained consciousness, Hunter offered, "It shall soon pass."

She nodded, seeming distracted, her gaze darting in every direction. "Where am I?" She turned a puzzled gaze to him. "Who are you?"

Taken aback by her incongruous questions, Hunter knew not what to say. Tongue-tied, he stared at her. Had the incident muddled her wits?

She frowned. "You look oddly familiar."

Was Détra trying to confound him? Suspicion filled his mind. "You mean to tell me you know me not?"

She shook her head. "Though I rarely forget a face, I confess I can't quite place yours. Have we met?"

"Met?" Hunter said, springing to his feet, wondering about her odd speech. "I am your lord and husband."

"What?" She seemed truly perplexed. Though the bed curtains impaired her vision her gaze strayed around the room. Then with a sudden move, she lurched out of the bed, and the coverlet slipped to the floor, exposing her thin chemise.

"Where are my clothes?" she demanded as she inspected herself. Then, with a sharp intake of breath, Détra jumped backward, as if to escape from herself. She snapped a handful of her glorious auburn hair in her hand and stared at it in petrified horror, then pulled on her tresses as if trying to pull out her own hair, yanking at it with considerable force, crying out with obvious pain.

Deus! What was she doing?

"What the hell is going on?" she cried.

Taken aback by her language, Hunter nonetheless reached for her. With a fear-filled gaze, she backed away from him, stumbling over her garment chest. The small silver mirror on top of it fell on the stone floor with a clink. Her gaze strayed to it. She hesitated for a moment, then lowered herself and picked it up. Straightening, she pressed the mirror against her chest as if gathering courage to look into it. Befuddled, Hunter watched as her trembling hands lifted the mirror to her face then stared into it, letting out a shriek the likes of which he had never heard before.

A moment later, she dashed out of the bedchamber with Hunter at her heels.

ISABEL RACED DOWN THE STONE STEPS INTO A LARGE room as if the devil were after her. Ignoring the presence of several people gathered there, she rushed to the freedom of an open door to the outside world.

Rain prickled her body with its cold needles, drenching her immediately as she blindly dashed across the vast expanse of yard.

Trembling with cold and horror, Isabel dared a look behind to gauge if she'd been followed. Lightning silhouetted a man against the castle behind him as he dashed after her. Her breath caught in her throat. The castle looked eerily similar to the ruins she'd visited and where she'd collapsed just moments ago. At least she thought it was moments ago. Automatically she lifted her wrist, looking for her watch, but it was not there.

In her momentary hesitation, the man reached her. "For Heaven's sake, Détra, what has come over you?" he shouted over the roaring thunder.

Who's this Détra person? Isabel wanted to ask, but the words died out in her throat as she raised her hands to fend off the man—hands as alien to her as the red hair that clung wetly to her face. As unnatural as the voluptuous breasts peeking from underneath her camisole. As unrecognizable as the stranger's face she'd glimpsed in the mirror before she fled the room.

Isabel fought against the crescendo of terror possessing her, against the lure of fainting that teased her senses, against the need to ignore the absurdity of her thoughts. Instead, she sought to find strength where none seemed to exist. This must be a dream, a horrible nightmare, and soon she would wake up from it.

The man was speaking to her, but she hadn't heard a word he said. She thought he looked eerily familiar, but certainly not her *lord and husband,* as he had claimed. And then she remembered where she'd seen him. *He* was the man in the vision she'd seen in the ruins of the old castle while holding the chalice with the bright blue stones, the man who had stood by the pregnant woman, looking at her with adoring eyes.

And she, horror of horrors, was that woman!

Good God! She had for the briefest moment during that vision wished to be that woman.

Had she wished the vision into life?

Horrified, Isabel snapped her glance down to her stomach. Relief washed over her to find it flat. She glanced back at the man, but there was no adoration in his gaze now, just puzzlement and concern.

"We must get back inside," he said, pulling her gently with him.

Stubbornly she sank her feet in the mud. She didn't want to go anywhere. The openness of the outside suited her much better than four suffocating walls. Yet, as if to discourage her, the heavy rain took a sudden turn for the worse and lightning began to strike with the regularity of a clock ticking the minutes.

"Unless you wish to catch your death," he said, a twinge of annoyance tempering his voice, "I suggest we return inside, Détra."

My name is Isabel, she wanted to scream, but the words didn't come out of her mouth. Just like it happened in her nightmares when she wanted to run but couldn't, wanted to scream but there was no voice. Yes, this was just like it—a dream, a nightmare. She was probably burning up with fever in some hospital bed, hallucinating. Shockingly, the explanation calmed her.

Ignoring him—he was, after all, a figment of her imagination—Isabel spun around and simply walked away. If she continued to walk and think of other things, like a nice cup of tea, he would probably go away. Her mind went through the motion of preparing tea—the water, the kettle, the tea. Moment by moment, action by action, thought by thought.

Strong hands snatched her from this idyllic scenario, lifting her with ease, as if she weighed no more than a feather. Frustrated, Isabel began kicking and punching him, but he ignored her protests and hauled her back to the castle.

He carried her with him up the steps to the second floor, leaving behind a trail of muddy puddles.

"Put me down, you animal," Isabel screamed, the sound of another woman's voice resonating eerily in her ears.

He continued to ignore her until they reached the room from which she'd just escaped and threw her down on the bed, his heavy body keeping her in place. He pinned her arms against the mattress and above her head. "Cease your struggles, my lady wife. It is not becoming of your position in this castle."

Shock made Isabel gape at him, for a moment doing exactly what he commanded. But when his words sank in—he saw another woman when he looked at her—Isabel resumed her struggles with renewed energy. She had to get out from under him! But the more she struggled the more pressure he applied, and his hard body plastered against hers until her lungs clamored for breath. The bastard was going to kill her! Realizing she was no match for his strength, she ceased her struggles but sought his face with a fury-filled glare. He met her gaze with a dark, prodding stare, but pulled back a little.

Able to breathe again, Isabel gulped in air as she moved her gaze away from the impenetrability of his dark eyes to the nose that looked like it'd been broken before, to the well-defined lines of his cheeks and the full bottom lip of his mouth. His face was handsome, in a rugged sort of way, intriguing in its maleness.

To her artistic eye, that is.

She promptly swept her gaze up to find his eyelids half closed, shielding his thoughts and his intentions as his mouth settled suddenly over hers.

It was a hungry, searing kiss that lasted just long enough for Isabel to enjoy a tantalizing taste of him and short enough to disallow any reaction from her.

Surprise clouded her judgment for the seconds the kiss lasted, but when his hands began pulling down the wet camisole that kept her barely clad, Isabel gathered her senses pretty fast. "What are you doing?" She pushed him away, furious he'd taken advantage of his strength and her temporary insanity to paw her.

Freeing her from the pressure of his body as he sprang up, he gave her a bitter grin. "I am not about to ravish you, if that is your fear." He threaded his fingers through his wet hair and drops of water slid down his neck disappearing in his drenched shirt. Isabel followed their trajectory with disturbing interest.

Now that he no longer covered her with his heated body, Isabel realized it was colder inside the room than it was outside the castle.

"I merely do not wish for harm to befall you."

Isabel sat up in bed and pulled the saturated fabric back into place over her chest. No, not her chest, she recognized immediately. The man had not touched her body, but the body of another woman—*his wife?* Good God, how could this have happened to her? Isabel struggled with the undeniable fact that this body was not hers.

Closing her eyes, she willed again the nightmare to end. When she opened her eyes a moment later the dark, handsome stranger still stood before her. And her body was still not hers. She pinched herself hard, but the pain she felt denied she was in the throes of an enduring nightmare, as she'd like to believe.

Reality or delusion, something really weird had happened. She couldn't dismiss the vision the chalice had revealed to her nor what was happening right now. She had been wide-awake when the vision occurred, as she appeared to be now.

Her shoulders slumped with the weight of her predicament and Détra's voluptuous breasts. This was not a nightmare, this was really happening to her, the product of her thoughtless wish. And this man—she darted a sly glance at him, realizing she didn't even know his name— thought she was his wife. He saw this Détra when he looked at her. How was she going to pull the wool over his eyes long enough to undo this bizarre situation? And how was she going to undo it?

"I don't feel myself," she whispered.

That much is obvious, his gaze seemed to say, but politely he inquired, "You remember naught of me?"

Suddenly Isabel realized two very important things. She was not only in another woman's body but also in another century—the Middle Ages by the looks of it. And though modern and medieval English should resemble each other very little, she and Détra's husband seemed to have no trouble understanding each other. Isabel had no doubt it was the chalice's doing. After all, what was a little translation compared to time travel and body switching?

Panic grew inside her. Should she tell him the truth? That she had somehow taken over his wife's body with the help of a magical chalice? Isabel immediately dismissed the idea. He would most probably think her insane and God knew what dire consequences such confession would bring upon her. These were the Middle Ages! Though people were much more mystical now than in modern times, dabbling in magic would equal worshiping the devil, or such nonsense. Isabel was not about to make her life more difficult than it already was.

"I'm afraid you are right," she said, though she neglected to explain that she didn't remember him because she didn't know him.

He narrowed his eyebrows in obvious doubt. "Do you remember anything at all or is it just me you forgot?"

What an odd question to ask. "I remember nothing."

He stared at her as if trying to read her mind or search her soul. Isabel shivered under his dark stare. "Your heart halted its beating for a while," he said, as if that would explain her amnesia. "I thought you dead. Do you remember that?"

"Dead?" Isabel staggered back. *Détra's heart had stopped?* Good God, had the woman died, her spirit lost somewhere as Isabel took over her body? Had her thoughtless wish sent Détra into an early demise? She immediately chased the thought away, not able to deal with such a scenario.

And then another terrifying thought assailed her. If Détra was dead, what had happened to Isabel's body? Was she dead also? If that were true, Isabel would be stuck here forever. There wouldn't be a body to return to.

She wouldn't accept that. She and Détra must have exchanged bodies. What other way could they undo this travesty? Was Détra freaking out in her body? Would she have the good sense to try to find a way to undo the exchange? Isabel was certain of one thing; like her, Détra would have no wish to be chained to a body, a place and a life that didn't belong to her.

So distracted was Isabel with her thoughts that she didn't even notice Hunter had helped her to a chair by the fireplace until he gently lowered her to its cushioned seat.

"All I remember," Isabel mumbled, "is waking up in a strange place, with a strange man, not knowing who I am."

He kneeled by her side. "I am no stranger. I am your husband. You have been through a terrible ordeal, but all shall be well soon."

Thankful for his understanding, albeit misguided, Isabel's gaze strayed around the room, catching sight of the chalice on the table. Her heart stopped for a moment and she stifled a cry of recognition. Good God! She'd been holding that chalice when she'd had the vision, when she'd made that stupid wish, when she'd fallen unconscious. Had Détra also held it here in her own time? Made a wish, maybe? Was the vision Isabel had seen, in fact, Détra's wish? Was Hunter aware of what had happened? He didn't seem to be.

Her attention was brought back to the man in question when he lifted a strand of hair away from her face, and his knuckles gently skimmed her cheek, eliciting in her too strong of a response for such brief touch from a stranger.

"Oh!" The half moan, half whisper escaped Isabel's throat as goose bumps spread down her arms. It must be this body, she reasoned. It just reacted to an obviously known touch. It had nothing to do with her. She hardly knew the man; she couldn't be attracted to him. Could she?

"You must get rid of this sodden chemise." His rough, callused palm drifted over her shoulder. "Your skin is cold and you tremble."

Isabel swallowed hard. The smoldering look he sent her way was undeniable. She'd been married before; she knew that look.

She pushed to her feet. "You're right, I'm really cold." She ambled to the table, to the chalice, but before she reached it, the man spun her around to face him. His hand rested on her shoulder again.

"You speak oddly. Do you feel well?"

"Well?" No, she didn't feel well at all. "Not really. I'd—" she paused. She must try to speak without contractions, more in tune with his speech. "I would like to rest a little. I am very tired." She smiled to look more agreeable. "Maybe later we could talk and maybe you could help me remember my past."

Of course she wouldn't tell him she planned to be far, far away by then.

DÉTRA HAD GRINNED AT HIM. SHE HAD NEVER GRINNED at him before. A stunned Hunter rose to his feet and moved to stand before his lady. The uncertain way she looked at him and around herself corroborated her claimed confusion. The lack of disdain in her eyes after she recovered consciousness, even when she fought him, also puzzled him. She looked none the worse and yet there was something indefinably different about her. Even her speech was odd, not the timbre or tone, but the rhythm and cadence of her voice, her odd choice of words, her less than formal speech.

Should he believe her claim of memory loss? Or was she trying to befuddle and dupe him, surely with the intent of continuing to deny his marital rights?

Hunter had not missed Détra's interest in the chalice the moment she sighted it on the table. Did she remember more than she wanted him to believe?

Looking into her green eyes, eyes oddly bereft of scorn for him, the vision the chalice revealed returned vividly to his mind. And the intoxicating thought took. Mayhap the chalice had granted his heart wish, after all. A second chance to begin anew with his lady wife.

Hunter was not a man to turn his back on good fortune. And fortune seemed to be smiling at him.

And yet Détra had asked for his help to remember. Should he reveal the unpleasant details of their marriage, knowing the truth would only deepen the chasm between them? Or should he use this opportunity to finally make good on what seemed a hopeless marriage, even if he colored the truth a little?

His conscience warred with his heart.

Noticing her trembling, however, he postponed the decision. She would sicken if she remained in wet clothing. "I shall send Maude to aid you," he said. They could speak later, when she was rested.

He reached for the chalice—he had not forgotten about it, and there was no way he would leave it with her—when she lay a hand on his arm.

"I do not even recall your name," she whispered.

Her touch bored holes through his garment, searing his skin and unleashing his desire. He fought against the urge to pull her flush to his body and kiss her lips in full for the first time. And Lord help him! He wanted her to kiss him back as badly. Wanted it with such force he could almost taste her from where he stood.

With the possibility she could finally fulfill his heart wish, his desire for her flourished, becoming fiercer and more demanding.

He cleared his throat before he spoke. "Hunter is my name." He was certain his voice faltered.

"Hunter," she whispered.

The sweet sound vibrated in his ears. Détra had rarely called him by his name.

Whether her gesture was meant to distract him mattered not at this point. He grabbed the chalice, and before he made a fool of himself, he left the bedchamber, closing the door swiftly behind his back.

"MY LORD?"

Hunter gathered his thoughts and pushed away from the door.

"The healer is here," Maude said. "How is my lady?" Her voice was laden with worry.

Maude must have just returned from the village if she had not seen Détra's mad dash through the great hall and her return on his shoulder, Hunter thought.

"My lady wife has recovered from her ordeal," he said.

"Oh, blessed is the Lord!" Maude fell to her knees, making the sign of the cross in thanksgiving.

"Amen," Hunter responded automatically, as he took in the healer's ragged appearance, her medicinal bag crossed over her chest, filled with lifesaving herbs and potions. Mayhap even a potion to recover lost memories.

"I thank you for coming," Hunter told the healer. "But your presence is no longer needed."

"Mayhap I should still have a look at her," the healer said, eyeing him with shrewd eyes.

"There is no need," Hunter retorted. "Go to the cook and have your fill of whatever you fancy, then go look for Godfrey, the steward, and he shall reward you for your troubles."

After a little hesitation, the healer nodded and left.

"May I see her?" Maude asked.

"Aye, but first I wish to speak with you." Now that he had gotten rid of the healer, Hunter turned his attention back to Maude. "After this morning's ordeal, Détra is in a most fragile state of mind. I bid you to aid her in regaining her strength and health, and refrain from speaking of disagreeable matters in her presence. I wish not to upset her unduly."

"Certainly, my lord. I shall do all in my power to aid my lady. I hold her in great esteem."

"I know you do." He paused. "So do I."

Maude caught Hunter's gaze for a brief moment—an odd fact considering servants rarely faced their lords. But before she lowered her gaze again, Hunter saw the pleading in it. "May I ask a boon of you, my lord?"

Hunter nodded, wondering what she could possibly want.

"Please be tolerant of my lady's ways. She has suffered much in her life. I truly believe she shall come to appreciate your caring for her."

Hunter cringed. Even the servants knew of Détra's coldness toward him. How much more did they know? Did Maude know about their unconsummated marriage? Shame washed over him and he had to bite his tongue not to lash out at Maude. It was not her fault her lady had been a most difficult woman to woo.

Mayhap he could enlist Maude's aid in his plan of conquest. The maid seemed on his side, judging by her last comment.

"There is something else you should know about your lady," Hunter said. "She remembers naught of her life."

"How can that be possible?"

Hunter shrugged. "I know not. A consequence of striking her head, I imagine. However, it is my wish that neither her health nor the fragile understanding between us be imperiled by rehashing unpleasant matters."

"It is most understanding of you, my lord."

Encouraged, Hunter continued, "Lady Détra and I are husband and wife, and I wish a peaceful and harmonious life for us. Can I count on your aid?"

Maude shot him a knowing glance. "I shall do your bidding, my lord. I wish the best for my lady."

Hunter nodded and stepped away from the door. He had a chance to right the wrong of his marriage with Détra, and by all that was holy, he would not waste it.

Chapter 3

CLUTCHING the edge of the table, Isabel stared in despair at the shut door after Hunter disappeared behind it carrying with him the only known means to her freedom. Damn! She thought she'd fooled him; obviously she thought wrong. Not even her last attempt to distract him had worked.

And now the chalice was gone.

She had to follow him.

Thought led to action and Isabel marched to the door, opened it a crack, and then swiftly closed it back again.

Hunter stood outside speaking with a couple of women. Their muffled voices barely carried through the thick wooden door, their words unintelligible. Was one of the women the one Hunter said he'd send to help her? How was Isabel to follow him with other people at her heels?

Isabel hung her head back against the door. She'd wait a little; maybe the women would go away.

The reality of Détra's fleshier body suddenly weighed her down. The waterlogged chemise chilled her to her soul. She hugged herself for warmth and comfort as her gaze caught sight of two wooden chests sitting on the floor a few feet from where she stood. Maybe she could find some dry clothes in there. It wouldn't do for her to get sick and get stuck in bed, or worse, be dependent on medieval medicine. She had no clue how healthy Détra's body was. Better not take any chances.

As she moved toward the more ornate chest, figuring that should be Détra's, she noticed for the first time how her thighs rubbed against each other in a very unfamiliar and unpleasant way. She tried to ignore the odd feeling.

This is only temporary, she chanted silently to herself.

The very large, rectangular chest adorned with paintings of rose vines on its face and flat cover undoubtedly doubled as a bench. Isabel removed the handheld mirror lying on it and sat it on the floor without looking into it again. Opening it, she rummaged inside, finding several gowns, chemises, woolen stockings, and a small leather box containing jewelry, a lock of hair, ribbons—small mementos of Détra's life.

Uncomfortable with going through Détra's personal belongings, Isabel put the small box back inside, lifted the first gown she saw, and closed the lid down.

She pulled the wet chemise over her head and let it fall in a wet heap on the stone floor. Two oil lamps, suspended in rings on the wall, cast an unreal glow on the flawless, pale skin, the large, full breasts, and the slightly rounded stomach of Détra's Rubenesque form.

Isabel muffled a cry. Good God, she truly hoped Détra was not pregnant. With trembling fingers, Isabel rushed

the dress over her head, shielding the unfamiliar body
from her view and the cold damp of the room. Her feet
were cold and dirty. She picked up the wet chemise from
the floor and used it to clean them, then put on the leather
shoes she'd found by the chest. They fit her perfectly. Of
course they did. They belonged to this body she had stolen.

Changes were not new to Isabel. In her wandering life
she'd learned to accept them, learned to find good in the
different and familiar in the unknown. But not even she
could appreciate the ludicrous twist of fate she'd brought
upon herself, Détra, and her unsuspecting husband.

She must undo this horrible mistake.

Blindly swirling around, Isabel ended up face-to-face
with the massive four-poster bed whose white hangings
opened like curtains, the largest and most decorated piece
of furniture in the room. The mere thought she'd be expected to share it with Hunter drove her to the far end of
the room where an arched window graced the wall.

An elaborate iron bar, used to keep the shutters closed,
leaned against the wall. The intricate ironwork in such a
utilitarian object intrigued Isabel, momentarily distracting
her from her dismal plight. She'd seen similar objects in
museums across Europe and had marveled at their beauty
and antiquity. She traced the vine that laced the bar whose
tips spiked to different directions like a two-pointed arrow
and felt an odd emotion of witnessing the inconceivable.

Her attention drifted to the pane made up of small
pieces of white-greenish glass that covered the window.
Subdued rain stroked the glass with rhythmic, soothing
pecks as the storm cleared outside. For a moment the
sound comforted her, but soon reality hit Isabel with full
force. She might need the storm to put things back to the
way they were. It didn't escape her that she might have
to re-create the scene exactly as it was, storm and all.

Good God! First she'd lost sight of the chalice and now the weather was changing. Was her window of opportunity already closing on her?

Desperation seized her and Isabel pushed against the unmoving glass pane, soon realizing the futility of her action. She took a step back and drew in a deep breath. From the corners of her eyes, she saw a kneeler underneath a wooden cross standing somberly by the arched window. She turned to it. Judging by the worn indentation on the leather kneeler, either Hunter or Détra, or maybe even both, had a strong relationship with God.

Though Isabel would never deny her spiritual side—no one could truly appreciate the whimsical beauty of art without being a little mystical—she could hardly remember the last time she prayed. Baptized Catholic, thanks no doubt to her mother since her father had been a confessed atheist his entire life, Isabel had retained only the rudiments of her religion.

Yet she didn't need to be a churchgoer to realize there was something decidedly unearthly to what had happened to her. Exchanging bodies with another woman was inconceivable, unimaginable, and impossible to say the least, and yet it had occurred.

Whatever power had made this travesty possible though, it could surely undo it. Unwilling to wait for her fate to unfold, Isabel turned her back to the kneeler and the myriad of details firmly establishing her presence in this foreign time and place—as if being in another woman's body wasn't enough to drive a sane person to madness—and bolted to the door. Before she reached it, though, the door swung open. Behind the young woman standing in the threshold, Isabel could see Hunter disappearing out of sight.

Damn! She couldn't lose sight of him now.

"My lady—"

Rushing past the woman at the door, Isabel cut her short with a wave of her hand. "Later," she mumbled, flinching at her own curtness, but she didn't have time to get acquainted right now; Hunter was already rounding the corner of the corridor and in a few seconds more she'd lose him.

Hanging behind at the top of the landing—she didn't want him to know he was being followed—Isabel glimpsed Hunter gliding down the steep stone steps. After he crossed the huge room and stepped outside through the massive oak door, she gave him pursuit. Not bothering to look inconspicuous to the other inhabitants of this alien world, Isabel crossed the room after Hunter. She had a mission in mind and nothing would stop her.

Outside, the rain had all but abated and only sporadic drops fell from the clearing skies where the sun peeked shyly between the retreating dark clouds. The weather had taken a decided turn for the better but a cool breeze was still blowing. With a little luck the rain would start again soon, and by then she should have already recovered the chalice.

The morning was growing late and the empty yard of earlier was now heavily populated. A quick glance to her right revealed massive stables and farther down a crowd of men practiced with swords and horses. The twin gates to the outside world lay open in the distance, guards standing sentinel by them. More guards stood at different points on top of the wall encircling the castle. There were plenty of people coming and going, yet there was no sign of Hunter.

Where the hell did he go? She'd kept at his heels, not possibly allowing him enough time to reach the stables or lose himself among the men in training. He certainly couldn't have crossed the vast expanse of yard between the castle and the outside gates. He could have entered, however, one of the many little huts distributed haphazardly in the huge yard. Or rounded the castle walls in the direction of the back of the building.

Isabel paused for a moment, considering which route to take. The back of the castle seemed the quicker, and safer, choice. Hiking up her skirts, Isabel skidded and slid her way to the back. There, a grassy hill sloped down to an orchard of apple trees. As fast as the wet, slippery grass would allow, Isabel rushed down the hill.

Peeking through the neatly planted rows of fruit trees, Isabel saw no sign of Hunter. She braved her way inside the grove. A few sporadic drops fell from the rain-laden leaves above, running down her face like solitary tears, while birds chirped cheerfully in the aftermath of rain. Isabel couldn't share their joy. She needed the storm back, lightning, thunder, and the chalice. She wanted to be back in her own body, her own time, and her own life.

She stopped, let her skirts fall over her feet, and jerked the unruly curls of hair away from her face, gathering the ridiculously long tresses in a makeshift ponytail at the back of her head. She realized Détra had no control over the jarring auburn color of her hair, or the profusion of curls, but why would the woman allow her hair to grow below her buttocks? It was such a nuisance. Isabel longed for her short, manageable hair.

She gathered her skirts again and trod on, avoiding a low branch hanging over the path. After a while she stopped again to take stock of what to do next. She'd already gone deep enough into the orchard and hadn't found Hunter. Maybe he hadn't come this way at all. She should just return to the castle. Darting a glance backward she discovered the castle was no longer visible behind the canopy of fruit trees.

"Do you seek me?"

Isabel jumped, swallowing down a shriek and swirling around, her hair splashing free again against her face.

Appearing out of nowhere, Hunter leaned a shoulder against a tree, his feet crossed in a leisurely manner, as if he'd been there all along watching her.

Damn! The man was proving difficult to fool. Not that she was very practiced in this game of deceit, anyway.

"Not particularly," she said, gathering her hair once again away from her face. Her gaze sought his person and she noticed he didn't have the chalice with him, and neither was it in the vicinity of where he stood. Had he hidden it in the orchard or had he dropped it somewhere in the castle or even along the way? How could she find out without asking him, or drawing attention to it?

Sensing his gaze upon her, Isabel brought her attention back to him. "After this morning's ordeal I needed a little fresh air," she said in explanation for her presence in the orchard. For effect, she took a deep breath, the pleasing after-rain earthy scent filling her lungs.

With an easy motion Hunter pushed away from the tree and ambled in her direction. The moment he invaded her personal space, Isabel's nostrils filled with the intoxicating manly scent of him—clean, fresh, and much more enticing than any artificial perfume could ever aspire to be. The heat from his body floated to her like vapors from a hot spring. She resisted the urge to fan herself with her hand.

"Last we spoke your need for rest was greater."

Isabel couldn't say whether his tone was doubtful or simply matter of fact.

"Needs change," she answered cautiously, feeling like a blind woman everyone believed could see. "My room suddenly became too dark and suffocating. I decided a walk would do me greater good than a rest."

"And thus you sought the freedom and privacy of the orchard," he offered.

Isabel nodded. That was exactly what she wanted him to believe. Maybe she still could pull this off. "I love the sun, the freedom of the openness—" She snapped her mouth shut. She'd forgotten who she was supposed to be. Détra might feel the absolute opposite from her. Likely, the woman hated being outside, judging by her pale skin, and loved dark and suffocating, judging by her choice of husband.

"Indeed?" he asked, noticing her reticence. "That is odd since I thought you disliked the outdoors."

Isabel didn't know what to say. She was caught in her first contradiction. How many more before Hunter became suspicious of her? But why would he? Hadn't she lost her memory?

"I guess I forgot about that too," she said.

Isabel knew that anything remotely connected with mental illness in the Middle Ages would be misunderstood and thought evil, but on what else could she blame the blunders she was bound to commit until she could reverse her wish?

"I know it is difficult to understand—I myself cannot understand it at all—but I remember nothing about my past."

"I see," he said with that enigmatic look of his.

Did he really?

Hunter's tolerance was crucial to Isabel's plans of making as few waves as possible until she could undo this bizarre situation. She wanted to disappear as if she'd never been here.

Though she knew little about the intimate details of Détra's and Hunter's lives, they seemed well suited for each other—in appearance, at least. They matched in color, she in a vibrant brightness, he in a dark sort of way.

Isabel's own pale coloring would contrast too sharply with him. They also seemed well matched in size; Hunter stood only a head taller than his wife did, though he was very tall indeed. Isabel's petite form would be dwarfed in his presence. And surely Hunter appreciated Détra's roundness and fleshy body—no doubt the female ideal of many centuries before and yet to come—unlike Isabel's small and trim frame.

And doubtless, Détra also appreciated Hunter's masculine handsomeness—ideal in any century. And so did Isabel. What woman wouldn't? There was nothing soft about the man. From the impenetrability of his black onyx eyes, to the rough-looking stubble that shadowed his bronzed face, to the great breadth of his shoulders, Hunter was the picture of a medieval warrior in all his glory.

Defined by his ability to physically defend himself and what was his, willing to go to any lengths to achieve his goals, most probably capable of unbelievable acts of bravery guided by some unspoken code of honor. . . .

What was she trying to do? Brainwash herself? Isabel shook her head to dispel the idealized image her mind created. Hunter was just a man, albeit a very alluring one. A man married to the body she now inhabited. She repressed a growl of frustration at the undeniable truth.

"I beg your understanding, Hunter, if at times I should act a little . . . odd. Hopefully this forgetfulness will only be temporary." She watched him as she waited for his response. When the seconds strung along, his silence began to weigh on her. Her body tensed, her stomach churned, and her mouth went dry.

After an interminable stretch of time, he finally broke the unsettling silence. "I am an understanding man."

Relief washed over Isabel. "Thank you," she said simply.

He lowered his head a little as if about to impart the

greatest of secrets. Isabel caught herself leaning toward him.

"I am pleased you got rid of your sodden chemise," he said, picking up a curl of her hair and twisting it around his fingers, his hand close enough to touch her face. "I wish no ill fate befalling you." He brought the strand of hair to his nostrils and inhaled deeply.

His confession and the intimate gesture unsettled Isabel. She straightened her back, looking for something to say that would dissipate the intimacy of such a personal moment. Noticing he still wore his wet clothes, she seized her chance to separate them. "Is your life less important than mine?" She stared pointedly at his clothes.

He cocked his head, as if unsure of her concern. His face assumed a serious demeanor, his penetrating gaze seeking her soul. And then a half grin slashed his handsome face, dispelling his all-too-serious façade, making him look younger than she'd first thought he'd be. How old was he, anyway? Suddenly Hunter was not the medieval warrior anymore; he was just a man. A man who belonged to another woman and to whom she was very much attracted.

"My lady's concern lightens my heart," he said, letting go of her hair and taking a step back.

Without warning, he undid his sword belt and let it fall to the ground. Pulling his shirt over his head in one sweeping move, he unveiled a muscled, bronzed chest generously sprinkled with dark hair.

The tantalizing view of his sinewy body pushed Isabel into action. She skittered back, snapping her mouth shut and lifting her hand in warning—as if the gesture had the power to terminate his shameless striptease.

"What're you doing?" she asked. "I didn't mean for you to undress." In her agitation she even forgot not to use contractions.

If he noticed it, he ignored it. He shot a perfunctory glance around before returning a daring gaze to her. "There is no one here but you and me, husband and wife."

Husband and wife!

Isabel swallowed hard at the reminder. She was in Détra's body and Détra *was* Hunter's wife. Good God! What a mess she'd made of things. What if Hunter and Détra often rendezvoused in the orchard? Isabel almost groaned at the possibility.

At the sight of Hunter's hand reaching for her, Isabel got ready to bolt, but instead of grabbing her as she'd expected, his hand reached above her head to pluck an apple from the tree. Letting out a breath she didn't know she was holding, she chided herself for feeling like an uninitiated teenager and not the twenty-five-year-old woman that she was.

With what she thought was a nonchalant pose, she stood her ground, but when Hunter offered her the apple with a daring, tempting gaze, Isabel knew she should've run when she had the chance. Excitement skimmed down her skin. She hadn't felt that way in a long time and she was tempted to accept the offering—not the fruit, but the promise behind that dangerous gaze.

Was that how Adam had fallen for Eve's trick?

Isabel refused to submit. She shook her head.

Hunter shrugged at her refusal and took a deep bite of the fruit. His teeth tore the crimson skin, sinking with gusto into the ripe meat, then his lips closed over the morsel. A drop of juice escaped from the corner of his mouth, drifting down his chin. The tip of his tongue reached for it, partly recovering the runaway droplet, then gliding over his lower lip, until it disappeared again inside his mouth. Isabel followed the trajectory with mesmerizing interest.

Unable—more like unwilling, she silently admitted to

herself—to turn her gaze away from his mouth, Isabel watched as Hunter continued to devour the forbidden fruit until all that was left was the core. With a flip of his wrist he tossed it to the ground, then licked the sweet juice off his finger.

Isabel knew she was gaping. She snapped her mouth shut for the umpteenth time, but when he reached for the drawstrings of his pants she knew she could either run or face the music.

She simply wasn't ready to dance right now.

"I believe it is time I returned to the castle." She stumbled over her long skirts in her attempt to flee. How she missed her blue jeans! "A lady's duties are never done, you know." She almost groaned at her witless remark. She must have lost her brain somewhere between his mouth and the waist of his pants.

Hunter caught her wrist and brought her flush to his body. "What of your duty to your lord husband?" he whispered against her cheek, the sweet scent of fresh apple mingled with his manly scent wafting to her, more delectable than any exotic fruit she'd ever tasted.

Trying to free herself from his hold, she said, "Certain duties should be reserved for more private quarters." She almost rolled her eyes at her prudish words. Phony as they sounded to her, surely they wouldn't to him.

"A moment ago you thought the orchard private enough." Hunter deposited a soft kiss behind her ear before wickedly licking her earlobe. By a miracle Isabel managed not to squeal, her weak knees a telltale sign that it'd been too long since she'd last made love to a man. And Hunter was no ordinary man.

She must get him away from her ears. There was just so much she could take.

Isabel pushed against him, swallowing hard as she noticed how his pants hung precariously on his narrow hips.

If he took a deep breath, the damn garment would plunge to his ankles. The image disturbed her the more because she couldn't erase it from her mind.

Dismissing the treacherous wanting forming inside her, Isabel averted her gaze from the growing evidence of his desire. Desire directed at Détra, not her, she reminded herself once again, gaining some control over her stumbling heart.

"Would you deny your husband a kiss?" Hunter whispered as he refused to let her go. His mouth traveled the oversensitive skin of her neck.

Trying to get her mind clear of the fog enveloping it, Isabel pondered that a kiss might not be too high of a price to appease him. Maybe he would be satisfied with that. Surely he wouldn't expect to make love in the orchard—after a thunderstorm no less—in the middle of the day? These were medieval times! The sexual revolution was centuries away.

Isabel realized she was mind babbling. Desire had transformed her brain into mush, and yet the longer she took to answer him, the longer his body pressed against hers, the longer he inflamed her desire with his touch, and the more difficult it was for her to think clearly. She should allow him one kiss and then he'd let her go, and she wouldn't be forced to cross the thin line between necessary duplicity and downright deceit.

"A kiss," she whispered, pulling him away with a final effort. Her gaze drifted from his inflamed eyes to his parted lips. Oh, whom was she kidding? If Hunter's kiss were half as good as she anticipated, she knew *she* wouldn't want to stop at only one kiss. "One kiss," she repeated, more to herself than to him, then closed her eyes and waited for the world to end.

*   *   *

A KISS FROM HIS BRIDE, WILLINGLY GIVEN, EAGERLY accepted. The tremble began in the pit of Hunter's stomach and journeyed up to his heart. He shook with the exhilarating prospect of Détra's surrender. Her acceptance, her love, the possibility of realizing that vision of happiness, meant everything to him, and now with Détra's lack of memories, it all seemed possible.

With a deliberate slow motion Hunter stepped forward and burrowed his hands underneath the soft mass of curls, resting his thumbs on her cheekbones. Her eyes flared open and she measured him with her gaze.

Eager to take from her what she promised, what she had forever denied him, Hunter was unprepared, however, for the desire flickering in the green depths of his lady wife's eyes.

Détra had usually avoided looking at him altogether, until this morning before the advent of the chalice, when she didn't hide the disdain in her gaze. And yet, there was no denying the desire revealed through her half-lowered eyelids, her parted lips, her sweet womanly essence mingled with the faint scent of rosemary that wafted to him, curtailing his breathing and making his body coil tightly. Hunter forced himself to take a deep, calming breath, lest he fall at her feet like a drooling idiot.

Surely his bride had not followed him to the orchard for a midday tryst, though the thought cheered him mightily. Could his mother's magical chalice be powerful enough to warrant such drastic change in Détra? A fool he was not, and yet he could not deny she was different. There was a new touch of daring mingled with vulnerability about her that he found quite becoming.

His rough thumbs caressed the soft skin of her face and to his delight she did not recoil from him. For a wife who had avoided her husband like the plague since their wedding night, Détra's acceptance of his touch was a much-welcomed relief.

"Are you going to kiss me," she asked, cutting into the fog of his thoughts, "or are you going to stare me to death?"

The merriment in Détra's voice confounded Hunter. The twitch of impatience grounded him some. His mind doubted her metamorphosis, but his foolish heart eagerly embraced it. It was too early to know whether she played him for a fool or not.

"Though your beauty enchants me and I would stare at you forever," he said, feeling giddy like the fourteen-year-old lad he once was, gazing at the unattainable object of his affection, "your kiss is a pleasure I would be a fool to forgo."

Giving in to the carnal invitation of Détra's plump lips, Hunter lowered his face to hers. There had been too many stolen kisses for him. He wanted this one to last forever. He grazed her lips ever so lightly and was unprepared for the jolt of intense pleasure the contact afforded him. He kissed one corner of her mouth, then the other. He caught her lower lip between his and suckled it, savoring the sweet nectar. She did not pull away; instead, she inched closer. Encouraged, Hunter slanted his mouth over hers, his tongue slipping between the sweet seam, daring, hoping she would open to him.

And she did! Her hands, fisted in a token protest, also opened up, and her palms flattened against the flesh of his chest.

With the blood roaring in his ears, Hunter probed deeper and her velvety tongue met with his. The shock traversed down his body, hardening him swiftly. The primitive need to be inside her fueled a desperate need to turn the flicker of desire he glimpsed in her eyes into a full-blown fire of lust. He slid his hands down her back;

his arms encircled her waist as he brought her body flush to his while his mouth devoured hers. Hunter warred against the need to rock his erection against her. That would be too much, too soon, he decided. He wished not to frighten his lady wife. She had already given him more in this kiss than she had since the day they were wedded.

But now that he had tasted her passion, he could not be satisfied with only one kiss. He wanted more, much more. His mouth slid down her neck, found the concave of her shoulders and tasted her to his heart's content. Her little murmurs of approval drove him insane. Never had Détra responded to his touch like this. The few crumbles of attention he received from her had always been stolen, demanded, delivered as if under siege. But now he could feel her desire, could smell it, taste it. Whatever the chalice had done to Détra, Hunter hoped it would never change her back again.

He slid one knee between her soft thighs while his mouth relentlessly tasted her, from shoulders to neck to mouth, back and forth again in a joyful ride. He dared to go further. He slid one hand up her side and cupped her breast. He rubbed his palm against her hardened nipples, and what had begun as a tender caress quickly escalated into a hungry, almost desperate touch.

With his free hand Hunter lifted her from the ground and she wrapped her legs around his hips. He stumbled to the nearest tree and secured her against the trunk while he pushed her skirts upward. As he sought to release himself from the confines of his breeches, he whispered against her mouth in utter ecstasy, "Détra, oh Détra."

It took Hunter a moment to realize his wife's body had stiffened, her lips ceased their wondrous caress, her hands pushed against him. "Stop, please, stop," she cried.

Dazed, his breath coming in short gasps, his heart

thumping uncontrollably, Hunter stared at her in utter confusion.

"Let me down, please," she begged, avoiding his gaze and trying to push her skirts down.

Understanding swiftly filled Hunter with the old shame of rejection. With his heart burning, he stepped back. He stood there, exposed, unable to hide the desire that throbbed at his loins and the shame that flamed his face, as she rearranged her clothing.

She had done it again. Had brought shame and humiliation to him. Only this time, she had gone too far. She had led him to believe she could care for him, want him. This deceit he could not forgive her.

"Why have you followed me into the orchard?" he asked, a bitter grin slicing his face. "Speak the truth, my lady wife. I cannot abide liars."

Détra visibly trembled. It would do her good to fear him. He was at the end of his rope, foolishly believing that a mere chalice could change the woman he wedded into the woman of his heart.

"I'm not your wife," she cried.

"What do you say?"

"I am not your wife," she repeated in a whisper as she lifted her gaze to him.

Was it regret he saw there? Hunter stepped toward her. He would know once and for all what manner of game Détra played.

"If not my wife, pray tell me, who are you?"

Chapter 4

I'M a twenty-first-century woman who made a thoughtless wish to be in your wife's place and now inhabits her body and lusts for her husband!

Isabel gritted her teeth to avoid shouting the words that choked her. As uncomfortable as she was with the pretense she must endure, she couldn't just blurt out the truth. To claim amnesia was risky enough in these medieval times; to proclaim body switching and time travel could be deadly. She wasn't about to have her sanity questioned and put her life at risk.

She would have to find a way to survive until she undid what her thoughtless wish had provoked. And though she didn't want Détra to suffer the consequences of her actions in this time, she'd have to think of herself also. Isabel only hoped Détra was coping well in the future. She didn't want to go back and find herself in a straitjacket locked up in a psychiatric ward.

"Speak, Détra." Chest heaving with labored breathing, hands fisted beside his powerful body, posture as stiff as a tree trunk, Hunter demanded her reply.

Turning her face away from him, Isabel's gaze rested on the mud-covered hem of her dress. She fussed with it, gaining some time to think. If not the truth, what could she possibly tell Hunter? She'd spoken out of turn when she denied being his wife. Damn his hot kiss that clouded her judgment and made her momentarily forget the seriousness of her situation and blurt out the truth about her identity. Now she was left to explain the unexplainable.

"You denied being my wife," Hunter insisted. "Surely you have something to say about that."

Reluctantly Isabel lifted her gaze to Hunter, but uneasy under his stare, she shifted in place, flipping an unruly curl away from her face. She couldn't take back her words—they were already out—so her only choice would be to build on what she'd already said.

Yet no brilliant thought came rushing to mind. "I may have spoken too soon," she began, hating the unaccustomed position of having to explain herself. "Though, obviously, I could not say with any degree of certainty whether I am or am not your wife—"

"Memories or nay," he interrupted, "the fact you are my wife remains unchanged."

"That fact alone cannot change the way I feel," she retorted. "You must realize how awkward it is for me to assume a life I remember nothing about with a husband who's a stranger to me."

"A stranger whose kisses you eagerly responded to," he immediately challenged. "Or do you deny that also?"

She had done that, hadn't she? She had responded to his kisses and then turned cold on him when he called her by his wife's name. Of course Hunter didn't know it wasn't his wife who had rejected his touch but an impostor.

Had Détra ever rejected her husband's amorous overtures before? Was a medieval woman even allowed such discretion? Weren't medieval women considered chattel to their husbands? A shudder ran down her spine and Isabel eyed Hunter cautiously. He was a powerfully built man, and a visibly angry one. Thankfully he also looked to be in control of his temper. For the moment, at least. How long would that control last when she continued to resist his advances? And resist him she must. It'd be wrong for her to take advantage of the situation, despite her attraction to him. Hunter thought she was his lawful wife, for God's sake! Isabel knew better.

"My body reacted to you," she blurted out in an attempt to distance herself from her questionable actions. "It was just a natural response; I had no control over it." As soon as the words stumbled out of her mouth, Isabel realized her mistake.

For a moment Hunter looked perplexed, but then probably realizing she'd given him the perfect argument, he stepped closer, invading her space again, filling the air with his scent, his heat. He cupped her face with his very large hands and a jolt of instant awareness struck Isabel.

"Surely," he whispered as his fingers burrowed beneath the curls of her hair and his thumbs caressed her cheek, drawing goose bumps down her neck, "that fact alone proves that even without memories your heart recognizes me as your lord husband."

Isabel pursed her lips—there was no argument against that. No woman in her right mind would forget Hunter's touch. With an emotion akin to regret, she peeled his hands from her face and stepped back, putting some very necessary distance between them.

"I am willing to accept that fact," she said, realizing

she must concede that much. "However, I ask you to be patient and wait to resume certain . . . aspects of our married life until I can recover my memory."

If she couldn't avoid playing the role of wife to Hunter—at least, until she found that damn chalice and reversed the travesty her misguided wish had caused—she would surely avoid sharing his bed. She would not add to her sins. No matter how attracted she was to the man.

His nostrils flared in obvious displeasure. "We have been wedded for two weeks and I am to accept a celibate life unless your memory returns?"

Hunter and Détra were still in their honeymoon! No wonder he was freaking out. No man—unless a priest or a eunuch—would consider an undetermined time of celibacy. Worse of all, Isabel was unable to reassure Hunter it would be only a temporary arrangement, that soon all would be back to normal.

The back of Isabel's neck and shoulders ached with tension. She rubbed them wearily. Hunter had every right to be angry and to demand an answer from her. After all, though he didn't know, it had been *her* thoughtless wish that caused this horrible entanglement.

For a moment, Isabel toyed with the thought of asking Hunter for the chalice's whereabouts. But how would she explain she remembered it and nothing else? She could give no logical reason for wanting it. She wasn't even sure Hunter was aware of the chalice's magical powers. And if she revealed she was she would also have to reveal her secret. A secret so unbelievable no one, in this medieval time or any other, could possibly comprehend, let alone accept.

Isabel shook her head. No, she couldn't chance it. Her situation was precarious as it was. Maybe later, in a more appropriate time and place, she could spring her request on Hunter without having to give too many explanations.

Meanwhile, she would just keep on working to keep Hunter at bay while she searched for the chalice.

"I agree my request seems unfair," Isabel said. Hunter snorted. "All right, I know it is unfair. However, it is equally unfair of you to expect me to resume our life together as if nothing has happened." Forestalling his challenge and his approach she lifted a hand between them. "Please, hear me out. This is very difficult for me." Her voice shook with the effort to control her emotions and to think coherently. "I have lost all cognizance of my own person. My request for some understanding and some time to remember, to situate myself, to accept and adjust—if necessary be—to this new life is not unreasonable."

A lengthy silence followed. Hunter stared at her as if he wanted to read her mind or touch her soul. Isabel understood she might be asking a little too much from a medieval man, but if Hunter cared for his wife the way it seemed he did, then he'd surely give her some breathing space.

"How long?" he finally asked.

Isabel let out a sigh of relief. "A month," she said promptly. Not that she had any intention of remaining in this body for that long. It was just a precaution in case things didn't go as smoothly as she hoped.

Hunter shook his head.

Obviously a month was out of the question. She wouldn't need that long to locate the chalice, anyway. How big could this castle be?

"Two weeks then," she backtracked. Two weeks should be plenty of time.

He hesitated. Isabel pressed on. "If by the end of that time my memory has not returned I swear I will abide by your wishes."

He came to stand before her. Their gazes locked as he

took her hands into his, as if daring her to reject him this time. She didn't.

"I grant you a week's time," he said as if that'd be the greatest sacrifice on earth for him.

"A week is not much time to recover one's memory," she complained.

"You are my wife. A week is a reasonable amount of time for you to accept that, memory or nay."

Realizing she was backed against a wall, Isabel had to agree. "All right. A week then." She better find that damn chalice way before that time was up. The way Hunter looked at her and the way she reacted to his touch didn't bode well for either of them.

With a slow motion he brought her hands to his lips and kissed her fingers with such tenderness, Isabel trembled.

This man loved his wife! The realization spread over her like a cold shower and instantly a pang of guilt tightened her heart. She had separated Hunter from his wife and she would do anything to bring them back together again. Surely, at this very moment, Détra was desperately trying to return to her own body, to her own life, to her beloved husband.

Meanwhile, for everyone's benefit, Isabel would keep up with her charade. Soon everything would return to normal and Hunter would have his wife back, not even knowing he'd kissed and desired a total stranger.

"Meantime—" Hunter's husky voice brought Isabel out of her musings as he lifted his lips from her hands. She sought his dark, impenetrable gaze and a light shone there, a light she hadn't noticed before. "—I shall endeavor to aid you in recovering your memory."

Had she truly expected him to fade into the background while she ostensibly sought her past when in fact she chased her future?

He kissed her gently, unhurriedly, unthreateningly. All Isabel could do was to accept it, to take it, to savor it. He lifted, letting go of her momentarily while he picked up his shirt from the ground and donned it quickly along with his sword belt.

He tucked her hand back into his. "Let us walk back to the castle, my lady wife."

There was no misinterpreting the promise in his words, in his gaze. A promise not intended for her. Isabel shook the sadness overtaking her. She didn't belong to this life, to this body, to this man, no matter her wish. She had no right to feel anything toward Hunter. No right whatsoever.

WITH DÉTRA'S HAND FIRMLY ENCASED IN HIS, HUNTER ambled toward the castle. He reeled inside, uncertain of what to expect next. In the orchard, when he had glimpsed the desire in the depths of Détra's eyes and tasted her wanton kisses, he had been certain the chalice had granted his heart wish.

Her apparent change of heart soon after, however, had swiftly shattered that illusion.

Was Détra truly forgetful? Or was it just another excuse not to consummate their marriage? She seemed sincere enough regarding her lack of memory—odd as that might be. Who had ever heard of such a malady? And yet, if the chalice had anything to do with it, and Hunter wanted to believe it did, he should accept her claim without a question. After all, what else could have happened to explain Détra's change? For she had changed. It was almost as if she cared for his feelings.

And therein lay a very important distinction between his bride of earlier this morning and this one walking by his side. A distinction Hunter fully intended on exploring.

As they plodded up the slippery grassy mound, Hunter

observed Détra. Struggling to hold her dress up from the wet ground, Détra took a moment to notice his stare. When she did, she followed his gaze to her exposed legs.

"Difficult thing to handle." She shrugged, letting her skirts fall and halting their progress, lest she trip on the length of cloth, no doubt. "I believe I need the use of both my hands." She shot him a beguiling smile.

Still unaccustomed to a smiling Détra, Hunter acquiesced, wondering about the odd rhythm of her speech—full of melodious tones nonexistent before this morning's incident, full of words Détra never used before, full with a casualness he would never attribute to his lady wife. Wondering about her garment—why was she not wearing a shift and stockings underneath her gown and head covering she always wore before?

As soon as she gathered her skirts in a more demure manner, regretfully hiding her naked flesh to his view, Hunter repossessed her hand and resumed their walk.

Contrary to her usual self, Détra allowed his handling of her, but after only a few steps she halted again, this time warring against the unruly curls that refused to obey her commands. She flung her head back. "Dam—" She shot him a guilty look. "Blasted hair."

Détra's annoyance at her glorious hair—her most cherished feature—intrigued Hunter. He had noticed, since this morning's ordeal, she often rearranged her tresses in an annoyed manner. Could it be because she usually wore it in a tight plait or covered by veils unless in the privacy of her bedchamber? Hunter infinitely preferred her hair loose, falling over her shoulders in vibrant waves and flying about with the breeze. He could still feel the silky texture between his fingers when both he and Détra were lost in their embracing kiss in the orchard.

Hunter's senses, reawakened by the glimpse of flesh, immediately reacted to the memory of those kisses. His lust stirred impatiently. A lust he now would have to wait a week to assuage thanks to his promise to his lady wife. And yet, what was a week when he had been waiting for what seemed an eternity for her surrender?

Besides, he would not lie idle in the meantime. He would continue to seek the desire he glimpsed in his wife's eyes until he turned that flickering into a full-blown lust for him.

Unbidden, memories of their disappointing wedding night—and all the nights that followed—came back to him. For years Hunter had dreamed of the day he would have Détra in his arms, in his bed. That fantasy had carried him through many a lonely night. And yet, when the time came for them to be together as husband and wife, Détra had rejected him.

But in the orchard this morning Hunter had discovered there was passion in his lady wife's heart, after all. Passion that had been buried underneath the dislike she held for him. Passion that he fully intended to awaken by the time this week was over.

However, he must keep in mind Détra's true feelings for him buried in the depths of her mind, feelings that would surely resurrect to life along with her memory. His only chance to entomb them completely would be to fill her heart and mind with memories she would long to relive.

And to do so he would have to deceive her into believing a fantasy that never was. A sudden pang of conscience speared his heart. He ignored it. It was for her own good, for the good of them both. He would do whatever was necessary to prove to Détra and everyone who ever doubted his value that though a bastard of unknown sire, he was worthy of being loved and cherished by his lady wife.

As they resumed their trek, Hunter watched the sun—

which had barely showed its face this morning—suddenly surge from behind a dark cloud in a cheerful presage of good things to come. At least he hoped so.

"The first time ever I saw you," Hunter began, spinning his tale, "I thought the sun had descended upon the earth, just as it is doing now."

She turned her gaze back on him.

"You were radiant," he said truthfully. "Still are. The most beautiful lady I have ever laid eyes upon." And that was the truth. He never forgot how the sun had framed Détra's hair in a fiery halo those many years ago, exactly as it was doing now.

"So, it was love at first sight," she said.

"It was for me."

She halted. A shadow of a jesting smile played on her face. "You mean to say that I was not immediately struck by the cupid arrow the moment my eyes laid upon your handsome visage?"

Humor? Another unexpected change.

"There was not much you could see considering I was covered in mud." He carefully chose his words. The closer he stuck to the truth the easier this would be.

She raised an inquiring eyebrow.

"I was involved in a brawl with another squire," he explained as he urged her forward.

"Oh, and what was the fight about?" she asked as they rounded the corner of the keep.

"I remember not," Hunter lied, not wishing to speak of matters that were best left unspoken between them. "It was a long time ago. It hardly matters now."

In the bailey, Windermere's people busied about their affairs, but as Hunter and Détra strolled by them, one by one they halted and gaped openly at them.

Détra seemed to pay them no mind. Hunter cherished every moment.

"It mattered enough for you to fight with this young man. It could not have been about me, considering we had just met, or was it?" she teased, her green gaze seeking his.

In a way it had been about her, though the fight had started for a completely different reason.

Accustomed to being ostracized—in his village he was shunned by the other boys for being considered better than they were, and in his fostering castle he was shunned for exactly the opposite reason—Hunter had learned early in life to ignore hurtful taunting. However, when cunning alone failed him he was forced to use physical strength to be left alone. And that day, when he first saw Détra, had been such an occasion.

Edmund, an apprentice squire like Hunter, but unlike Hunter, one of noble birth, was one of his most tenacious persecutors. Resenting Hunter's presence—for only those of noble birth were allowed or could afford to be trained for knighthood—Edmund missed no opportunity to smear Hunter's honor. His favorite gibe was to call Hunter a bloody bastard.

Hunter's bastardy was an undeniable fact and most at Hawkhaven, where Hunter fostered, were aware of that. Some even wondered whether Lord Reginald, his fostering lord, could be his father. Hunter wondered as well. After all, the man was Hunter's sponsor. However, such suspicions were never proved, though it gained Hunter the animosity of yet another squire—Rupert, Lord Reginald's son.

But calling Hunter a bastard had not been the cause of that particular fight. On that day Edmund had decided to add another insult to his tiring taunts. He called Hunter's mother a witch. And that Hunter could not ignore.

When Détra and her entourage had entered the bailey of Hawkhaven Castle, Hunter had already vanquished Edmund. Yet lost in the beauty of her sight Hunter had loosened his hold of the squire, who rose to his feet sneering at Hunter.

"You can worm your way into knighthood, Sir Bastard," Edmund had spat, "but no lady will ever take you for husband willingly."

In a way Edmund had been right. Hunter had wedded the woman of his dreams, but Détra had never accepted him as her rightful husband.

Hunter's hands balled up into fists—the old hurt fighting to surface, the old stoicism fighting to bury it. The tale he concocted to tell Détra forgotten.

"I see that it is not a memory you cherish," Détra said, trying to loose his hold of her. He then realized he had squashed her hand into his.

"As I said, it was a long time ago." He relaxed his hold of her.

"But I bet you won the fight," she said. A little mischievous smile played on her full lips.

Hunter eyed his lady wife skeptically. Her faith, though welcomed, was hardly expected. "Your trust in me is heartwarming." It would truly be were it heartfelt. "Let us just say," he continued, "that the squire I fought with will be forever known as Edmund the Toothless." Edmund's big teeth, made whiter by the contrast of his mud-covered face, had offered a target Hunter had found impossible to resist.

"I am sure he deserved it." His lady wife's smile and support warmed Hunter's heart. Though he shielded his heart from disappointment, he felt oddly pleased with himself.

"That he did."

"So that was how you conquered my heart," she said. "Not with your handsome face, but with your fighting skills?" Her appreciative gaze spanned the breadth of his chest. Unbidden, he squared his shoulders.

Nay, he had hardly won her heart on that beautiful summer day so long ago. In fact, Détra had been unimpressed with him. And why should she not? He was a scrawny squire, of unknown parentage and uncertain future. Even he knew that he was unworthy of her. But on that day, then and there, he had sworn to seek her for wife. And thus, Détra had become his unattainable dream. The one he admired from afar and worked day and night to be deserving of.

For Détra of Windermere was his heart wish. And though he had yet to win her heart, with the help of his mother's magical chalice, he might just have a chance at that.

"We were fortunate," Hunter said. "For my puny efforts to impress you would have hardly mattered had not the king blessed our union with his approval." He gazed at her, intent on impressing on her the inevitability of their fate. "Therefore, my lady wife, not even your lack of memories can set us asunder." He tried to keep the bitterness out of his voice but knew he failed when a shadow crossed Détra's face.

She laid her hand on top of his as they halted before the entrance of the great hall. "All shall be well soon, Hunter," she promised.

Was she trying to pacify him? Why?

"Aye, it shall." He would make certain of that. He motioned her inside and everybody in the hall turned a stunned gaze at the uncommon sight of their lady and lord walking hand in hand.

Chapter 5

A loner, a self-proclaimed nomad with no ties or family, Isabel had no firsthand experience with the kind of relationship Hunter and Détra must've shared before she'd messed things up for them. But knowing her own deep yearning for such closeness in her life, she keenly felt the weight of responsibility for the unhappiness her misguided wish had caused him.

Before she complicated his life, and Détra's, any further, she must retrieve the chalice. However, despite her probing, Hunter's brief account of his courtship with Détra had revealed nothing useful. She should've questioned him about the chalice and not immersed herself in his life.

After all, why should it matter to her whether Hunter and Détra's love was the epitome of a fairy tale or a tortuous road to happiness? Whether they fell in love at first sight or had slowly fallen in love with each other?

Whether they were together since they met or only recently received the king's approval?

What mattered was whether they would ever be able to enjoy their lives together again.

A knot formed in Isabel's throat. There was that annoying feeling again, the feeling of being an intruder, unwanted, unnecessary. Isabel swallowed down the bitter taste. She detested that role and yet she had played it too often. First with her parents, when she'd lived like a shadow to the two people who were completely content with each other's company. Then with Jack, her exhusband, when she'd tried so hard to fit in his orderly, perfect life, and failed miserably. And now she repeated history. Only this time she'd disrupted the lives of two strangers.

Guilt weighed her down. Isabel shook it off and walked beside Hunter into the great hall of Windermere Castle. She suddenly noticed the animated conversation trickled to a stop, and when she lifted her gaze, every pair of eyes in the room met hers.

Isabel's step faltered.

Memories of earlier this morning flashed to her. She had surely given them a sight to behold, running like a maniac through the hall and into the rain outside. Then later she had returned on Hunter's shoulders, screaming and kicking at him. Her third sojourn through this same hall, and possibly in front of these same people, she had followed Hunter outside in a more sedate if still conspicuous manner, for she hadn't acknowledged one single soul in her way.

And here she was again, walking hand in hand with Hunter as if nothing had happened.

Somehow Isabel didn't believe Détra's behavior was

ever that erratic, especially considering the way they eyed
her now, like she'd grown two heads.

God knew what damage her earlier performance had
done to Détra's reputation. This was her home and her
people. And yet Isabel couldn't blame herself on that account. She was doing the best she could under the circumstances. She must think of her survival first.

Hunter gently pulled her with him in the direction of
the stone stair, ignoring everyone. It was obvious he was
in no mood to socialize, and truth be told, neither was
she.

But it seemed someone was.

The man was shorter than Hunter, soft blue eyes, beard
a shade darker than his red hair, quite handsome in a
gentle sort of way. Not at all like the dark, rough-looking,
all-consuming Hunter, Isabel couldn't help but compare.

He stood to the side, obsequious yet concerned, then
bowed to Hunter and directed an intense gaze at Isabel.

"My lady," he said. "I have been worried. Maude told
me you were—" His gaze strayed to Hunter, and then
back to her. "—not yourself this day."

The understatement of the year!

"I am fine, thank you." What else could she say? And
who was he?

"May I be of assistance?" he insisted as if not believing
her words.

"As you can attest for yourself, Godfrey," Hunter interrupted, "my lady wife fares well."

Grudgingly Godfrey stepped back, though his gaze
sought Isabel's as if seeking confirmation.

Hunter's mood seemed to darken at that. "Lady Détra
needs her rest," he said. "I trust she shall not be disturbed." Without waiting for a reply Hunter pulled Isabel
forward.

As Isabel followed Hunter up the stairs she stole a

quick glance over her shoulder. Godfrey, and everyone
else in the hall, followed their progress with great interest.
Isabel turned her face forward. She didn't know what to
make of it. Frankly, she didn't care. All she needed to
worry about was finding the chalice and getting out of
here as soon as possible.

Only a few hours had passed since she'd awakened in
Détra's body, and yet it already seemed an eternity. The
longer she remained here the more embroiled she would
become in Détra's life.

And that was the last thing Isabel wanted.

When Hunter held the door open to the bedroom Isabel
crossed the threshold ahead of him and found a young
woman in the room staring at her with doe-like eyes. The
woman was petite and her light brown hair hung over her
shoulder in a tight braid that touched her knees. Chasing
away her deliberations, Isabel recognized her as the
woman she'd rushed by earlier when in pursuit of Hunter.
Had the poor thing stayed here waiting for her all this
time?

For a moment a dead silence blanketed them all. It
seemed no one knew what to do or say next. Then Hunter
came to stand beside her after he closed the door.

"This is Maude, your maid companion," he said. "She
is abreast of your condition."

Isabel nodded.

"Lord Hunter told me about this morning's awful mis-
hap," Maude said. "It is fortunate that you were only
mildly harmed by your fall. God was very generous in
sparing your life, my lady."

Hunter must've shared his belief of the bump on her
head with Maude. That meant that neither of them knew
about the chalice's magical powers, which in turn should
make it less suspicious for Isabel to ask about it, when
the right opportunity arose.

"Fortunate, indeed," Isabel agreed. "Though I was not totally unharmed. My memory is gone, after all."

Maude's uneasy gaze strayed to Hunter for a brief moment before alighting on Isabel again.

Was she being a little too flippant about her amnesia? Isabel wondered. Obviously it wasn't a readily understood illness in the Middle Ages. And even though the chalice's magical power was doing an excellent job of translating their words, words were infinitely easier to understand and adapt than concepts. Isabel made a mental note of being more careful when exposing modern notions.

"I shall do all I can to help you, my lady," Maude said.

Great! Now she had two people bent on helping her recover memories she never possessed.

"I am most grateful." Isabel plastered on her face the best fake smile she could muster in these trying times. She suddenly felt very tired and the dull ache in her head she'd been ignoring since morning intensified.

Hunter watched her with slightly narrowed eyes. If she didn't know better, she'd think he knew she was lying. But he couldn't know, could he? It was only her bizarre behavior. It'd frighten anyone who knew Détra well—especially her husband.

Maybe she should learn more about Détra, Isabel considered. If only to help her behave more like a medieval lady. She could blame just so much on her amnesia; there were things a person didn't forget. That didn't mean she was prepared to remain here longer than necessary. It was only a matter of survival, a matter she knew well.

Besides, she had to believe the duration of her stay was somehow under her control. Once she found the chalice she'd undo her mistake and all would return to normal. She wouldn't accept anything else.

Isabel turned her attention to Maude. She couldn't quite decide what to make of her. The woman was ob-

viously a servant to Détra, though one who seemed to care
for her lady. Could she also be a confidant, a friend perhaps? Isabel hoped not. The less she had to endure the
scrutiny of people who knew Détra well, the better off
she would be. Not an easy task considering everyone in
this place should know Détra well. She was their lady, for
goodness' sake.

How was Détra doing in her place in the future? The
cultural shock Détra would suffer would be infinitely
more devastating than Isabel's. The Middle Ages, though
a scary time, was not totally unfamiliar to Isabel—who
hadn't seen a medieval movie in the twenty-first century?—but what would Détra make of the technological
advances of the world? Would she be able to function
without the support of her husband and friends?

Hang in there! Isabel sent Détra a cosmic prayer.

As she would try to hang in here.

A ray of sunshine filtered through the glassy window.
Small particles of dust danced in the air, floating upward
as if reaching for heaven. Were she living her own life,
Isabel would be sitting by that window painting the afternoon away. And there would be no one to take her to
task. Had Détra ever spent her time in personal pursuits?
Somehow, Isabel didn't think so.

Sudden weariness took hold of her. "I am quite tired,"
she said, hoping both Maude and Hunter would take the
hint and leave her alone.

"A bath would do you wonders," Maude offered.

A bath did sound great, and if she couldn't get rid of
both of them, at least Hunter would go now, for surely a
medieval man wouldn't stick around while his wife
bathed. Hoping she was not mistaken, Isabel nodded
agreement.

By the looks of it, Maude had already expected to provide a bath for her lady, for all the necessary items for

the task were readily available at the room. Isabel didn't remember seeing any of these earlier before she'd gone in pursuit of Hunter. Using a small bucket, Maude began transferring the hot water from the caldron in the fireplace to a round tub that looked like the half of a huge wine barrel.

How was she going to fit in that small tub? Isabel wondered as she followed the steam wafting in the air. After that was done, Maude added cold water to the tub until she was satisfied the water's temperature was just right. She tested it by immersing her elbow into the tub every so often.

Finally, Maude moved to a small wooden box and from inside she withdrew a pretty blue flask. She dropped a dollop of its contents into the tub. A whiff of rosemary floated to Isabel and for some reason Détra's obviously chosen scent bothered her more than it should. It was like she was looking inside someone's medicine cabinet. It was so intrusive.

Isabel shook her head. Why would such a small transgression bother her, considering she'd snatched the woman's body?

"Let me help you undress, my lady."

Not in front of Hunter!

Before Isabel had a chance to voice her protest, however, Hunter came to stand before her.

"Allow me the honor." His eyes captured Isabel's in a dark, mesmerizing gaze.

Keenly aware of his proximity, Isabel read the command in his voice. An offer could be refused; a command must be obeyed. It was obvious Maude understood the difference for she swiftly backed out of the way.

Isabel wasn't as keen to mimic her behavior.

She gathered her skirts to step out of Hunter's seeking hands. "I would rather you did—not."

Hunter caught her in his arms, easily preventing her evasive maneuver, and brought her flush to his hard body, dangling her feet above the floor. Détra wasn't exactly a petite woman, yet Hunter seemed to spend no great effort holding her airborne.

"It is a pleasure I would eagerly partake," he whispered in her ears.

Isabel held her breath as goose bumps spread down her neck. She had no doubt Hunter would enjoy such a treat, but there was no way in hell she would allow him the pleasure.

She pushed away from him, her feet touching the floor again, and keeping a hold of her gown, she hurried to the window. From there she spun around to face him. "You seem to forget our agreement."

"I forget naught," he said. "Is it not your primary concern to recover your memories?"

She had no recourse but to nod agreement, even though she knew it was a trap.

"I merely wish to rekindle some of those memories for your benefit," he said, confirming her suspicions.

Damn! The man knew how to turn her words around. She had no need for rekindling of any kind, especially of memories she'd rather never have with him.

Isabel's head began to pound. "You promised to respect my request and keep your distance for the required time," she insisted.

He sighed, clearly annoyed.

Her headache intensified into a throbbing. Isabel winced and threaded her fingers through her hair—a now quite common action on her part, she realized. She pressed her palms against her temples, willing the pain to go away.

"What ails you?" He reached her in two large strides.

"My head is loudly complaining from when I hit the floor this morning."

"It is a malady from which you often suffer," Hunter revealed, though he checked the small bump on her head for good measure.

"Indeed?" Did Détra suffer from migraines? Good God! One more reason to get out of this body as soon as possible.

Hunter took her arm and led her to the chair by the fireplace and bathtub. Under the pressure of his hand, she lowered to the seat.

"Have you naught for your lady's aches?" he asked Maude.

Across the room, Maude busied herself pouring powder from two different jugs into a metal cup. She filled the cup with a honey-colored liquid, then brought it to Isabel.

"This potion usually helps your aching head," she said. "You drink it often."

Often? Détra's migraines must be really horrible!

Isabel hesitated—she truly didn't want to drink any unknown medieval concoction—but though unconvinced, she weighed the risk of declining a medicine Détra must have relied upon before, and apparently with no qualms. She'd have a hard time blaming this behavior on amnesia. After all, who wanted to suffer pain willingly?

A sharp pain lanced Isabel's temples again, helping her decide whether to accept the potion or not. Détra's body should be used to the treatment; at least she hoped so. Isabel would drink the potion.

But under no circumstance would she allow bloodletting!

Cup in hand, Isabel took a tentative sip—thankful the initial bitterness soon disappeared. She knew so little of medicinal herbs she wouldn't in a million years recognize what made up the concoction. She only hoped there would be no belladonna in it. Not that she would know the taste of it were there any in the potion she now drank. Under Hunter's watchful eyes, Isabel finished the drink.

Holding the empty cup in her hands, an idea rushed to her mind. She inspected the very ordinary metal cup with feigned interest. "Odd," she whispered. "I seem to suddenly recall a rather unusual chalice."

"What kind of chalice?" Maude asked.

"A beautiful one with sapphire stones—quite unique, in fact. I cannot quite recall where I saw it, but its enchanting image just came back quite vividly to my mind a moment ago." She handed Maude the metal cup with a dismissive shrug.

"Wait," she said as if the memory had just popped in her mind. "I think I saw it on that table this morning. Have you seen it, Maude?"

Maude shook her head. "I have never seen such a chalice in Windermere."

Maude seemed sincere enough. "How about you, Hunter?" Isabel asked as innocently as she could.

Hunter's face remained impassive. "Are you beginning to remember, my lady?"

Why was Hunter being evasive? What was he hiding? She'd seen him pick up the chalice from the table earlier and leave the room with it. He did it rather surreptitiously, but she saw him. Was she wrong in assuming he didn't know of the chalice's powers? Why would he want to keep it away from her?

"Is that not what we both want?" Isabel countered. "For me to remember?"

"Indeed. The sooner your memories return, the sooner we can resume our lives together."

There was no doubt in Isabel's mind what would happen if she started to *remember* too soon.

"Let us not get ahead of ourselves," she said, feeling a little light-headed. Did Maude add a sleeping draught to the potion?

"I go nowhere, my lady wife."

Hunter's words annoyed her. No matter what she said, he seemed to have a ready answer for her.

"Surely you have places to go." She waved her hand in the air in a dismissing manner. "You must have more important matters to occupy your time than watching me recover from a headache." She winced for good measure, which didn't take much acting skill considering her head truly hurt.

"I see naught more important than caring for my lady wife," he said gallantly.

"I appreciate your willingness but I would like to bathe and then take a nap. I am quite tired."

Finally accepting she would not change her mind, Hunter agreed. "As you wish, my lady wife. Rest well. I look forward to spending time with you when you feel less taxed. Maude shall take care of your needs in my absence."

He kissed her softly then left the room, closing the door behind his back.

Barely containing a yawn, Isabel undressed quickly and immersed herself in the wonderfully warm water of the bathtub. Fighting the lethargy taking over her body, she allowed Maude to administer to her. She felt better after her bath; even her head didn't seem to hurt so much, though her energies were depleted. A nap should do wonders for her.

She dried herself with a huge square of cloth Maude gave her, then sank into the soft feather mattress. She knew she'd cornered herself inside this room while Hunter would be free to hide the chalice he obviously didn't want his wife to have. Isabel hadn't missed he'd never answered her question about its whereabouts.

As oblivion shut out the world around her, Isabel's last conscious thought lingered on her mind.

What was Hunter of Windermere hiding from his wife?

HUNTER OPENED THE DOOR TO WHAT ONCE WAS A storage place in the garrison's quarters but now was a small chamber to use in times his need for solitude assailed him. He lit the two oil lamps on the wall and the utter darkness gave way to flickering shadows. His gaze swept the small space with a grim pleasure.

The chamber's Spartan furnishing suited him well. Like him, it had no need for pretentious luxury. Rushes covered the hard dirt floor, but no tapestry adorned its wooden walls. No hearth to warm the chamber in winter, no windows to bring in light, no stately bed but a small campaign cot and a large trunk for storage of his war-waging apparatus.

Hunter snorted. That he felt more at home in this hovel than at the great hall of Windermere Castle was a telltale sign that his dream of hearth and home was still beyond his reach.

He looked at the chalice he had retrieved from the orchard. Its azure stones no longer glowed, no blue mists revealed visions of his heart wish, no warmth seeped into his fingers, no matter how hard he had tried to make it come to life again.

Hunter stared at it, willing it to show its powers. Naught again. Annoyed, Hunter buried it in the depths of his war trunk, as he should have done since his first arrival in Windermere. It had been a mistake to have it in his bedchamber. And yet as the only item of value he ever possessed, apart from his warhorse and sword, and the only tangible remembrance of his mother, Hunter had wanted it close to him.

Besides, had the chalice not been there in the first place, in his and Détra's presence, mayhap its powers would never have been revealed, considering they had never before.

And for that reason alone, Hunter must keep the chalice away from Détra. As she might have been the catalyst for the unleashing of the chalice's powers, he could not chance she could be also the destruction of his heart's desire. After all, she had vehemently rejected the vision, and, therefore, him.

Détra's sudden remembrance of the chalice unsettled Hunter. He thought he had removed it before she had had a chance to see it earlier this morning. Obviously he was wrong. Or was Détra beginning to remember? He had hoped her memories would not return so soon, at least not until they could reach an understanding. Was this a warning the chalice's power had a time limitation to it?

A new sense of urgency took hold of Hunter.

As with everything in his life a gift had turned into a quest. Would that the chalice had transformed Détra into the wife of his heart instead of granting him just a short reprieve. Would he be able to win her heart in a short time?

A knock on the door distracted him. Jeremy, his squire, showed his face in the opening.

"My lord. Will you wish to shave this day?"

Hunter ran his hand over the hard stubble of his day-old beard. For a moment he thought of not bothering, then remembering Détra, he decided he wished to look his best for her. After all, he had a bride to woo.

"Aye," he said.

Jeremy disappeared to return moments later with the fixings for his shaving. That should be a duty for a page or a loving wife, but Jeremy insisted on doing this small task himself. Hunter understood well the boy's need to please him. Jeremy had lost his entire family when the hut they lived in caught fire in the middle of the night six years ago. He was the only survivor, and with no one to care of him, Hunter had taken in the boy and trained him as his squire. They had left Hawkhaven together and Jeremy had been grateful ever since.

Hunter cherished the thought of giving Jeremy the rare chance to rise above his station. A chance he himself had been given years ago.

"My lord," Jeremy said as he soaped Hunter's face. "The castle is abuzz with tales of you and Lady Détra."

"And what do they say?"

"That you have finally found your way into her graces."

Hunter was well aware of the impossibility of keeping secrets in a castle, and yet he had pressed Détra into keeping their unconsummated marriage out of gossipmongers' ears. Thus far he thought he had succeeded, for Jeremy would have told him long ago if such tales were carried about the castle.

But there was no hiding the cold distance between lord and lady. Détra was not a very demonstrative woman, even in the privacy of their bedchamber, let alone in the open view of servants and castle folks alike. No one had yet caught them in an intimate embrace, or even touching in public.

Not until this morning, that is, when he and Détra had walked hand in hand through the bailey and the great hall. No wonder the people of Windermere Castle were so shocked.

With the knife at Hunter's throat, Jeremy asked, "Well, did you?"

Hunter gave his squire a look that said, "Do your duty and shut your mouth," and immediately Jeremy returned his attention to his task.

Aware of Détra's objections to him before the chalice had stolen her memories, Hunter hoped to bring her to accept her place as his lady wife. He understood that even though a woman had the right to refuse being married by force, at least according to the Church, to refuse a king's orders would be foolhardy. Détra must have understood that for she had agreed to the marriage, albeit grudgingly. What she expected to gain in postponing the consummation of their marriage, he knew not. At first he had believed her excuses, but after this morning's confrontation he realized Détra must have had a plan in mind.

Surely she could not hope to obtain an annulment or a divorce. She had complained of lack of choices in her life, but even if she succeeded in the unthinkable, surely she knew the king would swiftly appoint another husband for her—one much less willing to forgive her sullen disposition.

Unless she had a particular man in mind!

The disagreeable thought took hold of Hunter. He had known of a prior bid to her hand, though he was unaware from whence it came. And yet the king had granted her to him. There was no reason to believe he would reverse his decree.

As Jeremy cleaned the remainder of soap and hair from his face with a wet cloth, Hunter plotted his plan. He had vowed to wait a week before demanding his lady wife's compliance to her wifely duties to him. Meanwhile, he would miss no opportunity to shatter the wall of mistrust between them.

Before her memories returned, Hunter would have wooed his lady wife into his bed, proved to all and sundry they were indeed a married couple, and hopefully found his way into her heart.

Chapter 6

HUNTER inserted the key into the rusty lock outside his private chamber in the garrison's quarters. He was the only one who owned such a key, thus the chalice would be safe here. He made certain the door was locked, then left in a hurry. Though Maude had informed him she had mixed a sleeping draught into Détra's potion and she would be sleeping at least until late into the night, most probably until dawn, Hunter wanted to be close at hand in case she woke up suddenly and started asking too many questions.

There would be plenty of people willing to whisper tales about their previous estrangement in his lady's ears—tales he would rather she heard from him in more appropriate circumstances.

Hunter thought of ways to avoid that situation. He could ask Détra to remain in her bedchamber, but that would be foolish. He had learned these past fortnight Détra was not a lady to linger in idle contemplation. She firmly believed in being involved in every facet of the running of her castle—excluding war waging, he hoped—and its people. The castle folks were very loyal to her and abided by her every wish. They obviously trusted her to care for their welfare. Hunter understood duty and loyalty, and he admired his lady's mettle. And yet he had to minimize her contact with her people somehow.

The tempting alternative of locking Détra in her bedchamber, away from prying tongues, however, was out of question. It would destroy the fragile understanding they were working upon.

His only choice would be to allow her controlled access to the keep and its people while he and Maude kept a close eye on her. He also thought it wise to keep Détra's malady a secret. He trusted Maude to keep quiet—in fact, he had already obtained her promise to do so—and he would convince Détra of the same. The fewer people knowing her loss of memory, the less they would speculate and the less they would meddle.

Hunter was almost out of the garrison's quarters when he passed Gervase, Windermere's premier knight. He briefly nodded at the man and continued on.

"My lord?" Gervase called, halting Hunter's progress. "I have disturbing tidings."

Hunter was instantly alert. "Speak."

"A band of Scots was sighted less than a day away from Windermere."

Hunter stiffened. Scots raids occurred with haunting frequency of late but never this far south. Windermere was miles away from the nearest Scottish border. What would they be doing here?

"How many?" Hunter asked.

"Five or six. The traveler who sighted them understandably did not get too close a look."

Hunter nodded. The Scots were a fierce people and Robert the Bruce—Scotland's chosen king—was a veritable stone in King Edward's boots. A stone the king hoped Hunter would remove by uncovering the identity of an English traitor Edward believed had fueled Bruce for years with vital information.

King Edward II despised the thought that not only had Bruce wrestled back nearly all of Scotland from English hands, but also that he and his outnumbered army had soundly defeated the English at the Battle of Bannockburn last summer. Therefore, Bruce's demand that England recognize Scotland's independence and his rightful place as its king fell solidly on Edward's deaf ears.

"There are not many of them to lay siege to any well-defended castle, especially not Windermere," Gervase said, interrupting Hunter's thoughts.

"That might be true," Hunter said. Could they have ventured this far not to raid but for a clandestine meeting with their informant? "However, it warrants to have them watched closely and to warn our neighbors." And their closest neighbor would be Lord Reginald and his son, Rupert. The old man's failing health had him confined to his bed; therefore, it would be with Rupert that the messenger would have to deal. That was a task Hunter would rather delegate to someone else.

"I shall send a scouting party out to access the proximity of our enemy," Gervase said.

"Nay."

"But, my lord—"

"I shall go myself," Hunter said. A scouting party would not be looking for a traitor, and Hunter had a hunch the man was in the vicinity.

"Send a messenger to warn Hawkhaven of the possible danger, and have my destrier ready," Hunter said. "I depart shortly." *And hopefully I'll return before dawn when Détra arises*, he thought.

ISABEL WOKE UP FROM A HEAVY SLEEP IN A DARK room with a flickering light. Feeling quite disoriented, she focused on the light, and as her eyes adjusted she noticed the fire dying in the fireplace and white curtains around her bed.

Her grandmother's bed didn't have curtains.

Isabel sprang up in bed and the covers fell to her lap. A chill settled over her body, and instinctively she pulled the covers up. At the first glimpse of her naked, voluptuous chest, awareness filled her with a rush of memories, placing her not only where she was but also in whose body.

The sheer weight of such acknowledgment took her breath away. She gathered the coverlet to her chest. This was no flight of fancy but brutal reality. Taking a steadying breath, Isabel put the last events in order in her mind. She remembered drinking a potion for her headache late this morning—at least she thought it was this morning— and resting her eyes closed for a moment. Judging by the lack of light infiltrating through the shuttered window and the silence and darkness in the room, that moment had lasted longer than she'd anticipated. Thank God her head no longer hurt.

Her gaze strayed to the place beside her in the bed and a sigh of relief escaped her at not finding Hunter there. At least she didn't have to face him now. Maybe Hunter, considering her feelings, had decided to sleep somewhere else for now. At least she hoped so.

Wrapping the covers around her body, Isabel rose to her feet. The floor was cold as she skipped to the door. She opened it and peeked outside in the dark corridor.

There was no one in sight. It must be the middle of the night. A great opportunity to go searching for the chalice, but without light and not knowing where to go it seemed a losing proposition. Isabel hesitated, then closed the door and returned inside.

She would begin her search in this room, though she didn't believe the chalice was here. After all, she'd seen Hunter taking it with him when he left this morning. However, he could've brought it back while she was sleeping. Even recognizing the thought was far-fetched Isabel still wanted to take a look in here. There was always the chance she could uncover some clue of its whereabouts or even learn more about Détra and Hunter.

The fire in the fireplace was now reduced to a few glowing embers and sparse kindling sparks that emanated no heat and little light. First things first. She picked up a few pieces of wood lying on the floor and dropped them inside the cavernous aperture. She poked the embers with an iron poke until the fire caught. She remained before the fire, soaking in its warmth, and then spinning around, turned her attention to the badly illuminated room.

She saw the oil lamps on the wall but had no clue how to light them. Her gaze fell on the table near the bed where a candle sat on a metal holder. She picked it up and brought it to the fireplace, almost burning her hand while attempting to light it. With it, she lit the oil lamps. Though their weak luminosity was but a small improvement, the chalice's shape and size would be easy enough to locate in the room, even if she couldn't see clearly.

Her gaze scanned the room. There were few places a chalice could be hidden—no crevices or nooks on the walls, no bookcases or closets, no safes or locked boxes. Her gaze fell on the wooden chests. She'd already gone through Détra's garment chest earlier, but maybe Hunter's would be more revealing.

No such luck. Besides his personal clothing there was nothing else in Hunter's garment chest.

She moved on to other areas, including under the bed, behind the tapestries on the wall, even inside the fireplace. The chalice wasn't anywhere in this room.

Isabel wasn't exactly disappointed; she didn't really expect to find the chalice in the room, but she was frustrated nonetheless.

Her feet were cold and so was her body as the fire began to die again in the fireplace. She'd forgotten how time-consuming it was to keep a real fire alive, accustomed as she was to gas fireplaces and heaters. She threw in all the rest of the wood she could find, stirred the embers, and then rushed to bed. There was nothing else to do but wait for morning to resume her search.

DAWN HAD JUST BROKEN INTO THE DARKNESS OF THE night and weak rays of light filtered through the thin slits of the shuttered window when Hunter found his way into his bedchamber. A fire burned low in the hearth and the oil lamps on the wall were lit.

He stoked the fire and extinguished the oil lamps before stretching sluggishly, working the kinks out of his aching shoulders after a nonstop ride for half of the day and most of the night.

Having stopped at his private chamber at the garrison's quarters and divested himself of his hauberk and accouterments of war before coming to his bedchamber, Hunter quietly removed the rest of his garments. Hoping to steal some rest before the castle fully awoke and his duties demanded his presence, Hunter opened the bed curtains of his marital bed.

His wife lay on her side, taking up most of the bed, one knee drawn up, the other straight, one hand buried underneath the pillow while the other rested close to her face. There was something about her—an abandonment, an ease never before seen—that disconcerted Hunter. She was the perfect image of a beautiful angel in a peaceful slumber.

So contrary to the Détra he knew.

That lady had always lain straight as an arrow and tense as a bowstring on the very edge of the bed, with as much distance between her and Hunter as she could possibly muster.

Mayhap the sleeping draught had temporarily freed Détra from her cares; or mayhap she expected not his return this night.

The latter was probably truer.

Whatever her expectations, however, Hunter was back and he was tired, and he would not turn around and return to his hard cot in his private chamber. He lifted the covers to bury himself underneath them and his breath whooshed out of him. Hunter sank down into the mattress. Sleep and exhaustion fled immediately.

His lady wife slept in the nude!

It took Hunter a moment to gather his surprise. Even though probably everybody in the Christendom slept unclothed, Détra had never done so before. In fact, he had never even seen her body without some kind of garment hiding it from his complete view.

Now he was certain Détra had not expected his return.

A mix of displeasure and longing filled his heart while undiluted lust filled his loins. He fought the desire flaring in him. He had promised her a week's respite, and he would give her that much, even if it killed him.

Hunter concentrated on the thought of her coming to him willingly after that time, as she had promised him, as he longed it to be, and as she had already done at the orchard.

Resisting the urge to pull her into his arms, he lay there, unstrung and unfulfilled, watching her steady breathing until he fell into a restless sleep.

WARMTH BECKONED ISABEL. SHE STIRRED AND SOUGHT the heat with her body. It was so close she could feel it. All she had to do was seek it and she'd have it. She scooted back until she backed up against a wall—a fiery, smooth, hard wall. Her eyes shot open. And she dared move no more.

This time awareness swiftly hit her in full. In a blinking moment she knew exactly where she was and who was sharing the bed with her. Light filtered through the closed curtains of the bed and distant voices outside announced the morning was already on its way. And yet here she was in bed with a man whose leveled breathing revealed he still slept, but whose warm, tight body was very much awake.

She'd fretted about the nights with Hunter, but morning had revealed itself to be a much more immediate threat.

Hunter stirred and his arms encircled Isabel, pulling her closer into his warm embrace. No doubt caught in the throes of some erotic dream, he cupped her breast with his hand, catching her stiffening nipple between his fingers. With a soft groan he nestled his hardness against the cleft of her naked buttocks and Isabel's treacherous body immediately began to respond.

Oh, why hadn't she put some clothes on before going back to bed? Isabel froze in place while the stirrings of desire wreaked havoc with her insides.

Hunter's breathing quickened and his warm breath fanned the back of her neck. *Oh no, not her neck! Not her weak spot!*

Having withstood as much as she could, and barely

suppressing a moan, Isabel leaped to her feet, carrying the covers with her.

A surprised Hunter jerked up in bed, then, seeing her, jumped out of bed to stand naked before her with unabashed male confidence. Isabel clung to the coverlet like a lifeline.

Good God! But Hunter was a fine man!

"What the devil is the matter?" he asked.

She swallowed hard, then averted her gaze to his face. "Your snoring disturbed my sleep," she lied.

He cocked his head as he stared at her in disbelief. "I do not snore." His gaze lowered to that part of him that still stood sentinel and added, "But I do recall a very vivid dream." He gave her a purely rakish gaze.

He was a dream!

Isabel backed away from him, from the sight of him, before she forgot herself. "We sleep no more."

She pivoted, ready to run, but he closed the gap between them in one big step and swirled her around to face him.

"The reality of having you in my arms should surpass any dream." He gave her that half smile. Did Hunter ever fully smile?

Conflicting emotions warred inside of Isabel. She knew she should back out now before his next move. Knew she should remind him of their agreement and stop what was bound to happen if he touched her. Knew that it'd be wrong for her to assume the role of his lover.

But even knowing that Isabel didn't move.

Her heart stammered in her chest when his fingers skimmed her naked shoulders. Her breath came in shallow gasps when his callused palms enclosed her neck and his thumbs rested underneath her chin, lifting her face to him. Her body trembled when her gaze fell on his mouth, on his parted, eager lips—inviting lips.

Oh, she knew she was playing with fire, but for the life of her she couldn't stop. She couldn't step back. Hunter was going to kiss her, and there was no force in this world that could stop them.

With uncharacteristic fatalism Isabel watched his mouth descend upon hers. And when their lips touched, she opened hers to his warm, hungry kiss, and she tasted his desire mingling with hers. Pushing guilt aside, Isabel surrendered to the kiss, her fingers threading his soft, silky hair.

His mouth slanted over hers, deepening the contact, his tongue playing with hers, delving, withdrawing, teasing. Isabel caught it and suckled it, tasting him, feeding his hunger and her own.

With a groan Hunter slid one hand behind her neck, fingers entwined in her hair, the other hand encircled her waist, bringing her closer, tighter into his embrace.

Oh, but the man knew how to kiss! Knew how far to go, how deep, how hard. And when his mouth descended to her neck, she let her head fall back and savored his touch, reveling in his unabashed desire for her, his wanting of her.

It had been so long since she felt this way with a man. And maybe she'd never really felt this way with a man before.

As his breath came in gasps, his touch became more urgent and his kisses more demanding. And Isabel was ready to respond in kind.

"Oh Détra," he whispered against her ears. "Your beauty consumes me."

Hunter's words abruptly snapped Isabel out of the enchantment his touch had woven about her. And though her body still thrummed with desire, her mind once again grounded in reality. This man was not her husband, his desire was not for her, and his love was not hers to enjoy.

Guilt returned with a vengeance. She'd already wreaked enough havoc in Hunter's and Détra's lives with her misguided wish. She might even be doing more harm than good by rejecting him, but she knew that if she made love to Hunter she'd never be the same person again.

Isabel stiffened against Hunter. Her body straightened as her hands pushed against him.

It took him a moment to understand her change of heart, and a moment longer to accept it, then he let go of her. His arms fell alongside his powerful and beautiful body, but he didn't step away. She hated confrontations but braced herself for his explosive reaction. Silence greeted her. Isabel lifted her gaze to Hunter but instead of the expected anger she found his blank stare.

And that hurt the most. She would've preferred angry shouts to this painful silence.

A knock on the door saved Isabel from offering babbling explanations she didn't want to give and Hunter most certainly wouldn't like to hear.

"Come in," Isabel said.

"Go away," Hunter bellowed at the same time. Then with a humph he spun around and marched to the door, naked as he was.

"No!" Isabel raced after him, gathering her cover as she ran, and placed herself between the door and Hunter. She kept her gaze firmly on his dark eyes. "You cannot open the door naked like that."

"A moment ago you thought naught of it."

A moment ago she wasn't thinking.

There was a long pause, then he shouted, "Who is it?"

"Maude, my lord."

Hunter took a deep breath, exhaled loudly, then marched to his clothing trunk. Glad he hadn't given her a piece of his mind, Isabel accompanied his progress with undisguised interest. His shoulders were of an impossible breadth, his back straight and erect, and the muscles on his tight buns flexed as he moved.

Fine man, indeed!

A man who belonged to another woman. A fact Isabel ought to engrave in her mind.

She waited until Hunter was decently clad before she opened the door to Maude.

"Good morning, my lady, my lord," Maude greeted as she entered the room, carrying several pieces of wood, which she dropped by the fireplace. She promptly revived the dying fire, then ambled to the bed, opening the curtains and tying them with a ribbon. She fluffed the pillows, straightened the sheets, and then folded a blanket that had fallen to the floor.

Meanwhile, still holding the soft coverlet to her body, Isabel moved closer to the warmth of the fireplace while Hunter finished getting dressed.

The rustling of Maude's skirts as she moved about the room and the crackling of the wood in the fire were the only sounds in the room. With a quick glance to Isabel, then Hunter, Maude moved to the table and began preparing a drink.

Moments later she offered the cup to Isabel. "Your morning drink, my lady."

"Thank you," Isabel said, unconsciously taking the cup and sipping the warm and soothing drink before she realized she hadn't even questioned what was in it. Tasting chamomile lessened her apprehension, though she couldn't be sure that was all that made up the concoction. It was eerily similar to her habitual morning tea, though she was aware tea as she knew it wasn't known in medieval England.

"A cup of mead might be just what you need to sweeten my lady wife," Hunter said.

Was he speaking metaphorically?

"Is that what this is? Mead?" Isabel asked.

"Nay, my lady," Maude answered. "It is a concoction of your own doing that you greatly appreciate in the mornings."

Well, the *tea* tasted all right and it was better than having nothing else to drink.

"Mayhap you should break your fast in your bedchamber this morning," Hunter said.

Was that a suggestion, an order, or a question? After what had just happened between them, she doubted Hunter was in a mood to share an intimate breakfast with her.

"I have matters that require my attention," he said, looking very displeased with her.

Spending more time with Hunter was the last thing she wanted right now. "I would not keep you away from your duties."

"Is my lady well enough to resume her duties?" Maude asked.

Duties? What were Détra's duties? Isabel had lived her entire life in rented rooms and small flats. Her only attempt at playing house had been when she'd been married. And that had been a failure. Surely Détra had servants to do the normal household tasks like washing, cooking, and cleaning. Would she be expected to embroider, weave, sew, or supervise servants?

All matters she knew nothing about. Isabel almost groaned.

Rescue came from the least expected source. "I advise my lady wife not to overdo," Hunter suggested. Had he seen her panic?

Isabel immediately latched on to Hunter's excuse. "I agree," she said. "I would rather postpone my duties until I feel stronger."

His penetrating gaze held hers captive. "I also believe,"

he said, "it would be best if we keep your loss of memory a secret from the rest of the castle people."

"Why?" Isabel asked. How could she pull this off without the excuse of her amnesia?

"Yours is a rare malady," he explained. "It would surely be misunderstood. Windermere's people are dependent on your strength for guidance and support. Your welfare is their welfare. It would do them no good to fret over your health and their future."

Isabel suddenly realized the scope of her misguided actions. She had not only stolen Hunter's beloved wife but also the lady of the castle to whom these people looked for support. One more reason for Isabel to undo this travesty as soon as possible.

"They are bound to find out when I fail to recognize them or not know about some matter I should know about," Isabel said.

"That is true," he conceded. "Therefore, it is wise for you to curtail some of your tasks and minimize such contacts. At least for now."

Not only did that make sense but it'd also work well for her. The less she had to do that involved knowledge of the medieval way of life, the better off she would be.

She nodded.

"Maude will be with you at all times. You can trust her. We have your well-being at heart. Never doubt that." He seemed to hesitate for a moment, then kissed the corner of her mouth before walking to the door.

His fleeting yet gentle touch served only to awaken in Isabel a craving to taste more of him. And to remind her, if she succeeded in finding the chalice today, which she hoped she would, she would never see Hunter again.

A lump rose in her throat. Why would that thought upset her so much? How could she miss a man she had just met a little over a day ago?

"Hunter," she called, and he turned expectantly at the door.

She wanted to say good-bye, wanted to apologize, wish good luck, but none of that would make any sense to him. She could at least take comfort in the thought that once Détra returned to her own body, and if she chose to tell her husband the truth, Hunter would have nothing to feel guilty about—they hadn't crossed that final line.

"You are a fine man, Hunter," she said, knowing how inadequate those words were to express her feelings for a man she should've never met but would never forget.

Chapter 7

YOU are a fine man!

Deus! Those were the first pleasing words Détra had ever spoken to him.

Hunter stood at the door's threshold stunned by the unexpected praise. Then abruptly he wiped the foolish grin off his face. Pleasing words, aye, but not strong enough to sweeten the bitter taste of her rejection. She was sadly mistaken if she thought she could incite him in one breath and deny him in the other.

Hunter pivoted and shut the door behind him.

As he descended the narrow staircase into the great hall, bewildering thoughts kept him company. On two occasions now since the incident with the chalice, his lady wife's seesawing behavior had baffled him—yesterday at the orchard and moments ago in their bedchamber. Both times she had eagerly responded to his kisses with a passion he had only hoped lived within her, only to abruptly step away, cutting him off without so much as a by-your-leave.

Détra's earlier objections to him—his bastardy, his humble beginnings, and their forced marriage—had been the impetus behind her earlier rejections, and that Hunter could at least understand. However, unaware of such facts as she was now, why would she continue to safeguard herself from him? Why would she melt in his arms then pull away from him as if demons chased her?

Demons or memories? The thought suddenly assailed him. Memories of him?

One moment she was his heart wish come true and in the next the cold reality he was trying so hard to change. Would that the chalice had worked its magic on Détra in a more definite way. As it was, he was uncertain what to make of her change, how much to believe or whether to trust her loss of memory at all.

Weariness settled over Hunter and he rubbed his burning eyes. He had slept next to naught since his arrival at dawn from his futile search, which had yielded no Scots, no traitor, not even any sign of suspicious activities. Yet, Scotsmen had been sighted less than a day from Windermere. What were they doing so far south of the border?

Frustration at the impossible mission King Edward had leveled on him prickled his skin. To find a traitor Hunter was unsure even existed, he must venture outside Windermere, therefore neglecting his duty to protect the castle and his need to put his marital affairs in order.

Sooner or later he knew he must pay a visit to the border lords and assess their situation. Later, rather than sooner, he decided. He had a couple of men in strategic places close to the border and he would continue to patrol the area around Windermere and go on short sojourns, like yesterday's, but he would refrain from leaving his wife for long periods of time. Especially now. He might not gain his wife's heart in such a short time, but he would consummate their marriage and solidify once and for all his hold on Windermere Castle.

Meanwhile, while he occupied himself with his many duties, Hunter would have to rely on Maude to watch Détra for him. The maid had shown him loyalty thus far. Hunter hoped he had not misplaced his trust in her. Hoped she understood she was not only to refrain from speaking of disagreeable matters to Détra but also not to reveal any matter that would go against Hunter's wishes.

Knowing he teetered on the brink of dishonesty, Hunter silenced his conscience. He had no illusions he could keep Détra in the dark forever, and yet he needed not forever. A week's respite was all she asked, and it was all he would give her. He wished for her acceptance, her heart, and her love, but failing in attaining those he would settle for her acceptance of him as her lord and husband, and of his control over Windermere Castle.

And he would accept naught less than that.

Hunter entered the great hall and sat at the lord's table on the raised dais. The hall was empty of knights, for the morning grew late, but a few servants rushed to and from their duties.

"Duty," Hunter muttered to himself, as a serving wench brought him ale and bread. After a short silent prayer of thanksgiving he broke his fast. Duty ruled his life. Duty to God, to king, to his lady wife.

Once he had hoped that last duty would be the easiest of his lot. And though lately he had almost believed it would, thus far it had proved his greatest challenge. Moments ago he had awakened from the most heavenly dream to a finer reality of a very pliant Détra in his arms.

However, like dreams, that idyllic moment had been fleeting.

His wife's rejection of him gnawed at his insides and

though it hurt as much as her earlier ones, there was a subtle change he could not overlook. The earlier coldness and animosity had given away to passion and regret, as if one warred with the other.

And Hunter would find out why.

Maude's interruption had prevented him from demanding an explanation, though it had served to make Maude a witness to an intimate moment between them. For surely Maude could not have missed their state of dishabille, Détra's flushed cheeks, and her kiss-swollen lips. And especially she would not have missed Détra's parting words.

Fine man, indeed, Hunter snorted as he brought the tankard of ale down to the table with more force than he had intended. One day soon Détra would know with certainty how fine a man he truly was.

ISABEL HAD SEEN THE DELIGHT IN HUNTER'S FACE AT her unexpected praise. But then his half grin had disappeared and he left the room without a word. Obviously her words had not mollified him enough. Could she blame him? Isabel knew exactly how he felt, for it was exactly how she felt: unfulfilled, nerves raw, body tense with frustration.

She had not intended on going this far with him again. She was not a tease. Yet she'd lost her senses both times he held her in his arms, when she savored his kisses, experienced his touch. Isabel had yielded to lust before—a physical relationship between two consenting adults was one thing, but this . . .

Well, this was something very different.

She pivoted, catching Maude staring at her. "Lord Hunter's tolerance with your malady is very admirable," the maid said. "Few men would be so accommodating."

Isabel agreed. "He has been very understanding."

And understanding would be crucial for Détra and Hunter to put their marriage together once Détra returned to her own body, as its lack had been crucial in the breakup of Isabel's marriage to Jack. Curious that the things she'd thought Jack had liked most about her had been the things he'd worked so hard to change in her. And what she'd wanted so desperately from him in the beginning had been what had driven them apart in the end.

And yet, when faced with unexplainable changes in his wife, most of which must be disagreeable, Hunter had tried his hardest to be understanding, accommodating.

Disquieted, Isabel strode to the chest that held Détra's clothing. "Can we get out of this room for a while?" she asked, rummaging inside. "I would love to see the rest of the castle." She wasn't interested in a historical tour, but in searching for the chalice.

"My lady, you have not broken your fast yet," Maude said.

The mere mention of food made Isabel's stomach rumble. She hadn't eaten anything since yesterday morning. "Maybe something light like cheese and fruits," Isabel said.

Maude nodded and left, and while she was away, Isabel took the opportunity to search the room for the dreaded chamber pot, or bedpan as it was called in a few countryside places it still could be found, albeit rarely, in Europe of modern times. She was sure there was some kind of privy available in the castle, but she'd have to get dressed to go look for it, and she just couldn't wait.

Finding what she needed, Isabel made quick use of it. She washed herself afterward with cold water, scrubbed her teeth with a wet piece of cloth, and combed her hair with her fingers. Considering Détra's mass of curls, Isabel didn't think a brush could have been of much use.

Isabel had stayed in very modest accommodations before, but the basic necessities were usually available. Suddenly, she realized how little a person really needed to
survive.

At least temporarily.

Using a ribbon she'd found among the clothes Maude
had laid over the garment chest, Isabel tied her hair at the
nape of her neck. That should keep the curls away from
her face for a while.

Inspecting the available clothes Isabel realized there
would be no panties or bras in Détra's wardrobe. She
picked up a long dress of fine linen with form-fitting
sleeves and dropped it over her head.

At that moment Maude returned with the food—
cheese, bread, a pear—and Isabel began devouring everything, realizing how hungry she truly was.

"I see you have already donned your chemise, my
lady," Maude said, picking up a gown from the top of the
chest.

Chemise? Isabel thought it a dress. It was quite different from the one Isabel was wearing when she'd awakened in Détra's body yesterday. That one had been of a
thicker material and looser like an old-fashioned camisole;
this one was sheer and quite soft to the touch. A definite
improvement.

The gown Maude held out for her was magnificent.
Tight-fitted to the waist, it flowed into a glorious skirt
with a small train on the back, like a wedding gown. It
was of a beautiful chocolate hue with golden threads
throughout in a material that looked like velvet, but silk-
ier. Its sleeves were tight to just above the elbow then
flowed into a bell shape.

A much too luxurious dress to wear at home.

"How about something simpler?" Isabel asked.

"This is a favorite of yours," Maude said. "It would surely please Lord Hunter."

Was Maude suggesting Isabel should be making more of an effort to please Hunter? Or was the maid simply giving her some fashion advice, as she was probably used to doing for Détra?

As if it mattered what Détra wore, Isabel thought wryly. Hunter was definitely a man in love and in lust with his young wife. And though she'd muddled things up a bit these past two days by rejecting his advances, once Détra returned she could easily pacify him.

And what a sacrifice that would be!

Isabel suppressed the stab of envy, for a moment toying with the idea of wearing the ugliest dress she could find.

Amazed at her pettiness, she shook her head. "The chocolate gown will do just fine."

Maude shot her a decidedly odd look. Was it the word chocolate that threw her off? So far Isabel hadn't had any trouble with their ability to understand one another, but there were instances when unknown concepts might not be easily understood, as in the case of chocolate—a confection nonexistent at this time.

With Maude's help Isabel was soon fully dressed—including woolen stockings and a pair of anklet boots. Remembering what she wore yesterday morning, Isabel shook her head, embarrassed. The wet camisole had probably revealed more than anyone in that place would ever wish to see of the lady of the castle. And the simple gown Isabel wore later without a chemise or stockings had been decidedly inappropriate. No wonder Hunter couldn't keep his eyes off her naked legs. Good God! She must've looked like a prostitute.

It was to his credit that he had not ranted about her state of dishabille.

The scent of rosemary wafted to Isabel, bringing her out of her thoughts. Maude stood by her side rubbing her hands together with some kind of oil. "What is that for?" Isabel asked.

"For your tresses, my lady. It will give them shine and fragrance and it will help in the taming of the curls."

"Thank you, Maude, but I've already tamed my hair this morning. Some other time maybe." Wearing Détra's scent bothered Isabel. It was foolish of her, she knew, but she wanted to put whatever sense of distance possible between herself and Détra.

"Is there any other scent available?" Isabel asked just out of curiosity.

"Not in this bedchamber," Maude said.

Of course, Isabel thought. She didn't think there would be access to a perfumery somewhere in the castle. It was just a thought.

"If you wish, I shall seek another, but it will take time. What is your preference, my lady?"

"Never mind," Isabel said. "If you are ready, I would like to begin our tour now."

"No veil, my lady?"

"No, Maude. Shall we?"

Isabel followed Maude out of the room and into the dark corridor. Wall torches provided illumination, but with no windows to bring in light, the place seemed to be immersed in perpetual darkness. They stopped outside a door a few feet down from her bedroom. Isabel could hear peals of laughter coming from inside.

"The weaving room," Maude said, opening the door to a room roughly the size of Détra's bedroom.

Unlike the corridor, the room was well illuminated by three rectangular windows with glazed glass panes. Before them two women sat on a pillow-covered bench working on their embroidery, while two others sat behind spinning wheels on the other side. One woman bent over a table rearranging and cutting pieces of fabric while yet another sat nearby sewing. A small child of perhaps ten years of age sat at the feet of one of the embroidering women. She, too, had a piece of fabric in her hand to which she was dutifully applying her needle.

The last time Isabel had seen that many women together in one room it had been in her former mother-in-law's house at Christmas. Like that day, the happy conversation stopped the moment she entered the room.

The women, ranging from the very young to the quite old, rose as one to curtsy to her. Had they heard of yesterday's events concerning their lady? Had they seen her mad rush half naked through the hall? Judging by their expectant gazes, they were probably wondering what would be her next folly.

Isabel smiled. The sides of her mouth ached with the effort, though she was getting very good at faking it.

"Good morning," she said, and they all responded in unison.

The young girl approached and offered Isabel her piece of cloth—a kerchief of some kind, with a pretty vine embroidered on the borders and a giant rose in its center. "Very pretty," Isabel said.

The girl beamed at her compliment. "Grandmother told me my stitches are not as pretty as yours but I am improving."

The young girl's stitches were surely a lot better than Isabel's could ever be, since Isabel and needles didn't mix at all.

"Well, I think they are very nice," Isabel said, and this time her smile came easily.

"You still have a ways to go, Louise," the old lady by the window said gently. "You must strive to emulate our

Lady Détra, however, whose stitches are the prettiest in the Christendom."

Hoping she'd never have to do a demonstration, Isabel accepted the compliment with a nod.

"Will you join us this morning, my lady?" the old lady asked as the young girl returned to sit by her feet, leaving the embroidered kerchief in Isabel's possession. "We could use your company and assistance."

"Maybe tomorrow," Isabel answered. "I have some other duties to attend." Good God! She was beginning to sound like them. "In fact, I just stopped by to see if I could find a misplaced needle." She folded the kerchief, and not knowing where to put it, tucked it underneath her tight sleeve as her gaze strayed from the women to the room. There were pegs on the wall, a couple of stools here and there, bolts of cloth in one corner of the room, and a small trunk on the floor, probably filled with sewing tools and scraps of material.

"I shall look for it, my lady," Maude said, moving to the trunk.

Isabel stopped the maid. "No, I will look for it myself." Then at Maude's inquiring gaze, she added, "I am not sure you will know exactly what I am looking for."

Isabel opened the trunk, rummaged inside, and then closed it with a thump. Nothing. Of course, what was she thinking? If Hunter was hiding the chalice from her, which she believed he was, he'd find a more original place than the sewing room.

"It is not here," Isabel said, lifting. The women eyed her in silence. "Maybe it is somewhere else."

She wouldn't despair just yet. This was only the second place she had searched in a very big castle. There were still lots of other places to look.

"Carry on," she told the women in her best ladyish manner as she fled the room, followed by Maude.

Thankfully, Maude refrained from commenting about her behavior, which Isabel knew was forced at best, and led Isabel to the round tower where the chapel was situated.

Isabel learned the priest had died last year and they were still waiting for the new assigned priest to arrive. Sometimes it took years for that to happen, Maude had commented. Meanwhile, they had to make do with sporadic visits from neighboring priests who said mass and heard confessions for the duration of their stays.

"Is a visit expected soon?" Isabel asked as she opened an intricately carved box at the center of the altar that guarded a beautiful golden chalice, but not the one she sought.

"It has been a while, though mayhap soon we shall be blessed with one." She shot Isabel a sidelong glance.

"Amen," Isabel said, knowing it would be what Maude wanted to hear, though Isabel and confessions wouldn't make a very good match at this point.

After that, they moved through other rooms sparsely decorated. At a glance Isabel could tell there was no sign of the chalice, and not many places to hide one either.

The upstairs held no more interest for Isabel. Time to move down the staircase and into the great hall, as the big room Isabel had seen yesterday was called. There were tables spread out over the cavernous room, tapestries and banners on the wall, and a big wooden table on a raised dais, but no sign of the chalice. At the far distant wall there was a door, however, that Isabel hadn't noticed before.

"Where does that door lead?" she asked.

"That is the chamber where Windermere's lord meets with his knights to discuss matters of safety and war. It is also where the steward manages the ledgers and rents."

A place where Hunter probably would spend a lot of time. Worth looking into it. Isabel ambled to the door and opened it. In the middle of the room there was a big table flanked by long benches on either side. Godfrey, the man who had accosted her yesterday on the way to her bedroom from the orchard, sat hunched over a book methodically making annotations on its page.

He rose at her entrance. "My lady," he bowed. "I did not expect you. How do you fare?" He glanced at Maude with a little more than casual interest and a little less open concern. Was there something going on between those two?

"Well, thank you."

"Forgive me, my lady, for not seeking you out this morning," he said. "But I was commanded not to disturb you with castle's matters."

Isabel knew well who had commanded Godfrey, unknowingly helping her deal with a situation she wasn't in the least prepared for. "My husband means to spare me the pain of a headache, and for that I am thankful to him; however, I hope that did not mean you had to deal with a problem you could not handle yourself."

"According to your wishes, I seek to keep you abreast of castle matters."

"Well, for the foreseeable future I would appreciate if you dealt with such matters on your own."

"Aye, my lady," he answered, straightening a little.

Scanning the room for hiding places, Isabel said, "Do not mind me. I am looking for a misplaced object." She moved around the room, opened a box here and there, moved larger objects to look behind them, but again, no magical chalice. She strolled to the table against the wall. Scrolls and maps, a dagger, a half-filled cup of wine, a carafe, and a couple of bloodred apples covered the top in an untidy heap. The memory of a sensual Hunter sinking his teeth in the juicy fruit at the orchard almost made her choke. She swallowed with difficulty.

She picked up an apple and turned to leave. "I guess it is not here."

"May I ask what it is you seek, my lady?" Godfrey asked. "I might be of help."

Isabel shook her head. "Thank you. I think I have an idea where it might be now. I will not disturb your work anymore." She forced herself to walk to the door and step outside as if unhurried.

"My lady," Maude asked as she caught up with her in the great hall. "What is it that you seek? Surely not a needle in a war chamber."

Should she trust Maude with her quest? What if she went to Hunter with the information? How would she explain to him her earnest interest in a simple chalice? Better not say anything, but now Maude expected an explanation.

"Nothing really," she confessed. "I thought it might be a way for me to familiarize myself with my surroundings without having to reveal my lack of memories."

"Oh," Maude said. "Very keen, my lady! Thus you learn what you need while you keep your malady hidden, as Lord Hunter advised."

"Exactly." Not really! "Where to now?" Isabel asked as they stopped in the middle of the great hall, which was beginning to fill with people. Several tables were set throughout the large room and servants were setting jars and cups on them.

Was it lunchtime already?

"There are the kitchens, the laundry chamber, the candle-making chamber, the garden, the orchard." Maude paused. "I assume we shall go outside the castle walls to the village."

Good God! The village? Could Hunter have taken the chalice outside the castle? That would complicate matters tremendously. But she still had several places to search right here before she ventured outside.

"No, Maude. Let us just stay within the walls for now."

But where within these walls could Hunter have hidden the chalice? Surely not in any place she could have easy access to, therefore the kitchens, laundry room, and garden should be scratched off her immediate list. Maybe the orchard, however. Had he taken the chalice there as she'd thought yesterday? And if he had, would it still be there?

Most likely Hunter had chosen a place where Détra wouldn't normally go, like the stables or knights' quarters. But if ladies weren't accepted in those places, how would she be?

Isabel's hand tightened around the apple she still held. She took a big bite as she thought where to go next. Her gaze turned to Maude. Wide-eyed, Maude stared back at her.

"You loathe apples, my lady," Maude whispered as if she'd caught Isabel eating worms.

Chapter 8

ISABEL swallowed down the last bits of the delicious apple with considerable difficulty. "I guess I just forgot about that," she said. If she could forget about her past why couldn't she forget about her dislike of apples? She'd have to explain to Maude and Hunter the ramifications of memory loss. Maybe they just didn't understand what that entailed.

A commotion at the entrance of the great hall distracted her and she turned to the door. A knight came rushing in and Hunter followed behind with a young man close at his feet.

"Forgive me, my lord," the young man chanted, upset to the point of tears.

Hunter was hurt. Blood dripped from his left hand, staining his white shirt and leaving a bloody trail behind.

The room suddenly closed in on Isabel as her heart slammed against her chest and her blood thrummed against her ears. She fought the painful memory suddenly filling her mind and heart, and shut her eyes to the sight of Hunter's blood, hoping it'd chase away the resurgent memory, but there was no running away, for one was as real and vivid as the other.

In one terrifying moment reality fused with remembrance in Isabel's mind and she was once again living that fateful morning so long ago. Back in the same bedroom she'd shared with Jack. In the same bed that cradled the creation and the destruction of precious life. Forced, once again, to witness with powerless anguish as blood spilled from deep within her womb, running warmly down her thighs to form a crimson pool on the white sheets of her bed, cruelly and unmistakably robbing her of her only chance at motherhood.

"My lady wife, I am in need of your assistance."

Dragged out of her trance by Hunter's calm voice, Isabel flared her eyes open. Unclenching her jaw, she swallowed down the bitter taste of sorrow and tore herself away from the lacerating memories. She had suppressed the agonizing recollection in such a way that not even in her sleep had she allowed the nightmare to accost her. She'd often dreamed of her baby but never the circumstances of his death.

And to have it come to her like this tore her inside.

With immense effort Isabel controlled her trembling and despair and faced Hunter. He stood before her, eyeing her expectantly, clearly waiting for her to tend to him.

Was one of Détra's duties to tend to the wounded?

Isabel scanned the room—the hall seemed to have filled out all of a sudden—and the people's collective expression clearly revealed they counted on her to do just that.

"It is naught but a scratch," Hunter said, as if to reassure her.

Isabel took a deep breath. "A scratch can fester as easily as a deep cut," she said, proud her voice didn't quaver. If she concentrated on helping Hunter's injured hand she might forget her heart's festering wound.

"Let me take a look at it." Isabel took Hunter's hand into hers. A deep gash, way beyond a scratch—and therefore her pitiful nursing abilities—slashed his left palm. Indecision stayed her mind. She had two options; she could either tend to his injury, as seemed to be expected, or bail out. To bail out she'd have to offer an explanation, and the only one that'd work would be her lack of memory. However, that presented a problem since the hall was full of people and she was supposed to keep her amnesia a secret.

Maybe she could fake her way through this. After all, it wasn't as if she was expected to perform surgery. However, being watched closely by so many pairs of eyes made her doubly uncomfortable. She'd gotten away so far with her lack of knowledge but the longer she remained in this time the more chances her luck would run out.

Ignoring the shiver coming up her spine, Isabel sought the embroidered scarf she'd tucked underneath her sleeve earlier and used it to stop the flow of blood in Hunter's hand.

"It is too beautiful a kerchief to waste on a man's wound," Hunter said.

Isabel acknowledged his attempt at small talk with a weak smile. Was he trying to reassure her or distract himself? "Need surpasses beauty," she said, then, turning to Maude, asked the maid to get water and clean rags. "And the potions, of course," she added, purposefully vague in her request. Surely Maude knew exactly what to use, and all Isabel would have to do was clean the wound, dress it with whatever herbs they used in the Middle Ages, bandage it, then send Hunter on his merry way.

She could do that!

"Forgive me, my lord," the young man said yet again.

"Lord Hunter shall deal with you later," the knight behind the young man said.

"I shall have a word with Jeremy now," Hunter said. "You," he addressed the knight, "may return to your duties or to your midday meal."

The man stiffened, obviously unhappy on being dismissed. As if realizing his curtness, Hunter added, "I wish to thank you for your concern and prompt reaction, Gervase."

Soothed, the knight bowed his head in acknowledgment. Hunter then turned to the visibly shaking Jeremy. "Follow me," he said.

They all walked to the war room. As they entered, Godfrey rose from his table. "At your service, my lord," he said.

"I give you leave to join the others at the great hall for the midday meal," Hunter said. "Later I shall speak with you about the rents and other matters."

Godfrey nodded and left.

Hunter turned to a downcast Jeremy. The young man, not wanting to wait for his dressing-down, rushed to kneel before Hunter. "I beg your forgiveness, my lord. I should have been more alert and noticed when you moved. It was my fault. I await my punishment," he said in one breath.

"It was not your fault," Hunter said.

Jeremy lifted a startled gaze to Hunter. "But it was. I should have—"

"Cease, Jeremy." Hunter pulled the young man up. "I was distracted, and a distracted warrior risks losing limb and life, his own and of others as well. Let this be a lesson to you. Never lower your guard in battle, for any reason whatsoever."

The young man looked at Hunter with what was certain adoration, drinking in every word.

"Now," Hunter continued. "Return to your duties. I want to see not a speck of blood on your sword when I inspect it later." The seemingly harsh words belied the kind gaze Hunter rested upon Jeremy.

"Aye, my lord. As always I owe you a debt of gratitude." He bowed deeply and then left.

Obviously, Jeremy felt responsible for the accident, and whatever had happened, it was kind of Hunter to ease his mind.

A kind gesture, an understanding word, a sympathetic ear: Deeds only caring people, like Hunter, were willing to give. Isabel's former husband's lack of generosity to her in the most traumatic moments of her life showed how little he'd cared.

Jack's accusing words still reverberated in her mind as clearly as if the man now stood before her, hurling those hurtful words at her.

"You must be happy now," he'd coldly told her, when days after she'd lost her baby she'd tried to share her pain, to talk about their loss. "You never wanted to be a mother, anyway," he'd accused. "Well, you got your wish. Your freedom is intact, Isabel. Enjoy it." He had stomped out of the house and out of her life.

Isabel admitted she'd been reluctant to get pregnant, utterly frightened of the immense responsibility of nurturing another human being, of having someone so dependent on her for its survival, its happiness. But when it finally happened, she had been elated and therefore utterly devastated at her loss.

Jack had not understood; he had only cast blame her way.

Isabel turned her thoughts to the present when she realized she was gripping Hunter's hand a little too hard.

He was looking at her with curiosity, probably wondering what was wrong with her.

"I am sorry," she said, relaxing her grip.

Maude returned to the room, carrying in her arms enough paraphernalia to rival a hospital emergency room. Of course there was no mechanical equipment but several bowls in different sizes, vials containing herbs and powders and God knew what else, rags, and a small leather box that Maude set on the table.

Still applying pressure to Hunter's hands, Isabel was reassured she'd seen no knives or cutting objects among Maude's apparatus.

And no leeches.

Isabel urged Hunter to sit and he straddled the bench by the table. Standing by his side, she removed the blood-soaked scarf. She held Hunter's hand over a large bowl and thoroughly rinsed the wound with water, removing any vestiges of dirt, hoping that would be enough to prevent infection. Though the wound no longer bled copiously Isabel picked up a clean rag and continued to apply pressure to the cut.

After a moment she glanced Maude's way, relieved to see the maid busy filling a cup with wine then pouring in it a light powder from one of her vials. She handed the cup to Hunter who drank it in one swallow. Isabel wondered if it was some kind of anesthesia. Hunter's stoic expression didn't necessarily mean he wasn't hurting, just that he chose not to show his pain.

"Do you have the healing herbs ready?" Isabel asked, trying to sound knowledgeable and praying Maude knew what to do and wouldn't question her further.

"Aye." But Maude made no move to hand Isabel anything.

Isabel glanced her way. "Well, where are they?"

"Will you not stitch the wound first, my lady?"

Isabel felt the blood drain from her face as understanding dawned on her. Maude expected her to do what? Good God, not even if they were in the middle of a desert with no help for miles would Isabel set needle to flesh. She couldn't even sew cloth, for goodness' sake.

"Cauterize it and be done with it," Hunter said.

Isabel groaned, knowing she couldn't possibly fake her way anymore.

"It is not too deep of a cut, my lord," Maude said. "You would be best served by having the cut sewn shut. Besides, my lady has the touch of an angel and her stitches are so small and tight you shall barely have a scar."

That did it! She couldn't possibly do what they expected of her. Isabel realized her selective amnesia was poor excuse for not remembering skills she used to possess. Maude hadn't even understood how she could eat apples when it was obvious Détra disliked them.

She lowered Hunter's hand to the table, then took a step back. "I cannot do that."

Cannot or want not? Hunter thought.

He swallowed down the question along with the shame clogging his throat. Was it not enough he had been bested by a mere squire in front of knights, men-at-arms, and servants alike while distracted by mundane thoughts of his lady? Had he also to suffer the ignominy of having Détra refuse to tend to his wounds?

Who had ever heard of such denial from a wife? Then again, Détra had been naught but contrary since the day they were wed.

Heat rose from his neck to his face. Confounded grief! He would be the laughingstock of Windermere Castle.

Hunter refused to even consider the possibility the castle folk might also know he had yet to consummate their marriage. Détra had sworn secrecy and yet, considering their last spat before the chalice had robbed her of memories, he had to wonder if she told him the truth then.

And thus here he was, still playing the waiting game. But not for long, Hunter swore. At the end of this accursed week, and if he could help, much earlier, Détra would be his wife in fact. He had discovered passion underneath her icy veneer and by God and king he would not let her forget that.

Détra showed him her shaking hands. "I would poke you silly," she said, looking distraught. "You are better off having Maude tend to your injury."

Détra seemed truthful enough. Would he be so fortunate that she cared? Nay, he would be a fool to believe her refusal to tend to him was for fear of causing him pain. She could not harm him with a needle any more than she had already done with her thoughtless words two mornings past.

Hunter would also hazard a guess that her reluctance had naught to do with being squeamish at the sight of blood. As the lady of the castle Détra had no doubt tended to many wounds of knights and servants alike, had surely assisted in childbirth, and probably witnessed the slaughter of animals. Blood was a constant in any of these events.

And yet the horror and sorrow in her expression when she first caught sight of his injury had not been false. She had stood there paralyzed for a long moment as if in the throes of some horrible nightmare. Or memory.

What was Détra hiding from him or mayhap from herself?

It suddenly dawned on Hunter how little he knew about his wife. His youthful fantasy of the beautiful lady who would love and accept him without qualms, the heart of his heart wish, had proved a fallacy. His experience with her since their wedding had been naught but hardship.

And yet, he could not deny that since the morning the chalice had unleashed its powers on her she had changed. Not to his idealized vision of her, as he had wished, but to a different Détra, nonetheless.

Even the way she rejected him now carried a hint of regret.

The damn cut on his hand throbbed more with every passing moment and every new aggravation. Hunter wanted this done and over with now. He turned to Maude. "Do as your lady bids you," he said through clenched teeth.

Maude opened the small box, from which she withdrew needle and silk thread, but before she moved to his side, Détra cried, "Wait!"

Hunter snapped his gaze back to Détra. Did she change her mind? Would she tend to him after all?

"Boil the needle first," she said. "And wash your hands with soap."

Hunter and Maude exchanged wary glances. What did Détra speak of?

"Clean hands and needles will keep festering away," she explained.

Hunter had never heard of such a remedy before. How could boiling a needle prevent in any way a wound from festering? Had the chalice not only robbed Détra of her memories but also addled her wits? Or was trickery hidden behind her claim? A prickle of doubt stung Hunter again. The morning of Détra's transformation he had been at his wits' end, and she had known it. Mayhap it was for that reason that she had revealed her true feelings for him with hurtful words she could never take back.

Could Détra have concocted the loss of memory to control him, counting on his honor to continue to play her waiting game? But what did she wait for?

Hunter pushed those nagging thoughts aside.

"Do it," he ordered Maude. What possible harm could a boiled needle and clean hands do him?

Maude nodded, then rushed outside, returning moments later with scalding water. Détra put the needle in a small bowl and poured boiling water over it, then watched carefully as Maude washed her hands with soap. Only then did Détra empty the bowl, leaving the needle in it.

"You may use it now," Détra said.

Maude picked the needle up and threaded it, then went to work on his already swelling hand.

Sitting by his side on the bench, Détra whispered, "Tell me what happened, Hunter."

Throughout the ordeal his lady wife listened to his tale of the incident and other small matters she kept prompting out of him, and before he knew it the task was completed.

Détra took over then, spreading a paste Maude had given her over his swollen palm, then setting on top of it a poultice of a large green leaf filled with crushed herbs before wrapping his hand with clean strips of linen.

Her touch was soft, her expression concerned, her moves sure. "We should change the bandages and the poultice every day," Détra said. "And try to keep it from getting wet." She smiled at him. A radiant smile she could not possibly feign.

She was a walking contradiction. And Hunter disliked the uncertainty immensely.

Disconcerted, he moved his hand and gaze away.

"Perhaps you should give Hunter that potion you gave me yesterday, Maude. He could use some sleep," Détra suggested.

"I still have many duties left in this day," Hunter said. Was she trying to get rid of him?

"But you are hurt. Can you not rest for a while?" Détra asked.

Mayhap they could spend some time together this day,

Hunter thought as he dismissed Maude. Détra followed Maude to the door, probably thinking herself dismissed too.

"My lady wife," Hunter called and Détra halted. She pivoted to face him. "I request you share the midday meal with me."

"In the great hall?" she asked, looking eager to escape the war chamber.

He shook his head. "Here. It is more private."

Détra's gaze flipped from him to Maude to the room in obvious indecision. That his wife was reluctant to spend some time alone with him, to share a private meal together, grated on his nerves.

"Sure," she finally said.

With a sinking heart Hunter knew she would rather be anywhere but here with him.

THEY ATE ALONE IN THE WAR ROOM, AMID PARCH-ments, ledgers, maps, and utter silence. Isabel was emotionally and physically drained and she wasn't up to idle chitchat. Was Hunter mad at her for bailing out of sewing his wound at the last moment? He was so quiet, Isabel wondered about his thoughts.

Wondered but wasn't fool enough to ask. She didn't want to start any conversation that required her to give an explanation of her behavior.

Isabel missed her uncomplicated life. Missed her painting, her long walks, and her solitude. She didn't know how much longer she'd be able to bear living in another woman's body, this woman's body. Everything felt wrong, from the heavy hair atop her head, to the fleshy body she dragged around and whose reactions she seemed to control very little, to the troublesome emotions that filled her heart.

Guilt for what she'd done, fear she wouldn't find the chalice, desire for a man who belonged to another woman, were all too intense emotions for her to bear.

Should she chance it and ask Hunter again about the chalice? She'd already broached the subject yesterday, though that had amounted to nothing. Still, now that he knew she remembered the chalice, what difference would it make if she mentioned it again? But what would she use for motivation? What would she say if he asked why she wanted it?

"How is your hand?" Isabel asked just to break the uncomfortable silence.

"Throbbing."

She was surprised he admitted this much. "Maybe you should rest a little."

"You keep saying that. Do you think me a weakling?"

A weakling? Was he teasing her? A man who took stitches on his hand without anesthesia? "I think you brave beyond comparison."

"You mock me."

"No," Isabel said quickly, touching his arm. "I care what happens to you, Hunter."

He turned those inscrutable onyx eyes on her as his hand covered hers. "Indeed?"

Isabel sucked in her breath. She tried to move her hand away without appearing to be rejecting him again. It didn't work. He held her hand in place.

"Was that the reason you refused to tend to my injury, because you care so much for me?" His voice was deceptively calm, putting Isabel on the defensive.

"You seem to forget my lack of memories," she retorted. "I was afraid I could hurt you more than I could help you." Then, tired of having to explain herself every moment, she added, "I'm trying very hard to reconcile with my duties as the lady of the castle, Hunter."

"I see," he said after a long pause. "Though you accept your role as the lady of this castle you continue to refuse to assume the role of my lady wife."

"If I had a choice our lives would revert to how it was before—" She almost said before she found the chalice. "Before I struck my head."

Hunter rose angrily. "Would you now?"

Why would he doubt her? "Yes, I would. Do you think I like not knowing who I am or not remembering my beloved husband? Do you think it is easy for me to be living this . . . this stranger's life?"

Fuming, Isabel sprang to her feet. She was at the end of her wits, and angry too. Angry with herself, with Hunter, with the world at large, and especially angry at fate for giving her a glimpse of a man she could love but could never have. A man she was deeply hurting.

"I want my life back," she cried. "I want to be sure of what I am doing. I want to be free to love whomever I choose."

"And who might that be?"

You! she wanted to shout.

"You," she whispered. Though love was not what she'd been looking for, Isabel recognized the possibility with Hunter. But what possibility? There was no possibility between Hunter and Isabel. Isabel didn't exist for him. Isabel was only the cause of all his turmoil.

Isabel realized Hunter was baffled by his wife's behavior, riddled by her rejection, disheartened by the turn of events. Had Détra been here she'd have tended to her husband's wound with care, ability, and love. She would be sharing his bed and his heart. Isabel had given him none of that. No wonder he was so vexed.

Vexed! Isabel couldn't believe she'd thought that word. She was being unduly influenced by her medieval surroundings.

Good God! She had to get out of here.

She left the bench to stand before the other table against the wall. "I realize this has been a very trying time for you," she said conciliatorily. "But it has been very trying for me as well."

His stance softened, anger disappearing, though a shadow still covered his eyes. He strolled to stand before her. Almost tentatively he brought her into his welcoming embrace and Isabel allowed her head to rest on his chest. She listened to his heartbeat thrumming against her ears while he kissed the top of her head.

Sensing his need for comfort, a need that mirrored her own, her arms encircled his waist and Isabel hugged him, as much offering as taking comfort from that embrace.

Hunter lifted her face to his and his gaze settled on her mouth. Isabel wanted to kiss him so badly her lips trembled. His fine body hardened against hers, unleashing her own desire.

She knew if she gave in to her desire for him, she'd never be able to forget him. And forget him she must. She stepped back, though still within the confines of his arms.

"Hunter." Her raspy, foreign voice surprised her again, reminding her of whose body she was in. "I want you," she said, deciding to be at least this honest with him. "I want you, but I cannot make love with you. Not now, not yet." She knew she was putting herself in harm's way by denying him yet again, but if she could only keep him at bay a day or so more, she still could find the chalice and leave him before her heart had been completely stolen from her. Before he had anything to regret.

"What difference can a few days make?" he asked, his own voice so husky it melted her insides.

"All the difference in the world." Détra should be back in her own body by then. "I want it to be perfect between us when we finally come together." They would never be together.

"It shall be perfect," he whispered, pulling her closer.

"Not if I feel I am making love to a stranger."

"I shall not be a stranger for long," he vowed. His hand caressed her naked neck, drawing goose bumps over her entire body.

Isabel didn't know how, but every time they were together they ended up in each other's arms. And every time she pulled back she hurt Hunter anew. Perhaps it was time to give in a little.

"Perhaps you are right," she said. "But we should take this slowly. One step at a time." She inched her way closer to him. "One touch at a time." She threaded her fingers through his tousled dark hair, surprised at how soft it was. Then she kissed him softly.

But Hunter would have none of that. He gathered her in his arm and deepened the kiss with undisguised hunger.

And she kissed him back in kind.

Kissed him because his mouth begged for kisses, his body tempted her touch, and his heart deserved to be loved. Kissed him in hello, kissed him in good-bye, and God help her, kissed him because she didn't know when or if she would ever feel this way again about a man.

And as she kissed him she lowered her hand to that part of him that throbbed against her.

Chapter 9

AT Détra's unexpected touch, Hunter staggered back against the table. The strong legs that had supported him and his hauberk in many a battle now quavered like badly mended sticks as she rubbed her palm against his arousal.

She had come willingly to him! Would she also be ready to surrender her heart?

Through the cloth of his breeches, Détra's fingers curled around his engorged member, squeezing it, rubbing it in rhythmic moves, scattering his wits.

He had suffered such unfulfilled desire for Détra since their wedding night that the promise in her passionate touch dazzled him. Halfheartedly he pulled away, but she refused to relinquish her power over him. His mind commanded him to stop her torturing touch before he lost control and spilled his seed like an untried boy. His body demanded he relish the pleasure of her rare touch.

Just a moment longer, he told himself, unconsciously allowing the moment to stretch indefinitely while her hand kept him captive and her tongue explored his mouth.

His heartbeat pounded so loud and fast in his throat he feared he would loose his heart in Détra's kiss, and when her hand buried underneath his breeches, searing his skin with her bare touch, unbridling long-sought pleasure, Hunter knew he had waited too long.

The urgent need that refused to be denied overrode his will and turned him into a mindless heap of sensation. His head fell back with the force of his release as his growl echoed in the four walls of the chamber like thunder caught in a cave.

Moments later, when he finally caught his breath, Hunter opened his eyes. He found Détra beyond his reach.

"You should have stopped," he chided mildly, aware he was the one who lost control.

"I wanted to bring you release." Her throaty voice was raspier than usual.

"That you did." His grin was a mix of satisfaction and embarrassment. He would give himself a few moments more, then, when able again, he would return the boon to her. Meanwhile, he needed to hold her close. He pushed away from the table and opened his arms to her. "Come," he invited.

But Détra didn't move.

"I shall not leave you dissatisfied," he insisted.

Détra stepped farther away from his grasp. "There is no need," she said. "It was enough for me to give you pleasure."

Hunter froze in place, awareness slowly replacing his momentary elation. It took him a moment to realize what her words signified, but when it finally dawned on him he staggered back as if she had slapped him in the face.

Had she shared such an intimacy with him only to con-

tinue to deny him? Fresh suspicion joined the nagging
doubts he already entertained about Détra. Doubts about
her lack of memory. Doubts about her apparent change.
Doubts she would honor her vow to surrender to him once
this sennight was over.

Hunter's smile disappeared, shame replacing embarrassment. Shame for his weakness and gullibility. Shame
for allowing his lady wife to manipulate him to her own
will.

Shame that Détra had rejected him yet again.

Feeling unmanned, Hunter rearranged his clothing. A
man could take just so much humbling, and God was witness he had suffered his fair share in his life. These past
days alone should last him a lifetime.

"Well, my lady wife," he said, forcing the pain from
his voice. "That was truly edifying."

He turned his back on her and strolled to the table in
the middle of the room, where he refilled his cup with
wine. He took a good swallow, trying to put his thoughts
in place.

"These past few days have been very trying for both
of us," Détra said. "I just wanted to give you some joy,
to let you know that I care, even though it might not look
like it."

Hunter spun around. The little wine left in his cup
spilled out with the force of his spin. Joy? Care? Was she
trying to justify the unseemly way she handled him? To
make excuses for her constant rejection of him? Mortifi-
cation burned his face. "Should I be grateful for the scrap
of intimacy you have just thrown my way?" he shouted.

She jerked back at his outburst. "That was not what
that was."

Not bothering to hide his frustration Hunter cast the
cup across the room. It hit the wall with a loud clink that
somehow seemed distant and detached. With two long

strides he reached her. He stood before her, towering above her, glaring down at her as he struggled to control his rising anger as desire swiftly fled away. He wanted to shake her until her teeth rattled. Wanted to push her down on the table and take her here and now, ending once and for all this game she played.

"Pray tell me," he hissed between gritted teeth. "What was that then?"

Détra withstood his glare with impossible composure. Hunter was torn between contempt for her coldness and admiration for her mettle.

"That was all I could give you at this time," she said.

Contempt won out. All she chose to give him, he silently corrected her.

"Indeed," he said. "But I expect more than a whore's trick from my lady wife."

She paled, her eyes narrowing in pain, and then anger. How dare she be angry with him? She had made a fool of him for the last time.

Hunter gripped her shoulders, ignoring the sting on his wounded hand. It was his God-given right to take her here and now. No one would dare interfere. No one would gainsay him. No one would berate him for forcing an unwilling wife to do her duty by her husband.

"There shall be no more waiting for us," Hunter said, tightening his grip on her.

Détra stiffened in his arms. Her breath came in small gasps and her eyes burned with anger, then shadowed with fear. Her hands curled around his forearms but she said naught.

Her silence made Hunter realize that though no one would condemn his deeds, his wife would. If he took her now when his heart was so full of anger and shame there would be naught but anger and shame between them. He had waited too long, bargained too much, and compromised his future to have her love and acceptance.

The chalice had given him a chance to right the wrongs of his marriage to Détra. He could not forget that.

He would give Détra one last chance. He would give his heart wish one last chance. But he would wait no more.

He let go of her. "This night I expect your full surrender," he said. "And God is my witness, do you reject me again, I shall not respond for my deeds."

Tearing his gaze away from her he marched to the door. As he opened it he made a show of rearranging his garments. There would be no doubt in anyone's mind that he and Détra had just enjoyed a tryst in the middle of the day.

And after this night there would be no doubt in his wife's mind that her control over him had ceased to exist.

ISABEL STARED IN BEWILDERMENT AT THE RETREATING Hunter. What had gone wrong? How could her attempt to mollify him have gone so awry? Instead of mellowing, the man had been furious with her, behaving as if she had committed a mortal sin when he seemed to have enjoyed her touch very much.

He had even called her a whore, the self-righteous bastard!

Indignity filled Isabel with rage. She swore she would be out of Détra's body before the sun set on the horizon this day. She still had a few places to look. And if she didn't find it and Hunter decided to behave like a Neanderthal tonight, she would fight him all the way.

Isabel blinked back tears of frustration and, with trembling hands, filled a cup with wine, then took a big swallow of the red liquid. The almost-tart taste burned her throat, but after a few more gulps her insides calmed.

She was through feeling guilty over this whole mess.
Her one stupid, unintentional mistake had snowballed into
a vortex of consequences totally out of her control. She'd
hoped she'd find the chalice immediately after she first
realized what her wish had provoked, thus reversing the
travesty and avoiding having to take another woman's
place in her husband's arms. She had even tried her
damnedest to do the right thing for everyone's sake,
though it was naïve of her to think she could keep Hunter
at bay without consequences. She should've been worrying primarily about her survival and safety, and not whose
feelings would be hurt, hers included.

Several deep breaths later Isabel finally accepted that
her intention of pacifying Hunter, albeit good, had back-
fired. And because of that her situation had turned from
difficult to precarious.

How deeply had she hurt Hunter with what to him must
have looked like her detached offering? She had almost
pushed him beyond his limits. Would he truly force her
into submission if she denied him again tonight?

And yet, despite his anger, his obvious disappointment
and frustration, he hadn't thrown her on the floor and had
his way with her when he had the chance. The thought
had crossed his mind, she knew it, but he had not done
it. And he could have with impunity, Isabel belatedly realized. No one would've stopped him. No one would've
dared. But if he didn't do it while in the grips of anger
why would he do it later, when he had calmed down?
Would she dare put him to test?

By the end of this day Isabel knew she would have to
make the decision she'd been postponing the moment her
eyes had set on Hunter. Until then, however, there was
still hope that the damn chalice would somehow turn up
and save her from more heartache.

*   *   *

THERE WERE ONLY THREE PLACES ISABEL BELIEVED
could be hiding the chalice—the orchard, the stables, and
the barracks, or garrison's quarters as Hunter called it.
Somehow, she didn't think Hunter would hide the chalice
in the kitchen, laundry room, or garden, though she would
search these places if her first three choices didn't pan
out.

After Hunter left the war room, Isabel took the opportunity to do some searching there, just in case. Her gaze
perused the room looking for hiding places and settled on
a small chest against the wall by the table. She lifted the
heavy lid. Several pieces of parchment, or animal's skins,
were tightly wrapped inside a cloth. She would have to
undo the bundle to see what was inside, and she decided
against it. She didn't want to disturb anything, though she
was curious what they contained.

There were also feather pens, bundled together and tied
with a ribbon. Their feathers were trimmed to almost
nothing and the tip was pointed and split, resembling a
fountain pen. Isabel pried open a tightly shut jar and discovered ink inside.

For a moment she was enchanted with the thought of
using these writing materials for drawing, but dismissed
the thought, realizing she had more pressing matters in
mind. Like finding a chalice and returning to her own
body.

However reluctant, she put everything back in the
chest, closed it, and moved over to the small table against
the wall.

She skimmed her gaze over the big book Godfrey was
working on earlier, realizing it was an account book judging by the names and numbers of entries, probably of the
castle's expenses and income. She picked up a few maps,

setting them down without the least understanding of what they depicted.

After combing the room for the chalice and finding no sign of it Isabel left the war room and crossed the half-empty hall, thankful Hunter was nowhere in sight. She really didn't want to face him right now. Seeing Maude hurrying to her, Isabel decided to give the maid the afternoon off. Somehow she didn't think Maude would approve of her searching plans.

"How do you fare, my lady?" Maude asked somewhat anxiously.

Had she heard Hunter's growl of satisfaction early on? Or his angry shouts soon after? Maude was probably wondering whether her lord and lady had been having sex earlier or blasting each other out. Isabel wasn't about to clarify matters for her.

"Fine," she said, a forced smile playing on her lips. "Where is my husband?" Knowing where Hunter was would simplify where to start her search.

"He is back in training, I am certain," Maude said.

"With an injured hand?"

"That would not stop him."

No, it wouldn't, Isabel realized. It hadn't stopped him from shaking her in the war room either.

"You wish to see the rest of the castle now?" Maude asked.

"No. I want to walk outside for a while."

Isabel moved to the door and immediately Maude fell in step with her. Isabel stopped. "If you do not mind, Maude, I would rather be alone for a while." At the maid's look of surprise, Isabel added, "Take time to do something for yourself, for your own enjoyment."

Maude looked utterly bewildered at her suggestion. Maybe medieval people didn't do anything for fun or even had time off. Isabel just didn't have time to deal with that right now.

"I will see you later." Isabel left the great hall and the confounded Maude behind.

The yard was quite busy with people coming and going. Even if the stables and barracks were empty of men at this time of the day there would be plenty of people to witness her entering either place. The stables she could get away with it, but the barracks would look mighty suspicious. Isabel imagined the place was for men only. What would the lady of the castle possibly want to do there?

She would check the orchard first.

Isabel spent a good part of the afternoon searching behind trees, checking a few suspicious spots on the ground where the dirt seemed to have been turned—maybe Hunter had buried the damn chalice. She looked through apple-laden branches, even climbed a tree or two—an almost impossible job with her very long and cumbersome gown.

Again she wasn't surprised when she didn't find the chalice.

Better luck in the stables, she wished herself.

Before she marched out of the orchard, she plucked a particularly appetizing apple from one of the trees and took a bite out of it. She loved apples, and these were the best she'd had in a long time.

The traffic in the yard had diminished considerably. Only a few men lingered about as the sun lowered on the horizon, throwing shadows across the big yard before it disappeared completely behind the mountains in the distance. Isabel ambled in the direction of the stables, a long, horizontal wooden structure conveniently located near the barracks. She entered the building unchallenged. The odor of horse manure and urine clung in the stuffy air, making her gag. Taking shallow breaths and holding her long dress up, she gingerly stepped over the soft hay-strewn floor—at least she hoped that was what it was—to peek inside the occupied stalls from a distance.

Most of the horses didn't seem to mind her presence, though she had no way of knowing their true mind—she and horses having never mingled before—but one of them eyed her with a distrustful look on its face and neighed loudly.

Startled, Isabel jumped back just as a young man suddenly rose from a dark corner of the stable, making himself visible to her.

Isabel gathered her composure. It wouldn't do to have someone witness her ignorance of horses. After all, medieval ladies should be well acquainted with them. It was their mode of transportation, wasn't it? It'd be like a modern woman not knowing about cars. Some might not know how they were built or how to fix them, or even how to drive them, but most wouldn't be afraid of getting into one.

The young man put down a bucket of manure he was holding next to three other filled buckets, and then came to her. Isabel eyed the buckets he left behind. Hunter wouldn't be so crazy as to hide the chalice in a bucket of manure, would he?

She would exhaust all her options first before even considering that particular hiding place.

"Eleanor missed you last night, my lady," the young man said.

Isabel assumed he was speaking of the horse, or more appropriately the mare. "I was occupied with other matters." Knowing Détra should know the young man and especially the mare, she added, "I hope you took good care of her in my absence."

"Aye, my lady. Me and Eleanor are best friends." He

patted the mare's nose and the animal gave a content snort.

"I am glad," she said.

The stable boy looked at her hand. "Will you give her the treat you hold?"

Isabel remembered the half-eaten apple in her hand. She had no problem parting with the fruit, but the thought of putting her hand close to those very big teeth wasn't pleasant. Nonetheless, she'd do what she must. Eleanor glared at her for a moment, refusing to take the treat, making Isabel very nervous. Could the animal sense something was wrong with her owner? Then, with a subtlety Isabel would never relate to horses, the mare took the apple from her hand without so much as nipping her fingers.

Pulling her hand back, Isabel decided the chalice wasn't there and she'd better leave the place. She thanked the stable boy, said good-bye to Eleanor, and then stole outside, eagerly gulping in the fresh late-afternoon breeze. In the distance she heard the grunts and shouts of men in training subsiding. Soon they would be returning to their quarters. Even knowing she probably didn't have much time before that happened, Isabel headed in that direction. Time was running out on her. If she didn't find the chalice today, her fate would be sealed tonight.

CHALICE IN HAND, HUNTER SAT ON THE COT OF HIS small chamber in the garrison's quarters. In desperate need of reassurance, he willed the stones to glow, the vision to reappear, but the chalice remained unchanged as it had always been with the exception of that morning two days past.

Did the chalice truly have magical powers? Would it

ever show them to him again? Or had it all been a dream, wishful thinking on his part?

Hunter refused to believe it thus. He could still see in his mind the vivid image the chalice had revealed. The significance of that vision had arrested his anger at Détra in the war chamber. The small possibility his heart wish could still come true had stilled his hand in forcing her to his will. The fact Détra had mellowed toward him these past two days when she had been so cold and distant in the weeks since their marriage had convinced Hunter there was still hope for them, that in some way the chalice had worked its magic on her.

Still, he was utterly vexed at yet another rejection from his wife—and yet the Détra of old would never have touched him the way she did today. Mayhap when he conquered her body this night, he would finally find his way to her heart.

Unless Détra was feigning her reaction to his touch and the passion he had glimpsed in her, Hunter was certain he could use her own desire to aid him in his plan. He had failed before for he had allowed his own lust to overcome his wits, therefore giving her control. He would do differently now. He would keep his desire in control while he brought hers to life. And he would keep her in such throes of passion, give her such pleasure, that when rejection crossed her mind, she would have no will to reject him.

And she would come back to him for more.

Hunter lifted from the cot and strode to the war chest, then deposited the chalice inside. It was time to seek her. As his hand rested on top of the chest lid he heard the door creaking open. He flung the lid down and spun to see who had entered his private chamber without his bidding.

Détra stood at the door, trying unsuccessfully to hide

her surprise in seeing him there. But what had she expected to find here if not him?

"Do you seek me?" he asked.

"I—ah—Yes, I was hoping to find you here."

"Indeed?" Then why did she look like she had seen a ghost?

"What was that noise?" she asked as if reading his mind. "It startled me."

"The sound of a lid falling over a chest."

"Oh." Her eyes widened as she glanced at his war chest, visible behind him. "What do you keep there?"

She seemed just mildly interested, but Hunter was mistrustful of her motives, especially with his chalice safely buried inside it. Yet she had no way of knowing that, had she? "Naught much," he answered dismissively. "Naught that would interest a lady, anyway. Only accouterments of war."

His gaze followed hers as she inspected his sparsely furnished chamber, taking in its lack of comfort. She glanced over the still-full round tub he had used earlier to bathe, the dirty clothes on the floor, the weapons scattered over the table, the war shield leaning against the wall, then stared at his full hauberk hanging over a stool by the cot. The rest of his knightly ensemble—mail coif, gauntlets, helm—rested inside the chest and out of her view.

She walked to the cot, sitting on it as if intending a long visit. She lifted part of the hauberk with her hand. "It is heavy," she said as if surprised, then turned her attention on him. "You must be a sight to behold in full armor." She gave him an appreciative look.

"*You* are a sight to behold, my lady wife."

She smiled at his compliment. "Have you been in many battles?"

He nodded, not interested in discussing his warring pursuits at this moment.

"Is there any tale you would like to tell?" Her gaze strayed to the war chest. "Any mementos you would like to share?"

Suspicion crawled inside of him again. "No mementos," he said. "I carry only memories with me. As for tales, I am no troubadour capable of weaving enchanting words to entertain a noble lady."

"Well, at least you are home safe. May I assume we are not at war at the moment?"

Her apparent lack of knowledge of England's current affairs lent credence to her claim of memory loss. However, that might be exactly what she wanted him to believe.

"We are at war, my lady wife," he said, wondering where this odd conversation would lead.

She cocked her head slightly to the side in a manner he had never seen in her until two days ago. "With France?"

"Edward guaranteed peace with France, at least for the time being, by marrying the French princess, Isabella. Scotland is our foe for now." Though she quickly subdued it, Hunter did not miss the fleeting interest that crossed his lady wife's face at the mention of Isabella or Scotland. He knew not which.

A connection between Détra and Queen Isabella would do them no harm. However, the thought Détra might have any association with Scotland or the traitor settled heavily in Hunter's gut. And though his duty to the king would be to pursue the matter, he decided to postpone it.

"Did you seek me to discuss England's foes?" he asked, perching on the chest across the cot, more on eye level with her. Thus far he was still uncertain of her purpose in seeking him out.

"No," she said quickly, then repeated slower, "No. I—I came to clear the air between us. What happened earlier was a misunderstanding. I unintentionally hurt your feelings and in return you lashed out at me, hurting mine." She lifted her dazzling green gaze to him. "Can we just forget about that and start fresh?"

He was very agreeable to the thought.

"How do you suggest we do that?" He wanted to hear her words of commitment to a new beginning, for if she hoped to convince him to wait any longer than this night to have her, she would be sorely disappointed.

"How about supper later on? We can talk then and perhaps find some common ground on which to stand together."

"Yours is a timely suggestion," he said, then moved from the chest to sit by her side on the cot. "Since I already had planned on sharing a meal with you this eve."

"Good," she said, rising. "Then I will see you later."

"There is no haste." He gently pulled her back down by his side, their thighs touching on the narrow cot. Why wait for this night when she was here now? "I would like to ask a boon of you, a small token of goodwill, if it pleases you."

She gave him an uncertain look.

"To cement our new beginning," he added.

"What do you have in mind?"

Her throaty voice pleased him immensely. "It would give me great pleasure," he whispered, watching as she swallowed hard in anticipation of his request, "to see your hair free of restraints. I very much enjoyed the sight of it in the orchard yesterday morning."

Her hesitation lasted but a moment. She reached for the silk ribbon confining her hair and untied it. She ran her fingers through her tresses until the curls cascaded free over her shoulders and back in a fiery mantle.

Hunter's groins tightened. So much for keeping his lust in control.

"Beautiful," he said as he captured a handful of curls in his hand, reveling in their softness, inhaling deeply the rosemary scent. With the tip of his fingers he trailed the curve of her shoulder and neck up to her earlobe, then down to her throat. Encouraged by the slight tremor of her body, he drew near, then kissed the sensitive skin of her neck, nibbling at it, indulging in the sweet taste of her. She moaned and turned her head slightly to the side in surrender to his touch.

With his right arm supporting her back Hunter trailed kisses along her cheekbones then settled over her parted lips, tasting her sweet nectar in repeated forays of tongue and lips. He caught her lower lips in his alternating between suckling and soothing.

"The very sight and taste of you give me pleasure," he confessed against her mouth.

She moaned again and he brought her closer to him, her breasts against his chest. Her hands encircled his neck, and as their knees fought for leeway, she swung her legs over his thigh, resting against his ever-growing arousal.

With the back of his injured hand he caressed her breasts. He could feel the nipples hardening even through the fabric of her gown. Frustration mounted, as she arched against him, clearly expecting more than his accursed injured hand could give her.

He lay her down, freeing his right hand for the caress. While he kneaded one breast, his mouth nibbled on the nipple of the other breast. Détra whimpered, arching to him. Their awkward position, made more difficult by the narrowness of the cot and Hunter's injured hand, frustrated him. He lifted from her and scooted down the cot, bringing her legs, knees bent, to the top of the thin mattress.

He planted her feet slightly apart, then his hands buried underneath her skirts. He sought her gaze and she looked at him with dazed eyes. Slowly he pushed her skirts up and over her knees to let them fall and gather in a bundle at the top of her thighs as she lay back on the cot. He undid the garters then rolled the woolen hose down to her ankles, his rough hands caressing the uncovered skin.

Deus! He was throbbing already.

He nudged her knees further apart, revealing the dark triangle at the entrance of her womanhood. With the tip of his fingers he raked the soft, warm skin of her inner thighs, feeling the goose flesh rise in response. She arched against him, scooting in the direction of his fingers. He obliged her.

When his finger entered her, heat and moisture welcomed it, closing around it. He placed his palm against her mound, rubbing it as his finger reached deep within her. Détra moaned, almost bucking out of the small cot. He moved his head between her thighs. She was now utterly open to his mouth and hand. He continued to thrust his finger inside of her as he kissed her inner thighs. Détra's moans came in quicker gasps as she undulated against his hand until her cry of release reverberated in the small chamber.

Hunter lifted from her, breathing as harshly as she did. He began removing his garments with jerky but quick moves.

He was ready to end once and for all the drought of his life, to consummate his marriage, consolidate his hold of Windermere, and finally possess the woman of his heart.

Chapter 10

ISABEL'S head flopped to the side, her face resting against the hard cot, her eyes open but unfocused. She lay in languid abandon, relishing the last waves of the orgasm that still thrummed inside of her.

"Détra."

She heard Hunter calling his wife's name and the sweet pleasure partly vanished. She didn't want to face him right now. Not as vulnerable as she felt.

Her gaze wandered and, spotting the war chest, she remembered her reasons for coming to the soldier's barracks. Not to find Hunter as she'd made him believe, but to search for the chalice that would take her back to her own body and life. The chalice that would save her from doing exactly what she'd just done: succumb to Hunter's touch.

Irony of all, Isabel truly believed she had found the

chalice. It had to be hidden inside the war chest. Where else would Hunter keep it?

And tomorrow it would be almost too late. Not too late for her return to her own body, but too late for what had already happened between them, for what was still to come.

Isabel felt Hunter kneeling between her legs, and though she didn't want to, she looked at him. He was magnificent in his maleness, rough-looking yet utterly handsome. Tousled dark hair, inscrutable onyx eyes, and the blue-black stubble of a beard shadowing his sun-bronzed face.

And he was naked between her thighs, his arousal eagerly reaching out for her.

Isabel swallowed hard, her heart stammering at just the sight of him. She'd postponed the inevitable for far too long. After their encounter earlier in the war room she knew Hunter wouldn't wait anymore.

Her time of reckoning had arrived. Isabel understood survival, understood she'd be doing more harm to Hunter and Détra's relationship if she denied him again. And yet she also knew that making love to Hunter would forever reverberate in her soul, wherever she was.

Suddenly the mask she hid behind fell, and Isabel finally admitted to herself she'd kept her distance from Hunter not only for Hunter and Détra's sake, though she'd considered their feelings, but for her own.

With her skirts tossed up to her belly, exposing her moist, recently satisfied, and yet still very eager body to him, Isabel knew there was no running away now. And she wouldn't. She would go to him willingly, no, more than that, she would go to him eagerly, for she'd thought of being with him many times since she'd first set eyes on him.

Wasn't that what had kept her hesitating? Her own

feelings for him? Feelings that could never be returned, for when he looked at her it would be Détra he saw?

He knelt there, softly caressing her inner thighs with his fingertips, watching her, as if waiting for her consent. Isabel almost screamed at him, "Go ahead, get it over with."

Sex devoid of emotion would be much easier to face than her wanting to make love to a man who belonged to another woman, especially knowing that man would be thinking of his wife when he came inside of her.

Isabel winced, the painful pang of guilt and jealousy spearing her heart.

"I burn for you," he said as he spread his own thighs and gently drew her hips to him, her feet resting on either side of his hips, her back and buttocks sitting on his powerful thighs, her center open to him. Unhurriedly, he rubbed the tip of his engorged penis at her exposed entrance and Isabel could feel her juices flowing, rushing to welcome him.

He burned for his wife! The thought intruded.

Isabel's pride rebelled against it. The body belonged to Détra but it was Isabel's mind, her heart, and her soul that commanded it to feel, to respond, and to accept what Hunter was offering.

She pushed aside the nagging doubt of her very convenient rationalization. Hell, she'd already come this far, had already crossed the line she'd sworn never to cross, she wouldn't turn back now.

Damn her soul but she would have all of him.

At that moment, Hunter entered her a little, jolting her back to him. He pushed in a little further, just enough for her to have a taste of him, to draw a deep breath in anticipation, but not nearly enough to satisfy her blooming craving. Then he pulled back, not quite withdrawing but leaving her bereft and scooting against him. He obliged her by thrusting deeper, yet again not totally. Her hips moved against him, wanting all of him inside of her. Instead, he pulled back again, wrenching a silent cry of frustration out of her.

"Do you want me?" he asked, slowly entering her again, inch by tantalizing inch. Isabel groaned, her insides burning, her breath stolen, her heart thrumming against her ears. Instead of speaking she pressed against him in answer.

And he pulled back again.

Oh, no, you won't. Enough already!

Holding on to his forearms, Isabel pushed herself against him, fully engaging his penis inside of her. She gasped as the sensations spread over her body.

"Does that answer your question?" she asked.

Seeming to have lost some of his damnable control, Hunter held her hips firmly in place, preventing her from moving as he struggled to control his breathing.

"Remind me to never doubt a lady of few words," he whispered in a husky voice that mollified Isabel somehow.

And then he smiled. And Isabel stared at him as if seeing another man. Handsome when serious, Hunter was utterly charming and adorable when smiling.

As if she needed further encouragement.

With his help Isabel lifted her upper body from the cot and sat fully on him, her arms encircling his neck, her hands burrowing in his hair, her fingers scraping against his scalp.

When his mouth settled over hers and she surrendered to his skillful kisses, she cursed the fabric of her dress that prevented her breasts from feeling the skin of his chest. Hunter's hands that a moment ago had stilled her movements now urged her on. The tension inside of her grew to a crescendo about to explode. All thoughts fled from her mind as she rode him hard, rode him until the world ceased to exist, until she forgot whose body she inhabited, until she cried out in spent ecstasy.

Hunter pushed her back on the small cot, following her, still inside of her, while she floated back to reality. And yet he gave her no time to settle down. He thrust inside of her with an impatience he couldn't hide, no tentative stroke now, no teasing. Isabel raised her knees to better accommodate him, already feeling the waves of pleasure rising again inside of her. And as his deep, hard, and intense thrusts continued, the waves crested and she cried out with him as he found his release.

AS HUNTER LED HIS WIFE OUT OF HIS PRIVATE CHAMBER in the garrison's quarter he could not contain the joy in his heart. Neither could he believe how passionate, how giving, how loving she had been with him.

How very much his heart had wished her to be!

Détra stood by his side, waiting for him to lock the door, not seeming to mind at all the few men gathered in the small hall of the garrison's quarters gawking at them with incredulity, surprise, and dawning understanding. For there was no mistaking what Hunter and his wife had been doing in that chamber. Her glorious hair cascaded over her shoulder in a disarray of curls—which she minded much less this day, having pulled the strands away from her face only once or twice. There was a glow of contentment on her face, a softness in her gaze when she looked at him, like a bride leaving her nuptial chamber accompanied by her much beloved husband.

Hunter reveled at the thought. Mayhap he had reached her heart after all. Mayhap his chalice had finally made his heart wish come true. Mayhap all would be well for them.

"Is there need to lock the door?" she asked. "I am sure

no one would enter it without your permission."

"This is my private chamber, and I wish to keep it as such." Especially while his chalice was still hidden inside.

Détra opened her mouth as if to speak, then, changing her mind, snapped her lips closed.

Nagging doubts assailed him again. Could Détra know more about the chalice than she had let him believe? She had mentioned it but once after that fateful morning when the chalice had worked its magic on her, and then only in a very fleeting manner. Had she known more, had she remembered the morning of her transformation, she would not have made love to him this day.

Hunter wondered. Wondered but was not foolish enough to bring the matter up for discussion.

Hunter led Détra out of the garrison's quarters and together they strolled through the dark bailey in the direction of the great hall. The night had fallen and now covered the earth like a giant mantle. Suddenly Détra halted her steps and looked up at the night sky.

"I have never seen so many stars together in my life," she whispered. "It is an awesome sight."

Hunter looked up, not seeing any more stars than usual, then turned his gaze on her. "None shine as bright as you." He felt a little foolish in his awkward attempt to woo her. He had never been very good with words or courtly manners. His life had been one of deeds, of war, of struggle. And yet, were he able, he would create an ode to his lady wife's beauty.

She turned to him, but in the darkness he could only see the nuances of shadows across her face.

It had taken him long enough, but she was finally his. Hunter pushed away the thought his joy might be temporary. When Détra remembered her true feelings for him would this night hold any special meaning to her at all? Or would it become a memory of betrayal?

Hunter pulled Détra into his arms. He might be at a loss for words, but there were other ways to express his feelings for her. His mouth covered hers with eager, hopeful passion. And God be praised, Détra responded in kind. The world ceased to exist around them. There were just the two of them alone in the dark bailey, two lonely stars that had finally met in the immensity of the sky and thus together shone brighter.

Would that this moment of harmony last forever.

Détra was the one who first stepped back. "I will never forget this night, Hunter."

"Neither shall I."

She shivered in his arms.

"The night grows cold, we had better go inside."

They ambled in the direction of the great hall.

As they entered the busy hall they were received with glances of curiosity much like two days ago when Hunter had escorted Détra from the orchard, but like moments ago in the garrison's quarters, their curiosity turned into acceptance.

Hunter was aware of Windermere's people's reluctance in accepting him, mayhap even justified if he considered the unsettling gossip he had heard about their previous lord. Not that anyone told him any tale directly, but Hunter had grasped enough from scraps of conversation here and there to realize Détra's former husband had not been a kind lord.

Could Détra's anger and rejection of him be a result of the way her former husband treated her? In that case, her loss of memory was indeed a blessing far more reaching than for his own benefit. Hunter would have to ask Maude about that. It would help him to know more about his lady wife, even if she could not remember herself.

They approached the main table and Hunter helped Détra to a chair beside his own. As he sat down he noticed a stranger standing below the lord's dais. The man's face was vaguely familiar.

"A messenger from Hawkhaven has just arrived," Gervase said. "I was about to send word to you."

Hawkhaven! That was where Hunter must have seen the man. He nodded to the messenger to approach him.

"Welcome to Windermere Castle," Hunter said. "What tidings bring you?"

"My lord." The messenger bowed before Hunter, then lifted. "Lord Reginald summons your presence at Hawkhaven with the utmost urgency."

What would his fostering lord wish with him? Could it have anything to do with the Scottish raiders?

"Is Hawkhaven under attack?" Hunter asked.

"Nay, my lord. It is a personal matter."

Personal? A chill skittered down Hunter's spine.

"Lord Reginald is ill and we fear he shall not be among the living for long," the messenger continued. "He wishes to speak with you without delay."

Hunter's conflicting emotions about his fostering lord warred inside of him. He owed much to Lord Reginald. Without the man's generosity Hunter would have never become a knight, therefore, never have gained his own lands and castle, and above all, never have wedded the Lady Détra.

However, such unexplained generosity had garnered Hunter the envy and hatred of most people at Hawkhaven, especially Lord Reginald's only son, Rupert. Mayhap, like Hunter, Rupert had also wondered about his father's reasons for giving such unheard-of opportunity to a bastard of unknown sire who lived as a villein on the outskirts of his castle.

The only possibility was that Lord Reginald was Hunter's true father.

A possibility that most probably had occurred to Rupert as well, for the young man had resented Hunter's presence in his castle from the beginning, ever working to undermine Hunter's training to knighthood.

And now Lord Reginald was dying. Could he be summoning Hunter to finally tell him the truth, guilt ridden for not recognizing Hunter as his son before? Hunter had wished for so long to learn his father's identity. Had begged his mother for it, but she had died, taking her secret with her. Being a bastard had been a heavy cross to bear, but not knowing his father's name had been a much heavier burden.

How would Rupert welcome such tidings? Would he accept Hunter as his half brother? Would Hunter?

"Rupert knows of his father's summons?" Hunter asked.

The messenger shook his head. "Lord Rupert was away when Lord Reginald sent me here, though he might be back by the time you reach Hawkhaven. You must not dally, my lord. Lord Reginald was adamant to see you immediately."

Whatever it was that Lord Reginald wanted to tell him he seemed to not want his son to be present. There was no point in speculating until he saw his foster lord and heard of his tidings in person, but his heart swelled with the knowledge that soon he would meet his father.

"I thank you for your prompt delivery of Lord Reginald's message. Avail yourself of a hearty meal and you may spread your mat in my hall this night. I will accompany you back to Hawkhaven at dawn."

The man bowed, then found a place to sit at a table below the dais.

"Gervase," Hunter called. "Select two knights and three men-at-arms for the journey on the morrow. I bid you to remain at Windermere to protect the castle in my absence."

"Would you allow me to serve you in this journey, my lord?" Jeremy, Hunter's squire, asked as he filled Hunter's tankard with ale.

"I might be in need of your services as long as you keep your sword away from my body."

The young man nodded with such vehemence Hunter was afraid his head would rip from his neck and roll down the dais.

"Who is Lord Reginald?" Détra asked.

"I fostered at his castle."

"Fostered? I thought Windermere was your home."

Hunter had to constantly remind himself Détra remembered naught of her life. "It is now," he said, taking a swallow of ale.

"Oh!" She seemed to take a moment to digest his words. "Is Lord Reginald your foster father?"

Hunter's attention snapped quickly back at her. He was never sure what Détra meant with the words she chose to use. At times he could not understand her at all; at other times, even the words he understood seemed to have a different meaning for which they were intended.

A result of her lack of memory, for certain. Still . . .

"My foster lord," he answered. "I have no father." He watched her closely at his disclosure of such truth.

"I am sorry," she said, looking truthful and contrite. "Lord Reginald seems anxious to see you; he must care for you."

Hunter doubted Lord Reginald cared for him at all. He surely had not shown Hunter any special treatment those long, lonely years at his castle. He had equipped Hunter with horse and hauberk, had trained him in the art of fighting, and had demanded his best, accepting no less than perfection from him, never allowing Hunter to forget what a great privilege he had bestowed upon him. But he had never praised Hunter or showed any pleasure in Hunter's accomplishments.

Hunter owed Lord Reginald his gratitude, his allegiance, but not his devotion. He would go to him, but if the man turned out to be his father, Hunter was uncertain he could grant Lord Reginald his forgiveness.

Yet he would give the man the benefit of the doubt, until he spoke with him.

"How long will you be gone?" Détra interrupted his thoughts and prolonged silence, probably tiring of waiting for him to speak.

"Hawkhaven is about twenty miles north of here; its lands border Windermere's. It should take me a day to journey there and one to return, and depending on what is needed of me, I should be away no longer than a sennight, mayhap less if I can help."

Détra turned to accept a goblet of wine from his squire, not seeming particularly heartbroken at his imminent departure. He would think after what happened between them this day she would at least show some regret he had to go away. Could she want him to leave?

Hunter lifted his tankard to his mouth and gulped down the remaining ale, watching Détra quietly take a sip of her wine. When she lifted her gaze to him, the sadness there mollified him somewhat.

Still, he was uncertain of Détra. And even though their marriage was finally consummated—a thrill ran down his spine at the memory—and his possession of Windermere assured, leaving Détra behind for an unforeseen time might not be the wisest decision.

What if in his absence someone revealed to his lady more than he wanted her to know? Hunter realized by hiding the truth from Détra he was risking much. However, if she knew the truth there would be no chance at all for them. He would cement their liaison first, make her understand they belonged together, make love to her until it became a need only he could fulfill, and only then would he consider telling her the truth. Now it was too early, too soon for her to know. They had barely scratched the surface of their emotions.

Still, the thought of Détra spending time with Rupert was not an agreeable one. Rupert had spent his entire life trying to outdo Hunter. He could reveal a lot about Hunter to Détra.

Hunter wondered which one would be the greatest risk. Take Détra with him or leave her behind?

ISABEL PICKED AT HER FOOD. THE TENSION IN HUNTER was evident in the way he squared his shoulders every so often, in his tight grip on the mug of beer in his hand, in the penetrating glances he shot her way as if trying to read her mind.

Considering he'd just received news of a friend's imminent death, his reaction was understandable.

At least she assumed Lord Reginald was a friend, though Hunter gave her no indication one way or the other. However, it was clear he was very bothered by the news.

What kind of role had Hunter's foster lord played in his life? Had he been a kind mentor or cruel persecutor? There had been pain in Hunter's voice when he spoke of having no father. Was his father dead or was there some issue that separated them?

So many questions she wanted to ask him, and yet his obvious reluctance with her other much less intrusive questions told her Hunter would be unwilling to speak in the presence of the mixed company at the great hall.

She couldn't fault him for that. Maybe later when they were alone in the privacy of their bedroom he'd open up to her and she'd be able to offer him the comfort he needed.

But being alone with Hunter again was something Isabel longed for and dreaded at the same time. She'd resisted making love to him as long as she could, knowing that after sharing such intimate exchange of love with him, she wouldn't be able to return to her own life unchanged. But Hunter had worn out her resistance with his skillful touch, and his unselfish lovemaking had touched her heart.

When his wife returned to her body Hunter wouldn't know the difference, and hopefully Détra would understand Isabel had had no choice, but Isabel knew she would forever be haunted by the memory of them lying together, loving each other in that narrow bed in the soldier's quarters.

Damn her soul but she didn't want to leave Hunter, though she knew she must return Détra to her rightful place at her husband's side.

With the prospect of Hunter gone from the castle tomorrow and therefore the opportunity to search the war chest in his absence, which she was almost certain contained the magic chalice, Isabel would finally put an end to this.

Yet the mere thought of never seeing Hunter again tore at her heart. Tomorrow Hunter would be gone, and maybe she would also. Tonight would be their last night together, the only night they would spend together. If she were condemned to a mere memory of him for the rest of her life, she'd give herself and Hunter a night worth remembering.

Chapter II

AFTER dinner Isabel followed Hunter to their bedroom. Inside, the fireplace was ablaze, the oil lamps afire on the wall, and lit candles spread out throughout the room. The nuances of light and shadow, the cool stone walls and fire warmth, and the open bed curtains invitingly created a magical atmosphere perfect for a romantic dalliance.

Had Hunter arranged this? Had he his own plans of seduction for tonight?

Isabel had seen him whispering with Maude at one time during dinner, and though she hadn't heard what they said, Maude had disappeared from the hall soon after.

"Maude will not be here to aid you this eve," Hunter said as if reading her mind.

Isabel spun around to find him inches away from her, the bedroom door firmly closed behind him.

"I shall care for your needs myself," he whispered as his hand encircled her waist.

Isabel had no doubt he would, as he'd done earlier in the barracks when his skillful touch had so consumed her with desire she had submitted to the inevitability of the moment.

Tonight she would be the initiator. She would make love to Hunter without thinking of the consequences. She would take care of his needs as well as hers, and perhaps in some small way leave a little piece of her with him when she left.

Gently peeling his hand from her waist, Isabel ignored the shadow that crossed his face. Soon her intentions would be clear to him and he wouldn't fear her rejection anymore.

"Perhaps tonight we may be of mutual assistance," she said, sprawling her palms over the impossible breadth of his chest, the heat of his skin searing her hands even through the fabric of his clothing, quickening her breath.

She gave him a light kiss on the lips, but when he wanted to deepen the kiss, she withdrew. "Earlier I allowed you to touch me as you wished," she said with a smile. "I demand the same rights now."

"A lady wife demanding rights from her lord husband?" he asked in a teasing tone, the shadow disappearing from his face.

Relieved—the last thing Isabel wanted was for Hunter to lash out at her in mistaken anger—she teased him with another light kiss. "Does that bother you?" She slid her palms down his chest to the hard planes of his stomach, leaving no doubt of her intentions.

"It pleases me," he whispered. "Though I cannot suffer such torment without promising retribution."

"I am counting on that." Isabel lowered her hand even

further down and undid the sword belt that hung sideways to his left hip. The heavy sword fell to the floor with a loud clank, yet neither of them bothered with it.

Hunter opened his arms as if offering himself to her. "In that case, my lady wife, I am yours."

Tonight he would be! Isabel thought.

Trailing her hands sideways on his stomach, her left hand brushed over his growing arousal. Hunter drew in a sharp breath. Isabel continued to slide her hands down his hips and thighs, burrowing underneath the hem of his tunic. As she pulled the tunic up she had to stretch her body and point her toes to be able to pull the garment over Hunter's head, and her face ended up only inches from his. Their gazes met and held for a moment, his dark eyes burning like live coals, hers no doubt as flaming as his.

Isabel gave him another kiss short in duration but lacking no intensity, and then her feet found support on the solid ground again. She gathered the hem of his soft linen shirt, which found its way over his head and down on the floor to join the tunic already in a pile there.

Pausing in her undressing of Hunter, Isabel admired his muscled chest generously sprinkled with dark hair. She raked her fingers through the curly hair, reveling in its texture and warmth. She roughened his nipples to pebble hard with the palm of her hands, then kissed them, running her tongue over them, then blowing hot air on the wet surface.

The next moment Isabel found herself plastered against Hunter's body. Her swelling breasts pressed against his chest, stretching the fabric of her gown, eagerly anticipating the moment they would both be naked, skin touching skin, since they hadn't totally undressed when they'd first made love.

Hunter reached for the back lacing of her gown while they kissed. Then, moments later, he grunted in frustration as the ties refused to give way. Isabel spun around in his arms, lifting her hair over her head and giving him free access to the back of her dress. He kissed her neck instead, momentarily forgetting about the lacing, as did she. Soon enough though, after a few impatient pulls, her gown hung loose on her body. Sliding his hands over her shoulders, he forced the gown to fall in a heap of velvety fabric at her feet.

Dressed only in a thin chemise, Isabel stepped out of the gown and pivoted. Hunter's injured hand rested at the small of her back, while his other hand settled over her breast, kneading it. He bent over her and covered the nipple with his hot mouth, suckling it through the thin fabric of her chemise, then taking the nipple between his teeth. Isabel moaned, feeling the pool of desire gathering inside of her.

But he was taking control again of their lovemaking and this time she wanted to give him pleasure first.

With trembling hands Isabel worked on the drawstrings of Hunter's pants while she tried to keep some lucidity of mind as he played with her breasts. That, and knowing he wore nothing underneath, turned her usually dexterous fingers into all thumbs. Finally his pants fell silently to the floor and she grabbed hold of his jutting arousal.

Hunter bucked as if burnt. He let go of her breasts momentarily, a look of doubt in his eyes.

What was he afraid of? A repetition of what happened in the war room?

To assuage any anxiety he might have, Isabel let go of him then stepped back and kicked her shoes off. She untied the lacing in front of her chemise, which opened invitingly, slowly lowering one sleeve down one shoulder, then the other. She pushed the fabric down to uncover the swell of her breasts, until a scrap of fabric caught her nipple, scraping it, sensitizing it beyond words, then spilling it free to Hunter's full view.

Hunter's mouth hung open as if he'd never seen his wife naked before. Then, with a groan, he hauled her flush against his body while his mouth took hungry possession of hers.

Isabel thought that after making love this afternoon the hungry edge would disappear from their lovemaking, but Hunter kissed her like there would be no tomorrow for them, and Isabel kissed him back knowing there wouldn't be.

She circled her arms around his neck and her hands entwined in his soft hair while their bodies melded together. Hunter introduced a leg between her thighs, and Isabel rubbed herself against the rough skin of his hair-covered thigh. Wild sensations shot from that point of contact and spread throughout her body, weakening her limbs, numbing her mind, and freeing her heart. Hunter's arousal nestled against her belly, hot, hard, and insistent.

He pressed against her as his hand reached behind her, between the cleft of her buttocks. As his mouth worked his magic on the sensitive skin of her neck and shoulder he inserted a finger inside of her, finding her wet and ready for him.

"*Deus!*" he cried, picking her up and shifting her legs around his hips. "You shall be the death of me, lady." And with that he entered her with one swift thrust.

Isabel moaned, locking her legs behind his back and clasping her hands together behind his neck for support. Hunter stood still for a moment, eyes closed, one arm around her waist, one hand beneath her buttocks, deeply and firmly buried inside of her.

And as they kissed—a tongue-dueling, lip-suckling, ravenous kiss—Hunter stumbled backward, a step or two, until his back rested against the wall. Isabel unlocked her legs from behind his back, opening herself to him as her knees almost touched the wall behind Hunter. He bent his knees a little, arching against her, and began to thrust in earnest. No shallow, slow motion here, no teasing and withdrawing, but hard, deep thrusts, betraying the hunger they both felt and that should've been already appeased.

Isabel's orgasm came so swiftly, so intensely, her cries drowned out Hunter's moans of release.

Afterward he held her in his arms until their trembling subsided and they caught their breaths. Slowly, Hunter lowered her to her feet and, spent, she collapsed against his body, her head lying against his chest, listening to the wild beating of his heart.

He had done it again. Had turned her into putty in his hands. It was a wonder Isabel had resisted him this long. And yet she'd promised herself to give him a night to remember, and that she would still do.

As soon as she caught her breath, that is.

HUNTER'S BUTTOCKS WERE GETTING COLD AGAINST the stone wall, but he dared not move lest he disturb Détra, who lay against him in languid abandon.

He had forgotten himself and taken his lady wife standing up against a wall, like a common courtesan, yet had it cost him his life he could not have reached the bed, so urgent was his need for her.

Fervently hoping she would not be vexed with him, Hunter kissed the top of her head. "It is most rare," he said into the perfumed curls of her hair, "that a man and his lady wife should share such wondrous lovemaking."

She pushed herself gently away from him, then looked up at him. There was an undefined sadness in her gaze. Did she disagree? Was it not wondrous to her?

"Most rare, indeed," she said, then, in unabashed na-

kedness, she ambled to the table where she poured water
into a bowl, then immersed a square of cloth inside. She
wrung it almost dry, then returned to him to gently rinse
his body as he had done to her in his chamber in the
garrison's quarters. He barely felt the sting of the cold
water on his hot skin, entranced as he was in following
the motion of her hands.

"Détra," he said in mild protest, bewildered at her gentle care.

"What you do for me," she said, "I reserve the right
to do the same for you."

Hunter would not gainsay her. Not in this matter, anyway.

When she finished, she returned to the table, rinsed the
cloth, and with her back to him did her own ablutions.
For a brief moment Hunter wished to cut her glorious hair
short, for it fell below her buttocks, covering the wondrous sight from his view.

Then he occupied himself with feeding more logs to
the hearth and extinguishing the fire in the candles and
oil lamps. Finally he strolled to her, and lifting Détra in
his arms, carried her to their bed.

He lay her down, climbed in, and let the curtains fall.
They were now protected from cold drafts in the warm
cocoon of pillows and furs and their bodies.

In the semidarkness Hunter gathered Détra in his arms.
He had never dreamed their coming together would be
this wondrous, suddenly realizing how appropriate a name
lovemaking was for the carnal act of joining two bodies
and two souls.

For after having been inside his lady wife's body this
night, Hunter felt part of her soul. And he would never
let her go.

There was no mistaking her passion, her wanting of
him, and the mere remembrance of her touch brought the

fire of desire burning anew inside him. He had waited so long to make her his, had longed for her for such a very long time, he could not get enough of being with her. He would offer no apologies for wanting his wife. Dismissing the dark cloud hovering above him that was her forgotten memories, Hunter secretly hoped they would never return.

He was surprised anew when Détra pushed him back onto the mattress. "It is my turn now," she said, licking her lips as if about to savor the greatest delicacy in the kingdom. *Deus!* And she was looking at him.

She kissed him teasingly—with her lips and tongue, suckling and soothing, seeking and withdrawing while her fingertips traced a path down his chest, bypassing his eager cock, down his groin and inner thighs, only to start upward again.

Hunter's breathing quickened in eager expectation.

Détra lifted her lips from his, then playfully bit his chin, the stubble of beard probably scraping her tongue. She did not seem to mind. She traced her tongue down his throat and chest, kissed and sucked each of his nipples—no woman had ever done that to him before—then darted her tongue inside his navel. She lifted, settling between his thighs, raking her long, glorious hair over his chest. The soft curls teasing him as sensually as her fingers had done before.

And when she strayed down his groin, and licked the very tip of his eager cock, Hunter leapt.

"You need not do this." His husky voice was barely audible to him. Had she heard him?

She lifted her head, pulling her hair away, and gazed at him. "I want to do this, Hunter," she whispered, fanning his wet skin with her hot breath. "This and more."

Deus! She would be the death of him!

Why should he not allow it? Why should he not revel in such an intimate touch? He relaxed his hold of her hair as his head fell back against the mattress. Isabel took him in her mouth, not the whole of him, just the sensitive tip, alternating between sucking it and licking it. Hunter's breathing stopped, his body trembled, and his mind muddled as his arousal grew. And when she gathered his balls and rubbed them tenderly as she continued to take him in her mouth, he thought he would die.

"Enough," he cried, finding strength to lift her and roll over on top of her.

"I was so enjoying it," she said in that teasing tone he would never have related to Détra.

"So was I, my lady wife," he whispered against her ear as he settled between her thighs. "So was I."

He kissed her neck, realizing how much she enjoyed that simple caress, as she craned it to give him full access. And when she began writhing beneath him, he took her mouth, realizing how much he loved kissing her. After tasting Détra he would never taste another woman again.

He found his way instinctively into her damp and hot entrance and he thrust deeply. He meant to take it slowly this time, but Détra lifted her thighs, placing her knees against his chest, making him reach deeper than he ever had before. He had to hold still for a moment to stop the crescendo of pleasure already building inside of him, not understanding how he had gotten so aroused so fast, so soon after he had already spilled his seed.

He pulled her legs down against the mattress, holding on to her thighs, taking control of his thrusts. Shallow, slow thrusts that made Détra writhe underneath him until he lost control again, and as her knees rose he thrust deep inside of her, fast and eager. He was vindicated, though, when her cry of release came moments before his own reverberated on the walls of the bedchamber.

*   *   *

ISABEL OPENED HER EYES AND IN A FLASH SITUATED herself. She sought Hunter with her gaze and found him out of the bed, already dressed, and kneeling down at the kneeler by the window in silent contemplation. Through the opaque bed curtains she watched him as her heart tightened in her chest. Very soon he would be gone, and so would she. And her life would never be the same again.

Hunter made the sign of the cross, then rose to his feet, obviously finished with his prayers. He looked her way and Isabel rose on the bed, then sat on its edge, her legs dangling off the mattress through the half-open curtains. Candles and the fire in the fireplace illuminated the room, but through the small gaps on the shuttered window she could see the gray light of dawn.

"Praying for a safe trip?" she asked.

"That and in thanksgiving." He looked at her in such a way that made Isabel think he was thankful for her.

A knot in her throat made speech impossible. Did Détra know how lucky she was? Isabel jumped to her feet, looking for something to cover her body, finding her chemise lying on the floor where she'd left it last night. She picked it up, dusted it, and then pulled it down over her head. "When do you leave?" she asked, pivoting, wanting to etch in her mind his handsome face.

He came to her and kissed her lips gently, and she savored the brief taste of him even after their lips separated.

"*We* leave as soon as you dress and break your fast, my lady wife."

"We?" Isabel stumbled back. "What do you mean, we? I thought you were going alone."

"I decided you should accompany me." He pulled her back into his embrace. "After last night how can I be without you for long?"

Isabel's heart began an anxious beat. There was no way

she'd go with him. She couldn't prolong this situation any longer. Her fantasy night was over and the reality of the dawning day was upon her.

"You told me you would be gone for only a few days," she said, once again disengaging from his arms and moving closer to the kneeler. She wanted to add she'd be here waiting for him when he returned, but didn't. She wouldn't be here; Détra would. "Besides," she said, "I thought you were in a hurry. I would only slow you down."

His inscrutable dark eyes settled on hers. "I go nowhere without you, Détra."

Isabel wracked her brain looking for a good excuse not to accompany him on this trip. She couldn't possibly spend any more time with Hunter; she was already too emotionally involved with him. What would happen to her sanity if she continued to play the happy wife? She was already dangerously close to losing herself in Détra's life.

She didn't want Détra's life! Her mind rebelled. She didn't want to live in the Middle Ages, in a castle filled with people dependent on her, doing chores she knew nothing or cared nothing about. She wanted her life, her freedom, and her painting back.

Oh, but she wanted Hunter, too, and that truth couldn't be denied.

But wanting him didn't mean she could forget that he belonged to this time, to this castle and people, and above all to Détra.

More than ever she needed to undo her mistake.

"I would rather not go," she pleaded. "I do not feel strong enough for such a long trip." That was a joke! She'd been strong enough to make love to Hunter time and time again last night.

A knock sounded on the door. In silence, Hunter

walked to it and opened it. He nodded to Maude to enter but kept Jeremy outside. Jeremy craned his neck and got a good view of Isabel in her chemise. Hunter must've given him a sharp look for he swiftly turned his gaze away.

"Wait for me in the garrison's quarters," Hunter told Jeremy. "Have my hauberk clean and ready for me."

"Aye, my lord." Jeremy disappeared and Hunter closed the door.

Maude was preparing Isabel a cup of herbal tea for which Isabel was profoundly thankful. She needed her tea desperately this morning.

Obviously not swayed by her arguments, Hunter said, "Aid your lady in dressing for our journey, Maude. Dawn is past and the morning will soon grow late. I wish to leave without delay."

"I still think I should not go," Isabel insisted as she took the cup from Maude. "Why is it so important that I accompany you?"

"Why is it so important that you do not?" he retorted.

Why was Hunter being so difficult about this? He looked almost distrustful of her. Could he be sensing she was lying to him? But how could he? Isabel took her time drinking her tea in silence. She had to convince Hunter to leave her behind. Would he believe another killer migraine? Or would he think it a little too convenient of an excuse, since she'd already made clear she didn't want to go on this trip with him?

Suddenly, the perfect excuse came to mind—her amnesia. God knew she had used it to cover a multitude of sins so far. One more wouldn't be out of place.

Remembering Hunter's story of how he had met Détra, Isabel asked, "Is not Hawkhaven where we first met?"

"Aye."

"Would I not be recognized there? And should I not

recognize people in return?" She waited for his answer, though his sepulchral silence was very telling. "Have you changed your mind about keeping my loss of memory a secret?" She directed an expectant gaze at him.

Hunter hesitated, probably torn between wanting his beloved wife with him on this trip and pondering how wise it would be to expose her *mental illness* to the world at large.

"Your acquaintance with Lord Reginald and his son is no deterrent to your visit, since there would be little interaction between you and them," he said. "Lord Reginald is probably incapacitated in bed and Rupert is absent from his castle at this moment. Your secret will be safe."

Latching on to her last argument like a drowning person would latch on to a lifeline, Isabel insisted, "You cannot be certain there will not be anyone else there who would recognize me. And you must realize by now that my memory loss goes beyond not remembering faces, names, or places. I feel like a totally different person. Would not someone notice that?"

There was a subtle change in Hunter's stance. He turned an intense gaze on her, as if seeing her for the first time. A shiver ran down Isabel's spine. She wished she hadn't made that comment. A few times last night Hunter had looked at her in an odd way. He hadn't said anything nor did he seem displeased at all, on the contrary. She had vowed to give him a night to remember and they would forever remember last night. Maybe that was it. Had Hunter noticed a difference in his wife's lovemaking? Though still honeymooners, Hunter and Détra had had two weeks to acquaint themselves in bed.

"I noticed that," Maude said.

Isabel turned a stunned gaze at Maude. Had Maude read her mind? How could she know what happened between Hunter and Isabel last night?

"You eat apples now," Maude explained. "You despised apples."

Apples? What had apples to do with anything? And then it came to her. Détra detested apples. Isabel loved them. That was the change Maude had noticed.

A confused Hunter turned to Maude. "Why would Détra despise apples? It is but a fruit."

Isabel was curious too.

"Lord William locked my lady in her bedchamber once, and for days all he allowed her to eat were apples. He jested the treat would sweeten his favorite mare."

Hunter stiffened beside an outraged Isabel. "Who is Lord William?" she asked.

"Your late lord husband," Hunter said.

Isabel's eyes widened. Détra had been married before, and obviously to a moron. Good God! How pleased she'd be with Hunter and how desperate she must be to return home. The old guilt assailed Isabel again.

She had to find a way not to go with Hunter on this trip. She stepped back and tripped over the kneeler. The cup flew out of her hand as she fell awkwardly over her hand, pain shooting up her wrist.

Hunter rushed to her, and, lifting her, he pressed her arm and hand in several spots.

"Ouch," she cried.

"It does not appear to be broken." A bruise began forming on her forearm where it had hit the kneeler as she braced her fall, but there was no swelling on her wrist.

"It is very painful, though."

"Wrap it tightly and it should be well soon."

Maude began ripping a thin piece of linen in strips, then wrapped them around Isabel's wrist.

Realizing she might've found the perfect excuse to bail out of the trip, Isabel said, "Looks like I might be staying behind after all." She tried to sound disappointed, but what she felt was sadness. "I could not possibly ride with an incapacitated hand." Had she fifty good hands she couldn't fake her way around horses, having never ridden one in her life. And that was surely the medieval mode of transportation they'd be using.

"It might be too sore for you to hold the reins of your mare," Hunter agreed. "I shall have a conveyance ready for you."

Desperation crept up on her. No matter what obstacles she put up, Hunter easily destroyed them.

"My lord," Maude said. "Mayhap it would be best if Lady Détra remained at Windermere. I shall watch over her while you are away."

"I have no doubt you would, Maude. However, I wish my lady wife by my side." Then turning to Isabel, he asked, "Surely you would not deny me that pleasure, would you?"

The sheer determination on Hunter's face was a barrier Isabel knew she couldn't transpose. He wanted his wife with him and she had no good excuse to refuse him, besides the terrible risk of losing her heart completely to a man who belonged to another woman.

"I would deny you no pleasure," Isabel said.

Chapter 12

HUNTER waited outside Hawkhaven's gates to be admitted into its bailey. The huge fortification delineated against the dawning sky brought back bitter memories of his many years of struggle but also a great sense of pride. He had survived—more than survived, he had prevailed—on his quests to achieve knighthood, to gain lands of his own, and to wed Détra.

But had he won her heart?

After the night they spent together, when she had held naught back, matching his passion and even surpassing it at times, Hunter hoped he might have won at least a part of it.

And yet he could not forget how she had fought not to accompany him on this journey. The tiresome indecision of never knowing exactly whether Détra was telling him the truth vexed Hunter. More and more he believed her claim of loss of memory, and yet there was much his lady wife was not telling him.

He stole a glance over his shoulder. Détra sat uncomfortably in the cart she shared with Maude. The slow-moving cart and the several stops they were forced to make had delayed their journey considerably. What should have taken but a day had lasted well into the night, and now at the dawning of a new day they had finally arrived at their destination.

At one time during their journey he had convinced Détra to ride on her mare while he led her mount. She had sat stiffly, looking utterly uncomfortable, as if she had never been on a horse's back before. That much surprised Hunter for he knew for a fact Détra was an accomplished rider.

Could her loss of memory encompass skills she used to possess? Not only could Détra not remember what she should never forget, but she also, at times, acted as if she were a completely different person.

In fact, she had admitted as much before they left on this journey. How fragile was his wife's mind? Had he been unwise in bringing her with him? And yet, to leave her behind among people who knew her well and would be more than willing to share the secret of their short past together would have been foolish. He could very well imagine what she would do if she learned that their love was naught but a chimera of his heart.

Nay, he had done well in bringing her, even with the potentially hazardous prospect of Rupert being in residence. For Rupert knew naught of Hunter's marital struggles with his lady wife. All the man could reveal to Détra was Hunter's humble past, and that Hunter had every intention of sharing with Détra soon.

The gates finally opened and they rode inside the bailey. After a brief exchange of greetings with Thomas, the premier knight of Hawkhaven, they were ushered into the great hall. He left Détra and Maude with Thomas and made his way to Lord Reginald's bedchamber.

Heart beating fast in his chest, Hunter hesitated outside the door. Too long he had waited to hear the truth, too long he had longed to put a face, a name, to his unknown father, and yet though he had thought himself prepared, he now discovered he was not.

The memories of the years of taunting he suffered in this very place and the fact Lord Reginald not once had come to his aid filled him with bitterness. What manner of man could watch his own son being humiliated time and time again and never rise to defend him?

Hunter fought the dormant anger rising in his heart. He would not allow the debilitating emotion to override him. No revelation from his foster lord could change his life now. He was a knight, a lord of his own castle, a man wedded to his love. Soon his castle would be filled with his children and Hunter would love them, care for them, and cherish them like a father should his children. And in doing so he would erase the memory of his own lonely childhood.

Taking a deep breath, Hunter straightened his shoulders, then pushed the door open. There would be no more delay. He would know now or forever bury the thought of his father in his heart.

The bedchamber reeked of urine, blood, and illness. Taking shallow breaths, Hunter walked inside, resisting the urge to dash across the chamber and jerk the window open for some very needed fresh air.

A circumspect physician was just finishing scraping blood-engorged leeches from Lord Reginald's chest into a bowl. He lifted, looked at Hunter, and then shook his head before leaving the bedchamber. An old maidservant propped pillows behind Lord Reginald's back, then helped him drink from a cup. Then she too left.

Hunter was alone with his foster lord.

His dying father?

He stepped closer, halting by the old man's bedside.

The tall, strong, virile man Hunter once knew had enfeebled to almost skin and bones. His once full, sandy hair had thinned to a few snowy-white strands. His massive hands were naught more than a skeleton folded over his heaving chest. Lord Reginald had aged beyond his years.

"It has been a long time," the old man whispered. His once booming voice that made every squire, and even knights, tremble now barely reached Hunter standing not a pace away from him.

"Indeed it has, my lord."

"You look well," Lord Reginald said. "I, on the other hand, am dying."

"I am certain you shall live for many years to come," Hunter lied.

Lord Reginald waved his hand in dismissal. "It matters not. I am ready for death, having grown tired of physicians, leeches, and bitter potions." His chest heaved, and he gasped for air.

Powerless, Hunter watched Lord Reginald's struggle. After long moments the old man's breathing finally eased a little. He opened his eyes and stared at Hunter. "I heard tales of your bravery in battle," he said. "Saved the king's arse at Bannockburn, did you?" A cough cut short his weak laugh. "I always knew you had it in you, Hunter. You cannot negate your blood. I like to believe I had something to do with the man you have become."

Hunter stiffened and waited. Was that how it would be? Lord Reginald claiming credit for what Hunter had accomplished before he revealed he was Hunter's father?

However, instead of the expected confession, Lord Reginald rambled on, "Heard you were recently wedded.

Lady Détra of Windermere, I believe. Beautiful lady . . .
Was she not wedded before?" He paused, catching his
breath. "A harsh man, if I recall well. Terrible choice,
good riddance, I say! I am certain she is well pleased with
you."

Lord Reginald's dark eyes, such contrast to his sandy
hair, stared at Hunter in speculation.

Did he know of Détra's reluctance toward him? "She
is content, I believe," Hunter said.

"As well she should be. From what I hear you had
your choice of land and yet you settled on Détra's small
castle. A beautiful woman can sway a man's mind in ways
he cannot even comprehend. You should never allow your
heart to decide matters of property, my boy."

My boy!

Hunter's heart swelled with the intensity of his desire
to hear the words that would forever unbind him from the
ghost of a faceless father.

"Windermere provides a more than adequate income,"
Hunter said. "I have no doubt I made the right choice.
Besides, what is a man if not his heart and honor?"

Lord Reginald snorted. "A man's heart tends to lead
him astray if he is not heedful. You have won the king,
the castle, and the lady. It will take more than heart to
keep them all."

"Is that why you summoned me to your bedside? To
warn me about my heedless heart?" Hunter asked impatiently. The man was dying, every word he spoke an effort; why play games with him? What purpose would that
serve but to torment Hunter further?

"Danger looms, Hunter. What is unknown to you
might be used against you."

What was that now? A vague warning of danger?
"Danger always looms, my lord. It is part of a man's life.

I am certain I would not have lived to see this day had I not been aware of that."

"I know what you seek," Lord Reginald whispered and Hunter leaned forward. "Your father's identity."

Hunter felt the blood drain from his face. "If you have knowledge of that, I pray you share it with me."

"First I will have your pledge," Lord Reginald said.

"To what, my lord?"

"To protect Rupert against his enemies." He paused. "Even yourself, if need be."

That even at the hour of his death Lord Reginald thought of Rupert first lanced Hunter's heart. But what had he expected? A tearful plea for forgiveness?

Naught in Hunter's life had ever come without a price. It was obvious Lord Reginald was no repentant man looking to amend his past misdeeds toward Hunter; he was a man after protecting his own, and clearly Hunter was naught to him.

For a moment Hunter considered turning his back on Lord Reginald and the truth. Let the old fool die with his secret, let Rupert care for himself. But Hunter knew he would not do so. He wanted to know if his foster lord was also his father. Wanted to hear the truth from the man's own mouth. Wanted to end once and for all the quest he had failed to achieve.

Grasping Hunter's arms with his bony hands, half lifting himself from the bed with a strength his frail body belied, Lord Reginald hissed, "Swear it or you shall never know." Their faces were only inches apart and Hunter could smell in the old man's breath the putrid scent of death.

"I swear." Hunter's words escaped through clenched teeth, knowing his vow would someday haunt him worse than not knowing his father's name.

Lord Reginald let go of Hunter's arm and fell against the pillows with a labored sigh of relief.

"Are you my father?" Hunter asked.

WITH WOBBLING KNEES AND POUNDING HEAD, ISABEL followed a servant up the stairs. Her entire body ached, especially her head, thanks to the longest journey of her life. Her means of transportation had been no more than a simple cart pulled by horses, and riding in one had been the worse traveling experience of her life. No amount of pillows could've softened that hard wooden floor she sat and lay on, and the thing rattled and shook as much as a hovercraft crossing the English Channel.

Once inside their bedroom Isabel went straight to the bed and sank on the soft mattress. She watched as Maude directed the servants carrying her trunk to put it down by the bed, then as they left with promises of sending refreshments, Maude began the unpacking. Not the clothing, for that would remain in the trunk, but their personal belongings and the small box of potions and herbs Maude didn't seem to live without.

Isabel was thankful for that and waited impatiently for Maude to mix a potion for her headache. As she waited she scanned the room. Standard medieval accommodations—a bed, a table and chair, and a fireplace. The walls were bare of decoration but there was adequate illumination with the window shutters open and burning wood in the fireplace.

As Maude brought her a cup, Isabel gulped the contents down, not even minding the bitter taste.

"You have not added a sleeping draught, have you?" Isabel belatedly asked.

"Nay, my lady."

"Good." Although she could use a good nap, Isabel

wanted to be awake when Hunter finished his conversation with Lord Reginald. Hunter had said very little about what he expected to hear from the man, but he was visibly tense throughout the trip. Isabel had a feeling this conversation was much more important to Hunter than he had wanted her to believe.

A serving woman appeared with a carafe and cups, and a round piece of bread filled with some kind of meat stew. "Would you have some fruits, by any chance?" Isabel asked. "Apples, pears, anything . . ." She wasn't used to heavy breakfasts. Tea and fruit were her usual fare.

The woman nodded, put down the tray she brought, then left.

Isabel fell back on the bed, stretching her body, her muscles screaming for a massage. She'd settle for a long, hot bath.

At her request, Maude stepped outside in search of a servant, leaving the door slightly ajar. Meanwhile Isabel sat up again, took off her shoes and the woolen stockings—she'd have to wait for Maude to help her with her gown—and then ambled to the trunk to rummage inside for what to wear after her bath.

Suddenly, a man grabbed her from behind, spinning her around and sealing her lips with his in a move so fast Isabel didn't have time to utter the scream lodged in her throat.

She struggled to free herself from his grip but he didn't seem dissuaded one bit by her efforts. Finally, he pulled back a little and Isabel slapped him so hard her hand prickled.

The stranger let go of her. "Détra!" The man had the gall to look shocked as he rubbed the imprint of her hand on his fair face.

Détra? He knew Détra? Who the hell was he, anyway?

At that moment, Maude returned. She rushed to Isabel's side as if to rescue her, though Isabel wasn't sure whether Maude had witnessed the kiss or the slap.

"Leave us," he ordered Maude. "I have matters to discuss with your lady."

"My lady," Maude said, not moving an inch away from Isabel. Her gentle hazel eyes were open so wide Isabel thought they would pop out. "It is very improper for Lord Rupert to be alone with you in your private bedchamber. What would happen if your husband walked in on you?"

Isabel's heart raced. Something was very wrong here.

"Has the bastard laid a hand on you?" Rupert demanded, taking her injured hand into his. There was no misunderstanding Rupert's proprietary indignation.

Isabel pulled her hand free. Who was he accusing of hurting her? Surely not Hunter! "I fell and hurt myself," she said. She wanted to add that it was none of his business, but held back.

It was obvious Détra and Rupert were acquainted. However, how well acquainted they were or how much Maude knew was uncertain.

What was certain was that Lord Rupert had touched her with a presumption that spoke of intimate familiarity, and Maude's attempt to protect her reputation seemed a little more than a simple matter of propriety. Her look of pure fright couldn't be just hurt medieval sensibilities.

Isabel's curiosity was piqued. But more than curiosity, an odd feeling of danger, of something being terribly wrong prickled her skin.

What if there was some shady business going on between Détra and Rupert? And yet what could she do if there were? And what gave her the right to interfere in these people's lives?

How could she not, after what she and Hunter had shared?

"Tell your maid to leave," Rupert said, bringing Isabel

out of her musings. "I must speak with you."

Isabel wanted to know what Rupert had to say, but she couldn't risk being alone with him. Maude was right; what would Hunter do if he found her alone with another man?

"Maude, would you please fix me my morning drink?" Isabel asked. As Maude moved to the table, Isabel ambled to the window on the other side of the room. Rupert followed her.

"I understand Hunter is here speaking with my father," he said after a sly glance at Maude. "I know not what he does here, but while he is occupied I must speak with you."

Isabel didn't like how sneaky that sounded. "I am all ears."

"Have you heard from King Edward?" Rupert whispered.

Isabel was blindly navigating uncharted waters here. "I have not heard from him lately," she said cautiously.

Rupert shook his head. "I have just learned that my petition for our betrothal lay on the king's desk unread even as he granted Windermere and you to that bastard Hunter." He threaded long fingers through his sandy hair. "Lord, I could kill him with my own hands," he spat.

Isabel trembled. Did he mean to kill the king or Hunter?

Rupert's ire wasn't faked. One could never dismiss a jilted man's hatred. The question was what role did Détra play in this?

"Forgive me," he said, probably seeing the fear on her face. "I meant not to frighten you, but that bastard has been stuck in my craw for too long now."

Isabel said nothing. She wasn't even sure who Rupert was most angry with—Hunter or the king.

"It will be sweet indeed when the king grants your petition for annulment of this travesty of marriage." He took Isabel's hands into his. "I know how difficult it must be for you to continue to keep him at bay, but you must not give in. As long as your marriage is not consummated, we may dream of being together soon."

If her life depended on it, Isabel wouldn't be able to speak. She stared at Rupert in horror. Good God! Détra wanted to annul their marriage? What would she do when she returned and realized that was no longer an option?

So much for not interfering in other people's lives.

And what about Hunter? Isabel hurt for him.

Misreading her grief, he touched her face softly. Fearing he was about to kiss her, Isabel swiftly stepped back.

He smiled bitterly. "I vow by all that is sacred in the Christendom, we shall be together soon, Détra. Hunter shall not have you. Not even over my dead body."

Rupert stomped out of the room, and as soon as the door closed behind him, Isabel wobbled to the bed and sank down onto the soft mattress.

Good God! Nothing was what it seemed.

Isabel tried to put her thoughts in order, but her mind was numb with the horror of the situation. Her head throbbed with pain and her heart squeezed with ache.

Hunter loved Détra, who loved Rupert, who loved Détra in return. Isabel loved Hunter, but she was a nonentity in this time. She didn't exist. Hunter was married to Détra, who wanted to dissolve their marriage, which Isabel had helped consummate.

Isabel covered her face with her hands.

"My lady. Here is your drink."

Isabel uncovered her eyes. Maude knelt before her with a cup in her hand. Isabel took the cup, and in silence sipped her tea, gathering her thoughts.

"Tell me what you know, Maude," Isabel finally pleaded.

Maude trembled and lifted.

Isabel followed her, spinning her around. "You must tell me. I remember nothing."

"Lord Hunter really cares for you," Maude said.

"I know that," Isabel whispered. "Tell me what you know about Rupert."

Maude looked everywhere but at Isabel.

"Please," Isabel begged. Maude was the only one who could elucidate this mystery.

"Your marriage to Lord William was a very unhappy one," Maude said.

"I gathered that by the apple incident you told me."

"Oh, it was so much worse than that, my lady. Lord William was a cruel man." She spat on the floor. "May his soul burn in hell."

Isabel was surprised at the vehemence of Maude's words.

"It is a blessing you remember naught of him," she continued. "Suffice it to say, no one in Windermere mourned his death."

Isabel wanted to rush Maude on, not really interested in Lord William, but bit her tongue, giving Maude freedom to tell the story as she saw fit.

"Soon after the funeral Lord Rupert began visiting you. You have known him for years, both your fathers being acquainted. You were lonely, my lady. You were reeling from years of ill treatment when Lord Rupert courted and wooed you like you had never been wooed before."

The more Maude spoke the worse Isabel felt. Maude's choice of words was revealing in itself. It was as if she was trying to excuse Détra's behavior.

"You knew the king would eventually find you another husband, and fearing another Lord William in your life, you made the decision to wed Lord Rupert."

"You mean to say I would have to accept the king's choice of husband without any recourse?" Freedom was such an important part of Isabel's life she couldn't fathom the thought of not being able to make her own decisions.

"The Church preaches you cannot be forced into marriage," Maude said with a snort. "But who is foolish enough to defy a king's command?"

Isabel admitted it didn't sound too bright a decision; still it didn't make it right.

"So I wanted to marry Rupert, but the king gave me to Hunter. How come you never told me the truth? Does Hunter know about Rupert and me?"

"Oh, nay, I believe not. Lord Hunter truly cares for you, my lady."

"And Lord Rupert does not?"

"It matters not now. Your marriage to Lord Hunter is consummated; there is no turning back on that."

Isabel stared at Maude. "When was my marriage consummated?"

Maude hesitated.

"When, Maude?"

"I believe it happened in the garrison's quarters two days past."

It was true, then. Détra had wanted out of this marriage and unknowingly Isabel had closed that door. She felt a measure of responsibility toward Détra and yet, her heart cried out for Hunter.

"It is for the best, my lady. Lord Hunter is the man to make you happy."

Indeed he was, but obviously not the right man for Détra. And yet Détra was the one married to Hunter, not Isabel.

Isabel's shoulders slumped. It was all so senseless. And there was nothing she could do to help anyone, least of all herself.

*   *   *

RUPERT LEFT DÉTRA'S CHAMBER IN A FOUL MOOD. SHE
had seemed different, more distant somehow, and he liked
it not at all. At least she seemed steadfast on her desire
to annul her marriage to Hunter, and yet there was hesi-
tancy in her, whereas before there had been only eager-
ness.

Though Rupert and Détra had concocted the unconsummated marriage plan together, Rupert had not truly
expected Hunter to stay away from Détra. That he had
truly surprised Rupert. No man in Hunter's place would
have hesitated to demand his marital rights from a reluctant wife, especially when property was involved in the
matter.

Mayhap Hunter had finally recognized he had no rights
to be wedded to a highborn lady, no rights to even aspire
to knighthood, bastard villager that he truly was, let alone
be anyone's lord. It would have been infinitely best for
all involved had Hunter remained in the village to live the
humble life due to him. The only life he deserved.

However, thanks to his father's unbound and inconceivable generosity, Hunter had achieved it all—knighthood, lands, and Détra. The woman who should be his by
rights.

Rupert had heard the king had given Hunter his choice
of holding and heiress. Could Hunter have chosen Détra
out of spite for him? To prove his superiority over Rupert
as he had tried many times in the past during the years
they trained together at Hawkhaven? The immense hatred
for Hunter that simmered for years inside Rupert bubbled
to the surface.

Hunter would not be victorious. If he could not count
on the king's decision, Rupert would line up another plan
to get rid of Hunter. A plan that would not only return
Détra to Rupert but also take from Hunter all that he had
so undeservedly acquired.

Rupert rounded the corner of the corridor and strode to his father's bedchamber. Knowing Hunter would be inside with his father, he did not knock but pushed the door open.

"Are you my father?"

Rupert froze in place for a moment, then, face flaming, tramped inside noisily. "What do you do here, Hunter? I thought you occupied with your new bride. Has the novelty of having a lady in your bed instead of a common wench worn off already?"

Straightening, Hunter slowly turned to face Rupert.

Rupert smiled. A superior smile he particularly liked to use when facing Hunter. Hunter's obvious frustration at his interruption pleased him immensely. He would not allow Hunter to wrestle a misguided confession from an old dying man and use it to make claim on Hawkhaven. Bastard Hunter would remain what he was—a bastard. Hunter had stolen enough from him already. He would steal no more.

"Back already?" Hunter said, his smile as false as Rupert's. "What? You could not find any more unwilling servant wenches to force yourself upon? What about a sword fight with a farmer boy? You have always enjoyed when the odds were in your favor."

"Bastard," Rupert spat, pushing against Hunter.

"Dim-witted fool." Hunter pushed back.

"Cease, boys," Lord Reginald cried. "I have no time for your foolish games." He wheezed, breathing clearly an effort for him. "Rupert, I wish to speak with Hunter alone."

Leave his feeble-minded father with Hunter? "What can you possibly have to discuss with him that you cannot discuss in the presence of your only son?" Rupert asked.

"Matters that do not concern you," Hunter answered.

"Indeed? There are no matters concerning my father

that do not concern me." He was Lord Reginald's only son and therefore his only legitimate heir. He would allow Hunter no more undeserved favors. "What brings you here, Hunter? Need to prey upon a dying man for further favors? Has he not given you enough? Must you bleed him to death?"

"Cease, Rupert," Lord Reginald interrupted. He coughed, then caught his breath again. "*I* summoned Hunter here."

Rupert turned a stunned gaze to his father. "You called on him? Whatever for, Father?" Fear knotted Rupert's stomach. Though Rupert had often wondered about his father's generosity toward Hunter, he had never accepted his father could be that bastard's sire. Surely there was another explanation.

"Are you my father?"

The question he overheard Hunter asking when he entered the bedchamber came ringing back to mind. A question to which Hunter would never find answer for Rupert would never allow his father to utter such frightful words.

Rage boiled inside of him.

Without warning Rupert punched Hunter in the face. Hunter staggered back, blood running from the corner of his mouth. He lunged at Rupert, hitting him in the stomach and stealing his breath away.

"Cease!" Lord Reginald's cry rose above the ruckus Rupert and Hunter were making. "Cease, you fools!" Lord Reginald began coughing in earnest, unable to stop and catch his breath.

Rupert and Hunter halted. Rupert shoved Hunter out of the way and rushed to his father's side. Hunter walked to the foot of the bed.

Lord Reginald's cough worsened, lifting his feeble body off the pillows. Blood spilled from his mouth to stain crimson his chest and the coverlet.

"Call the physician," Rupert cried, and for the first time in his life Hunter obeyed him.

The physician arrived moments later, and Rupert moved to the side to give the man room. His father's cough thankfully ceased after the physician administered to him. Then, a moment later, the physician lifted.

"How does he fare?" Rupert asked.

"Your father is dead."

Rupert staggered back. He understood his father had been the force behind him, and though he expected him to die soon, he was shocked at the sorrow and the fear clogging his throat.

He turned a shaken body to where Hunter stood and the man's pale countenance gave Rupert some measure of satisfaction, for Rupert believed in the depths of his heart that Hunter mourned not Lord Reginald's death but the secret that died with him.

"Now you shall never know," Rupert whispered. There was justice in the world after all.

Without a word Hunter stalked out of the bedchamber.

Chapter 13

HUNTER stomped inside the guest chamber, slamming the door with such a fury Isabel jumped to her feet. She followed him with her gaze as he marched to the table and filled a goblet with wine, gulping down the liquid without taking a breath or probably even tasting it.

Isabel exchanged weary glances with Maude. Had Rupert confronted Hunter, somehow letting their secret out? The mere thought of having to explain herself to Hunter made her queasy.

Searching for the right words to strike up a conversation, Isabel ambled toward him. She touched his shoulders. "What is the matter, Hunter?"

He spun around, as if just noticing her in the room. His face lost some of the frustration and anger. He threaded his fingers through his dark locks, a gesture she hadn't seen in him before. "Lord Reginald has died."

There was such hurt, such pain in his voice, Isabel's

heart constricted. "Oh, I am so sorry." She enveloped him in a comforting embrace. Sincere in her sympathy for his pain, she was nonetheless relieved his grief was not for having discovered Détra's secret. Hunter remained stiff in her arms for a moment, then with a big sigh that came from deep within him he laced his arms around her waist and pulled her tight to him.

They stood quietly embraced for several moments until Isabel broke the silence. "Do you want to talk about it?"

Hunter gently pushed her away. "Not now."

Understanding her silent support was all Hunter wanted at this moment, Isabel suppressed the many questions she wanted to ask him about Lord Reginald and their relationship. Hunter would talk if and when he was ready. She wouldn't push.

Maybe she could distract him. She pointed to the bathtub. "How about a bath? It is ready for you though I think it might need more hot water. I can ask Maude to get you some." Isabel knew Hunter was tired and dusty from the trip and emotionally drained with the recent news. A bath might help him relax. It sure had done wonders for her body, though her mind still swirled with worries.

Hunter looked over her shoulder to the bathtub, then nodded. "No need for more hot water."

"You may go, Maude. I will take care of my husband's needs." Before she left, Maude gave Isabel an encouraging smile.

Maude wanted Détra and Hunter to be together, Isabel realized. Maybe there was a way for Maude to help Détra adjust to a life with Hunter when she returned. And although she worried about Détra, the last thing Isabel wanted was for Hunter's heart to be broken.

"How is your hand?" Hunter asked, probably surprised at seeing her wrist wrapped with much less bandage than she had insisted at Windermere. Yesterday she had overplayed her injury a little, wanting to find an excuse not to ride and therefore miss the trip, but today Isabel decided she'd have to be dead to make the journey back on that cart. The fact she didn't know how to ride a horse hadn't changed, however. Maybe, and the thought appealed to her greatly, she could ride back with Hunter.

"It is much better today." She moved her wrist in a few directions to prove her words. There was a slight discomfort but not much pain at all. Maybe the potion Maude gave her for her headache was such a great pain reliever that it had numbed her wrist as well. "How about yours?" she asked.

"It needs a change of dressing."

"I will do that after your bath."

He nodded, and Isabel watched as he undressed with an economy of movement most men were known to possess. Garments fell in sloppy piles as he pulled them off his body on the way to the tub. In all his glorious nakedness Hunter stepped into the water. Isabel sat on a small stool behind the tub, the same one Maude had used to help her bathe earlier.

"Is the water warm enough?" she asked, making small talk to avoid the real issues hammering in her mind.

He sank down, resurfacing with wet hair. "Warm enough."

Grabbing a small measure of the soft soap from a small pot by her feet, she rubbed her hands together, then began washing Hunter's hair, enjoying its silky softness while her fingers massaged his scalp. He surrendered to her touch, breathing deeply, the silence in the room not heavy but complementary to their feelings. Having spent most of her life under the chaos of her parents' music practice sessions, Isabel appreciated the comfort silence could offer.

She tilted Hunter's head back a little, then taking care

no soap got into his face, she used water from an extra bucket on the floor to rinse his hair. With a soapy cloth she washed Hunter's shoulders and back, then kneaded the knots of tension that stubbornly resisted her efforts even as she lingered on them. She used the water from the tub for the rinsing of his back.

Pulling him against the back of the tub she reached from behind him to wash his wide chest and hard stomach. He leaned against her, his wet head soaking her as he watched her with those inscrutable dark eyes of his. Isabel went as far down as his navel, then made the journey back up his chest to his shoulders and arms, which he lifted for ease of reach. By the time she lifted from the stool she was soaking wet and wondering if she couldn't do a better job of bathing Hunter if she shared his bathtub.

She switched positions to the front of the tub, his gaze following her all the way.

"Is this a new manner of garment?" he asked eyeing the huge towel she had wrapped around her body.

Isabel held the sides, spreading them open like the skirts of a dress. "Simple, but comfortable," she said, kneeling down before him.

"Even rags would look ravishing on you." His dark eyes shone. With appreciation? Unspoken love? Unshed tears of grief?

Now facing him, Isabel massaged one large foot, then the other, surprised he was not ticklish.

"Have I ever bathed you before?" she asked as she worked her way up one muscular calf, then another.

He hesitated. "Never," he finally said.

Her hands reached his thighs and she had to lean forward over the tub to reach higher. "Never?" she asked as she massaged each thigh with circular motions, feeling every hard muscle underneath her palms.

"We have been wedded but for a short time."

Not so short a time that explained why Hunter and Détra hadn't consummated their marriage before Isabel appeared in the picture. What had Détra said or done to keep Hunter at bay for more than two weeks? And why had Hunter allowed Isabel to believe it wasn't their first time when they'd made love in the garrison's quarters?

Was it purely male pride? Or was it a deliberate gesture to bring about exactly what had happened between them? Not that she'd been an unwilling partner. But Détra would have been.

Isabel pushed aside such thoughts. Now was not the moment to bring the subject up, but if she remained in this body much longer, she would ask Hunter about it.

Her hands brushed Hunter's arousal. She lifted a questioning gaze at him. In response Hunter rose, pulling her up with him, her towel falling to the floor as his wet chest rubbed against her breasts. He kissed her hungrily, with a desperation she hadn't felt in him before. Still holding her, still kissing her, he stepped out of the tub, picked her up in his arms, and took her to the bed. His lips left her as he lowered her on the mattress and positioned himself between her thighs. She opened to him and he entered her with one deep thrust.

Understanding Hunter's need to exorcise his pain, Isabel was ready for him, lifting her knees and giving his thrusts greater depth. She could feel the violent beating of his heart against her breasts, the tension in the muscles of his shoulders her massage had failed to dissolve, and the pain in his heart as he desperately sought relief for his grief inside of her.

She nibbled on his chin, licked the underside of his throat as her hands stroked his back, and arched against him to meet his thrusts with her hips. His cry of release began as a rumble deep in his throat that intensified as his strokes gained desperation. It finally exploded into a roar of such power, such anguish that the walls of the chamber vibrated with its resonance.

After the final tremble of unrepentant ecstasy rocked him, Hunter collapsed spent over her, gasping for breath. After a moment, aware of his great weight, he lifted, supporting himself with his arms against the mattress. He hovered above her, his forehead touching hers, his eyes closed for long moments. Then he rolled to her side and, taking her with him, tucked her head underneath his chin.

The moments strung along in silence for so long that Isabel thought Hunter had fallen asleep. And then she heard his whisper. "He might have been my father."

Isabel's heart began a staccato beating. She lifted from his arms and gazed at him. "Lord Reginald?"

He nodded.

Oh God, that was why he was hurting so much.

Isabel pushed her back against the pillows. "Do you want to talk about it now?"

He gave her a sidelong glance. Then, almost as if deciding that having come this far he might as well go on, he pushed himself up, sitting by her side. "There is not much to tell. I was born in the village nearby Hawkhaven Castle, and for all accounts should have remained there till the end of my days." He paused, looking at her as if to gauge her response, then continued, "One morning, when I was fourteen, days before my mother passed away, she packed my meager belongings in a cloth and sent me to the castle where Lord Reginald took me in and trained me into knighthood."

What was Hunter saying? Isabel was still unsure. "Was Lord Reginald your natural father?"

The intensity in his gaze made his dark eyes shine ebony. "I know not. He died before revealing the truth to me. Now I shall never know who was my father." His voice choked with bottled-up emotion.

"Oh, Hunter. How awful! But maybe there is another way of finding out for sure."

He shook his head. "I am a lowborn bastard of unknown sire, Détra. And that shall not change."

There was such pain in his voice Isabel ached for him. He waited for her reply as if his world depended on it. Now she understood why Rupert kept calling Hunter a bastard. He knew it. And she hated Rupert for it.

Taking Hunter's hands into hers, she kneeled before him, praying she would find the right words to reassure him. "Being born a bastard—" Hunter flinched at hearing her say the word, but she needed to say it, needed to get this out into the open so he would never have to worry about it again. "—is a matter of circumstance totally out of your control. It has nothing to do with honor. Behaving like a bastard is a matter of character and choice. You might not know who is your father, Hunter, but you never were and shall never be a bastard in the true sense of the word. You are the most honorable man I have ever met and I am thankful and honored to know you."

And then she kissed him with the desperation of having found the man of her life but knowing he couldn't belong to her. With the longing to give him the love that burned inside of her but she couldn't confess. With the need to erase his pain and sorrow.

And he kissed her in return. Their roles were now reversed. She was the one in desperate need of love. And he was the one giving it to her.

And she took it. Every drop of love he sent her way, whether she deserved it or not, whether it was intended for her or not, until they lay spent in each other's arms.

*　*　*

THE BLACK-SHROUDED COFFIN CONTAINING LORD RE-
ginald's body was carried from the death chamber, where
he had been prepared for viewing and mourned, into the
chapel of Hawkhaven Castle by an escort of four knights.
Messengers had been sent to neighboring lords and
friends, and those who lived nearby came to pay their last
respects, joining Rupert, Hunter, and Détra inside the
chapel for the mourning office.

After the mass was over the small cortege stepped into
the bailey, where it seemed the entire village stood waiting, holding lit candles in their hands. As was custom,
Rupert had given alms to the villagers to follow his father's coffin to Hawkhaven Castle's private burial grounds
located on a small hill behind the chapel. Hunter recognized a few faces from his childhood spent in the village,
though he had seen little of them while fostering at the
castle and naught since he left Hawkhaven to follow King
Edward on his war against the Scots.

None of the villagers acknowledged his presence and
Hunter understood why. To them he was almost a traitor,
having abandoned his humble origins to join ranks with
the highborn, when in truth Hunter had lived for many
years in a limbo belonging to neither.

Détra squeezed his hand and Hunter's heart filled with
joy. With his lady wife's acceptance, he had finally found
his place. His mother's chalice had indeed granted him
his heart's desire. Even the pain of not knowing his father's name hurt less now that Détra stood by his side.
He glanced at her, grateful for her presence, engulfed by
her support and acceptance. Her devotion and concern
elated him. Barely a week ago, this new Détra had come
into his life and he already loved her more than the idealized image he had carried in his heart for so long.

And yet, the old Détra had despised the thought of
being married to him; should he risk telling her the whole

truth about that? Would she repudiate those earlier feelings for him and continue to accept his lowborn status?

Hunter wanted with all his heart to tell her the truth, to banish the shadows and subterfuges between them. But still he hesitated. Mayhap he would give them a little while longer.

The cortege continued on its way to the graveyard led by the priest carrying a wooden cross. Rupert, Hunter, and Détra followed the coffin, then the neighboring lords and friends, Hawkhaven's knights, men-at-arms, and servants, and finally the villagers and their lit candles.

The usual laments and wails from the widow and family were oddly absent. Rupert, Lord's Reginald only kin, walked in abject silence. The priest made the sign of the cross over the burial spot, sprinkled it with holy water then dug a shallow trench in the shape of a cross. As they prayed, a couple of villagers dug on the spot marked by the priest and Lord Reginald's coffin was lowered to his final resting place. The lit candles were placed around the grave and later a tombstone would be added.

People started to move back to the great hall where food and drink would be served for the guests and in the bailey for the villagers. Hunter lifted his head and caught sight of Rupert speaking with that despicable character, Toothless, who years earlier had insulted his mother's name and paid for the affront with the loss of his front teeth. As if sensing his gaze, Rupert lifted his eyes to him. The hatred and resentment in Rupert's glare were so intense it seemed to form a wall between the two men.

Hunter never understood why Rupert detested him so. Hunter had been the one forced to live under the shadow of Rupert's privileged status as the lord's son. And even now, in the end, Rupert had won. His father had died without acknowledging Hunter.

As if reading his mind, a derisive grin curled Rupert's lips.

Hunter had to fight the bitter resentment forming inside. He would not allow Rupert and his father's cowardice to nullify all he had accomplished on his own. He was no longer a poor, needy village boy. He was a man who had carved a niche for himself, garnered admiration and gratitude from knights and lords alike who fought alongside him, even the king himself, who awarded him Windermere Castle. He was lord of his own lands and he was wedded to the beautiful woman of his heart.

Apart from his father's name, Rupert had naught over him.

Turning his back on Rupert, Hunter led his lady wife back to the castle.

It was time they went back home.

RUPERT FOLLOWED HUNTER'S RETREAT WITH SUCH HA-tred he was sure his heart would turn to stone if he did not sway his gaze away.

"I wager you will be glad to see him gone," Edmund, called Toothless, the perennial squire, hissed through the gap of his front teeth.

"I should think you shall shed no tears either." When Hunter had knocked out Edmund's front teeth those many years ago, he might have taken what little wit the man had possessed. Still, Edmund had served Rupert well and blindly. A trait much preferred to wit when one was involved in secretive matters as Rupert was.

"He should not have been here at your father's funeral," Edmund said. "I understand not why you allowed it, my lord."

"I had my reasons." He did it for Détra. So he could be with her under Hunter's nose. It had not happened the way he had planned, though. She had avoided him like the plague, mayhap fearing her husband's ire. One more reason for Rupert's foul mood. As if the death of his father was not enough.

"Look at him." Edmund spit through the gap of his teeth. "Strutting about as if he belongs in our midst. Were it not for his witch mother the bastard would never have left the village where he belonged."

Staring at Edmund from the corners of his eyes, Rupert wondered whether the lackwit suspected who might be the bastard's father. Rupert had never voiced out loud his fear that his father could have sired Hunter, and when Lord Reginald had chosen to remain silent even as he brought Hunter up to live in his castle, Rupert had done the same. He had wondered, however, and feared that one day Hunter would be acknowledged and steal his inheritance.

That was why Rupert had returned home from the castle where he was fostering at the time Hunter came to live here. He had wanted to give Hunter no chance to worm himself into his father's grace. He grinned, pleased with himself, for he had done exactly that. Lord Reginald had died carrying his secret to his grave.

Still, wanting to make sure Edmund knew naught of his thoughts, Rupert asked, "What is your meaning, Edmund?"

"Black magic, of course, my lord. How else would Hunter be so fortunate in his endeavors?"

"Black magic?" Rupert asked, wondering if Toothless had gone insane.

"It is believed Hunter's mother made a pact with Satan." Edmund lowered his voice at the last word as if fearing the Prince of Darkness himself would hear him. "And that Hunter is the devil's spawn himself."

That Rupert could well believe.

Nodding knowingly, Edmund continued, "It is clear the power of his chalice derives from malevolent influences."

"What chalice?"

"The one he so jealously guarded his entire life. It was given to him by his mother days before she delivered her soul to the devil at the hour of her death. That was the day he came to be at Hawkhaven Castle. Coincidence? I think not."

A chalice with magical powers. Could it be? For the first time Rupert took Edmund's babbling into consideration.

"Have you seen it?"

Edmund jumped. "The devil?"

"Nay, you idiot, the chalice."

"Aye, once. A very valuable-looking piece with sapphire stones a village's witch could never be in possession of by legitimate means."

Edmund's story gave Rupert pause. There was a certain truth in the fact that fortune had always smiled upon Hunter. Since the day the bastard had set foot in Hawkhaven he had excelled, even without any prior skills with swords or horses. He had absorbed knowledge like a sponge, with ease impossible for such a baseborn youth. And after gaining his gold spurs he had earned the king's gratitude by saving the man's life. And as a reward, he had wedded Détra.

Could it be true? Could the chalice be the source of Hunter's good fortune? The exhilarating thought took hold. Outwitting Hunter had been a difficult challenge Rupert had faced his entire life, but stealing the man's power in the form of a chalice should be child's play.

Oh, he would enjoy seeing the proud Hunter lose everything he had so undeservedly obtained.

"Why have you never mentioned this to me before?" Rupert asked. Had he known earlier he could have absconded with the chalice years ago, thus avoiding all the problems he faced now.

"I guess I forgot."

Forgot. Rupert sighed. That would be just like Edmund. Should he truly put stock in such an idiot's words?

And yet the fact Rupert had never heard or even glimpsed the chalice would not necessarily mean it did not exist. Surely knowing how invaluable the chalice was, Hunter would not broadcast its existence to the world.

But there would be one other person who would know if it truly existed. Détra.

WITH HUNTER DOWN IN THE STABLES MAKING THE last preparations for departure and Maude just about finished packing their belongings, Isabel paced the floor, wondering what she should do about Hunter.

She'd known him for a very short time but she'd never felt so close, never cared so much, never lusted so madly for a man before. If there were any way she could be with Hunter without having to steal his wife's body and life she would do it without a second thought. But was there another way? And how would she find that out?

She was reaching for straws here. There was no other way but return Détra to her body as soon as possible. Yet the thought she'd be returning a woman who couldn't or wouldn't even want to love Hunter like he deserved to be loved—like Isabel would love him had she the chance— drove Isabel insane.

What could she do then?

Could she be unselfish enough to try to fix the situation so that Hunter and Détra could be happy together?

Her stomach turned into knots. Good God, she didn't know if she had it in her.

And even if she did, what could she do? Tell Hunter

about Détra and Rupert's relationship? Would he forgive Détra? Would Détra want forgiveness? That would be the biggest hole in her plan. She could do nothing to change Détra's feelings.

Frustration balled up inside of Isabel. Cruel fate played a trick on all of them. No one could be happy in this story. Isabel had to give up Hunter, the man she loved, or steal another woman's life to be with him, both options not exactly a direct path to happiness. Détra and Rupert couldn't be together as they obviously wanted to be, for Détra and Hunter's marriage could not be annulled now that it was consummated. Hunter was married to a woman whom he loved but who didn't love him in return.

What would happen when Détra returned to her body? What would she do? Would she leave Hunter for Rupert? Isabel couldn't condemn the man she loved to such an unhappy ending. If only Détra would give Hunter a chance, she'd see what a wonderful man he was. But Isabel had no right to tell Détra whom to love.

The best Isabel could do would be to play this out as closely as it would have happened without her presence. And to do that she needed more information about Détra. Depending on what she learned she'd find her course of action.

She moved to where Maude was finishing with her packing, and bent over the chest. "How well do you know Détra?" Isabel asked, realizing her mistake even before Maude lifted and raised her eyebrow in surprise at her. "I mean," she quickly amended, "how well do you know me? Sometimes I think of myself and the old Détra as two different persons, since I remember nothing of my past."

"It is a peculiar and troublesome situation," Maude said with kind understanding. "To answer your question I believe I know you quite well, my lady. My mother was

your nursing maid and we were raised practically together."

Détra and Maude seemed to be of a same age. That
should've made it easier for them to be close, maybe even
friends, and yet there was that difference in class between
the two of them. How would that work in the Middle
Ages? Isabel needed to make sure she could trust Maude's
answers. "Have I ever confided in you? I mean, not with
castle matters but with private concerns."

"You have confided in me from time to time."

"Have I ever told you I loved Rupert?"

Maude hesitated. "Not in those exact words, nay."

"In what words exactly? This is very important,
Maude."

"Well, you thought him charming and handsome. He
made you laugh." Obviously Détra hadn't had much to
laugh about while married to that horrid William.

"But have I ever said I loved him?"

"Nay," Maude said. "You told me you had chosen to
wed Lord Rupert because you wanted to make the choice
this time around and not be forced to wed a man you
knew naught about."

That was exactly what Isabel wanted to hear. It seemed
that in a time when women had very little choices, Détra
had hoped for some control over her life, especially after
a dreadful marriage experience. Isabel couldn't blame her,
but she couldn't condone the decisions she made concerning Hunter also. Was the woman blind? Couldn't she
see what a wonderful man he was?

"Had I not lost my memory," Isabel continued, "and
we were in this very same situation—my marriage to
Hunter being consummated, and me having made the earlier decision to be with Rupert—what would I do now?"
Isabel knew she was putting too much stock in Maude's

words, but all she wanted was reasonable doubt that would justify her meddling in Détra's life.

"I know not, my lady."

So much for her expectations.

Time to tackle the subject from another angle. "How easy would it be to annul my marriage to Hunter?"

"Nearly impossible."

"So, this marriage is valid and pretty much indissoluble."

"Before the eyes of God and king."

"All right. With that in mind, what would be the consequences of my abandoning my husband to be with another man?"

Maude's scandalized gaze should be answer enough for Isabel, but she wanted to hear the words, and so she waited.

"Excommunication by the Church, for certain—"

Maybe Détra could live with that, since, in a way, she'd already committed adultery.

"King's persecution, since you would go against his wishes—"

Could Détra afford to ignore a king's ire?

"And Lord Hunter would most probably give you pursuit and blood would be spilled. My lady, I beg you not to do that."

Now, that could be a deterrent to Détra. Whichever way Détra's heart lay she would know Hunter or Rupert, or even both, could be killed in a confrontation of that kind. Would Détra risk that?

"Thank you, Maude. I think I know what to do now. Can you call Rupert here? And while I am talking with him, please, can you keep an eye on Hunter? I do not want him to surprise us together."

"My lady, meeting with Lord Rupert is folly."

"Not if it will help end this situation once and for all."

Still looking unconvinced, Maude nonetheless left to do what Isabel had asked.

Isabel wasn't sure at all what she was about to do was right, but it seemed Détra's fate had been sealed the moment Isabel and Hunter had made love. In the twenty-first century Détra would have every right to divorce Hunter and marry Rupert, but in these medieval times she'd be putting herself and everyone else through a lot of grief and danger and still not be able to live the life she wanted.

Besides, from where Isabel stood, Détra didn't even love Rupert. If she'd just give Hunter a chance . . . Not that that made Isabel feel any better, but if she must return Détra to her own body, at least she could try to guarantee Hunter's happiness.

Chapter 14

RUPERT saw Maude as she was leaving Détra's guest chamber. "My lady wishes to speak with you," she said and then disappeared down the steps.

"As I wish to speak with her," he spoke to the empty corridor behind him. So, Détra had finally decided to grant him the pleasure of her presence. He was beginning to suspect she was avoiding him.

He opened the door and walked straight to where Détra stood by the bed. He took her in his arms and kissed her hungrily, though only briefly for she immediately squirmed out of his embrace.

"What manner of greeting is this?" Vexed by her cold welcome, Rupert's foul mood returned. "Why have you avoided me?"

"Do you want to raise Hunter's suspicions?"

"And yet you summon me to your bedchamber while your husband is nearby."

She hesitated, then moved away from him. "I could not leave before expressing my deepest sympathy for your loss."

His mood ameliorated somewhat, though not entirely. He followed her. They stood behind the closed door. "It was a great loss indeed," he said. "It is the thought that we shall be together soon that makes it bearable."

A shadow crossed her eyes. Rupert stiffened. In the past Détra had been pleased when he spoke of their future together. What had changed?

"Rupert," she began, and the way she said his name did not bode well in his mind. "I hate to tell you this, especially in this difficult time you are facing, but there can be no future for us."

Reining in his temper, Rupert asked, "And why ever not? What has changed, Détra?"

"The marriage has been consummated." She spoke with more fatalism than he would have accorded a woman whose amorous plans had been thwarted.

Fury rose in Rupert's heart. He whacked the door with his fist in sheer frustration. The thud echoed in the bed-chamber and from the corner of his eye he saw Détra jump. Oh, he had known that sooner or later Hunter would demand his marital rights—in fact, were Rupert in his place, he would have forced her on their wedding night. And yet to learn Hunter had taken his pleasure upon Détra was more than he could bear.

Rupert took a deep breath, controlling his anger. He had to find a way to extricate Détra from Hunter's talons. "When did it happen?"

She stepped back. "What does it matter—"

"Were there witnesses?" He advanced toward her. "Are you with child?" There was no way Hunter would take Détra away from him. She belonged to him. The man had taken enough. His fortune was about to run out.

"I am not sure—"

Had she not even considered she might be carrying the bastard's child? Détra was no pure maiden; playing the innocent did not suit her at all. "Did he force himself upon you or did you welcome him gladly to your bed?" What Rupert really wanted to know was whether Détra's feelings about her husband had changed. Before Hunter had arrived to claim her in marriage, she had been adamant about wanting to wed Rupert. A few days ago when they spoke while Hunter was away from Windermere, she was still sure that was what she wanted, and yet now she relented?

"He is my legal husband," she said.

"Now you offer excuses for him." Rupert grabbed her shoulders and kissed her again, a brief but possessive kiss. "Has Hunter pleased you so well in bed you have forgotten about us?" His hand cupped her breast, and he rubbed himself against her.

She pushed against him. "Our fate is out of our hands, Rupert."

Not yet, it is not. Hunter will not take what is mine!

If the story Edmund had told him about the chalice was true, then there was still hope. "We shall be together," he insisted. "Make no mistake about that."

"Rupert," Détra said in a conciliatory manner, much more to his liking. "You are a handsome, powerful man." He puffed his chest. "There should be no shortage of beautiful ladies who would be more than happy to be your wife."

Her puny attempt to pacify him failed miserably. "I shall want no other."

"I am not free anymore," she cried. "Would you risk making an enemy of God and king?"

"I can handle the king and Hunter is not God. He is but a bastard who rose far too high above his station and must be brought down. And I am the one to do it."

He was about to ask her about the chalice when Maude dashed into the room. "My lady," she cried. "Lord Hunter is on his way up the stairs."

"You must go," Détra said, pushing him to the door.

For a moment Rupert considered staying and confronting Hunter, but decided against it.

When he had the source of Hunter's good fortune in his hand he would not only destroy the bastard and recover Détra and her property but he would also become a most powerful man. A man who could choose his friends among kings.

That would make Rupert most powerful, indeed.

THE TRIP BACK TO WINDERMERE CASTLE WAS UN-eventful for the most part. As Isabel had planned beforehand, she rode with Hunter, while poor Maude took the cart by herself. Secure in the safety of Hunter's arms, her back cushioned against his wide chest, inhaling his male scent and feeling his heat and his strength envelop her, Isabel almost forgot about the horrible bind she was in.

Her parting conversation with Rupert hadn't gone the way she'd hoped. Not that she had expected him to meekly accept his affair with Détra was over, kiss her good-bye, and wish her good luck, but she'd hoped for at least recognition of the inevitable—that their affair was doomed unless they alienated the whole world. And she had made it clear to Rupert she wasn't willing to do that.

Frankly, Isabel didn't think either Détra or Rupert were prepared for such drastic measures. What bothered her was not knowing whether Rupert was the kind of man who would accept defeat graciously. It surely hadn't looked that way when she talked to him, but he had been angry and hurt then. Isabel hoped Rupert wouldn't go medieval and call Hunter on a duel or something worse like an ambush, or hire a mercenary murderer.

Uneasiness skittered down her spine. Should she warn Hunter? How could she do that without revealing his wife's betrayal? Isabel shook her head. She was letting her imagination get away with her. Besides, Hunter was a strong warrior. Surely he was capable of taking care of himself.

Isabel squeezed Hunter's arm, reassuring herself with his presence. He pulled her even closer to him. "Are you tired?" he whispered in her ears, the husky sound vibrating deep within her.

"A little." She moved in the saddle, her buttocks grazing against his loins, as it'd happened several times during the trip, and Hunter groaned softly.

"Mayhap we should stop for a while," he said.

Isabel smiled, knowing exactly why he suggested that. Throughout their journey he had stopped several times, even suggesting she might be more comfortable in the cart with Maude or on her own mare for a while. Every time she had politely declined. She understood his discomfort for she wasn't immune to their close proximity either. Her body might respond in a less visible way but she felt just as aroused as he did. And yet, not knowing how long they'd remain together, she didn't want to miss a moment of being with him, close to him, touching him.

"How far are we from Windermere?" she asked instead of answering his question.

"A couple of miles, no more."

"Maybe we should hurry home then, instead of stopping for a rest." She nestled her head against his shoulder and nibbled on his rough chin. "So I can ride you instead of this damn horse."

She heard and felt his deep intake of breath as his arm

tightened around her waist. He shouted to his men that he
would be moving along ahead of them.

"Hold on, my lady," he whispered in her ears. "I fear
this shall be a very rough ride."

Isabel smiled. She was counting on that!

Hours later, after a wild lovemaking, Isabel watched
Hunter sleep, wondering how she would ever live without
him. His confession of his birth circumstances had moved
Isabel deeply and brought them closer. She knew in this
time and age being a bastard was a stigma difficult to
ignore, and yet Hunter had confided in her, trusted her
enough to reveal such an intimate and painful part of himself. As she'd told him then, she was proud of him, yet
she knew Détra might feel differently.

If only she could communicate with Détra. Find out
whether she was trying to return home.

Of course she was trying to return home. Even if Détra
didn't love Hunter she'd have many reasons to want to
be back in her own body and life. She was probably going
insane in a world she couldn't possibly comprehend or
accept. And she had Rupert here. Détra still didn't know
there was no hope for them.

The fact she hadn't succeeded yet meant little. Détra
might have lost possession of the chalice in the future, as
it had happened to Isabel in this time. She might not even
understand the chalice's power or she might be incapacitated. Isabel had this horrible picture of Détra detained
in a mental health facility.

Not a good situation to be returning to, and an even
worse one to condemn someone.

Isabel quickly snuffed the little flame of hope trying to
fire her insides. Even if she could bring herself to disregard every argument against remaining in Détra's body,
Isabel would forever live in fear that Détra would find a
way to make the swap. It was hard enough for her to think

of leaving Hunter now. How much harder would it be to lose him later, maybe even years down the road, when they had grown even closer, more in love, perhaps even having had a child together?

The mere thought of losing a child again made Isabel nauseated. She had no choice. She had to leave now and the sooner the better.

Silently, Isabel rose in the dark as Hunter lay in peaceful slumber. She searched his clothing for the key to his chamber in the garrison's quarters and found it easily enough. Too easily. Maybe fate was telling her something.

As soon as morning broke, Hunter was supposed to leave on a scouting trip. Isabel would use the opportunity to search his private room for the chalice. If her guess was right, and she was sure it was, she'd find the chalice in his war chest.

Isabel heard Hunter stir and swiftly climbed back in bed, hiding the key under her pillow and hoping Hunter wouldn't notice its absence until it was too late.

Sleep eluded her. Having memorized every nuance of his handsome face Isabel remained awake, watching him in the dark. She would make a painting of him as soon as she was back home. Sorrow squeezed her heart with an iron fist and a tear rolled down her face when she realized a picture would be all she would have of Hunter. A picture and the memory of the man she loved and could never have.

DAWN ARRIVED WITH ITS ASHEN RAYS INFILTRATING the room through the open shutters of the window. Isabel had slept little and fitfully, but was once again awake when Hunter rose silently. She unobtrusively watched him dress, then feigned sleep when he approached and kissed her softly before leaving the room.

Isabel waited until she was certain he was gone before rising from the bed and dressing in a hurry. Now that she had the key, she was afraid that if she waited a moment longer her courage would desert her and she'd be forever condemned to a life of uncertainty and guilt.

Maude arrived with her morning tea to find her already up and dressed. Isabel gulped down the tea without even tasting it, and then she hugged Maude.

"Thank you so much for all your help and understanding," Isabel said. "In the next days I will need you more than ever, Maude. Please point me in the right direction. Do not let me forget my obligations to Hunter and remind me there is no hope for a relationship with Rupert. Will you do that for me?"

Maude lifted a confused gaze at Isabel. "My lady, you frighten me."

"I know and I am sorry, but swear to me you will do what I ask you."

Maude nodded.

Isabel walked to the door.

"Where do you go?" Maude asked.

"I shall be right back."

Good-bye, Maude!

With the key burning a hole in her hand, Isabel left the bedroom and hurried down the stairs, to step into a great hall that was beginning to stir to life. Servants collected the pallets they'd slept on, opened trestle tables, and then set them on the floor. Isabel crossed the hall silently and undisturbed and stepped outside into the awakening day. In the weak light of morning she could see Hunter at the gates conversing with the guards—maybe giving them a few last minute instructions before he left.

She waited until he crossed the gate, then dashed across the bailey to the garrison's quarters. A few men washed their faces in a trough on the outside wall and an uninhibited one relieved himself not far from them. Isabel ignored them all and entered the small hall. A few heads turned a surprised and shocked gaze at seeing her there.

"Good morning," she said. As if this was her morning routine, she marched to Hunter's private room. No one stopped her or questioned her, though many would be wondering what she was doing there. Isabel would let Détra explain her presence in the place later.

She inserted the key in the hole and it turned with a rusty noise. Opening the door, she stole inside. It was dark there and Isabel almost kicked herself for not remembering to bring a lit candle. She still hadn't learned how to produce fire. However, she knew where the war chest was, saw its dark form against the wall, and dashed to it. She opened the heavy lid and began rummaging inside. She didn't need light. She would feel with her hands the chalice's shape. She touched every object inside the chest, moved them around, took them out, but none resembled a chalice. Frustrated, she sat on her haunches. She was so sure the chalice was here. Where else could it be?

"Looking for something?"

Isabel's heart stopped. She turned and saw Hunter standing at the door, his silhouette delineated by the lit candles in the hall behind him.

"I thought you were gone," she said stupidly.

"Evidently." He walked in, pulled her up to her feet, lit the oil lamps on the wall, and then closed the door. "What do you seek, my lady wife?" he asked, facing her.

For a moment she thought about finding an excuse, but she was getting tired of that. It was time to put the cards on the table. She might never find the chalice otherwise. And she couldn't remain in this body a moment longer.

Isabel straightened her shoulders and, looking right at him, she said, "I search for the chalice I asked you about some time ago."

Dead silence greeted her words. Hunter stood there with a blank expression and stiff posture, like a condemned prisoner waiting for the firing squad to end it all for him.

Well, at least he hadn't immediately denied the chalice's existence.

Encouraged, Isabel continued, "I believe the chalice has something to do with my loss of memory."

"A simple chalice?" He sounded nonchalant, but by now Isabel knew Hunter would show only the emotions he wanted the world to see.

"A magic chalice," she corrected.

Hunter moved to the war chest and with one knee bent, the other on the floor, he began putting back the objects she had taken out. "What makes you believe the chalice is magic?"

Expecting him to laugh at her suggestion, or even dismiss it with derision, Isabel was surprised he considered the possibility. Again, the feeling Hunter knew more than he led her to believe assailed her.

"I know the chalice was in the room that morning I fell and struck my head," she said. "Though I do not believe that was what truly happened."

He rose, pivoted, then faced her again. He didn't seem angry, almost resigned, in fact. "What do you believe happened?" he asked.

"I am not sure," she said evasively. How far should she go with the truth? She had to make Hunter believe she truly needed the chalice and the only way to do that was to prove it was indeed magical. That is, if he didn't already know that.

"All I know," she said, "is that something decidedly odd concerns that chalice. I remember warmth seeping from it into my fingers, I remember its blue stones glowing like stars and a blue mist enveloping me before I lost

consciousness." Here she hesitated. Should she speak of
the vision? One thing was for sure, had Détra seen it she
wouldn't have been happy about it. Had she rejected it?
Could that, coupled with Isabel's wish, have been the true
instigator of their body swapping?

Isabel didn't have to go there right now. "When I woke
up I did not know who and where I was," Isabel continued. "I believe the chalice is responsible for what happened to me, and if I find it, I will also find the answers
I seek."

"Are you so displeased with your life that you want it
changed?" he asked.

She shook her head. "That is not it."

"Then what is it?" he asked, taking her into his arms.

Isabel stepped out of his embrace, albeit reluctantly. If
he kissed her now they would end up making passionate
love and Isabel would be once again derailed off her mission. She'd been delayed long enough.

"I need my memories back. Please, Hunter, humor me
in this. If you know the chalice's whereabouts, please tell
me."

Looking displeased she had evaded his touch, he said,
"Unpleasant memories are better left buried."

"We cannot run away from who we are," she said,
anguish chafing her throat. "The past has a way of catching up with us."

Hunter knew that all too well.

Sooner or later Détra's memory might return. How
would she react when even after he had professed his love
for her he continued to mislead her? He might be doing
more harm than good at this point by keeping the truth
from her.

After all, he could not deny Détra's changed ways
since that fateful morning the chalice had shown them
both the vision of his heart wish. Had she not proved it

by accepting his bastardy? Would knowing her old feelings for him end the understanding they had found together?

Suddenly Hunter realized it was not the truth he feared so much anymore, but the possibility the chalice could revert this Détra he loved more than his heart could ever have wished into the lady of old.

When the chalice had erased Détra's memory, it had given Hunter a chance to win her heart. Their marriage was now consummated and his hold on Windermere guaranteed. And he was so close to winning her heart. She had yet to profess in words her love for him, but she had done thus in so many other ways. Hunter was not about to risk all he had achieved with Détra, but he would tell her what she wanted to know.

"If the past matters so much to you," Hunter said, "I shall give it to you, but I offer no apologies for loving you, though I have misled you to believe all was always well between us."

With a sigh, he closed the lid of his war chest, then perched on it. Détra moved to the cot and sat on it. They faced each other.

"You were very unhappy to be wedded to me," he confessed. "In fact, that very morning you lost your memory you had told me in no uncertain terms I was beneath you."

A bastard son of a village witch shall never be my lord nor husband.

Hunter could not repeat such painful words. And yet, when he had confessed his bastardy to Détra she had not only been unfazed by it, but also accepted him with no reservations.

Dormant hope filled his heart.

He plodded on. "You were holding the chalice that morning when you fell." It would be best to leave the chalice's powers out of it. Best for her to believe the fall had been the perpetrator of her loss of memory. He wanted Détra to be satisfied with what he told her and desist of demanding what could forever change their lives.

"When you awoke remembering naught, I let you believe all was well between us."

He rose, then reaching her with one large step, knelt by her feet, and took her hands into his. "For that I beg your pardon."

He waited for her reply, seeking her grim countenance for a softening toward him.

"I cannot tell you how the old me would react to such confession," Détra said. "I will not say you were justified in lying and making the choices for me that I should have made for myself. Love is trust, Hunter—" Her voice choked with emotion and Hunter felt like a knave for his half-truths.

After a moment, she continued, "What I will say is that I understand there are times in life we do things we are not proud of."

"Does that mean you forgive me?"

"It means I will not stand as judge over you. However," she added, "not knowing what was in my heart and in my mind in the past, I cannot stand before you with my naked soul and therefore we cannot be ever assured of our true feelings for each other."

"I want you just the way you are now, Détra. I have no doubts of my feelings for you and I know not what you mean by such words."

Was the woman denying him? The thought made his insides tie into a knot. Had he been overly trusting in her change?

"I mean that sooner, rather than later, we should tell each other the deepest truth of our hearts. We should clear every doubt that poisons our minds. We should forgive each other's shortcomings and then we should pledge our love anew. Only then will our lives be fulfilled."

Hunter rose to his feet and strolled away, his back turned to her. What was she asking of him? He pivoted and found her standing before him.

Deus! But he loved this woman. Détra had never cared enough to speak to him about their feelings like she was doing now. He took her in his arms and kissed her. She softened in his arms and kissed him back. When they finally parted, his breath came in gasps. He wanted her with a desperation that had become part of his life. He turned to lead her to the cot, but she held her place.

Unsure, he gazed at her.

"I need to know who I am," she said. "And I need the chalice for that. Would you give it to me?"

Hunter staggered back. He wanted to give her the chalice. Wanted to believe all would end well. But something in her demeanor, in her gaze—sadness, regret, he could not quite ascertain what—halted him.

"Where is it, Hunter?" she asked. "Where is the chalice?"

After a long silence, he said, "At the bottom of the lake."

Chapter 15

THE room spun wildly around Isabel, and with rubbery legs she staggered back, backing against the cot. She slumped down on it, sitting in stupefied silence, body frozen but mind in turmoil.

Had she misheard him? Did Hunter really say the chalice—the only way for her to return to her own body—was buried deep at the bottom of a lake?

The memory of her finding the chalice in the future by the lake's shore gave credence to Hunter's revelation. How else would the chalice appear in that location centuries in the future if not for someone putting it there in the past?

And with the chalice gone she would be stuck in this time, with Hunter. The thought took hold. Would she dare hope this could be the answer? The temptation to accept her fate was to remain here with Hunter was great.

But not great enough!

Isabel jerked to her feet and stalked across the room. Stark wooden wall greeted her. How could she even consider taking over Détra's life without knowing what happened to her in the future? And how could she be happy with Hunter without knowing when or if Détra would find a way to return to her own life, her rightful place at Hunter's side?

Desperation clamped her heart with an iron vise, and Isabel felt the strength seeping out of her limbs. She fought the oblivion threatening to overcome her, but the walls closed on her and she forgot how to breathe.

She was trapped. Without the chalice she would forever live in fear of being jerked away from Hunter, and there was nothing she could do about it.

"Détra." Hunter's disembodied voice reached her as if from afar. He gripped her shoulders and led her to the cot where he gently lowered her down, one hand supporting her back.

"Speak to me," he demanded.

She clung to his forearm with clammy fingers. "Why did you get rid of it?" she asked.

A shadow fell over his face. He rose and moved across the room, away from her. With rubbery legs Isabel followed him. "If you do not believe in the chalice's magical powers," she said to his back, "why did you send it to the depths of a lake? Why keep it away from me?" She needed to understand, to make some sense of what was happening to them.

Her hand on his shoulder, she turned him around to face her. "This is too important to me, Hunter. Without the chalice I have lost the only way to my past."

"I understand your need for answers, but why can you not forget the past and begin anew? We have each other, Détra. Is that not enough?"

"I cannot begin anew as long as my past hangs over

me like a dark cloud." *As long as there's the threat of Détra returning,* she silently added.

His fingers raked his hair and he sighed heavily, clearly in the throes of some inner struggle. She kept her gaze firmly on his face while his gaze strayed around the room, then finally settled back on her.

"Very well," he said. "I see you cannot be dissuaded. The chalice's powers are beyond my control. Not knowing what effect it would bring upon you, since it had already robbed you of your memories, I made the decision to keep it away from you and everyone else. Hence the lake."

"How can you make such a decision for me?"

He grabbed her shoulders. "You are my lady wife, my heart's wish, and my life. It is my duty to protect you. I shall not allow any harm to befall you."

"The chalice took my life away, Hunter," she insisted. "Only the chalice can give it back to me."

"Not your life, just your memories," he said.

"And what is a life without memories?" she insisted.

Hunter's hands fell from her shoulders and he trod to the stool in the corner of the room. He peeled his hauberk from his body as if it weighed nothing, then dumped it down on the stool. The stool fell over and the clinging of metal rings echoed in the small room until the heavy hauberk lay silently on the floor.

With one sweeping motion he brought the stool and the hauberk up straight, then removed the padded tunic covering his chest, leaving a linen shirt in place. He pivoted, his gaze seeking her. "I shall give you back your memories without putting you in harm's way."

Isabel wanted to scream in frustration. Wrong answers were always the result of talking in circles and that was what she'd been doing since the beginning.

"The chalice was given to me by my mother on the

day she sent me to Hawkhaven Castle to begin my training for knighthood," Hunter began. "She promised me the chalice would one day grant my deepest heart wish." His face split into a bitter grimace. "At the time all I longed for was to know my father's name. Which I never learned, as you well know."

He moved again, as if he needed action to be able to get the words out. He took his sword belt and leaned it against the wall, then perched himself against the war chest.

Even without his armor and half undressed Hunter presented a rough, dangerous, and utterly masculine picture. Isabel had to shake her head to escape the enthralling image.

"I did not believe in the chalice's powers," he continued. "Not then, and not for a long time, but I kept the chalice with me as a reminder of a dearest mother I once had. I was vindicated in my disbelief when I obtained the gold spurs of knighthood, not through any magical powers, but after years of struggles and adversity. Knighthood led me to be called to King Edward's service in his war against Scotland, which led to my saving the king's life in the battlefield, which led to him awarding Windermere to me and you for my wife."

Hunter told his story in a matter-of-fact, detached way. And though Isabel had many questions she decided not to interrupt until he was finished.

"However," he continued, "after only two weeks of marriage I discovered I had wedded and been in love with a dream that did not exist, and it mattered not how much I wished otherwise, my lady wife wanted naught to do with me."

"Do you know the reason of . . . my rejection?" Isabel asked. Did Hunter know of Rupert?

"You mean, besides the fact I am a lowborn bastard of unknown sire?"

He didn't know!

But that didn't erase the pain in his dark eyes, even though Hunter tried to sound nonchalant. How much deeper would he hurt if he found out Détra had betrayed him? Damn the woman for her callousness.

"Whether you know your father or not makes no difference to me," she said. And yet her reassurance meant little, for Détra obviously thought differently.

A brief smile crossed his face and warmed her heart.

"That fateful morning," he continued, "I thought I would be condemned to live my life with a wife who despised me. That was when the chalice chose to reveal its power for the first time in a vision of my heart wish—a joyful portrait of a happy life with you." He laughed a humorless, dry laugh. "A prospect you swiftly rejected, of course. You grabbed my hand and the chalice, and something went wrong. We were both jerked into unconsciousness, and when we came to, you remembered naught of your ill will toward me. Selfishly, I chose not to enlighten you and used the opportunity to prove to you, and to myself, the vision could come true."

Finally understanding what had happened relieved the guilt Isabel had carried solely on her shoulders all this time. The vision she'd seen had been Hunter's wish for a perfect life with his wife, which had prompted Détra to reject him at the same time Isabel had wished to be in Détra's place. It hadn't been only her misguided wish that had provoked the body switching; they'd all had a part in it.

And yet, Isabel was the only one who knew the truth on all sides. That knowledge, however, didn't make things any easier on her—on the contrary. It tore her apart to know Détra would reject Hunter again once she returned.

And she would return. Détra might not want Hunter but she had other reasons to want her life back, reasons Hunter was unaware of.

Hunter strode to where she stood and took her hands into his. "I never meant to hurt you," he whispered. "I ask that you seek in your heart to forgive me. And I vow to spend the rest of my life proving to you that we belong together."

Were the circumstances different Isabel might've been less than understanding of Hunter's motives and actions, but considering Détra's deceit of him, and Isabel's own less than truthful self, she thought it wise to defer judgment. It was obvious the three of them had behaved in a less than truthful way, and yet neither Isabel nor Hunter had made any claim to sainthood. And she certainly wouldn't presume to speak for Détra. They were all flawed, imperfect human beings, and as such subject to making mistakes. Even huge ones.

But unlike her, Hunter had come clean with his secret.

Guilt at her own deception stabbed at her. The last thing in the world she wanted to do was hurt Hunter, but he would be hurt when she left, and the means would matter little to him. He would be losing the wife he thought loved him.

He waited for her answer with a stoic expression frozen on his face.

Hunter didn't know she was not his wife, he didn't know her love was not the one he sought, he didn't know that her surrender, her acceptance, and her forgiveness would mean nothing once Détra returned.

The pain Isabel felt in her heart was almost physical. The desire and the need to tell him the whole truth bubbled inside of her, swelling her heart to the point of explosion. But how could she ask him to believe in the impossible? It was one thing to accept a chalice possessed magical powers—people sometimes relied on amulets for good luck, even in the twenty-first century—but time travel? Body switching? That was beyond the realm of possibility, especially for a medieval man, especially in these circumstances. Hunter would surely think she was concocting the story to hide some nefarious reasons to reject him again.

Isabel's worst nightmare had come true. She, who for so long had sought a place to belong, who had tried so hard not to interfere in other people's lives, could not find happiness living another woman's life. Could not keep on lying and deceiving for the sake of survival. Could not live forever in fear she'd be wrenched away from the man she loved without as much as a warning, never really knowing when Détra would make her move.

Or if she ever would.

How could she live like that?

And yet, how could she accept Hunter could never be hers and pretend she could survive without him? Isabel couldn't deny her feelings for Hunter, couldn't turn her back on him when he needed her. And damn it, if Hunter wanted her forgiveness, she would give it to him.

Give it to him even knowing it was Détra's forgiveness he sought, and not hers. That she could keep his hurt at bay only temporarily. That his pain and shock would be devastating when Détra returned and he learned he had lost the love he had found with her.

But even knowing all of that, she couldn't deny him her love. Isabel squeezed his hands, and instead of speaking, sought his mouth hungrily, desperately, trying to dispel the world surrounding them, to banish the ghosts haunting her, the myriad of problems they would still have to face.

But not now, not this very instant, not while Hunter held her in his arms and kissed her back with no less desperation or passion. He drove her against the wall, rubbing his growing arousal against her. His hands caressed her breasts, pinching the nipples between his fingers. He lifted her legs and she wrapped them around his hips, her heart tightening in her chest.

Burrowing her hands underneath his shirt, Isabel trailed her fingernails up and down his back. She bit his chin, and licked the underside of his throat. Nibbled on his earlobes, then darted her tongue inside his ear.

Hunter shuddered and made a motion to move back to the cot.

"No, Hunter," she said. "Please, right here, right now." She couldn't wait, wouldn't wait a moment longer to be one with him again.

Hunter fumbled with the ties of his pants, then poised at her entrance, he whispered against her mouth, "I love you," and thrust deep inside of her.

The world swirled around Isabel and her thoughts scattered as he plunged deeper and faster. Her body became a mass of sensations and emotions too overwhelming to bear until, in an explosion of release, her cries joined his in the echoing walls of his private room.

Slowly Isabel floated back, but before reality intruded, she whispered against his ear, "I love you too, Hunter."

A thrill of joy skittered down Hunter's spine at Détra's longed-for words of love, the first time Détra professed her love for him made even sweeter coming in the wake of his confession of deceit to her.

Emotion clogged Hunter's throat. Naught he could say could surpass this magical moment and thus he tightened his hold of her in silent joy.

When he thought he had enough strength back, he withdrew from her and to his delight she moaned in disappointment. He carried her to the cot and brought her down with him. She lay on top of him, her head resting on his chest and her beautiful curls in wild disarray over their bodies as their breathing attained a more tranquil rhythm.

The distant, cold woman he had wedded was a far cry from this passionate, vibrant, loving woman he held in his arms and in his heart. But even more unimaginable, she had surpassed his idealized dream of her. Hunter now realized that the love he held for Détra of his youth paled in comparison to the love he felt for her now.

It was almost as if she was three very distinct women. The one of his youth, the one he wedded, and the one he loved. He was fortunate enough to finally have found the true Détra.

Hunter's only regret was that she could not have the memories of her past. And yet, mayhap leaving her memories behind was what had allowed her to become the new Détra she was now.

Hunter shrugged aside his convenient reasoning. He could not be more pleased with her change or with the fact she had finally accepted the chalice was no longer available to her. He loved her too much to even consider risking her getting hold of the chalice that could transform his lady wife into her old self. He knew it was selfish of him, but he would do naught to jeopardize Détra's acceptance of him.

He sent a silent prayer of thanksgiving to Heaven that he had looked over his shoulders this morning when he was leaving the castle walls. Had he not done that, he would not have seen Détra dashing across the bailey to the garrison's quarters. He would not have followed her and confronted her. He would not have unburdened his conscience of the truth. And he would not have heard her declaration of love.

Oh, how glad he was that he did!

* * *

MAKING LOVE TO HUNTER HADN'T IN THE LEAST quenched her thirst for him. Isabel had a feeling she would never have enough of him. But now she wanted to be alone, wanted to think what she would do next. She told Hunter she didn't feel well and wanted to return to her room. Despite her protests he insisted on accompanying her back to the castle. As they crossed the bailey, her half lie gave rise to a full truth when her insides began to churn with pain and her lower back to ache.

Isabel realized immediately what ailed her.

Life wasn't miserable enough for her at this moment; she was also about to have her period, if she wasn't missing the telltale signs. She didn't even want to think what women used for sanitary pads in the medieval age, though she would soon find out.

The great hall was filled with people eating. Isabel hadn't realized the morning had wilted away. She saw Maude and Godfrey seated together, and felt bad that Maude left her place at the table and rushed in her direction immediately upon sighting her.

Such devotion intrigued and bothered Isabel. A particularly bad cramp tore at her at that moment, and she grimaced, wondering whether Maude would have a potion for PMS along with a ready supply of sanitary napkins.

"My lady, are you unwell?" Maude asked.

"I think I might be in need of your assistance," Isabel answered, "but you must finish your meal first."

"I am finished, my lady."

Isabel wasn't sure of that but she did need Maude's help. She turned to Hunter. "I will be fine with Maude."

He reluctantly nodded. "I shall be here or outside training with the men if you need me."

"You are no longer going on your trip?" she asked.

"It is too late to join my men. Not that I regret having remained behind." He smiled wickedly and kissed her, then turned and strode to the lord's table, as Isabel had heard the long table on a platform in the great hall was called.

What had made him change his mind in the first place? Isabel wondered as she followed his progress with her gaze. Had he seen her sneaking into the garrison's quarters? Isabel wanted to kick herself silly for being so careless, though she'd been sure he'd left already. Not that it would've mattered, anyway. The chalice wasn't in his private room, but at the bottom of a lake.

Isabel suppressed the despair threatening her again. She'd been single-minded about finding the chalice and reversing her wish, but now that it was lost to her, she wondered if the chalice might have held another answer to her problem. She didn't understand its powers, didn't know what it was capable of. She shook her head, dispersing the thought. No use in reaching for stars while she was securely chained to the earth.

She turned to Maude, who patiently waited for her, and together they took the stairs. As soon as they entered the bedroom, Maude asked, "What ails you, my lady?"

Not sure how modern words would translate, Isabel simply said, "It seems it is that time of the month for me." She almost rolled her eyes at her choice of words, feeling like an extinct dodo in some fantasyland.

"Are you in pain?"

Isabel nodded.

"I have a remedy for that."

It seemed Maude had a remedy for just about anything. Would that she had one to conjure up lost magic chalices.

"You are very efficient," Isabel said, watching Maude prepare her a potion. "I am very appreciative of your efforts."

Maude smiled and handed her a cup. "You taught me all I know about the healing herbs, my lady."

Isabel gulped down the contents of the cup without hesitation while Maude fussed inside the big leather trunk, then returned with several strips of cloth.

"I made some new ones for you," she said as she handed Isabel what looked suspiciously similar to modern sanitary pads. They were longer and wider at the ends, and of course, made of several layers of linen or some other soft fabric. Lacking the adhesive strips of their modern counterparts, the pads had strings attached to their four ends, which Isabel assumed would be for tying around the hips to keep the pad in place. It amused her that even after centuries would pass sanitary pads would not evolve much. At least not in principle.

"Mayhap soon you shall have no more need for these," Maude said.

For a moment Isabel didn't understand what Maude was trying to say, but when it became clear, she gasped. Isabel and Hunter had made love several times during the past days without using any birth control. Obviously pregnancy had not happened, considering her current need for the sanitary pads. But had it happened, how would Détra react to the news? She'd probably be furious. Détra wouldn't want to carry a child from a man she didn't love, a child conceived without her knowledge or participation, a child who would forever seal her fate with Hunter.

Isabel's heart ached with the longing for such a child, especially one with Hunter. The irony of it all! She, who'd tried everything to conceive and failed, must now find ways to prevent conception. She couldn't make such an important decision for another woman, and she couldn't bear losing a child again. To lose Hunter would be hard enough.

Appalled, Isabel realized what she must do.

"Maybe I am not ready to be a mother just yet," Isabel lied, knowing she couldn't be more ready.

Surely women in the Middle Ages practiced some kind of birth control. Apart from the unreliable coitus interruptus and the rhythm methods, which would need Hunter's agreement, what other contraceptive was available to the women of the Middle Ages?

Isabel eyed Maude cautiously. If there were some kind of herb or potion to prevent pregnancy her maid would know about it. But how would she approach Maude with such a sensitive subject?

"I would like to have my memories back before having a child."

"What if your memories never return?" Maude asked.

"I have a feeling they will, eventually. As a matter of fact, Hunter has opened the door to my past by telling me of my earlier feelings for him," Isabel said.

"He did?" Maude seemed surprised.

"Yes, he even told me why he had lied. It seems I did not care much for him then."

"But you care for him now, do you not?"

"Yes, but let us not forget about Rupert. He could ruin everything between Hunter and me."

"My lady, you are not considering telling Lord Hunter, are you?"

"No, I have no intention of telling him about Rupert. That would serve no purpose at this point, but all the same, I would rather not conceive a child until I am certain this situation will not come back to haunt me later."

Maude was silent.

Too silent!

"Can I have children?" Isabel asked abruptly. If Détra was as barren as she was the matter would be moot, and she wouldn't have to approach Maude with a request for birth control potions.

Maude shrugged her shoulders. "Only God is privy to that knowledge."

Why was Maude being so reticent? Was she hiding something too? God, could anyone in this place tell the truth? Immediately Isabel realized how hypocritical that thought was.

"I have been married before," Isabel said. "And yet, no children. Is this an act of God, or have I manipulated the situation a little?"

"My lady," Maude tried to reason, "do you conceive a child now with your husband there shall be no haunting ghosts in your future."

Maude couldn't be more wrong. And because Maude wouldn't give her a straight answer, Isabel knew Détra had not left anything to chance.

"If I wished to wait a while to conceive," Isabel insisted. "How would I go about doing that?"

Maude hesitated for the longest moment, and then she let out a sigh of frustration. Clearly Maude didn't approve of what Détra did and Isabel was going to do. "There are ways . . ."

"What ways?"

"Well, jumping up and down after the deed is thought to be very effective."

Isabel looked at Maude in disbelief. She couldn't be serious. But Maude held her gaze with tremendous fortitude, not a hint of a grin on her face. She was serious!

Repressing a laugh, Isabel asked, "Anything else?"

"I was told that you should undulate your hips during the deed, and kneel down and sneeze after."

Isabel liked the undulating hips part, but surely not as a birth control. "I was thinking more on the lines of a medicinal remedy."

"Bloodletting is also a common practice," Maude suggested.

Isabel knew sooner or later bloodletting would make an appearance. She would have to be more direct in her inquiry.

"Do you know of a potion that could prevent pregnancy?"

That firmly silenced Maude's babbling. And Isabel instinctively knew Maude was hiding something.

With her fingers underneath the maid's chin Isabel lifted her face. "What is it, Maude? I hope you can trust me with whatever is bothering you."

The maid sighed. "The concoction you already drink every morning, my lady, prevents a baby from forming in your womb."

Isabel was momentarily stunned into silence.

"Why did you not tell me that from the beginning instead of all that silliness?" she asked.

"I thought it might change your mind about having Lord Hunter's child."

It was obvious Maude wanted her to get pregnant, wanted her to be happy with Hunter. The thought warmed her insides. Someone was rooting for her. Rooting for Détra, her mind cruelly reminded her.

But it didn't seem reasonable to expect Détra to change her mind. Even before her marriage to Hunter had been consummated she had already figured out all. Détra might want to return to her own life, but not in a million years would she accept Hunter as her husband or a child from him.

The thought soured Isabel's already knotted stomach. The last thing she wanted in the world was Hunter's unhappiness. But when she left, that would be exactly what he would get.

Chapter 16

A week had gone by since they'd arrived from Hawkhaven Castle, since she learned the truth of what really happened that fateful morning she woke up in Détra's body, since she learned the chalice was lost to her.

In a bizarre sort of way, the many pieces of the puzzle had fallen into place. And yet, despite that knowledge, or maybe even because of it, Isabel's situation had become even more difficult to bear. It was hard to be the guardian of the truth, caught in the middle of two worlds, two lives, living on borrowed time.

With the chalice out of her reach, Isabel expected to be yanked out of Hunter's life at any given time, maybe in a most inopportune time, like when she was making love to Hunter. The uncertainty of her situation was fraying her nerves in such a way she had cried on his shoulder last night. Cried, for goodness' sake, after making love with the man she loved.

Poor Hunter was totally baffled at her behavior. He could never in a million years guess the reasons for her tears. Maude had wanted to give her a calming potion, but Isabel had refused. Not even Valium could make any difference. Besides, even though Isabel had discovered the wonders of alternative medicine, she was already relying on it too much. Migraine, PMS, and the big one, birth control. Every day was a struggle between her conscience and her heart. Wanting a child so badly and knowing she could have it tore her apart. What difficult choices one had to make in life!

Belying the urgency gnawing inside, Isabel descended the stairs into the great hall with an unhurried step. It was almost supper time and she had spent today like the days before, trying her best to learn more about castle life, finally realizing there wasn't much she could or wanted to do to occupy her time.

In frustration she had delegated Détra's duties to more competent hands. From the kitchen cooks and helpers to the servants that kept the castle clean and functioning, to Godfrey who oversaw everything as its steward, to Maude, whom Isabel had elevated to healer of almost every wound, everyone seemed very diligent about their duties.

She knew the castle wouldn't fall into shambles without her input; on the contrary, she'd probably do more harm than good if she tried her hand at housekeeping, or more appropriately, castlekeeping.

Discounting the year she'd been married and the cottage she'd inherited from her grandmother, Isabel had never even owned a house. House, apartment, flat, hotel room—all had been places to live in for a while and then leave behind as she moved on.

Like she would eventually do with this place.

Every time life hadn't conformed to her wishes in the past, Isabel had moved on, leaving behind her troubles. But trapped within the confines of these walls in a situation she wouldn't have consciously chosen, with the outcome beyond her control, Isabel knew this time she couldn't run. And even if she could, she wouldn't be able to leave her troubles behind. She would forever carry with her the memory of Hunter, her love for him, the dream that could have been but never was.

Isabel's heart rebelled at being forced to accept she would lose Hunter one way or another, by her hands or Détra's. And every time she dwelt on the impossibility of her situation, her mind went back to the chalice, to the magic powers of the chalice. Like a sinking ship, she was ready to hold on to any possibility, minute as it was, for survival.

The chalice had to hold the answer. But with it in the depths of a lake what good would it do her?

Isabel feared another migraine if she persisted on dwelling on such an insoluble situation. Good God, how she missed painting. In times of troubles, in times of joy, her painting had been an integral part of her life, and yet even that had been stripped from her.

Suddenly remembering the writing supplies she'd seen in the war room a few days ago, Isabel crossed the still empty hall in that direction, a new sprint added to her step at the prospect of spending a few hours drawing.

She needed that distraction badly and she couldn't believe she hadn't thought of it before.

She opened the door to the war room and found Godfrey inside, but instead of pouring over a ledger as she'd expected, the man sat at what looked conspicuously like a drawing table. How had she missed that before?

"My lady." Godfrey jerked to his feet, visibly unsettled by her presence. "I did not expect to see you here." He lowered his hands alongside his body, as if to hide his ink-stained fingers from her view, as he stepped in front of the drawing table.

"What are you working on?" she asked, peeking over his shoulders to the drawing table where a small piece of parchment, no bigger than a four-by-six sheet, was held in place by the tip of a small knife. A beautiful decorative border depicting angels decorated the page and in the middle of it, a half-completed text, written in Latin.

Each letter was drawn with careful thought and detail, some with a flourishing swirl upward, others downward, but all the same size. The first letter of the paragraph, however, received a special treatment in intricate pattern, size, and color to distinguish it from the rest of the letters.

Isabel didn't understand Latin, but she knew a little Italian, and the first verses were pretty easy to surmise.

Ave Maria, gratia plena: Dominus tecum. . . .

Hail Mary, full of grace: our Lord is with thee. . . .

A prayer book! Isabel's mouth fell open as she witnessed the creation of medieval art. She'd seen pictures of it, but this was the real thing, in real time. Goose bumps spread over her body and her heart sang with joy.

"I am not derelict in my duties, my lady." Godfrey was still explaining himself. "The ledgers are done for this day and I have finished with the tallying for the week and—"

Isabel waved his explanations away with a motion of her hand and picked up one of the parchments on the floor. That such a beautiful work would eventually be lost to the world saddened her almost to tears.

What a terrible loss that would be!

"Is this your work?" she asked, in awe of it, aware of

the degree of attention and talent needed to do such small paintings and writings.

"I can explain, my lady," he stuttered. "I know you told me to destroy it, but—"

"Destroy it?" Isabel cried, jerking back and glaring at him as if he'd gone insane. Was Détra mad to order such an incredible work of art destroyed? By the look of surprise on Godfrey's face, Isabel realized she'd spoken too fast and with too much vehemence.

She collected her temper. "And yet you did not."

"Forgive me, my lady," Godfrey said. "I should have never presumed to gainsay an order from you. I just—"

Godfrey didn't seem to find the right words to explain his actions, and yet Isabel understood him well. Had he even a drop of appreciation for art in his heart, he couldn't have destroyed this work any more than she could have.

"Tell me," Isabel asked, "why do you think I gave you such an order in the first place?" She couldn't understand what would rattle Détra so much that she'd do such a thing.

Not knowing of her loss of memory, Godfrey eyed her oddly, obviously baffled by her question.

"Lord William commissioned the Book of Hours for you," he said as if that should be self-explanatory.

Ah! The good old Lord William again. After learning of the apple incident, Isabel doubted the man's good intention in doing something so nice for Détra. Obviously Détra thought the same and wanted nothing to do with anything associated with her former husband. Isabel couldn't blame her. God knew what other humiliation she'd suffered at the man's hands.

But to want to destroy such a beautiful work of art? Isabel couldn't allow such travesty.

"I will do as you ordered," Godfrey said, picking up the pile of parchments on the floor.

"Do not be hasty." Isabel took the parchments from his hands as she considered the ramifications of letting Godfrey in on her amnesia. Surely it couldn't make that much of a difference at this point. And it would help him understand her change of heart, for Détra would have a change of heart now.

"Remember a few days ago when you showed concern over my well-being?" Isabel asked, moving away from him and depositing the parchments on the table by the wall.

"I was assured you were well, my lady."

"I am," she said, turning to face him. "But that very morning I had suffered an accident that robbed me of my memories."

"My lady." Godfrey rushed to her, pulling a chair for her to sit, as if she were sick or weak. "How could that be possible?"

"It is a mystery," she said, refusing the chair. "But I am fine. No need to worry. I just do not seem to recall much of my life before the accident." She paused. Now that she'd explained her reaction, she'd have to explain her change of heart. "And I am sure I spoke in haste when I asked you to destroy the Book of Hours. Whatever were Lord William's intentions, it should not matter to me anymore. The man is dead, right?"

In bewilderment Godfrey stared at her, then nodded.

"I am glad you did not destroy it, Godfrey," Isabel said in further reassurance.

Relief relaxed the muscles on Godfrey's face. "Would you allow me to continue to work on it?" he asked tentatively.

"Absolutely."

His face broke into a big smile. "Thank you, my lady. Thank you. I am certain you will be pleased with the work once it is done and I vow not to allow it to interfere with my duties to Windermere Castle. They shall always come first."

Isabel nodded. "I am sure of that." She paused. "Maybe I can help you with your work."

"With my duties?"

She shook her head. Not exactly! "With the book." That was a chance of a lifetime. And though she had no experience with that kind of work, it would be just glorious to be able to try her hand at something new.

Godfrey hesitated. "I mean not to discourage you, my lady, but scribing and illuminating are difficult tasks."

He didn't seem to have much trust in her artistic talents. Obviously Détra wasn't interested in that kind of work, though she seemed efficient enough in just about everything related to the keeping of the castle. At this point, Isabel had ceased to worry about discrepancies between Détra's behavior and hers. It was obvious everyone should have noticed by now a distinctive difference between the two women. Besides, she'd already gone out of her way, even at her own peril, not to cause Détra trouble. She needed to do this for herself.

"I am well aware of that, Godfrey," Isabel said. "I just feel inspired of late to pursue different interests. Besides, it cannot be any more difficult than the intricate patterns of embroidery I am used to doing." Though she knew nothing could be further from the truth, she spoke with conviction to allay Godfrey's doubts.

The look on his face told Isabel she hadn't succeeded, but to his credit he didn't roll his eyes or contradict her.

Ah! The advantages of being the lady of the castle.

"I offer my assistance with the inscriptions," he said. "But I confess I have little talent with the illuminations. Brother Gene did all of those before he passed away."

Isabel picked up the parchments again and skimmed through the pile, realizing the illustrations, or illuminations as Godfrey called them, were finished.

Disappointment filled her.

Godfrey must have noticed it for he said, "There is still the cover leaf to be done. Mayhap my lady would like to paint a picture."

Isabel's overburdened heart gave a leap of joy.

"I most definitely would." She hadn't done any painting in weeks and she was feeling the effects of withdrawal. Besides, she needed an outlet for all the worries in her heart; otherwise she would explode with frustration. God knew painting was Isabel's most cherished gift. She wouldn't turn away from such a pleasure.

"I will need your help with the supplies," Isabel said.

Godfrey nodded. "I have some colors already prepared, my lady, but if you need others, I shall provide them to you."

"Excellent!" Isabel couldn't help the excitement rushing over her. She needed that, badly indeed!

"Mayhap we should begin on the morrow?" he asked. "The day grows old and the light of candles and oil lamps might not be enough."

Isabel wouldn't hear of postponing such pleasure until the next day. She wanted to start immediately. "I would like to get a head start," she said, already deciding in her mind what would be the most appropriate image for the cover of a Book of Hours.

WONDERING IF HE WOULD FIND DÉTRA PORING OVER the ledgers in the war chamber, since there was where Maude said he could find her, Hunter crossed the hall with large strides.

Since she had found out the chalice was out of her reach, Détra's mood had been rather frazzled. Not that he could blame her—she had been through quite an ordeal in the past few weeks—but Hunter hoped she would return to her duties and therefore find some contentment in her new life.

He knew, however, through Maude, that Détra struggled in performing the duties that came so easily to her in the past, and that in frustration she had delegated them to others. Clearly, her lack of memories was taking a heavier toll on her than Hunter had thought.

Guilt speared him. It was his fault she could not remember, his wish that had provoked such a change in her. If she was unhappy with her life, how could she be happy with him?

Only the chalice could change that. Did he have the right to keep it from her?

Mayhap Détra would still find something to occupy her time and mind. He opened the door to the war chamber and found her bent over a table, totally entranced with her work. She did not even notice his presence until he stood beside her.

She lifted her gaze from the parchment to him. "Hunter," she said, breathless as if she had been running. Her eyes glowed and a smile of pure joy shone on her face.

"What do you do?" he asked.

"I paint." With undisguised pride she showed the beautiful painting of Our Holy Mother Mary she was working on.

It was beautiful, indeed. "I knew not you were interested in idle pursuits such as painting."

The smile disappeared from her face and, frowning, she jerked to her feet. Immediately Hunter realized her displeasure. What had he said to vex her thus?

"Idle pursuit? Is that what you think this is?" She glared at him.

Hunter glanced at the painting again, recognizing her gift, and then at the many parchments on the table, realizing that together they would compile a Book of Hours. "I mean no disrespect," he said, feeling at an utter disadvantage. He knew naught of artistic pursuits. "But I was unaware painting or prayer held any interest to you." He certainly had not seen her spend any time on either pursuit before.

Displeasure rose with the color of her cheeks. "You know me not at all," she accused.

Indeed that was a fact of which he was more and more aware as time passed. He knew little of the Détra of old and even less of this Détra of new.

There was no doubt in his mind and in his heart, however, which one he preferred.

Not since his mother's death had Hunter felt so cherished and loved, and he treasured the intoxicating feeling. He would not allow his lack of knowledge to destroy what he had found with Détra.

"Then help me know you better," he said. "And I shall endeavor not to displease you with my comments."

She sighed, sitting down at the stool. "I have no need for false praise. All I ask is that you do not dismiss as inconsequential something that is very important to me."

He picked up the pile of parchments on the table and inspected them.

"I did not do those," she said.

He nodded, then looked at the illumination she was working on. Immediately he could see a subtle difference. Hers was more vivid, more real, with more feeling. For that was how Détra was. She had turned from a withdrawn, hostile wife, into a loving, attentive one. A wife with no qualms about touching or kissing him no matter in whose presence. A wife not ashamed of his humble beginnings.

Hunter's heart seemed to fill his chest. How he wished

he could make some enlightened comment about her wonderful work.

"I am just a warrior, Détra," he said simply. "But even I am in awe of such a gift."

She looked at him for a moment, judging his sincerity, and he withstood her stare, for he meant what he said. She smiled, and her whole face glowed with pleasure.

"I have no doubt of your valor as a warrior and I have been extremely pleased with your skill as a lover." She smiled wickedly at him. "Of course, it would be too much to expect an art connoisseur as well." She shrugged her shoulders. "Perfection is, after all, overrated."

He would show her perfection. He pulled her into his arms and kissed her. What could be more perfect than the two of them together?

THEY WALKED HAND IN HAND INTO THE GREAT HALL and sat at the lord's table. They had shared a meal there several times in this past week, and only a few curious gazes still lingered on them.

Serving wenches brought small basins with water so they could wash their hands, then in the absence of a priest, Hunter broke the bread with a prayer of thanksgiving so everyone could finally eat.

The meal progressed amid animated conversation in a joyous atmosphere that Hunter had seen only recently in his hall. When he had first arrived in Windermere he had found the castle and its people immersed in such gloominess, he had thought at first he was the cause. Later, he had learned that the oppressive life William, their former lord, had pressed upon them had been the true culprit of their unhappiness. That they now seemed freer, happier, pleased Hunter immensely. He felt a measure of pride for his contribution.

Even Détra, who had been in a morose mood this past week, seemed to be enjoying herself this night.

Hunter was pleased Détra had found a distraction after all.

After supper, Godfrey played the lute, stringing along a love song. Hunter had the impression he was singing to Maude. Were they sweet on each other?

When the strands of the melody died, Godfrey turned to Détra and asked, "Mayhap our lady would enthrall us with her enchanting voice."

Everyone in the great hall lifted an expectant gaze to Détra, and so did Hunter. He had heard her singing a long time ago at Hawkhaven and he had never forgotten that day. She had an angel's voice.

But at the horrified look on Détra's face, Hunter frowned. Surely it could not be modesty what prevented her from rising and entertaining them with her voice. Détra had not a bashful bone in her body. Besides, she had showed him the illumination of Our Holy Mother Mary with unabashedly pride.

Why would she balk at singing when her talent was evident?

Uncertainty rose again in his mind. There was so much about Détra's change he did not understand. Détra had forgotten how to ride a horse or tend wounds, and knew not how to embroider or make candles, according to Maude. And yet she painted beautifully when she had never done before, loved apples when she had detested them before, and loved him when she had hated him before.

Even the way she walked and spoke, the way she smiled, the way she looked at him, made him think of a completely different person. He could not comprehend such changes in connection with loss of memory. One did not forget certain aspects of life.

And yet Détra had. His doubts resurfaced.

"You need not sing, if you do not wish," Hunter said. "They will understand, however much they long to hear your beautiful voice."

Beautiful voice! That was one thing Isabel had never possessed.

Daughter to two singer/musicians, her parents had expected her to be able to sing, but no matter how hard she'd tried she could hardly hold a note.

Finally her parents had accepted her talents lay elsewhere. Isabel had embraced her painting with undisguised relief, though in the back of her mind she often wondered whether her relationship with her parents would've been closer had she been able to sing.

And now these people expected her to sing for them? Of course, Isabel realized she was in possession of Détra's voice, not hers. And by Hunter's accounts the woman could sing. And yet, Isabel didn't know any medieval songs.

"I do not remember any songs," she said.

Hunter nodded, then addressed the people at the hall, "My lady feels unwell to sing this night."

There was an audible noise of disappointment. Isabel had offered that same excuse so many times already to avoid doing something she was inept at that these people must think her the biggest sissy alive—a sure contrast to the Détra of old.

Something odd stirred inside of Isabel. It wasn't exactly jealousy but an emotion she couldn't quite define. She didn't want to one-up Détra, she wanted to know what it felt to have the voice to sing, to enthrall people with a song like her mother had done, if only this one time.

Gathering her courage, she went through several songs in her mind, discarding one after the other, even though she knew anything she sang would sound weird to them. Finally she settled on an old song her mother used to love—"Coming In and Out of Your Life," sung by Barbra Streisand.

With butterflies fluttering in her belly, she rose and everyone's attention turned to her. Hunter cocked his head and he smiled reassuringly at her.

"I will try a new song," she said. "One you probably have not heard before. I hope you will like it."

She took a deep breath and fixed her gaze on Hunter who pulled his chair back to better look at her. And then she began singing, at first tentatively, then with more assurance as she realized Détra's foreign voice was indeed very beautiful and very melodious.

The heartfelt lyrics, lyrics only someone in the throes of an impossible love could truly appreciate, spoke of loving someone you must leave, of having found the greatest love of your life knowing it couldn't last, of lies and secrets and good-byes. It was her feelings, her emotions out in the open for all to see. Until now she hadn't understood the poignancy of the old melody.

When the last words came out of her mouth, tears rolled out of her eyes, and utter silence blanketed the great hall.

Hunter rose and took her hands into his. He heard her emotional outpouring, but did he understand she was saying good-bye? Did he understand that every minute she was with him she would be saying good-bye?

"I love you," she whispered.

Hunter squeezed her hands into his, not knowing why her words of love were filled with such sorrow. His heart constricted. Détra should not be sad, loving him should not hurt her, and her lack of memories should not make her feel incomplete.

Deus! What had he done to his lady wife by withholding the chalice, and therefore her memories?

A disturbance at the front doors distracted Hunter. He turned and one of his men-at-arms rushed in accompanied by a stranger. Nay, not a stranger, Hunter realized, stiffening, but the same messenger who days ago had brought him Lord Reginald's summons.

What did Rupert want?

"My lord." The man bowed before him. "Hawkhaven is under attack. You must come to our aid immediately."

He was under no knightly obligation to Rupert. The vow Hunter had made to his father to protect Rupert had been made on the assumption Lord Reginald would reveal his father's name. He had not, and thus Hunter need not respond to Rupert's summons.

Gervase came to stand beside Hunter, waiting for his command.

"My lord," the messenger continued, noticing his reluctance. "Lord Rupert was not in the castle when the Scots were sighted this morning. Messengers were sent to different locations to try and find him, but he might not return in time. We are undermanned at this moment. We need your help. Please, you cannot refuse our plea."

"Who sent for me?" Hunter asked.

"Sir Thomas."

Hunter had always liked Thomas, Hawkhaven's premier knight, since Hunter was a young squire, and he and the people of Windermere held no blame for Hunter and Rupert's animosity.

"Gervase," Hunter called. "I want you to remain behind, in case this is not an isolated attack. We are close enough to Hawkhaven to be in danger." He then listed a few names he wanted to accompany him. "Have the men ready to leave at my command."

He turned to Détra. Her face was a mask of worry. "You shall be safe here," he said.

"But what about you, Hunter?"

"I am a warrior, Détra. I know a little bit more about battles than I know of paintings." He smiled to reassure her.

"I must make preparations." He kissed her, then with his mind already on the upcoming battle, Hunter left the great hall for the garrison's quarter, where Jeremy would help him don his hauberk and collect his weapons.

He saw Détra again in the torch-lit bailey where his men gathered, waiting for his signal to leave. She stood on the front steps of the castle, looking more beautiful in a glowing gold dress than he had ever seen her. Bringing his destrier close to the bottom of the steps, he kissed her good-bye.

"Pray for my safe return, my lady wife."

"I have something for you," she said and tied a green veil with golden threads on his mailed arm. "Promise me you will come back to me, Hunter."

He pulled her close to him and kissed her again. Knowing she would be here waiting for him gave him the strength to leave her.

"Wait for me, my lady wife. I shall come back to you."

Chapter 17

AFTER a restless night, half spent in vigil, Isabel woke up at dawn break. Staring up at the canopy of her bed, she remained unmoving for a while, her thoughts on Hunter. Isabel was not one to pray but she had spent half the night begging protection for Hunter of every angel and saint known to her.

With a heavy heart she rolled her head to the side and clutched the sheets in the empty space beside her. While she lay here warm and safe Hunter was putting his life in danger.

Jerking the covers aside, Isabel rose. Hunter's safety, though a priority, was only one of her worries. While she impotently waited for her life to unravel, Détra could be at this very moment finding a way to return to her own body.

Isabel hated this uncertainty. Hated that she was at the mercy of Détra's will, and above all hated the thought she might not see Hunter again, might never know what happened to him.

A sharp pain squeezed her heart at the thought. Isabel shook her head, as if by doing so, she could scatter away her worries. As she came around the bed, she saw Maude preparing her morning drink. Quickly donning a chemise she found on top of her garment chest, Isabel walked to the table.

"I am so worried about him, Maude."

"He is in God's hands, my lady."

Maude's fatalism shook Isabel. She had always believed in free will and making her own choices and forging her own path, and yet she had been ready to accept that she could do nothing to change her fate. Hunter's life might be in God's hands, but she was sure he'd be fighting for it with every skill and every ounce of power he possessed. Why should she do differently with their fate and future? Her mind might have conceded fate had played a big part in what had happened to her, but her heart refused to accept she and Hunter could never be together.

Isabel didn't know who was the woman with Hunter in the vision of utter happiness the chalice had revealed. For all she knew it could be her. After all, what she'd learned of Détra surely indicated it wouldn't be her. Of course, Isabel couldn't be sure Détra wouldn't have a change of heart once she returned and fulfill Hunter's heart wish after all.

God forgive her, but *she* wanted to be the one to make Hunter happy. More and more, Isabel realized the answer to her plight must address the wishes of all of them— Hunter's, Détra's, and hers. And the chalice was the link between them.

But with the chalice safely buried in the depths of the

lake, her chances of getting to it would be less than finding a needle in a haystack.

Maude handled Isabel a cup, and at the first sip Isabel was swiftly reminded of the potion's use. Guilt, desperation, and longing mingled inside of her already overtaxed heart.

"Why did he have to go, Maude?" she asked. "It was not his castle under attack, he did not have to fight someone else's battles, especially not Rupert's." She knew she was being petty, but she didn't need this added complication to her situation. And of course were Hunter still here, nothing would've changed. Only that she might've found the courage to tell him the truth about herself, and together they could search for the chalice.

That is, if he didn't lock her in the tower, thinking she'd gone insane.

"My lady, Lord Hunter is a warrior who has survived bigger battles than this one. He is also an honorable man. He fostered at Hawkhaven. He knows most of the people there. He would not have refused their plea for help."

"What if he knew of what went on between Rupert and me? Would he still have gone?"

"Oh, my lady, let us pray he shall never find that out."

Maude was right. If that secret came out, no one would benefit from it. But even without knowing it, a confrontation between Hunter and Rupert might still happen. There was no lost love between the two men, on account of Rupert's father. And despite what Isabel had made herself believe she wasn't totally convinced Rupert had accepted their affair was over.

"I do not like Hunter in the midst of a battle and I sure do not like that he is at Hawkhaven with Rupert. Something tells me I should not trust him."

Maude was conspicuously silent. Isabel turned to her

and under her questioning gaze, Maude finally said, "You should have never trusted him."

Something in Maude's voice made Isabel wonder. She lowered the cup to the table. "Do you know something about Rupert that I should be aware of?"

Maude shook her head. "I know the Lord's commandment says, 'Thou shalt not bear false witness against thy neighbor,' but I never trusted Lord Rupert." And then almost as an afterthought she added, "He was present at the hunting outing where Lord William died."

Was Maude implying Rupert had anything to do with William's death? Even if Rupert had the motive and opportunity to kill Détra's former husband, would he have done so? Had he wanted Détra that badly? Isabel's heart sank. Would he kill Hunter to have Détra now?

There must be another explanation. Isabel couldn't bear the thought she might've sent Hunter to a killer's lair without warning. "Rupert could not have been the only one at that hunting outing."

"He was the only one who pursued the widow not a day after the husband was buried," Maude said. "Not that anyone mourned Lord William's death. Still . . ."

"You should have told me about your suspicions, Maude. I could have at least warned Hunter of the extra danger that might be awaiting him at Hawkhaven."

"And what would you have said, my lady?" Maude asked. "Would you have told Lord Hunter the truth?"

If she'd had to choose between Hunter's safety and Détra's secret, she would've had no doubt which one she'd choose.

"He must never learn of your secret, my lady," Maude insisted.

Isabel was surprised at Maude's vehemence. "Are you thinking of my reputation or my future with my husband?"

"Both are important to me and everyone in Windermere, but it is not only your happiness at stake here, my lady. Lord Hunter has a gentle soul in the heart of a warrior. We respect his strength and his kindness. Unlike your former husband, Lord Hunter will protect and care for you and for Windermere's people."

Having lived a very independent life, Isabel had never considered how closely interlaced these people's lives were. They depended on Hunter for protection, for guidance, for justice. They relied on their lady for stability, encouragement, and harmony.

If Isabel remained here, could she fill their needs? Did she even want the responsibility? Amazingly the thought didn't frighten her as much as it once did. Though it was a moot point until she knew whether she would remain here or not. And she wouldn't know for certain until she either found the chalice or Détra returned on her own.

As Maude helped her dress, Isabel broached the subject with her. "I was considering a little walk by the lake this morning. Would you like to come with me?"

Maude looked oddly at her. "How do you know of the lake? It is hidden from view."

Damn it! If she couldn't see the lake from the castle and she wouldn't remember it, how could she know about it? Then again, why would Maude question her about it? The maid hadn't questioned her actions before.

"Hunter told me about it," Isabel said truthfully.

"It would be foolhardy to go outside the castle gates, my lady, considering the Scots are but a day's ride from Windermere."

The lake wasn't far from the castle, less than a mile if Isabel remembered well. They could be back in about an hour. Isabel was hoping Hunter had thrown the chalice on the edges of the lake near the place she'd found it in the future. That would be her only chance of finding it.

"I shall take the risk," Isabel said. "You do not need to come with me."

"I mean no disrespect, my lady. You have changed much since the morning you lost your memory—"

"I do feel like a totally different person," Isabel agreed.

"That is why . . ." Maude hesitated. "It is not my place . . ."

Maude shook her head and moved away.

Isabel wasn't sure what kind of relationship Maude had had with Détra before, but the maid was the closest to a friend Isabel had ever had, and she wanted to know what so distraught her.

Isabel followed her. "Speak your mind without fear."

"You used to meet Lord Rupert by the lake."

The air whooshed out of Isabel's lungs. "Good God, Maude! I am not looking for Rupert, if that is what you are thinking. I have no interest whatsoever in that man. I go to the lake because Hunter told me there is where the chalice I seek is. I asked you about it some time ago, do you remember?"

At Maude's nod, Isabel continued, "I believe the chalice is magical and can bring back my memories." That was all Maude needed to know for now.

"There are many bad memories in your past, my lady. Are you certain you want to find them? You have found joy with Lord Hunter, have you not?"

"Yes, but—"

"Please, do not put your happiness in jeopardy."

"My happiness will be in constant jeopardy if I do not find the chalice." Isabel paused. "I know you cannot understand this now, and I hope that one day I will be able to explain it to you, but for now I ask that you trust me. That you believe I have Hunter's best interest at heart. I love him, Maude."

"Then why do you prevent his child from growing in your womb?"

What could she say to that? Guilt and regret and longing tore at her heart.

She must have looked stricken, for Maude immediately apologized. "Please forgive me, my lady. It is not my place to dispute your decisions. And I do not, but I care for you and for Lord Hunter and I do not wish to see the hard-earned understanding between you two destroyed by yet another secret."

"And neither do I," Isabel said. "But I need this chalice, and with or without your help I will go to the lake to search for it."

With a long-suffering sigh, Maude nodded agreement.

THE MORNING WAS BEAUTIFUL, THE SKY BLUE, THE SUN shining, the birds singing, and a soft breeze blowing about in a total mirror image of Isabel's inner turmoil. How could the day be so radiant when her life was falling apart?

With the gates closed until Hunter's return, Isabel had a hard time convincing Sir Gervase of the wisdom of her short excursion. She finally wore him down. Guarded by two men-at-arms, her little entourage found its way to the lakeshore on a healing herb exploration—Maude's brilliant excuse.

The lakeshore had changed much, or more appropriately, in the future it would change much. Where in the future there'd been a clearing, now tall and dense trees grew all around the shore. Isabel couldn't even be certain of the exact spot she'd found the chalice in the first place. What was she thinking? She wouldn't find the chalice without knowing exactly where it was.

While Maude busied herself collecting plants to give

credence to her excuse, Isabel walked down the pebbled shore looking at the immensity of the lake with doleful thoughts. One of the guards accompanied Maude and the other followed Isabel at a distance. Although disliking being guarded and watched like a prisoner, Isabel understood the benefits of having a soldier protecting her.

She reached a bent near the lake and lowered herself to pick up a pebble when a shadow fell over her. She lifted her gaze to see Rupert standing before her.

Isabel swayed with the shock, and glancing over her shoulder, she discovered the guard was no longer in sight. Where in hell did he go?

"I asked your escort for a moment alone with you," Rupert said. "It has been much too long since we talked."

Isabel didn't like the sound of that. Did Rupert have people inside Windermere watching her? "What do you do here, Rupert? Do you not know your castle is under attack?"

"Attack?" To his credit he looked surprised. "Surely you are mistaken."

"There is no mistake. Hawkhaven is under attack from Scots raiders and Hunter is over there defending what is yours."

"It is just fitting then, for he holds what is mine." Rupert pulled her into his arms.

She struggled against his grip only to have him tighten his hold. "Let me go, Rupert," she demanded. "You have no right to touch me."

He cocked his head to the side, a bitter grin slashing his face. "How fickle is a woman's heart. Not long ago you reveled in my touch. Now that your husband has bedded you, you have changed your mind."

Not wanting to infuriate him further, she said nothing.

"What would you say if I told you of your husband's spurious nature?"

"I will not listen to you bad-mouth a man who is not here to defend himself."

"Not bad-mouthing, my beloved, just speaking the truth. All Hunter has achieved in his life was obtained through witchery. Naught came to him through effort or deserves."

Taking her silence as encouragement, he went on, "There is a magical chalice—"

Isabel drew in her breath. What did Rupert know of it?

"Oh, I see you know of it. Is that what has changed your mind? You think to make use of the chalice for your own benefit? Tsk, tsk, Détra, Détra. What a conniving little bitch you are. So perfect for me."

Discarding the last vestiges of civilization, Rupert gripped her throat with one hand, bringing tears to Isabel's eyes. "Where is it?" he demanded.

"I do not know what you are talking about."

"I think you do. If you wish no harm to befall your beloved husband, you had better tell me where it is."

Gasping, she pulled at his hands. "It is at the bottom of the lake," she finally cried.

"You think me a fool, my beautiful Détra, but when I get hold of Hunter's source of power and fortune, we will see by whose side you would rather be." He kissed her harshly, then pushed her away.

Isabel stumbled and fell backward, her buttocks and hands smarting from the fall and the pebbles on the ground, and her throat and jaw still feeling the pressure of Rupert's fingers. As she watched him disappear in the woods, she realized how dangerous the man really was. And he was on his way to Hawkhaven. She needed to send Hunter an urgent message.

Rising to her feet, Isabel rushed back to where last she'd seen her guard, bitter words of reproach burning her tongue. And yet before she had a chance to speak, the guard smiled at her, a smug, knowing grin. He knew about Détra and Rupert, Isabel realized, and secure in that knowledge he didn't fear her reproach or that she might tell Hunter about him slacking on the job.

Seething, she stepped on his toes, then circumvented him. Out of nowhere someone jumped in front of her, scaring her witless. She spun around only to witness another assailant slit her guard's throat. The guard fell to the ground with merely a cry in a pool of his own blood.

Isabel's scream lodged in her throat. Sandwiched as she was between two savages, with the lake on one side and the woods on the other, she had to make a split-second decision. Lifting her skirts she dashed into the woods. She hadn't reached far when she was caught from behind and pushed to the ground. She hit her chin on a small rock, the pain shooting up her jaw as her breath swished out of her lungs with the impact and the weight of the man pinning her to the ground.

The man pulled a dizzy Isabel to her feet and threw her over his hard shoulder. Recovering some of her senses, Isabel fought her assailant, but to no avail. The man had arms the breadth of a tree trunk and held her firmly in place. A few moments later she saw the other guard who was supposed to be protecting Maude motionless on the ground. Of Maude, there was no sign.

Isabel's heart froze. Was Maude dead? She couldn't fathom even the thought. She looked at her captors, there were three of them, and tried to commit their faces to mind, with the exception of the one who carried her, whose face she couldn't see now. Were these men Scottish? They weren't dressed in kilts as Isabel had expected but a shirt reaching their knees and a mantle tied to one shoulder.

What could they want with her? Was Rupert involved with this?

In silence the man holding Isabel threw her over his horse like a sack of potatoes, a heavy hand on her back holding her down. He kicked the horse forward and Isabel's head bobbed and then began to swirl, fear and nausea an explosive mix. Hard as she fought she couldn't hold the bile sliding up her throat and she vomited over the horse's flanks, the man's legs, and the rapidly moving ground.

She closed her eyes and her ears to the expletive coming from her assailant's mouth.

THE BATTLE WAS OVER BEFORE IT HAD BEGUN.

Hunter and his men had arrived at Hawkhaven's outskirts at dawn after a hard ride through the night, catching the group of about thirty Scots by surprise and swiftly defeating them, despite being outnumbered.

Though naturally pleased with the results, Hunter was concerned. Apart from laying waste to the village there had been no indication the Scots expected to engage in battle. They had made no visible attempt to breach the castle's gates, scale its walls, or even dig a tunnel to allow their entrance into the castle they besieged. They had camped outside Hawkhaven as if in expectation of a tournament. Could they be waiting for reinforcements? Surely they knew the castle was undermanned.

Something was very amiss here. A sense of foreboding, not unlike what he had experienced a few times in battle, assailed him.

As Hunter and his men victoriously entered the open gates of Hawkhaven Castle, they were greeted with cheers of joy from the villeins and castle people alike in joyful celebration of their victory.

However, even as he dismounted and greeted Sir Thomas and received his many heartfelt thanks, Hunter could not shake the feeling of impending doom.

Rupert's absence, however blessed to Hunter and the very reason he had been summoned and had come to Hawkhaven's aid, seemed odd.

He intended to get to the bottom of it.

As soon as he was seated at the lord's table in the great hall with a tankard of ale in his hands, he asked Thomas, "What do you make of this attack?"

"I know not, my lord." The man looked as puzzled as Hunter felt. "With Lord Rupert and most of Hawkhaven's knights away we were in a predicament. That was why I summoned your help when Scots were sighted coming our way. I am as surprised as you are that they did not attack us immediately. Mayhap they were waiting for reinforcements or for direct orders from Robert the Bruce."

Hunter very much doubted the Scots would have come this far south without their king's knowledge or consent. "Have you sent word to Rupert?"

"Not quite certain of where to locate him," Thomas said. "But I sent messages to all the places I thought he would be."

"Therefore you are not certain he is even aware that his castle has been under attack?"

Thomas shook his head.

"Rupert left no indication of when he would return?"

"Nay, but he is often absent, my lord. This time, however, many other knights were absent also. Some are with Lord Rupert, others with King Edward."

Hunter understood the knightly fee every lord owed to the king, and how some chose to pay him with coin, while others with services. And yet, Rupert should not leave his castle undermanned or at least let his knights know where to find him. It was foolish of him. And yet, who knew what guided Rupert's mind?

"We shall remain here until the morrow, in case the Scots return with reinforcements. But by morning I must return to Windermere. I cannot leave my own holding unprotected."

"Thank you, my lord. We are very grateful for your intervention."

Hunter downed the rest of the ale, then rose. "I will check on my men. I suggest you post extra guards for the next days, at least until Rupert returns."

HUNTER WALKED TO THE STABLES. MOST OF HIS MEN were tending to their horses, but Jeremy was busy talking to a couple of boys. Seeing Hunter, Jeremy dismissed them and came to his encounter.

"What have you learned?" Hunter asked as they walked, for he knew that was what Jeremy was doing, gathering information.

"Lord Rupert seems to be absent from his castle quite often," Jeremy said.

"That means little. He has other holdings that require his attention."

"Aye, but he often cannot be found. It has happened in two previous occasions when his presence was needed at Hawkhaven."

Interesting, but not what Hunter was looking for. "Any facts to explain his absences?"

"Speculations, my lord."

"Let us hear them."

"It is said that Lord Rupert covets another lord's wife and that accounts for his sudden disappearances."

"Whose wife?"

"That no one knows."

Too simple, but just what Rupert would do. Rupert cared about himself and no one else. He would not think twice about cuckolding even his best friend, if he had a friend. "Anything else?"

Jeremy hesitated.

Hunter halted and eyed Jeremy curiously. The boy never held his tongue before; why would he now? "Out with it."

"John, one of the stable boys I talked to, overheard an interesting conversation between Lord Rupert and Edmund Toothless the very day you left Hawkhaven after Lord Reginald's burial."

Hunter's attention was piqued. "Who or what was the subject of that conversation?"

"You, my lord," Jeremy said. "You and your chalice."

Hunter's heart skipped a beat. "What do you know of that?"

"I have seen your chalice before," Jeremy revealed, and Hunter schooled his features not to show his surprise. He had thought no one but his mother, himself, and Détra knew of the chalice.

"You never spoke of it," Jeremy continued, "thus I understood I should not also. What I knew not, and Lord Rupert has also just found out, was that your chalice has some unnatural powers. Is that true, my lord?"

Damn Rupert to hell! It had always been thus between them—Rupert could not stomach that Hunter might have something he did not, especially if he believed the chalice had powers. The man would not rest now until he took the chalice from Hunter.

"Nonsense," Hunter said, resuming his walk and leaving a surprised Jeremy behind. "It is but a chalice my mother gave me before she died. It has sentimental value but no magical powers."

"Lord Rupert believes otherwise." Jeremy caught up

with Hunter. "If I were you, my lord, I would watch that chalice very closely from now on."

BEFORE DAWN ARRIVED ON THE FOLLOWING DAY, Hunter was up and ready to depart Hawkhaven. Jeremy joined him and Thomas to break their fast in the great hall, while his men ate in the garrison's quarters. Amid reiterated words of gratitude from Thomas, Hunter and Jeremy stepped outside into the dawning day.

An arrow hissed by Hunter's ears and he dove down, bringing Jeremy with him. Rolling over on the ground, Hunter shouted orders to his men, who had gathered, waiting for him, and they scattered about the bailey looking for cover and also for the unknown archer. From the viewpoint of the guards standing sentinel in the tower over the walls came the signals; there was only one man sighted and he was rapidly disappearing into the woods.

Hunter rose to his feet and ordered one of his men to give pursuit to the messenger. Jeremy picked up the arrow that had hit the stone wall and fallen onto the ground and gave it to Hunter. A parchment was attached to the shaft and tied up with a lady's ribbon. With cold hands Hunter untied the knot and opened the parchment.

He felt the blood drain from his face.

"What is it, my lord?" Jeremy asked.

"The Scots have Lady Détra," Hunter said, still not believing what he had just read.

"Fear not, my lord, we shall rescue her."

"Aye, that we shall." But the Scots wanted him alone and also his chalice. What would the Scots want with his chalice?

Chapter 18

THE pele tower was eerily silent and dark. Hunter halted at a safe distance and observed the battlement roof for any surprises. In the fading moonlight he saw naught, though he was certain a man hid there pointing a sharp arrow at him. Leading his horse and a mare for Détra, Hunter approached the square building with its thick walls and narrow second-floor windows, built to withstand short sieges.

Towers such as this abounded in the north of England in response to the constant Scottish raids onto English soil, and this particular one was in the lands of the powerful earl of Lancaster.

It looked to be empty.

A perfect hiding place.

Unchallenged, Hunter reached the only entrance to the tower, an iron-fortified wooden door on the ground floor.

He dismounted and pushed the door ajar. The gates to hell opened with a creaking sound.

He knew he would be walking into a trap but for the life of him he could not do it any differently. The note had demanded Hunter come alone, and he had, at least for the last part of the journey. Fearing for Détra's life, he ordered his men to stay a safe distance way.

Hand clenching the hilt of his sword, Hunter crossed the threshold into a dark room with no windows. The lone light of a torch glowed on the far wall. Beneath it, Détra sat on a stool, her hands tied to her back, her glorious hair in disarray, her mouth sealed with a cloth.

At the sight of him she jumped to her feet and the terror in her face told him he need not look over his shoulders to know they were not alone.

Two men stepped up behind him. Hunter could smell the sweat and dirt common to men in battlefields. They did not speak and Hunter did not turn to acknowledge their presence. He kept a reassuring gaze steadily on Détra to soothe her fears, though his insides coiled with emotions—relief she was alive, fury at the sight of dried blood on her swollen chin, and fear he would fail in saving her from the miscreants' hands.

"Fear not, my lady wife, all shall be well," he said, taking a step in her direction.

"Brave words for a man in your plight."

Hunter halted. His gaze settled on a man descending the last steps of a narrow staircase in the right corner of the tower. The man came to stand near Détra, his features shadowed. He was a big man and Scottish by the intonation of his voice.

Hunter had half expected to see Rupert here, or at least his lackey, Edmund Toothless. After his conversation with Jeremy at Hawkhaven and the ransom note demanding his presence and the chalice, Hunter had suspected Rupert was involved in Détra's abduction. And he might still be. Coward that he was, Rupert would have his minions do his dirty work for him, but a Scottish minion? Grave suspicions assailed Hunter.

Was there more about Rupert than Hunter could ever have imagined? He pushed the thought aside. Détra's safety was his priority now.

"A man who abducts defenseless women would know naught of courage," Hunter spat.

The Scot snorted. "What does an Englishman know of courage when even your king hides behind young lads' arses?" He laughed at his own crude insinuation of King Edward's penchant for boys, but Hunter refused to be drawn into such an inconsequential discussion.

At his silence, the Scot stepped closer to Détra. "Where is the chalice?" he demanded.

Détra's eyes widened in horror. She was probably thinking they were as good as dead now since Hunter would not be able to produce a chalice that should be at the bottom of the lake.

"Release my lady wife first."

The man laughed again, a ruthless, grating laugh. "You are in no standing to make demands, English. Give forth the chalice or I shall slit her pretty throat." The man pulled Détra's head backward by her hair, then slid his dagger underneath her chin.

Hunter's blood boiled with impotent anger. With effort he controlled his ire. He would not put Détra's life in more danger than it already was. He needed to bide his time. The odds of him winning a confrontation with three armed Scots were against him but not out of his reach, if he chose the right moment.

Slowly Hunter withdrew the chalice from the depths of the sachet he had brought with him and lifted it in the air, exposing its beauty to the Scot's sight.

Hunter glanced Détra's way. Her face was a mask of shock and disappointment, and pain speared his heart with the ease of a sharp dagger.

Now she knew he had lied to her again, and this time, he warranted, she would not be so willing to forgive him. Even though Détra had professed her love for him, even though she had changed in ways he could not even fathom, Hunter had feared the chalice would return her to her old self. And thus he had kept it away from her, hoping he would never have to reveal the chalice still existed. And yet, faced with the choice between his happiness and Détra's life, there had been no choice.

The Scot let go of Détra and she bounced back, almost falling to the floor. She caught herself and found her balance with difficulty. "So much trouble for a cup," the Scot said, reaching for it.

Before he could grab it, though, Hunter rammed the chalice up and into the man's face, hitting him square in the jaw, shoving him back and off his feet. Swiftly, Hunter unsheathed his sword and lunged at him, thrusting the blade deep into the man's chest. Spinning around he stood between the two other Scots and Détra, protecting her with his body.

As the attackers charged at him Hunter shouted at Détra to run to the door, moving in an arch and keeping her at his back. His sword slashed in the air and thrust forward, cutting through flesh and steel alike, keeping the attackers at bay until Détra reached the door.

From the corners of his eyes he saw her struggle to open the door that fortunately was unlatched and only closed. With her hands tied to her back, she used her foot to widen the gap, and then dashed through the aperture to freedom outside.

Hunter's relief was short-lived, however, for the momentary distraction almost cost him dearly. One of his attackers delivered a mighty blow to his shoulder. Hunter staggered back with the force of the impact, and though he knew the blade had not cut through his thick hauberk, pain reverberated through his shoulder down to his sword arm.

Smelling victory, both Scots lunged at him. Holding the hilt of his sword with both hands Hunter swiftly sprang to the side at the last moment, and with one vaulting thrust, the blade rented through one of his attackers' bellies like a knife through cheese. The momentum carried Hunter as he whirled around and buried the sword in the other attacker's neck, almost severing his head from his shoulders.

Blood sputtered in all directions, bathing Hunter in crimson. Panting, he gathered his breath, and with pain screaming in his shoulder he dashed outside after Détra.

The weak gray light of dawn was not strong enough to disperse the thick fog enveloping the clearing around the pele tower; neither could it reveal the identity of the man holding Détra captive in his arms.

Hunter's heart sank. Détra had not gotten away.

He lifted his sword, ready to fight yet another Scot, but men began appearing out of the mist and soon he was encircled in a fence of pointed swords.

Knowing he could not possibly fight his way out of so many assailants, Hunter lowered his weapon, but kept it in his hand, waiting for a better opportunity.

The man dragged Détra inside the circle and halted a few steps from him. Hunter had seen him before; even in the darkness he would recognize such a face. Détra had fallen into the arms of yet another Scot.

Only this time, she had fallen into the talons of the Scottish king, Robert the Bruce, himself.

*   *   *

FROM THE BATTLEMENT ABOVE, RUPERT WATCHED IN
dismay the appearance of Robert the Bruce. What was the
man doing here so early? He was not supposed to come
until the morrow. Bruce would spoil all his well-laid-out
plans. Rupert had dreamed of having Hunter beaten to an
inch of his life, stealing his magic chalice, and therefore
his good fortune, and then releasing the beautiful Détra
from the evil hands of the Scots and Hunter's talons.

Now Bruce would no doubt take both Détra and Hunter
hostage and demand high ransom for their return and Rupert would be left with naught.

Rupert watched as Bruce walked inside the protective
circle of his men, holding a struggling Détra by his side,
and stopped a few paces away from Hunter.

"Does she belong to you?" Bruce asked. His strong
voice streamed up to where Rupert hid.

"She is my lady wife," Hunter answered.

"Is that how the English treat their wives?" Bruce
asked, obviously referring to Détra being gagged and
bound.

"I have the Scots to thank for the ill handling of my
lady."

Bruce let go of Détra and she ran into Hunter's open
arms.

"No one in my service would manhandle a lady,"
Bruce said.

"Then you know not the men under your service,"
Hunter hissed as he removed Détra's gag and the ties on
her hands.

"Are you hurt?" were the first words out of Détra's
mouth as she touched Hunter's chest and face.

"Nay. It is not my blood you see, my lady. A bath
should take care of that. And you?" he asked.

She shook her head and embraced him tighter. Hunter
combed her hair back with his fingers, whispering in her

ears. Rupert's stomach churned. He had envisioned Détra seeking comfort in *his* arms, not the bastard's.

Then they stood side by side, arms interlaced, two lovers against the world. Rupert almost puked.

Bruce ambled to Hunter, inspecting him with detailed attention. "Your name?"

With an arm over Détra's shoulders, keeping her close to him, Hunter said, "Hunter of Windermere."

That was a distinct pause. "Formerly of Hawkhaven?"

Hunter nodded.

How did Bruce know of Hunter? What could this mean? Rupert leaned closer to the battlement, his ears attuned to every sound floating up to him.

"Come inside, I must speak with you," Bruce said. "Worry not about your lady. I give you my word"—he grinned—"and the word of a king should account for something—that your lady will not be harmed by my men."

As Bruce and Hunter entered the tower, Rupert scampered off the battlements and onto the stairs. He must listen to this conversation at all costs.

ROBERT THE BRUCE, KING OF SCOTLAND, ALBEIT UNrecognized by England, stepped over three Scottish bodies, inspecting them briefly before his men removed them, then sat on the same stool Détra had sat on when Hunter arrived.

"I know not one of them," he said. "But then again, I cannot know every man who fights under my banner. And not every Scot fights for me, as you should well know."

Bruce no doubt alluded to the dissenting factions still existent in Scotland and to the many Scotsmen fighting on King Edward's side.

But Hunter said naught. If Bruce expected to ply him

for military secrets in exchange for his and Détra's lives, he would be sorely disappointed. Even if Hunter were aware of King Edward's plans against Scotland, and he was not, he could never betray the king to whom he had sworn fealty. He must find another way to save Détra. He was a knight, a lord of his own holdings who would be able to pay a handsome ransom for their freedom. Bruce would be interested in that.

And yet Hunter was surprised Bruce was aware of his existence. "How did you know where I hailed from?" he asked.

"I know of you from a long time past," Bruce said.

Bruce's puzzling remark baffled Hunter. Could Bruce remember him from the battlefields? But that would not explain he knew Hunter was from Hawkhaven.

Bruce's gaze strayed to the floor, and seeing the chalice lying by the stool, he bent over and picked it up.

"It has been long since I last saw this."

Hunter's head snapped to attention. How could Bruce know of his chalice? Dread filled him to think that his chalice was somehow connected to the Scottish king. Was Bruce behind Détra's abduction?

Should he deny ownership of the chalice? In doubt, Hunter said naught.

Bruce stared at him. "I gave this chalice as a gift to a beautiful young woman I once knew, a woman who lived in Hawkhaven's village."

Though his heart leapt at the possibilities filling his mind, Hunter still said naught. His mother had never told him who had given her the chalice. Hunter had always assumed it had been a gift from the lady of Hawkhaven, Lord Reginald's wife, who was fond of his mother before she died. That was another reason why Hunter was always so secretive about the chalice while he still lived at the castle. If Rupert had known about it he would have demanded Hunter give it back to him. As the only possession of his mother, Hunter hated the thought of parting with the chalice.

Bruce rose from the stool to stand before Hunter. "I know this chalice belongs to you because I know that woman was your mother."

Hunter blanched. What was Bruce saying? The question for which he had sought an answer his entire life hovered on his lips, a moment away from slipping into the open. Snapping his mouth shut, Hunter held the words within, refusing to allow the rising hope to surface again only to be destroyed yet another time.

Was he so desperate to know his father's name that he would jump to conclusions with any stranger that knew his mother?

Hunter stared at Bruce, scrutinizing him as if seeing the man for the first time. He noted the similarities between them—same height and build, dark hair and eyes— but those were common traits to many, and proof of naught.

He wrestled his gaze away, refusing to believe the truth that might be staring him in the face.

At that moment two Scots entered the tower. "One of the men was not dead yet, my lord," one Scot said.

Bruce rose his eyebrows. "What did he have to say?"

There was an odd exchange of glances between Bruce and his man. "The man behind the abduction is still at large. It is best if we secure the tower, my lord."

Bruce nodded and when Hunter made a move to follow the men up the narrow staircase, Bruce stopped him.

"Let them search the place first."

"If the perpetrator of my wife's abduction is here I want to be the first to find him, and the one to kill him."

Not releasing his hold of Hunter, Bruce said, "The tower is surrounded by my men; no one can exit without being seen. If he is in here, he will be yours."

Knowing he was not exactly in a position to make demands, Hunter nodded and stepped back.

Moments later one of the Scots came down. "No one is here," he said. "I left James in the battlement to watch out for coming English troops. You may continue your conversation without fear of ears listening to what is none of their concern."

Bruce nodded, and when his man left, he turned to Hunter.

"It was with great sorrow that I learned of your mother's demise," he said. "I cared much for her. And I made sure she was well taken care of."

Now Hunter understood why they never struggled for food. The wagging tongues in the village accused his mother of selling her favors, but Hunter knew better.

"Apparently you cared not enough to make her your wife." The pain of watching his mother pine away for a man she could never have resurfaced with renewed force. But even as Hunter accused Bruce he understood the impossibility of their union.

Bruce and his mother belonged to different stations in life. His mother had been the daughter of a blacksmith; Bruce was the son of an earl, now a king himself. Nobles sometimes claimed their bastards from such liaisons, but they rarely or never married the women who bore their children.

"I understand your resentment," Bruce said. "But I was a young lad, much younger than you are now, when I first met your mother. We were together for only a few days and we both knew there would be no future for us. I only learned of your existence days before she died. And even then I could do naught but provide for your future."

So it was Bruce who paid Lord Reginald to foster him. But what was the link between Hawkhaven's lord and

Bruce? Though their acquaintance in itself meant little, for many Scotsmen held lands and friendships in England and many Englishmen held the same in Scotland. Only in times of war those divisions mattered.

But there was no little significance in Bruce and his mother's relationship. "What exactly are you saying, Robert the Bruce?" Hunter demanded. He wanted the words.

"I am saying, Hunter of Windermere, that I am your sire."

And there they were! The words, the truth Hunter had sought his entire life.

Finally free from the shackles of uncertainty Hunter realized he knew not what to do with this newfound knowledge. He stared at Bruce, his father, and all the resentment, the hurt, the longing meant naught anymore. He knew his father, at last.

Bruce made the first move and they embraced awkwardly at first, then in a vise grip, both choked with emotions too strong for speech.

When they separated, Bruce said, his voice raspy, "A man is forced into many hard choices in a lifetime, and I have had my share of them, but the hardest choice of all is that I shall never be able to acknowledge you as my son."

"You have just done that," Hunter said.

"Yet no one else shall ever know," Bruce said. "For your own safety, no one must ever know."

And Hunter realized it truly mattered not whether he could shout the joyful tidings from the battlements of his castle to the world to hear. He knew who his father was and that was enough for him. Especially now that he had Détra's acceptance. An acceptance he had jeopardized by lying to her again about the chalice's whereabouts.

"We must part now," Hunter said. "I must care for my

lady wife. When next we meet, most probably in the battlefield, I shall turn my back to you."

Bruce nodded. "And I to you."

IN THE BATTLEMENT OF THE PELE TOWER, RUPERT
watched the sun rising on the horizon, seething at being
under the guard of a Scotsman. He should be grateful,
though, that his participation in Détra's abduction had not
been exposed to Hunter. Had it not been for Douglas,
Bruce's faithful friend, having recognized him, Rupert
would probably now be dead. He had no illusions Hunter
would forgive him for having abducted Détra.

Rupert was also grateful he was dragged from his
eavesdropping position after he had overheard part of
Hunter and Bruce's conversation, and not before.

He had heard enough that strong suspicions rose in his
mind.

The possibility Bruce could be Hunter's father pleased
and annoyed Rupert at the same time. Pleased him, for
what better weapon to use against Hunter than his possible
kinship to Bruce, self-proclaimed king of Scotland? And
annoyed him, for Hunter should be the spawn of some
unknown lowborn villein and not the son of a nobleman.

And yet a nobleman who surely would never claim his
bastard.

However, the mere possibility, especially backed up by
the physical evidence of the chalice, should be all Rupert
needed to cast serious doubts in King Edward's mind
about Hunter's loyalty to him and to England. Mayhap
even enough to have Hunter stripped of Windermere and
his marriage to Détra annulled.

The thought cast a warm glow on Rupert's mood.

A while later, when Hunter left the pele tower unharmed and, along with his wife, departed the clearing un-

hindered, Rupert's suspicions grew stronger.

Hunter had landed on his feet again, Rupert seethed, but his good fortune was about to end.

Rupert followed the guard down the stairs. It was time to speak with Bruce.

ISABEL DIDN'T DARE GLANCE OVER HER SHOULDER AS she sat stiffly on her mare while she and Hunter rode away from their captors. She counted the seconds in her mind, expecting at any moment to be yanked back by Scottish hands. Only when they'd ridden for quite a good while, and she had lost count of time, did she begin to believe they were truly free.

And only then did she allow herself to react to the horror of the last few days. The trembling of her lips spread like wildfire throughout her body. Never in her life had she been exposed to such violence, and never would she forget such a horrific experience.

Used to feeling relatively safe in a world whose rules she understood, Isabel was shaken to her core by the thought she could've died for no reason whatsoever.

But since when had violence made any sense? She was deluding herself to think she was safer in the future, where her views were colored by the fact she'd never been a victim of crime. Unfortunately, poverty, crime, wars, and terrorism still existed in the future. She'd just been lucky it had never affected her directly.

As she was lucky Hunter had been here to save her. The memory of the three dead men—men Hunter had killed—came back to her, and a bout of nausea threatened to overtake her.

"Hunter," she called, swallowing down the bitter bile. "I need to stop."

Without waiting for his help, Isabel slid down her

mount to her feet and unsteadily rushed to the edge of the woods flanking the road. Hunter caught up with her and held her head low as she retched miserably, her empty stomach rebelling at the pain.

When she was done he led her to the shade of a tree. She sat down, her face in her hands, her body shaking with sobs. Hunter held her until she calmed down, then he rose and went to his horse, returning to her side with a canteen of water. He took his gloves off, poured some water in his hand, then gently washed away her tears and the dust on her face.

"It is over, Détra."

"Is it?" she asked, glancing to the road from where they had come from. "Will they not follow us?" She didn't think she'd ever feel entirely safe again.

"Nay. There is no need to worry."

"How can you be sure?" She still couldn't believe the Scots had let them go.

"Bruce gave me his word."

"Bruce? As in Robert the Bruce, King of Scotland?" Isabel's mouth fell agape. "How did you get England's archenemy to release us?" Good God! Had Hunter been forced to compromise his integrity or loyalty to his country to save their lives?

Hunter jerked to his feet and offered her his hand. "We still have a long journey ahead of us. We should not delay."

She took his hand and rose to her feet. "You did not answer my question."

"There are things better left unsaid, Détra."

"There are too many things left unsaid between us," she said, acutely aware she had no moral backing for righteous demanding of the truth from Hunter when she herself had lied to him from the very beginning. But weren't most of their problems derived from their lies? If Hunter hadn't lied to her about the chalice's whereabouts, she wouldn't have gone to the lake and wouldn't have been kidnapped. God only knew what had happened to poor Maude. Isabel didn't even want to think about that. She had to hope Maude had gotten away.

"I want no more lies between us," Isabel said, determined to come clean as well. She couldn't bear the thought that Détra might return and reveal to Hunter that Isabel had lied to him all the while she was here.

Hunter was also tired of lies. He was well aware of the many secrets he had kept from Détra, and the consequences of keeping them. And he would lie no more. And he would begin by telling her his deepest secret.

"Bruce let us go because I am his son," Hunter said without preamble.

"What?" Détra staggered back in shock. "When did you find that out? Is that why he kidnapped me? To get to you? Good God, Hunter, you finally know!"

Hunter shook his head, smiling at how her mind jumped from one thought to another. "Bruce had naught to do with your abduction. I know not what he was doing at the pele tower and I did not ask, but while we were inside he told me the truth. And, aye, it is wonderful indeed to finally know."

"How can you be sure he was telling the truth?"

"He had proof."

"Proof?"

He told her then of the chalice Bruce had given to his mother, of him not knowing about Hunter until his mother had died, of paying Lord Reginald to foster him into knighthood. "For obvious reasons," Hunter continued, "Bruce cannot claim me as his son, but he had wanted me to know the truth. And now that I know, and that you know, no one else must know. This is a secret we must keep forever, Détra."

"I understand, and I am glad you trusted me with such a secret. How do you feel about knowing who is your father? Does it change anything for you? I mean, in your heart?"

Hunter pondered on the question for a moment. Aye, it changed everything. Knowledge of his father's name gave Hunter power to accept once and for all his past and look to the future with his lady wife. That was if she forgave him again.

"Aye, I am truly glad to know my father's name, but, Détra, to the world I must remain a bastard. Can you accept that?"

"A princely bastard? Sure," she teased.

He grinned at her jest.

"It does not matter to me who is your father," she said. "What matters is who you are." She hugged him tight.

Détra's acceptance meant the world to him, but they still had matters to resolve. He still had to find out who abducted her and why. Not to mention the small detail of his keeping the chalice from her. He would have to broach that matter soon, but before that he needed to know more about her abduction. "How did the Scots get to you?" he asked. "Was Windermere attacked?"

She shook her head. "I was at the lake."

"At the lake?" His voice rose. "Why did Gervase allow such folly when he knew Scots were but a day's ride from Windermere?"

"It was not his fault, Hunter. I convinced him that I would be safe. Besides, he sent two guards to protect us."

"The safety of Windermere and its people in my absence falls onto Gervase's shoulders, not yours, Détra. You could have been killed."

Bristling over his harsh tone, Détra spat, "Had you told me the truth of the chalice's whereabouts I would not have been there in the first place."

"Was that what you were doing at the lake? Searching for the chalice?"

Deus! It had been his fault that Détra was abducted. She could have been killed. The pain on his shoulders seemed to intensify, and Hunter suddenly felt older than his years, more tired than he had ever felt in his life.

"Why did you lie to me about the chalice, Hunter?" she asked.

No more secrets. No more lies between them.

"I was fearful the chalice would return you to your old self, to the Détra who hated me, who wanted naught to do with me, and thus destroy my dream of a perfect life with you."

His hands shot through his hair. "Now I know there is no perfect life, no perfect dream. That you should not wish for what cannot be yours. For even when dreams come true they might not be exactly as you wished them to be."

"Sometimes reality can be better than dreams," she said.

"Aye, and you have exceeded mine." He touched her face, still beautiful even marred with dust and tears. "You are not happy with me, my lady wife. Your relentless search for the chalice proves you cannot be happy until you are what you are, not what I want you to be."

He walked to his horse and picked up the sachet containing the chalice, then returned to her side. Giving it to her, he said, "Here it is. I give your life back to you in the hopes you would still want to share it with me."

With trembling hands, Isabel squeezed the sachet.

"Whatever happens, though," he warned, "our union shall stand. Naught shall change that. I vow to be fair, to protect and care for you even if you cannot be my heart wish, but I shall not release you from our bond of marriage." He then released his hold of the chalice.

"I could never dream a man as wonderful as you, Hunter, but I do not want a dream. I want the reality. I want you to want me." She patted her chest, indicating her heart. "The real me, not a dream. And the only way for this to happen is for me to open my heart to you as you have opened yours to me. To trust you with my secret as you have trusted me with yours. And to be forgiven as I have forgiven you."

Chapter 19

DÉTRA had a secret! Only one with memories could have secrets. Had she recovered her memories?

Hunter desperately needed to be alone with his lady wife. But from the moment, two days ago, when Détra had revealed she held secrets in her heart, secrets she was willing to share with him, they had not had a moment of privacy. The untimely arrival of his men had interrupted their conversation and the opportunities to speak alone during the journey had been scarce.

The waiting gnawed at Hunter and his mind swirled with questions and doubts. It had been such a relief to have finally cleansed his conscience and opened his heart to Détra. But her revelation that she too was plagued by secrets unsteadied him.

That she was willing to share them with him was encouraging. That she had forgiven him despite her memories, thrilling. But that she still insisted on having the chalice baffled him.

If not to recover her memories, why would Détra need the chalice?

Hunter wished not to mistrust Détra; God knew he had relied much on her forgiveness thus far. Nonetheless, he had kept a close eye on her during the journey, wondering what she would do with the chalice. She had done naught, but kept it close at hand, as if it were a precious relic.

The sight of men-at-arms camped outside Windermere Castle's walls caused no uproar in Hunter's mind as he recognized the king's banner. What would Edward want with him that warranted such an unexpected visit?

"Who are these men?" Détra asked worriedly.

Obviously not all memories had returned to his lady wife. "The king's men," Hunter said.

"Not Bruce's," she whispered.

"Nay. England's king, Edward II."

She nodded and followed him through the gates of the castle and into the bailey. Hunter helped Détra down from her mount, steadying her. She looked exhausted and frustrated. As was he.

"Do you think we can find out about Maude before we see the king?" she asked, looking around the bailey for Maude.

Seeing Godfrey, Hunter motioned him closer.

"Do you have news of Maude?" Détra asked as soon as the man was within hearing distance.

"She is safe and well, my lady."

Détra let out a loud sigh of relief. "Thank God!"

"Indeed," Godfrey said, looking as relieved as Détra was. "My lord, the king of England awaits you inside. And also Lord Rupert."

Détra's smile disappeared. "What does he want here?" she asked.

"I know not, but knowing Rupert he brings no joyful tidings," Hunter said. "We pay our respects to the king, Détra, then hope he will give us leave to rest before having to regale him with every gory detail of our ordeal. I shall not worry about Rupert."

They found Edward sitting comfortably at the lord's chair in the great hall, savoring Hunter's best wine, nibbling on cheese and bread, and conversing with Rupert. Hunter could not set aside his suspicions Rupert was behind Détra's abduction. Even if he had been with the king the whole time, it would not necessarily preclude his possible involvement.

"My lord." Hunter briefly went down on one knee at the king's feet then rose. "It is a pleasure to see you at Windermere. Please forgive me my delay. I trust Godfrey has taken care of your needs in my absence."

Edward nodded. "He has been very efficient."

Pleased, Hunter turned to Rupert. "I did not expect to find you here."

"I came to offer my aid in finding Lady Détra and repay you the inconvenience you have gone through on my behalf," Rupert said.

"Judging by the blood stains in Hunter's hauberk," the king interrupted, "I would hardly call it an inconvenience. Tell me Hunter, are you wounded or is this your enemies' blood?"

"My enemies', my lord. The king's enemies'," he added for good measure.

"As I thought." The king smiled. "Woe to the enemies of England and my crown. And hail to Lord Hunter's mighty sword." He lifted his goblet in a toast. Rupert made a perfunctory gesture and Hunter bowed to the king's compliment, since he had no cup in hand.

"Obviously, had I been informed in time, I would have

saved Lord Hunter the trouble of dealing with the Scots attacking Hawkhaven," Rupert said.

"It was not for lack of trying that you were not informed," Hunter said. "It seems you were nowhere to be found."

As Hunter had expected, the jab hit home. Ruffled, Rupert jerked to his feet. "My men knew exactly where to find me. There should have been no difficulty in such a task. I shall find out who is responsible for this failing and punish him accordingly."

Hunter was not in the mind for Rupert's excuses. Had he not been fighting Rupert's battle, Détra would not have been abducted, he was certain.

Then again, neither would he have met his father, or cleansed his conscience with his lady wife. Surely those had not been the results Rupert had hoped for. It had, however, made an incredible difference in Hunter's life.

If only he could prove his suspicions of Rupert.

"Be that as it may," the king said, "you are fortunate, Rupert, your castle still stands. And you should be more grateful for Hunter's aid. Especially in the light of our earlier discussion."

Hunter's innards tightened. What discussion? Anything coming from Rupert would only mean woe to him.

"I lament you paid such a high price for your generosity, Hunter," the king said.

Unease skittered down Hunter's spine. "I know not what you speak of, my lord."

Edward pointed to Détra. "In your absence your lady wife was abducted, I was told. It is fortunate indeed that you have rescued her unharmed." The king inspected Détra briefly. "At least I assume she is unharmed."

"Unharmed but utterly weary," Hunter said. Détra looked about to fall on her face. "In fact, both of us are rather exhausted and would like to retire momentarily."

Expecting to be given leave, Hunter was surprised at Edward's momentary silence.

"I realize this is a most unfortunate time," the king finally said. "But I must return to Berwick Castle without delay. Thus, let us speak now and be done with it, shall we?"

Hunter accepted his sovereign king's command disguised as a request with certain trepidation. Had the king heard of his encounter with Bruce? But how could he? Hunter directed an accusing glare at Rupert. Did he know?

"As you wish, my lord," Hunter said. "But mayhap you could give leave to my lady wife. She has been through a terrible ordeal and I am certain she is not interested in tales of battles."

"I am not insensitive to Lady Détra's plight," the king said, reclining back against his chair and taking a sip of his wine. "But I fear her presence is necessary since what I wish to discuss at this time is a certain petition she has made of me."

Petition? Hunter glanced at Détra and she looked ready to swoon, her skin a shade paler than usual. Before Hunter could succor her, she slumped down on the bench, wordlessly. The sachet, containing the chalice, fell at her feet.

Could this be the secret Détra wished to share with him? What could she possibly have wanted from the king? Hunter deeply disliked the implications.

Keenly aware of Rupert's presence, Hunter suggested, "Mayhap we should speak in private, my lord."

"It is a matter that concerns Lord Rupert as well."

Hunter's heart skipped a beat as Jeremy's words flooded his mind. *It is said that Lord Rupert covets another lord's wife.*

It took all of Hunter's strength not to spring on Rupert and skewer the man with his sword right here and now.

Deus! But he had been blind. Having never bested Hunter with the sword, the swine had resorted to stealing his wife.

But what role did Détra play in this? Was her frightened silence proof of guilt? Had his lady wife, the woman of his heart, betrayed him with his worst enemy?

A vein began pulsing on his temple. With extreme effort Hunter kept his features steeled.

"I am certain you would have preferred a more timely response," the king said to Détra. "However belatedly, here I am. Would you care to reiterate your petition?"

All eyes turned to Détra.

Knowing the terrible predicament she was in, Isabel swallowed hard. Détra's secret was about to be unearthed at the worst possible moment. Isabel had thought she might never have to address Détra's betrayal, at least not before she told Hunter of her true identify. How could he believe anything she told him after today?

Wasn't it enough of an emotional roller coaster she and Hunter had endured these past weeks? Did this added complication have to happen now?

Realizing all she could do at this point was damage control, Isabel steadied her gaze on the king. He was the man she must convince now. Hunter, she would have to try later. As for Rupert she didn't care a bit what happened to him.

"I would rather you disregard my petition, my lord."

Rupert looked about to have an apoplexy, which gave Isabel a small measure of pleasure.

"May I ask what this petition entails?" Hunter's voice was deceptively calm, and he showed no outward emotion but a slight tightening of his hand over the hilt of his sword that did nothing to calm Isabel's nerves.

"Your wife's desire to annul her marriage to you," Rupert gleefully informed him.

Isabel would've kicked Rupert in the groin with no pity

whatsoever, had he only been closer. The man was the true incarnation of a bastard. Should she inform the king about Rupert's presence at the lake when she was kidnapped? Or would that set Rupert off and make him bring attention to Hunter and the Scots?

"A petition Lady Détra has just revoked," the king corrected.

At least King Edward seemed interested in keeping the peace between his lords, Isabel thought, somewhat relieved.

"Am I to assume," the king turned to her, "that you are content with your marriage to Hunter of Hawkhaven?"

"Most definitely, my lord. Hunter is a wonderful man and I am grateful you made him my husband. I apologize for wasting your precious time with my temporary lack of judgment, and I beg your forgiveness."

"Mayhap you should beg your husband's forgiveness, Lady Détra."

"I intend to do so, my lord."

"You are aware that Lord Hunter is within his rights to chastise you in any manner he shall see fit. I will not interfere in a marital matter such as this," the king advised.

"And I shall accept my punishment." Isabel didn't exactly agree Hunter had the right to "punish her" but she thought it best to behave according to the customs of the time. At least in front of the king. Later, she would have to pacify Hunter somehow. She had no intention of being physically abused. Not that she truly believed Hunter would hurt her. He was just not that kind of man. Maybe after she told him the truth of her identity he would understand.

Or lock her up for life.

"You have leave to retire now, Lady Détra. Your husband and I need to speak of matters of war."

Dismissed, Isabel rose. She wanted to speak with Hunter, say something that would make him feel better, but he stood stiffly and avoided her gaze. Unsteady, she pushed herself away from the bench.

"Am I to get no satisfaction in this matter?" Rupert insisted.

"I have already spoken, Rupert," the king said. "I suggest you find another lady to fulfill your desires. This one is irrevocably wedded to Lord Hunter. You may leave now, Lady Détra," he reiterated.

Isabel stepped out from the bench and involuntarily kicked the sachet, sending it rolling down the stone floor. She dashed after it, but Rupert reached it before her.

"Mayhap I can give you some reasons to doubt the wisdom of your choice," Rupert said, holding the sachet in his hand.

"This does not belong to you," Isabel said, trying to get it back from him.

"Nay," Rupert said. "It belongs to Hunter, am I right?" He brought the sachet and placed it on the table before the king.

Edward pulled the sachet closer to him and peeked inside. His eyes narrowed shrewdly. "What is the meaning of this?"

"The proof Lord Hunter has abused your trust, my lord," Rupert said. "At Hawkhaven I learned some very intriguing facts about the attack on my castle."

Rupert paused for effect and waited for the king's command to continue.

"I was told the Scots never really attacked the castle nor made any attempt to breach its walls or besiege it in any manner whatsoever. It was only when Lord Hunter arrived with his men that a confrontation seemed to happen. My men were never even engaged in the battle and the Scots were quickly disbanded, albeit outnumbering Hunter's men two to one."

Rupert put his hands on the table across from the king and leaned over. "Hunter's daring single-handed rescue of Lady Détra from the Scots—"

"And how do you know I faced Détra's captors single-handed?" Hunter interrupted. "Were you there, perchance?"

Rupert smirked. "Thomas heard you speaking of the ransom note, which reached you at my castle, and your telling your men to stand behind, for the captors wanted you alone."

If Hunter had any doubts over Rupert's involvement with Détra's abduction, he had no more. Hunter had given no such command to his men while at Hawkhaven; all he had said was that the Scots had Détra.

"Now tell our liege lord," Rupert continued, "how the Scots knew to send the note to you at Hawkhaven and not Windermere?"

"Rupert knew where to find Hunter," Détra said, stepping closer to the table. "I saw him at the lake near Windermere and I told him Hunter was at Hawkhaven defending his castle."

"Indeed I was at the lake for a secret rendezvous with the lady." Rupert tried to turn Détra's words against her. "And once she told me of the attack on my castle, I immediately returned to it. There was where I learned of all I now speak to you, my lord."

"Liar," Détra spat. "I had no assignation with this man. In fact, I told him plainly that I was happy with Hunter and wanted nothing to do with him. Rupert made threats and accusations against Hunter and vowed to take Hunter's chalice. Moments later, I was abducted."

"Are you saying Lord Rupert is responsible for your abduction?" Edward asked.

"All I can tell you, my lord, is that when Hunter came to rescue me, one of the Scots who was holding me hostage demanded Hunter's chalice in exchange for my life. I am just connecting the facts in my mind."

"Nonsense," Rupert replied. "The lady has changed her heart about me, that much is obvious. But I shall not allow her to besmirch my honor."

Hunter remained silent throughout the whole exchange. Pleased Détra had come to his defense. Mortified she had met with Rupert at the lake. Furious Rupert had obviously been involved in her abduction.

He was inclined to believe Détra when she denied having sent for Rupert, however. He would never believe that fiend over his lady wife. And yet, she had not denied her earlier feelings for Rupert, only that she had changed her mind.

His heart ached with her betrayal.

"We digress from the matter at hand, my lord," Rupert insisted, still trying to find some fault in Hunter's honorable behavior, when he was the one at fault. "We discuss not my amorous involvement with Lady Détra but Hunter's delinquent actions." He pointed to the chalice in the king's hands. "This chalice has been in Hunter's possession most of his life. His mother gave it to him before she died. It is common knowledge; Hunter cannot deny it."

"I deny naught," Hunter said.

"However," Rupert said, ignoring Hunter, "there is a rumor that the chalice once belonged to Robert the Bruce himself and it was given to Hunter's mother as payment for certain services she provided for him in the past. It seems Hunter's mother was a camp follower in her younger days."

Bristling at all the innuendo he had thrown at his lady wife and the blatant lie about his mother, Hunter could

no longer hold his ire at bay. He lunged at Rupert and
buried his fist on the man's face. Rupert was a little
shorter but stockier than Hunter was, but he was hurled
to the floor with the force of Hunter's blow.

"Cease," the king commanded, rising and visibly annoyed. "I cannot have my lords fighting among themselves."

Hunter stepped back, albeit reluctantly, and gasped
with fury. Rupert pulled himself up, blood streaming from
his nose.

"What are you implying, Lord Rupert?" the king asked
bluntly.

"I say that is enough reason to doubt Hunter's loyalty
to England and to you, my lord."

"The fact the chalice once belonged to Bruce is not
evidence of Hunter's lack of loyalty," the king said. "My
father gave this chalice to Bruce long ago, so it once belonged to England."

"Still, the fact of Hunter's possible blood ties to Bruce
should give my king pause," Rupert insisted.

Hunter knew he must say something to counteract Rupert's venomous words, but what? He considered the implications of lying to Edward, and though lies had brought
him naught but sorrow, what would the truth bring him?
The king was a shrewd man and he might know much
more than he was letting on. If Hunter were caught in a
lie he would be as good as dead.

Besides, he knew what Rupert would ultimately do—
accuse Hunter of treason. Had Rupert been at the pele
tower? Had he overheard his conversation with Bruce?
But Bruce's men had inspected the tower and found it
empty. Or had they?

"My lord," Hunter said. "I deny not that the chalice
has come to me through my mother, as Lord Rupert has
told you, but I knew naught of its origins until two days

ago when I went in search of my abducted wife. I found her in the hands of a handful of Scots. While I fought and defeated the miscreants Détra fled outside their place of hiding and fell into the hands of Bruce himself. I thought we were done for, but denying his involvement in my lady wife's abduction, and at seeing the chalice and recognizing it, Bruce revealed to me he had, indeed given it to a woman of Hawkhaven Castle years ago—my mother. Obviously Bruce must have held her in great esteem, for he freed us in her memory."

"By God, how can anyone believe such nonsense?" Rupert spat. "Bruce let you go in memory of a village woman he tumbled with years ago? Bruce let you go because you are his flesh and blood and are conniving with him against our king."

The accusation hung in the air heavy with its dire implications.

Hunter sustained the king's gaze. "The evidence might look damning against me," Hunter said. "But I offer evidence of another sort on my behalf. I have served you long and loyally, my king. I have saved your life against Bruce himself, and I would do so again without hesitation. I have proved my loyalty to you in the battlefields and outside of them."

Hunter glared briefly at Rupert. "Considering Rupert's obvious interest in my lady wife, and her rejection of him, I would take any of his insinuations with a grain of salt. And I could return his unfounded accusations with suspicions of my own against his person. But I shall not do so until I have undeniable proof of my words. I shall not waste my king's time."

The king considered Hunter's words in silence, probably deciding the best way to execute him, Hunter thought grimly. To have come so far in life and then lose it all because of the hatred of one man was inconceivable.

The king's gaze strayed from Hunter to Rupert, measuring the men's contributions to him. Fortunately, Hunter knew having saved the king's life weighed heavily on his side.

"Paternal ties are difficult to prove unless the father makes his claim," the king finally said, and Hunter almost sighed with relief. The king wanted to believe in him; Hunter just needed to convince the king to give him a chance to prove his innocence.

"Has Bruce claimed you as his son?"

"He has not, my lord." And that was true; he would never do so to anyone else but him. "My loyalty is pledged to you, my lord."

"Very well," the king said. "For your valued service to me and for having saved my life, I shall grant you a chance to prove your innocence by delivering to me the real traitor. Do you fail in that . . . Well, I shall assume the worst. Do you disappear, your lady wife and this castle shall be awarded to Rupert. As an added incentive, your wife shall remain here in Windermere under my men's guard. I have spoken." King Edward rose. "We depart shortly."

"Thank you, my lord."

"Do not fail me, Hunter," the king said. "I grow very tired of betrayals." He called on Rupert and together they left the great hall.

A GREAT SILENCE FELL OVER ISABEL AND HUNTER AFTER the king and Rupert left.

He stood with his back to her; his right shoulder slightly slumped as if he carried the weight of the world on it, and his breathing so shallow she thought he might be unconscious.

Isabel could only imagine the thoughts going through

his mind and the emotions in his heart. She lifted a hand to soothe him, comfort him, but though he stood only steps away from her he was like an impregnable fortress utterly out of her reach.

She knew the only way to make Détra's betrayal less painful, and maybe acceptable, would be to reveal her true identity. But Isabel doubted the wisdom of springing such news on Hunter in a time he had to accomplish a most difficult task—to find the traitor and prove his innocence. She couldn't add to his burden, but she must find a way to soothe his pain.

"I must leave," Hunter said without turning. "The king awaits me."

"No," Isabel cried, holding on to his arm and halting his step. "Do not leave me like this, Hunter."

He pivoted. "How shall I leave you, Détra?"

"Not in anger, not with hurt, but with forgiveness, with hope for a future together, with the certainty that I love you, with the desire to return to me."

"You speak pretty words, my lady, but is that what is truly in your heart? I know not anymore."

"I know you are hurting," she said. "All I can say in my defense is that I am not the Détra you married, the woman who betrayed your trust. I am a totally different person and I love you with all my heart."

He considered her words for a moment, then he asked, "When did you remember about Rupert?"

"I never did, Hunter. I still do not remember him, and that is a blessing, I am sure."

"But I thought that was the secret you wished to tell me." Isabel nodded. She couldn't even hint at the real secret now.

"Revealing a secret implies knowledge, Détra, and knowledge comes from memory. How did you know of Rupert if not through your memories?"

"He told me about our . . . agreement when you and I went to Hawkhaven for his father's funeral. Unaware of my loss of memory he blabbed on about my petition to the king. That was how I knew what the king was talking about."

"That was why you kept me at bay, avoiding the consummation of our marriage, so you could obtain an annulment and be with Rupert."

"That is what he told me, but I do not remember."

"Have you been with him since our marriage?" he spoke through gritted teeth.

"No," Isabel cried. "No," she vehemently denied. "I would not let that man touch me if my life depended on it."

Some of the tension seemed to go out of him.

"I must go," he said again, though he made no move to leave.

She stepped closer. "Come back to me, Hunter." And then she kissed him. At first he did nothing—his lips didn't part, his arms lay rigidly by his side—but when, with a painful heart, Isabel was about to step back, he gathered her into his arms and kissed her with the desperation that seemed to be a constant in their lives.

Chapter 20

ISABEL stood in the middle of the bailey as Hunter, King Edward and his men, and the detestable Rupert disappeared in a plume of dust behind the gates of Windermere Castle. The sound of the horses' hooves thundering on the dirt path soon vanished in the air. But the fear in Isabel's heart for Hunter's safety wouldn't end until he returned home safely and avenged.

Only then could she concentrate on restoring the trust Détra had shattered with her betrayal of Hunter.

Isabel hoped she'd somewhat eased Hunter's pain at Détra's betrayal with her actions in front of the king and Rupert, and her reassuring words of love before his departure. Yet, having been on the betrayed side in a relationship before, Isabel knew only time could heal such wounds.

And time was one thing Isabel didn't have.

Isabel gathered her skirts and pivoted. She walked the

short distance to the great hall's entrance, mindless of her exposed ankles.

An Italian guy once had told her she had a very sexy walk—"Like the waves in the ocean, full of sensual moves." Isabel smiled at the memory, amazed it had come to her at all; she couldn't even remember the guy's name.

Suddenly her life before Hunter seemed a million miles away. And it might as well be, for time was as great a distance as miles. And yet, Isabel realized with some shock, she didn't miss her world. Surely she bemoaned the loss of certain amenities like electricity and tampons, and the thought of being seriously ill in this time wasn't a very comforting one, but apart from that, she didn't miss much at all. She'd never been into high technology, she hadn't even owned a computer or cellular phone, and the last car she drove she'd left behind in America years ago.

The only thing she loved and missed was her painting, and despite the lack of availability of painting supplies in this century, there was nothing that would prevent her from continuing to enjoy her art.

Isabel pushed those thoughts away; her adaptation to medieval life wasn't an issue at this point. After all, she bitterly reminded herself, she'd already gotten too used to a life that didn't belong to her. Her only chance to remain here with Hunter would be to find out that Détra didn't want to return to her own life.

And the only possibility of learning that would be through the chalice. Fortunately she wouldn't have to chase after it anymore. Isabel entered the great hall and her gaze immediately fell on the table where the chalice had been moments ago.

It was no longer there.

Good God! Had Hunter taken it with him? But he had given it to her. Had he changed his mind?

Refusing to let panic overtake her, Isabel scanned the

hall. A serving girl was walking to the war room, her back to Isabel.

"Miss?" Isabel called rushing after her.

The girl spun around and in her hands she held the chalice.

Isabel sighed with relief.

"My lady," she curtsied. "I am to bring anything I find to Godfrey for safekeeping," she said, as if fearing Isabel might think she was stealing the chalice. "Methinks the king forgot this," she added.

"The chalice belongs to Lord Hunter," Isabel explained. "I will take care of it for him. Thank you."

Without hesitation the maid delivered the chalice to Isabel, curtsied, and then left the hall in a hurry.

Tightly gripping the chalice in her hand, Isabel took to the stairs. She needed some privacy to try to figure out how to make the chalice's powers work. She'd like to wait for Hunter's return, but what if Détra managed the exchange while Hunter was away? Isabel couldn't chance that. She had to tap the chalice's powers now.

But what if instead of giving her answers, the chalice sent her back to the future?

Indecision momentarily paralyzed Isabel in the middle of the stairs. With exhaustion threatening to buckle her legs, she took the last steps with wobbling knees. She needed some rest.

Isabel pushed the door to her bedroom open and suddenly all fatigue fled her. Maude was inside. With a shout of joy Isabel dashed to Maude, taking the petite woman into her tight embrace.

"Oh, Maude, I am so happy to see you," Isabel cried as she hugged Maude tight, then pushed her away to look at her and make sure she was truly unharmed.

Maude inspected her with equal concern. "Oh my lady, I was ill with worry for you. I knew you were home and

I have been on pins and needles waiting to see you, but we were told to keep away from the great hall while the king was here."

Isabel pulled Maude with her so both of them could sit on the garment chest, which doubled as a bench. "Well, now we can talk, and I want to know what happened to you."

"I must beg your forgiveness, my lady, but when I saw the Scots coming in my direction at the lake, I ran away. I thought the guards would be able to protect you, and I wanted to go for help. When Sir Gervase and his men found the bodies of the two guards but not a sign of you, they set pursuit, but could not find you. When they returned empty-handed, I—" Maude broke into tears.

Isabel had never seen Maude crying—the woman was as stoic as Hunter was. Her heart tightened with emotion. Maude cried for her! Isabel had grown quite fond of the maid, the closest to a friend she'd ever had.

"What is important is that we are both safe," Isabel said, squeezing Maude's hands.

Maude nodded, wiping her tears. "You look frightful, my lady. A bath would do you wonders. I have also prepared some food, if you are hungry."

"Hungry? I am starved. I will take the food before the bath, even though I stink dreadfully."

Laughing, Maude ambled to the table and returned with a goblet of wine and a tray with cut apples, cheese, and small pieces of cold chicken. On the table, a bowl filled with apples made Isabel smile.

"Now you tell me what happened to you," Maude asked.

As Isabel sipped her wine and nibbled on the food she recounted the horrors of her abduction, Hunter's daring rescue of her, obviously omitting Hunter's secret, and then the events earlier at the great hall.

"Lord Hunter is now aware of your secret?" Maude asked.

Isabel nodded. Maude was too nice to name the secret. "He knows of his wife's betrayal with Rupert."

"And how did he react to the tidings?"

"I think he was stunned at first, but he did not go on a rampage."

"That simply is not his way," Maude said.

"I know, but there was a great disappointment and sadness in his gaze I will never forget, though I made sure he knew I love him and I want nothing to do with that man. I made that clear to everyone, including Rupert and the king."

"Then, let us pray Lord Hunter vindicates his honor and returns to you soon," Maude said.

"Hopefully by then his raw anger and pain might be somewhat diluted and he will be able to forgive me."

After she finished eating, Isabel peeled her clothes off of her body. One thing was certain, if she remained in this time, no matter how weird she would look, she'd always take her daily bath. She heard medieval lords carried their beds wherever they traveled. Isabel would carry her bathtub.

Immersed in hot water, with Maude washing her hair, safely enclosed inside the castle's walls, Isabel closed her eyes and enjoyed the warmth, comfort, and pleasure of being home.

Her eyes flared open. Home? Was that how she thought of this place? The feeling was as odd as it was enticing, as intriguing as it was frightening. Home! She closed her eyes again and the next time she opened them, the water was cold. She must've dozed off for a little while.

Maude waited, sitting at the stool with a huge drying cloth in her hand.

Isabel rose from the tub, dried herself, then sank her

exhausted body onto the soft mattress. With heavy eyes, she watched as Maude left the room, then succumbed to a much-needed rest.

Hours later, when she awoke, the room was immersed in darkness. She must have slept all day, she realized. Her first thoughts turned to Hunter. She said a silent prayer for his safety and success in proving his innocence, realizing she'd prayed more in these past days than she had in her lifetime.

Suddenly restless, she rose, had to wait a moment for a sudden dizziness to vanish, and then ambled to the table to light some candles. She poured some water in a bowl and washed her face.

Never before had her life been so out of her control. No sooner was one problem resolved than another fell in its place in a continuous domino effect.

And that last domino to tumble would be her fate with Hunter.

She pivoted and her gaze fell on the sachet containing the chalice, resting by the garment chest where she had left it this morning. As she dried her face she walked to it and picked it up.

Chalice in hand, Isabel went to the fireplace, which burned low. At first she stood there, holding the chalice close to her heart, not knowing exactly what to do. Should she wish for something or just stare at it until it revealed a vision? Fear, anticipation, and hope warred inside of her. Finally, gathering her courage, she lifted the chalice and looked at it.

The sheer beauty of it once again astounded her. She traced its lines with her fingertips, seeking the warmth she knew lived inside its pewter walls, but only cold metal touched her skin. She stared at the blue stones until her eyes burned, but no glow emanated from it, no mystical mist swirled from its depth, no revealing visions.

Isabel concentrated on Détra's image, then on her own body in the future, but the chalice remained unchanged. She thought of Hunter, her love for him, her desire to be with him. Nothing. Maybe she'd have to duplicate the exact conditions of that morning—time of the day, weather. The only predictable thing would be the morning, for the sun still rose day after day, but the weather would be out of her control.

Regardless, she would try the chalice's powers again in the morning. She returned to bed, but instead of falling back again asleep, she tossed and turned, thinking and worrying about Hunter and wondering about the chalice.

The next morning, before Maude came to her, Isabel tried the chalice again, and again nothing happened. She tried it every morning after that with the same results.

A week later, Isabel woke up at dawn to a terrible storm raging outside. Hunter hadn't returned yet and Isabel was getting anxious. Obviously it would take him more than a week to find the traitor, but the wait was killing her, especially when she was so afraid Détra might return at any time. The combined anxieties were driving her to the edge of sanity.

She jerked to her feet, trembling with the uncertainty of Hunter's fate and her own doubts about their future together. She had tried everything with the chalice, but it refused to work. Maybe this day, with the weather raging outside, it might come to life.

Isabel donned the same shift she'd been wearing when she first woke up in Détra's body, found her mark by the fireplace, and staring at the chalice, waited for it to give her some clue of what would happen.

She stood there for what seemed an eternity. Dawn turned into morning and found Isabel still in the same spot, fingers grasping the chalice, eyes bleary from staring at its unchanging blue stones for what seemed hours.

The chalice wouldn't work.

Isabel stumbled back to her bed, not knowing what to think. She lay down and stared up at the canopy of her bed. What had she done wrong? Was the same thing happening to Détra in the future? And then an insidious thought took hold of her. If neither she nor Détra could undo the exchange, they would be stuck wherever they were.

Dare she believe it? Should she believe it? She needed to be sure, for she wouldn't be able to live with the uncertainty.

Maybe she hadn't done everything she could to make the chalice work. What was she missing? She rose again, her gaze scanning the room, looking for a clue, anything that could point her to the right direction. A lightning bolt streaked the room with a flashing light, illuminating Hunter's garment chest.

Hunter! Of course, Isabel suddenly realized, the three of them had been involved in the incident with the chalice—Hunter and Détra here, Isabel in the future. Their wishes had interlaced and connected, and thus the transfer had occurred. It could only be reversed when the three of them connected again.

The knowledge did little to calm Isabel's nerves. Again she was the only one aware of all the facts. Détra's fate was in her hands.

Isabel's shoulders slumped with the weight of the responsibility.

She couldn't rationalize stealing Détra's life because she was the one who loved Hunter and therefore should remain with him. She must give Détra a choice in the matter.

What Isabel had feared all along was true. Her love with Hunter was doomed. And now she had to not only convince him she was not his wife but also that they must give Détra the choice of returning or not.

IT TOOK HUNTER THREE DAYS TO FINALLY LOCATE Bruce and a brief conversation with him to have his suspicions of Rupert confirmed. It took a little longer to decide what to do with that information. He needed proof, and there was none to be had. Without that, it would be Hunter's words against Rupert's.

The solution was brilliant in its simplicity, so simple Hunter almost overlooked it.

He would have to catch Rupert red-handed.

By now, however, Rupert would have realized his connection to Bruce was severed, and his position with King Edward uncertain. Being a man who liked to ally himself to powerful lords of opposing forces, Rupert would be on the prowl for a new association.

And less than a month later, Hunter's patience, probing efforts, and a little exchange of favors with knights with whom he had served under Edward, finally paid off.

A secret rendezvous had been arranged at dawn the next day between Rupert and one of Lancaster's men on the outskirts of Berwick Castle where Edward was temporarily residing. Lancaster was one of the most powerful lords of the realm and had Edward under his power. He was also responsible for Edward's lover's imprisonment and, some say, his death. Edward would never overlook Rupert's association with the man.

The time between the end of night and the dawning of a new day drew near. Wisps of fog swirled in patches like floating ghosts. Hunter and four of the king's men hid in the forest nearby the meeting place.

A call of an owl resonated in the air. Another immediately followed, and then silence. Hunter knew the sounds had naught to do with nature. The meeting was about to begin.

If everything went well Hunter would be cleared of any suspicions of disloyalty to the king and would be on his way back to Détra this very day.

A horse rode down the path into a small clearing in the forest. The rider dismounted and waited. From where Hunter was he could not make out the man's face, for it was covered with a hooded cloak, but he had no doubt of his identity. Hunter recognized the man's mount.

Odd how men rarely remembered to disguise their horses.

Another rider came from the opposite direction. He too dismounted. They conversed in hushed tones, then a parchment exchanged hands.

At that moment, Hunter and the king's men rushed out and surrounded them.

"Hunter," Rupert spat. "What do you here? I shall have your head for interfering with his majesty's affairs. I am delivering a message from King Edward to the earl of Lancaster."

Rupert's feigned outrage might convince those who knew him not. Hunter would not believe Rupert's innocence were he swearing it with his hand on the Holy Grail.

Hunter jerked the parchment from Rupert's accomplice's hands, and to his surprise and shock the parchment held the king's seal. A trickle of cold sweat pooled at the back of his neck. *Deus!* Had Rupert duped him?

He steeled his features. He had come this far; he could not retreat now. "And yet you meet in the dead of the night, outside the castle's walls, instead of just riding to Lancaster's holding and delivering the king's message yourself."

"It is not your duty to decide how I perform my tasks for the king."

"But it is my duty to protect my king from betrayal."

Rupert snorted. "This from a man whose loyalty is still in dispute."

"And yet, here I am, at the king's service," Hunter said.

"And so am I."

"We shall let the king confirm that," Hunter said, holding the parchment in the air. "Take these two men into custody," Hunter ordered the king's men.

"Bastard," Rupert spat, struggling against their hold.

Hunter did not flinch. For the first time in his life the word held no power over him. It slid off him like a dull knife against his hauberk.

Unfettered, he realized it mattered not that his father would never claim him and no one would ever know. He knew it and the knowledge gave him strength. That and his lady wife's acceptance even before he had told her the truth.

He stared at Rupert, the man's hatred for him no longer important, but for a moment the thought of him with Détra twisted his innards. Remembering her assurance that she did not even remember Rupert, that they had not been together at least since the morning of the chalice, Hunter realized that that too would no longer hold power over him.

Whatever had happened between Rupert and Détra had occurred before they had consummated their marriage, before she had pledged her love to him, before her utter and complete change into this new Détra he so loved. As Détra had told him, it had been a different woman who had betrayed him, not the woman she was now, the woman he loved beyond words, the woman of his heart wish.

"My lady wife once told me," Hunter said, "that being born a bastard was a matter of circumstance and had naught to do with honor, but everything to do with character and choice. I only now understand the true meaning of her words. Obviously, King Edward understands the difference well. But, you, Rupert, never shall."

"Think you I am at your mercy now? A cuckold bastard with a damn savage for a father?" Rupert spat on him.

Hunter stepped back, adroitly avoiding the spittle. "Nay, not at my mercy but at Edward's. And you know well he shall have none for you. A traitor's death is what awaits you, Rupert. What you deserve."

Lunging back against the two guards who held him, Rupert broke one arm free and grabbed a dagger from beneath his cloak. With a swift move he thrust it in his own heart.

"I shall not give you the satisfaction of seeing me tortured, hanged, and quartered as a traitor," he rasped as he fell to his knees, then crashed to the ground.

Hunter's shock lasted only a moment. He leapt to Rupert, but those were to be the man's last words. Clearly the evidence in the missive Rupert wrote to Lancaster was strong enough to warrant Rupert's desperate gesture. Whichever way Rupert died mattered naught to Hunter. Like the coward that he was, Rupert had chosen to die by his own hand rather than defending his convictions.

"Take the letter, Rupert's body, and his accomplice to King Edward and inform our lord I am returning to Windermere."

He had been gone too long. It was time to go home.

NAUGHT COULD MAR HUNTER'S JOY. NOT THE FOUL rain that pelted against his face with the force of a tempest. Not the mud sinking underneath his palfrey's hooves and making his progress slow. Not the delay of his men to recognize him and open the gates of Windermere to their lord.

He had come home, and Détra was inside waiting for
him.

There would be no more accusations, no more confessions or need for forgiveness. All was in the past and there
it would remain. Both he and Détra had made mistakes.
There would be no more rehashing of old sorrows.

Their lives would begin anew this day. Détra was
everything he ever wanted in a wife, and more. He could
not begin to comprehend the depth of her change, but he
would not dwell on that. Much of what had happened to
Détra would probably remain inexplicable and he cared
not. In fact, he could not even remember the Détra of old,
apart from her hatred of him. Those memories were buried
beneath the onslaught of joy and happiness she had given
him.

Hunter bid everyone in the bailey and great hall not to
announce his arrival. It was still early in the morning and
he wanted to surprise his lady wife in bed. With Jeremy's
help Hunter got rid of his hauberk in the great hall, dried
up some, then took the steps two at the time.

The thought of holding her in his arms, the smell of
the sweet scent of her hair, the feel of the silky texture of
her skin put an added sprint to his step as he floated up
the narrow staircase.

Deus! But he had missed her and had dreamed of
naught else but to return to her.

Hunter reached the top of the landing and stopped, his
waterlogged garments forming a pool at his feet. His heart
beat so fast he thought it would come out of his mouth
with his first words of greeting to Détra. He composed
himself, took a deep breath, ran his hands through his wet
hair, wiped his face, and then took a step forward.

"My lady, if I may be so bold," he heard Maude saying
as he approached the door. "Mayhap you should cease
taking this potion. To deny Lord Hunter's seed to grow

in your womb now is not something he would forgive."

"I know," Détra replied. "And I wish I could stop, but I cannot, Maude. Not now, not yet, not until I know for certain what the future holds for us."

Hunter's heart stopped its beating. Détra was preventing the conception of their child? The ultimate betrayal sunk deep into his heart. He could feel the blood draining from his face, the strength from his body. Anger, swift and furious, took hold of him, and he embraced it, for if he dwelt on the pain instead, he would fall on his knees and mayhap never get up.

He slammed the door open with such force it almost completely unhinged it as it hit the opposite wall. Détra and Maude jumped to their feet as Hunter marched inside.

"Hunter, you are back, you are safe," she cried, moving to embrace him, but he stopped her cold.

Without a word he slapped the cup from her hands and watched her follow, with a stunned gaze, its trajectory to the floor.

"Leave us," he shouted to Maude.

"My lord, please."

"Leave us now."

"You may go, Maude," Détra said, her arms falling alongside her body. "I shall be fine."

The woman did not even fear him!

Pain, dishonor, shame filled Hunter. He had to move away from her, get her out of his sight, or he would not be responsible for his actions. He marched to the door and slammed it shut behind Maude's back. The door hung askew on its one remaining hinge. He pivoted and faced her, a safe distance away.

"Of all the deceits I have encountered in my life," he spat. "This is the most unforgivable."

"Hunter, I can explain—"

"Do not speak," he interrupted through gritted teeth.

"The mere sound of your lying voice wounds me deeply. I want to hear no more lies, Détra. No more false profession of love, no more deceitful avowals of forgiveness, of acceptance, no faithless assertion of changes."

"They were not lies, Hunter." She took a step toward him. He froze her in place with his glare. "They could never be lies, not my acceptance, not my forgiveness, and most of all not my love for you."

"Do you deny what I have just heard? That you have been preventing my child from growing in your womb?"

She hesitated, then whispered, "No."

His heart shattered into a thousand pieces. "Then you must take me for a fool if you think I will believe your protestations of love."

"Oh, Hunter, you are no fool. I am, for thinking I could have a man who belongs to another woman."

Her words stunned Hunter. "Who do you want, Détra? Confess your sins once and for all."

"You, Hunter. I want you with every fiber of my being, but you belong to another woman. You belong to Détra of Windermere. And I am not she. My name is Isabel Herbert and I have taken your wife's place."

Chapter 21

HUNTER knew not whether to throttle Détra or laugh at her. He was more inclined to throttle her. Laughter would be no simple task, considering the betrayal she had just delivered him.

"So now you are an impostor," he said, relying on a seriously depleted forbearance not to explode in anger.

"In a manner of speaking," she answered.

Hunter approached Détra, and taking her face into his hands, inspected the beauteous lines of her countenance. The thrill of touching her was lost in the throes of his aching heart.

"Years passed between last time I saw you and the day we were wedded," he said. "But you have changed little. Think you I would not have noticed had another woman taken my wife's place?" He let go of her. "You think me a bigger fool than I am, Détra."

"I did not exactly switch places with your wife."

He frowned. "I thought that was exactly what you said."

She shook her head. "It is more complicated than that. Détra and I have exchanged bodies."

Had his lady wife gone insane? Or was this a last desperate attempt to pull the wool over his eyes to explain her reprehensible behavior?

About to lose his patience, Hunter ran his hands through his hair. Tiredness weighted his shoulders down. He had thought they were past secrets, past hurts. He had rushed home hoping to begin his life anew with his wife, with a woman he believed loved him. And now this . . .

"I would think you able to spin a more believable tale, Détra. You wound my pride for thinking me such a simpleton." He turned to leave, but she held on to his arm.

"Please, Hunter, hear me out."

"Why should I?" he shouted. "When all you have told me thus far are lies? When you think me such a fool to believe in your outlandish tale?"

"I know it is difficult to believe, but I am telling you the truth. Yes, I have lied to you before, but so have you lied to me. I gave you a chance to explain your actions. I think you owe me the same courtesy."

"I owe you naught." He jerked his arm from her hold. "The fact you prevent my child from growing in your womb is proof that your deceit cannot be explained or forgiven."

"Oh, Hunter," she said, shaking her head. "If you only knew how difficult this has been for me, how much I want to have your child. . . ."

"Oh," he said caustically. "And that is the reason you take a potion to prevent its conception."

"I only did so because I am not sure what is going to happen to us, and I do not want to make that decision for Détra."

He grabbed her by the shoulders. "You are Détra."

"No, I am not. I wished to be Détra, but I am not. And that is how this bizarre situation started, Hunter, with our wishes. Do you remember yours?"

Hunter let go of her. "What is your meaning?"

"Your heart wish, the vision the chalice revealed, Détra's rejection of it that fateful morning? Well, somewhere far away I was also seeing that same vision and wishing to be in Détra's place."

She massaged her temple with the heel of her hand. "There is no easy way to tell you this, so I might as well just tell you all."

"That would be helpful," he said. "And I am certain, amusing."

She ignored his sarcasm. "Maybe you should sit down."

"By all means." He sat on the chair by the fireplace and stared at her. She looked so beautiful his insides ached with the need to touch her, to bring her into his arms. He reminded himself that Détra had betrayed him in the most horrible way.

"As I told you, my name is Isabel Herbert." She sighed. "And I come from many centuries in the future."

Hunter jerked to his feet. "I shall listen no more."

Again she held him in place. "I beg you to listen to me, Hunter. Do you think me a fool to concoct such an extraordinary story to dupe you?"

"Is that not your intent?"

"No," she vehemently denied. "As fantastic as it sounds, I am telling you the truth. And if you just give me a chance to explain, you might understand. If you believe the chalice has magical powers, if you believe it has changed me, then you cannot discard the possibility that Détra and I have exchanged bodies, or that I come from a distant future. With magic there are no impossibilities, right?"

Hunter's mind rebelled against the absurd explanation, though his heart skipped a beat at the thought it could be true. The thought that his lady wife was indeed a different woman altogether, a woman who loved and accepted him as he was. A woman with whom he could truly begin anew.

He recognized the chalice was magical and it had changed Détra in ways he could not even begin to comprehend, but body switching? Journey through time? How powerful would the magic in his chalice need to be for such unbelievable tasks?

Nay, he told himself, stunned that he would even consider the possibility. Détra was just trying to blind him to her betrayal and the truth of the situation: that she truly did not love him.

And yet, involuntarily, Hunter sat back down in the chair instead of taking his leave of her.

"I found your chalice by the lake centuries in the future," Détra said. "I was in this very room, or what would be left of this room in the future, when the chalice revealed to me the vision of your heart wish. I saw you and Détra together, so happy, so in love, and I unthinkingly wished to be in her place. The next thing I knew I was waking up centuries in the past, in this castle, in a stranger's body, married to you. At first I thought I had gone insane, that it was a nightmare, that I was delirious, anything but the truth. You remember how I reacted that morning, do you not?"

Hunter did remember. "You told me you had lost your memories," he said.

"What else could I say? I did not know you or what would happen to me. I did not have Détra's memories, so I did not know how to act. What would you have done if

I had told you that I had switched bodies with your wife then?"

"And what do you think I shall do now?"

"I trust you know me well enough now, Hunter, to give me the benefit of the doubt. Open your mind, please. At least admit the possibility that I am telling the truth."

"Thus I am supposed to believe you have journeyed through time to steal my lady wife's body and be with me?" He rose again, marched to the table, and poured a goblet of wine. He emptied the goblet in one gulp, then refilled it. He gripped the edges of the table, his mind in utter turmoil.

"Not intentionally, but that was what happened," she said to his back, having followed him to the table. "Think, Hunter," she urged him. "Think about all the changes in Détra after that morning with the chalice, and then you tell me you still believe I am she."

Hunter turned slowly to face his wife. Unbidden, snippets of memories flashed in his mind. Memories of the many changes in Détra he had not understood but had intentionally overlooked as they had come with her acceptance of him.

The way she wore her hair loose, despite being obviously annoyed with its unruly curls, when she had before kept it tightly hidden under veils and braids. The way she swayed when she walked, when she had always marched with serious determination. The way she slept, free, unbound, unafraid of his touch. The rhythm of her speech, her choice of words, the way she had run words together for a time, though she had ceased doing that in a while now. Her smiles . . .

Hunter remembered her inability to accomplish tasks she had been proficient at before. Her disinterest in the running of the castle, delegating tasks, when before she had relished her duties with stubborn determination. Her newfound talent and interest in matters she should know naught about. Her painting, the odd song she sang to him weeks ago. Her sudden like of apples.

And the most important changes of all—her forgiveness of his deceits, her acceptance of his bastardy birth, her professed love for him.

Even if she had lied about her love for him with words, she could not have pretended her passion while in bed with him. She had desired him like no woman had before.

A tremor skittered down Hunter's spine. *Deus!* Could it be possible? He did believe the chalice's powers had transformed his lady wife into his heart wish. He had no way of knowing how it had accomplished that.

Hunter shook his head. Confusion, indecision, and a wanting to believe in her meshed inside his mind. Was he mad to consider the possibility? And yet, how could he not?

Hunter lifted his gaze to Détra and sought the truth beyond the surface of her beauty and what he knew of her, deeper in her eyes and in her soul.

And it was like seeing her for the first time.

Suddenly Hunter knew this woman standing before him, looking at him with such love in her gaze, could not be the Détra of Windermere he once knew.

"How could this be?" He choked on the emotion filling him.

Isabel's eyes teared up. Hunter believed her!

"The chalice is the catalyst of my being here," Isabel said. "The chalice, your wish, mine, and Détra's. I think, in fact, that you have wished me into life." She laughed a little nervous laugh.

"If you are not Détra . . ." he started. "But if this is her body, then how do you not possess her memories, her feelings?"

Isabel didn't know how to explain metaphysical matters to a medieval man, especially when she wasn't an

authority on the subject. All she could do was tell him
what she believed had happened.

"Even though when you look at me you see Détra, it
is my mind and my soul—Isabel's mind and soul—that
reside inside. My essence, not hers. Therefore it is my
feelings, my memories, and my emotions that govern her
body. Without the soul the body is only an empty vessel,
Hunter."

"And where is Détra's . . . soul now?"

"In my body in the future . . ."

Hunter shook his head. Isabel wasn't sure if in denial
or just stunned at the mind-boggling truth.

"I know it is difficult to comprehend. I guess it is easier
for me because I know who I am. But I swear to you, I
am telling you the truth." She touched his arm, and this
time he didn't flinch. Encouraged, Isabel continued, "It
was I, Isabel, who made love to you, Hunter. It was to
me that you told your deepest secrets. And it is I who
loves you with all my heart, mind, and soul."

He stared at her for a few moments, then pulled her
into his arms, hugging her so tight she could barely
breathe, but she didn't complain. She wouldn't complain
even if she passed out for lack of air, for she needed to
feel his arms around her, to hear his heart beating so close
to her, to be with him. For only God knew whether they
had the rest of their lives together or only this very day.

"Isabel," he whispered against her hair.

The sound of Hunter's voice saying her name for the
first time was Isabel's undoing. She sobbed against his
shoulder, unable to stop.

"I believe you, do not cry. I believe you," he chanted.

Finally getting hold of her emotions, Isabel stepped
back from his embrace. She had yet to tell him the worst
part.

"What?" he asked, obviously noticing she wasn't finished with her story. "Is there more to this tale?"

She nodded.

"Deus!" He paced the room for a moment, then sank down on the garment chest, patting the empty space beside him. "Come, sit by me, and tell me all."

She complied. "Détra is stuck in the future."

He took a moment to digest the information. "Is she harmed?"

"I do not know. The future is a very different place, Hunter. I am not sure Détra is capable of adapting to such drastic changes. Think of huge machines flying in the sky, carrying people from one place to another. Think of being able to speak in a small box and hear a person's voice from the other side of the world. Think of carts moving about without horses. These are just a few of the changes Détra would have to adapt to."

He took a moment to digest her words. "Will those things harm her?"

"No, but it is the acceptance of those things that worry me."

"You adapted well here, even though it is obviously much different from your time."

"Well, I had some knowledge of what a medieval time would be. It is a matter of record in the history books. Détra does not have the same advantage. To her everything will be utterly incomprehensible."

He frowned. "What is *medieval*?"

"That is how this time will be known in the future."

He nodded. She sensed his curiosity. He had many questions in his mind, but he reined himself. "If Détra adapted to the changes, how would she survive there? Do you have kin, husband, father, to care for her?" He gazed at her intensely.

Was he jealous of her past? Isabel smiled. Hunter had indeed accepted she was a different woman.

"I have no husband nor father," she said. "I own my own home and have means to live comfortably. Besides, in my time, a woman is allowed to live her own life. We do not need anyone to take care of us."

Hunter seemed relieved, maybe for more than one reason. "Then Détra shall be fine there. I always thought she would rather be on her own than a wedded lady."

"If Détra adapted," Isabel insisted. "She would be fine, but that is not my only concern, Hunter. Despite what you might believe, Détra may wish to return home."

"Why would she?" he asked. "Détra hates me, was very unhappy here, complained about having no choices. I think she would not wish to return at all."

"We do not know that for sure, do we?"

"What are you suggesting, Isabel, that we bring her back?"

"If that is what is supposed to happen, yes."

He jerked to his feet. "Surely you jest. After all we have been through together, you tell me you wish to leave me?"

"No." She rose to stand before him. "No, I do not want to leave you at all, but we cannot build our happiness upon Détra's misfortune."

"For all we know Détra is thrilled with the exchange. No husband, no father to make choices for her and means to support herself. I think she has made her choice."

"I cannot take over her life, Hunter, unless I am sure that is also her choice."

"Why would the chalice bring you here if it was not meant for us to be together?"

Good God! Hunter was making this so difficult for her. She wished she could just forget about Détra and take what he was offering her, but she couldn't. Her conscience would not allow it. Damn it!

"I wish I had the answer to that question. All I know

is that we have no right to make this choice for Détra, as we would not wish for her to make our choice for us."

"If Détra returns, none of us shall be happy."

"That is a risk we must take."

He didn't answer her.

"Sometimes we must make the difficult choice because we know it is the right thing to do, the only thing to do," Isabel said.

Hunter thought of all the hard decisions people in his life had to make. His mother's silent acceptance of a doomed love, his father's choice of Scotland above all else, his own choice to never share his sire's name with anyone but his lady wife. Détra had bemoaned her lack of choices, and Isabel was forcing him to recognize what he could no longer ignore.

Lightning struck outside, its blinding flash crossing the room, reminding him of the fateful morning when he had thought the chalice had given him his heart wish. And now he would have to let Isabel go, for if he did not, she would never be happy with him.

And he loved her enough to make that choice.

"We should not delay," she said, lifting the lid of her garment chest and withdrawing the chalice from within.

"What is the haste, Isabel? A few more days would make no difference." He wanted to be with her as much as he could.

"Ah, but it would," she responded. "The longer we wait, Hunter, the harder it will be for us to part."

Hunter took the chalice from her hand and deposited it back where it was, closing the lid.

"Hunter, please, we must—"

"Soon enough, Isabel," he said. "Soon enough, but not before I make you mine for the first, and mayhap the last time. I shall have that memory of you if I can have naught else."

Gently he began undressing her, slowly removing the layers of her garments, revealing peeks of alabaster skin here and there until she stood gloriously naked before him. She had suffered much lately, had even lost some weight. He wished to protect her, to cherish her, to love her for the rest of his life and never let her go.

What capricious fate would give her to him only to whisk her away?

Without taking his gaze from her he undressed himself.

They stood naked in body and in soul before each other. Stripped of secrets, with naught to hide and naught to fear but their uncertain future. Hunter pushed the thought aside. He would think of naught else but of Isabel in his arms. He lifted her hair, settling it behind her shoulders, the curls cascading over her back like a sun-kissed waterfall. He cupped her face and kissed her, nibbling at her lips, teasing with his tongue, burning in his mind and heart the sight and taste of her.

He kissed her chin, her throat, slid his lips over her sensitive shoulders. She moaned in response. So responsive, so trusting of him, so loving.

His hand cupped her breasts, squeezing them, teasing her nipples to peaks, then his mouth settled on a breast, suckling, licking, tasting to his heart's content. He continued down on his pleasurable journey to paradise.

He nudged her legs apart and, grasping her soft buttocks, he licked her hot center, savoring the taste of her. Her hands burrowed in his hair, urging him on, and then she lifted one leg, setting her foot on the garment chest, in sure acceptance. Her hips undulated against his mouth, and when he thrust a finger inside her, she convulsed with pleasure. As her cries softened, Hunter withdrew his finger and mouth, rose, and lifted her onto him, burying deep within her.

Her cries began again, and as their mouths met, her

legs embraced his hips, and he began to thrust. And as he felt his seed rushing into her womb, he cried out her name against her mouth. How could he live without her?

Hunter sank to his knees, still inside of Isabel. And he knew that he would never love another.

"I love you," he whispered in her ears. "Not your body, not my dream of you, but you, Isabel."

She trembled in his arms. "I love you too, Hunter."

He remained inside of her, holding her to him, postponing the inevitable moment of truth.

Another flash of lightning streaked the bedchamber. The weather outside was turning into a violent storm.

Isabel looked at Hunter. "It is time."

He rose, bringing her up with him, then slowly withdrew from her. And Isabel never felt so bereft. He walked to the table, filled a bowl with water, picked up a rag, and returned to her. He cleaned her gently, she did the same for him, and then they got dressed.

They did not speak but moved like automatons—unfeeling machines to the outside world, a burning mass of emotions inside.

Isabel picked up the chalice. Hunter found his place and moved her to where she should be. They would have everything exactly as it was. And yet nothing was as it was.

"I shall not wish for Détra's return," Hunter said. "And I shall not wish for you to leave me."

"We must wish for what is meant to be, Hunter. If our destiny ends here, then we shall have our memories."

"I want you to know that I shall never love another."

"I want you to be happy."

"There will be no happiness without you."

She understood, for she felt the same. "Then we must make the most of our lives. But I ask you not to blame Détra for what happened. We are all responsible."

"You are a better person than I am, Isabel. For if I knew you could live with your conscience and still remain with me, I swear I would have no qualms in keeping you."

"No, you would not. You are a good person, Hunter. You are worthy of any woman's love. Never forget that."

Isabel lifted the chalice and Hunter reluctantly set his hands on it, motioning her to put hers over his. The warmth came swiftly, traveling from her fingers up her arms and her body. The blues stones glowed, and the blue mist began to appear. Isabel looked at Hunter and saw her own fear reflected in his gaze.

She returned her attention to the chalice, to the mist. It swirled between them and an image began to appear. She waited impatiently, for this vision looked different than the one they had seen the first time around. In it, Détra appeared in the future, in Isabel's body. At least Isabel assumed it was Détra, but it could as easily be Isabel. Mounted on a horse, she stood outside the ruins of Windermere Castle. There were other people around, construction workers. Isabel realized the castle was being restored. A man wearing the hard hat that engineers and architects wore in a site walked to the woman on the horse. She bent over her mount and kissed him, then smiled happily at him.

He brought his hands forward from behind his back and presented her with the chalice.

There was surprise and shock on her face, as if she didn't believe her eyes. And then, she sat up transfixed, looking into it.

What was she seeing?

At that moment the image wavered as the mist swirled around Isabel and Hunter in a crescendo of speed. The blue light of the stones brightened unbearably, then the room fell into total darkness, and Isabel and Hunter fell unconscious to the floor.

*   *   *

HUNTER REGAINED CONSCIOUSNESS FIRST. HEART stammering in his chest, he gathered his wife in his arms. He tried to make sense of the vision he had seen, but all it had revealed to him was the image of the unknown woman—Isabel he assumed—in the future. Who was that woman kissing another man? Détra or Isabel?

Hunter stared at his wife, praying for her to be Isabel. And the moment she opened her eyes, and her gaze settled on him, Hunter knew without a shadow of a doubt.

"Isabel," he cried.

Smiling, she nodded.

Choking back tears, Hunter kissed Isabel, his lady wife.

Epilogue

UNDER the gray light of a winter afternoon, Isabel put the last finishing touches to the portrait of Hunter she had been working on for days now. She had chosen to depict him in a full-body portrait.

She stepped back to admire her handiwork and her heart filled anew with her love for Hunter. When she had awakened in his arms, those many months ago, and he had known before she even spoke that it was she and not Détra with him, Isabel had known that there would never be anything that could tear them apart.

That day they had talked about the significance of the new vision the chalice had revealed to them, and had come to the conclusion that Détra was indeed happy where she was. That she had found her place, seemed adjusted and obviously in love.

And the fact that Isabel had remained in the past cemented their belief all was as it was supposed to be.

Hunter and Isabel had also discussed what to do with the chalice. Hunter had wanted to keep it, but Isabel tried to explain to him that if they didn't throw the chalice in the lake, she might never find it in the future and never come to be with him. That was a difficult concept to understand. She wasn't even sure she was right, but they both agreed they couldn't take the chance.

And so the chalice rested safely in the depths of Lake Windermere.

Hunter popped his head in the door, distracting her from her thoughts. "Is it finished yet?" he asked.

She nodded.

"May I see it now?" he asked, not moving from the door.

Despite his previous insistence Isabel hadn't let him peek at her work in progress, but now that it was finished she waved him in.

He approached her, kissed her first, and then looked at the painting. He stared at his image, obviously taken by surprise. "Do I really look like this?" he asked.

Isabel inspected her work critically. Surely there couldn't be anything wrong with the way she'd chosen to portray him. Hunter's dark hair was a little tousled, like when they just finished making love, his dark eyes impenetrable but glowing, a shadow of a beard giving him that ferocious look his gentle soul hid behind, and a half smile giving a glimpse of that soul.

She had dressed him in his hauberk and a royal-blue vest covered his chest, giving a touch of color to Hunter's darkness. His hands gripped the hilt of his sword pointed to the floor in front of him.

If that image didn't represent Hunter, she didn't know what would. Maybe a nude portrait of him would have been a better choice, but that would be the subject of another painting.

"Did you not like it?" she asked.

"I am just a simple knight, my lady wife. That you see me as such is more than pleasing."

She smiled, relieved. "And how else, but in all his handsome glory, would I see my lord and husband and the father of my child?"

He kissed her, obviously pleased with her words, then lifted her oversized body in his arms.

"You stay on your feet for too long, my lady wife. You must rest." He took her to her chair by the fireplace and lowered her on it, then added logs to the fire.

While caressing her swollen stomach, Isabel enjoyed the warmth, the smell, and sounds of burning wood. Hunter stepped away and she followed him with her gaze.

He looked at her with such love, such devotion, Isabel trembled under his stare. She returned his gaze full of the same love and devotion, and suddenly she realized that was the exact image the chalice had revealed to them.

Hunter must have come to the same conclusion, for he walked to her and knelt before her.

"My dearest Isabel, you are my heart wish come true."

She smiled. "And you are mine."

Award-winning author
Elizabeth English

The Borderland Trilogy

The Border Bride
0-515-13154-7

The Laird of the Mist
0-515-13190-3

The Linnet
0-425-19388-8

"English's romance is captivating."
—*Booklist*